PIRATES

THE LIGHTHOUSE KIDS

Spirits of Cape Hatteras Island

PIRATES

Jeanette Gray Finnegan Jr.

ISBN 978-1-59715-142-9
Library of Congress Catalog Number 2016940498

First Printing

CONTENTS

PROLOGUE

The pirates discussed in this book were the ones who operated off the coast of Cape Hatteras. Pirating was a way of life for thieves who preferred the sea. With the end of conflict between England and Spain, fought mostly at sea, many sailors who found themselves no longer employed in the service of their country at war, and not trained for employment on land, chose the exciting life of oceangoing marauders. Ships used for both private and trade purposes were an inexpensive way of travel, since land travel was difficult.

With the whole Atlantic seaboard alive with commerce, some chose as their area of activities New England, particularly the islands near Martha's Vineyard and the shores off the edge of Providence Town in the state of Rhode Island. Others concentrated their efforts stalking those sailing out of New York, Philadelphia, and the capes of New Jersey. Southern pirates made their home near Charleston, South Carolina, and farther down to the coast of Florida. The pirates in this book were familiar with the shores of all of the above, but they spent most of their time in the area of North Carolina.

They unloaded their cargo in North Carolina cities; walked the docks of Hatteras, Bath, and Portsmouth Island; and had camps in the sparsely inhabited swamps of Ocracoke, the village located at the extreme south end of the island of Cape Hatteras. They lived short and largely unpleasant lives and made names for themselves in history. The period from 1700 to 1725 is labeled the golden age of piracy. In studying the lives of these troubled young men, it seemed less than a golden age for those involved.

As Hatteras Island lived through that period, residents now honor their ancestry by celebrating every year with a festival, the Pirates Jamboree.

Those who chose the life of a "sea robber" experienced the bounty of the land and sea surrounding it. The sea provided an escape and employment. The land was always available for supplies, and most of the time friendly people were willing to buy the spoils (bounty). At this time in the history of Cape Hatteras, the island also included a land bridge to what is now Ocracoke Island. This pirate era touched the coasts of North and South Carolina with a threat equal to the Indian wars and skirmishes raging inland, reaching to settlements stretching from the coast to the Mississippi River. Hatteras Island did not have those conflicts; theirs came from the sea.

By the time the scourge of criminals found their trade, there had been two hundred years of ships crossing the ocean from the mainland of Europe to North and South American shores. Shipping was easy and profitable, forging a connection over what had historically been a prohibitive body of water. A fortune could be made from robbing ships, similar to the activity of inland thieves as they made their living robbing stagecoaches and banks. Pirates also became infamous people, as they carved out on the sea their place in history.

The tools depicted in this book represent the common types used during the era. Everything mentioned was authentic to the time. So many stories come from that period of history, all over the New World—pirates being only a small story of this nation's growth. But this story was interesting, coming from such a small sliver of sand: twenty-six miles long, less than one mile wide, and separated from the mainland by miles, stretching out to sea thirty miles beyond the coastline of civilization.

Very few people have written about this community of people living off the U.S. coast, and how they grew and prospered in their villages.

They were denied help from the mainland because of distance and the complications of access. Thus, these people became independent.

We did have access—maybe once a week, weather permitting—to a mailboat able to dock in canals dug out by locals for just such a purpose. At low tide, local fishermen rowed out to meet the mailboat and unloaded the mail along with other supplies and necessities of all types, which included schoolteachers, the occasional salesman, news by word of mouth, and catalogues with wonders beyond belief. These catalogues served many purposes, among them, things wanted that we could not duplicate. For the little girls like myself, those included the opportunity to cut out paper dolls, plus the furniture for a dollhouse, locals could order musical instruments, and gain knowledge of the current fashion. But this was our adventure, just one of many. Enjoy it, I did, living it and reading about it.

These five books are for the locals who will want verification of the stories they heard, and the "strangers," as my 102-year-old mother calls everyone who was not born on this sandy soil. These strangers now outnumber the locals, but they are here because they have also fallen in love with the attitude, style, quiet, and serenity that comes with living on the edge of the world. Welcome. We could not have advanced without you.

This third book, on pirates, is part of the excitement that comes with such a place. In spite of all the glamorization from film and script, those poor souls lived a harsh life. It would be nice to think they eventually learned of the wonderful life they supposedly lived. The truth is far less glamorous.

The Adventure Begins

Luke slapped and cracked his whip until his wrist was sore. He was both remembering the skill he once had as well as keeping a watchful eye on his little brother and his cousin, as they, too, heard the loud snap of their own Christmas whips. The annual Pirates Jamboree was to be held in the early spring on the island, and there were organized contests, in various skills, suitable for all ages. The kids of the lighthouse compound knew they would be entering a competition formerly reserved for grown men. They also knew that they were surprisingly good and had an excellent chance of winning, so they ignored the pain and continued.

Luke had been taught by the great Manteo. His mother, Weroansqua, was the chief of the Croatoan Indians who lived on Cape Hatteras Island. Even though much time and many dream adventures had passed, the knowledge Luke acquired from his time with Manteo had returned easily. He was now in the process of teaching the skills to Blake and Ellie.

Every year in the spring, the seven villages held their annual Pirates Jamboree on the grounds of the Cape Hatteras Lighthouse. Men began growing a heavy beard around January, and most already looked like pirates, as they either had obtained the look they wanted or went further to grow an even more lusty growth of hair. For some, the look was the challenge. To others, the preparation took on another goal. It was a desire to be crowned "king," the one most resembling the pirate Blackbeard, known to have frequented the area.

Some thought that treasure was buried somewhere in the vicinity of neighboring Ocracoke, or Hatteras, as these two islands were connected during that time, and Blackbeard frequented both areas as he sold his cargo to the island's people. Gold and chests of precious gems were more a wish than a fact. The pirate's buried treasure has always been the stuff of fiction. If the pirates did come away with "money" for their efforts, they quickly squandered it.

Pirates of the Carolinas captured merchant ships, which carried not gold or silver bars but rather products like sugar, rum, molasses, rice, and cloth. Gold and silver were the cargo of ships sailing from the Caribbean to Europe, after having raided the mines of the South American Indians. Ships as far north as the Carolinas were transporting usable trade items to the colonies, which the pirates attempted to convert to gold.

The unsuspecting passengers of those ships were robbed of their valuables at the same time the cargo was stolen, and the thieves, after sharing equally with each other, mostly wore or gave away their jewels. Chests of jewels were captured, usually by the pirates working the Red Sea, when they attacked ships coming from the Orient traveling west to Europe.

Colonies of the Carolinas were willing to buy the commodities from the pirates for far less than they would otherwise pay. These ill-gotten gains offset the taxes the government required to buy the same goods. Otherwise, those items were not available at all.

The islanders looked forward to the festival that commemorated the pirates who supplied them long ago with goods they could otherwise not have afforded. By this time the pirate had been romanticized in film and print. Kids loved to dress as what they had learned was in pirate style, and patches were cool. They were not aware that what they saw on the movie screen, or read in books from the Bookmobile, were glorified renditions of what a pirate's life was actually like. They had already seen the film *Treasure Island*, and of course they mulled over the pictures of pirates in books like *Robinson Crusoe* and *Captain Blood*. They could not wait for Grandpop's Sunday paper, which had a comic strip called 'Terry and the Pirates.' The dress and bold style was what they wanted to emulate. They would later learn what real pirates did, but the true facts were long forgotten in order to glamorize it for the masses. At the festival, activities included horse and dune buggy races on the beach, some even entering into race cars that were far from the stripped-down buggy, but rather modern cars operated by some very talented drivers. The Midgett brothers even went so far as to boast their skills in a Cadillac. These boys had already set the bar for talented sand driving, with their handling of the Old Blue Bus through soft and unforgiving sand trails from one end of the island to the other. That heavy old school bus at the hands of one of the brothers made the trip up and down the island in a feat others could only attempt to copy. Younger boys had designs on their father's family car for races, but of course had yet to inform the owner that his new car would soon be up to the running boards in sand and salt.

The children could see the practices from their second-story bedrooms, as some of the island boys met at dark to cross over the dunes and race down the beach at low tide, unbeknownst to their parents. Tires slacked, motors revved, one of the local girls would wave a flag to start, and the sand flew behind the very same cars that carried their parents to church.

The Coast Guard had its hands full with the dory races that sent the boats out past the breakers to a prepositioned marker (buoy), rowing around it and back. Their competition, the local fishermen—also skilled in conquering the mighty ocean as a result of casting their nets for fish, and anxious to test their rowing arms and backs against these military men—would determine who was the stronger team. The challenge was to pull against the unrelenting ocean to go forward, past the incoming breakers, against the tide, and of course, manage the tide coming back, hoping not to get swamped by a huge wave rushing from behind and sweeping them to shore, possibly with such force as to capsize the boat in the wash. This was an all-day affair, two teams timed, and in the afternoon, the two with the best time would, as Pop said, "have at it!"

The Coast Guard had their huge horses to pull the dory almost to the breakers, helping them avoid getting mired down in the soft sand of the wash, which could prevent them from getting off the beach even to start. Young men from the village had already asked Captain Charlie if they could enlist the help of Ol' Tony and Big Roy, his two government horses. Resembling Clydesdales, they were draft horses with wide hoofs and strong legs, and fearless, since they were used to pulling a heavy dory to sea. This evened up the contest. The villagers were serious about this contest, just as they were when they matched up against the seamen during baseball games. Other local fishermen from Hatteras, Kinnakeet, and Rodanthe searched the villages for strong steeds to pull their dory. They looked for horses that would confront the surf without balking, to get the dory in position to brave the breakers. It was a seven-village festival that marked the beginning of spring and provided bragging rights all the way through the summer baseball season.

Women all through the villages were busy making the beautiful costumes they imagined a pirate or his wench would wear: elaborate garb for the men and fancy dresses for the ladies. Queen of the Pirates was also a prize to be won by the lovely young girls of the island. The king and queen were usually from different villages, and popularity typically figured in the mix. Ellie had her eye on Jack and Lindy's friend Tinker, Mr. White's beautiful redheaded daughter, who would make a striking queen. Ellie also knew her and actually could not imagine anyone prettier. But the island could boast of many beautiful, striking girls, and everyone in each village had their favorite. Nature had collected its finest on this concentrated little strip of sand. There were the Burrus girls, the Austin girls, the Fulcher girls, Scarborough, Hooper Jennette, Barnett, Gray, Miller, and Midgett—the list was long, with each village able to field more than a dozen worthy candidates. Beauty was sprinkled all over the place—in the sky, on the land, in the sea, and in the countenance of its women. Maybe that was the way of an island.

The jamboree was a much anticipated event for the villagers. Winter was over, and flowers were beginning to spring up alongside the road and in people's yards. The trees turned green, pines sprouted up and out, and deer grazed near the road between villages. In backyards, they were easily spotted as they showed off their fawns, some even displaying the little knobs of antlers beginning to grow. Dogwood trees sprinkled throughout the woods began to bring forth their special white flowers and mixed with the lacy pink mimosa flowering trees. It was a magical time.

Ellie and Blake were also getting used to their wondrous black horse, named Blue for the way the light lifted the color from his glistening, extremely black hair. He was young, but they were also, so it was a good match. They begged Grandpop to let them race Blue on the beach, but Captain Charlie put his foot down on that one. Neither Pegasus (Gus) nor Blue were allowed. Both were too young, according to Grandpop, so the kids just resigned themselves to watch the horses race in the afternoon. Sitting on the beach, they mentally compared their steeds to the ones showing up from the villages—various kinds of horses, banker ponies included, lined up to test their speed. Some boys did not want to show the speed of their animal to anyone, and they anticipated a surprise win. However, the boasting at school allowed most to know which horses would be in the final running. The boys from Kinnakeet were certain that one belonging to a guy in their village would win, as there was a particularly good rider among them, Freddie Scarborough, and he was fortunate enough to have a fast horse.

Luke and Blake raced each other every afternoon to prepare for the foot races. Ellie's job was dropping the flag to start the race, just like she had seen the teenage girls do for the car races. Grandpop dusted off the croquet set and squared off the area for horseshoe throwing. Targets were made for shotgun marksmanship, and there was even an area to show off one's skill with the bow and arrow.

People went about their business, and it seemed that spirits were lifted as spring came to the island a little more each day.

Activity around the lighthouse was extremely bustling during these times, as it was the scene of the final contests. For the dory racers, that particular stretch of beach in front of the lighthouse had its own characteristic wave action, going over its own particular shoals and holes, requiring the boaters to be familiar with the challenges presented by the ocean floor at that spot. Each stretch of beach was unique, and the boater needed to be familiar with the challenges presented by the ocean floor at that particular location in order to maneuver out to the buoy and back. Most launched in a familiar place, whether Hatteras or Rodanthe, but nobody launched at the lighthouse, so the challenge was real for all contestants.

Something was going on every afternoon after school, and the kids could hardly wait to get in on it. The absence of cars did not deter them from freely moving around the island. It was easy to get from one place to the other by horse and two-wheeled cart. As cars arrived on the island, those who did not have access to one simply stood by the side of the road or walked slowly forward until a person driving a car stopped a short distance in front of the pedestrian and offered a ride. The person would jump on the running board of the passenger side and travel along, exchanging gossip along the way and hopping off at the destination. Those who preferred to walk would just wave the car along.

Men and boys usually smiled, jumped on, hooked their hand under an open window, and chatted until the car slowed enough for them to hop off. For people whom everyone knew loved to walk, the driver would blow the horn in greeting and wave. Walking was an island mode of transportation that most enjoyed. Therefore, lots of children walked over to the compound after school to watch the preparations with Luke, Blake, and Ellie. It was normal to kick off the shoes and walk everywhere. Walking in groups was also fun, either in the village or on the back road or through the woods. There was much to do as one ambled down the road. Distance was no problem. Especially in the summer, there was always a group of barefooted boys and girls in the personal yard of the lighthouse kids. Most were teens, as the younger ones were not allowed near the water unattended by an adult.

Island horses, cattle, and hogs roamed free on the land with only a nicked ear or mark to distinguish to whom they belonged. Horses and cattle especially were familiar with the ocean and beaches, as they knew that thrashing around in the waves, or wash, in the summertime would give them relief from the many varieties of varmint that plagued them during the hot and sticky season. A good roll in the salty ocean would soothe the bites from green flies, horseflies, and mosquitoes that bothered them all day every day this time of year.

Later there were also dipping vats, located at special places in the villages, where cattle and horses were run through regularly to rid them of the pests, especially ticks. Each animal was swiped with a green paint brush as it emerged from the trough to indicate that it had been dipped.

Diseases of various names dated back to the Bible (Exodus 9:1–7), when Egyptians attempted to control the illnesses that plagued their cattle. Finally, in the late 1800s, it became apparent that ticks on animals caused sicknesses, so the federal government required that vats be built all over the southern states. As a result, there were statewide dipping laws. At one point, it was against the law to transport southern cattle north, and Virginia refused in 1909 to allow cattle from farther south to pass through the state. As the culprit was finally determined to be ticks, it resulted in dipping vats being scattered about the island.

Livestock roaming free on the island also began to affect the growth of forests, as they grazed on the tender shoots of the plants and trees that tried to grow in order to replenish what was also being destroyed as each storm came through, uprooting large trees. Fences of all kinds were soon needed, no matter how small, for the island to continue to be green. Without them, the absence of new growth allowed the blowing sand to take over.

Luke, Ellie, and Blake were taught early on that caring for their personal horses was vital to have them live any length of life at all. They never missed their chores of brushing and grooming Gus and Blue. They also learned to manage the saddle that Mr. Burrus had given them. Uncle Jack had done a good job of softening it up with oil, and Grandpop rigged up a contraption that allowed the three to move it from the horse to the fence with ease. The saddle was for Blue, as Luke preferred to ride Gus bareback, usually with a blanket as his saddle. This transportation took them away from the compound to the village for comic books from Mr. Hollivey's store, visits to their friends, and of course, the mansion on the hill in the woods. They were beginning to become quite familiar with that old house, its grounds, and the outbuildings. The warmer the weather, the more mobile the kids became. Their adventures stepped up the pace from only once in a while to practically every weekend. Luke was the ringleader.

By the time summer rolled around, each one of them had been in the mansion's rooms so much that they could list the items of every room. They knew where to find the key and were careful to be discreet, never touching, only looking. The pirate artifacts never ceased to amaze and puzzle them. Luke was forever pulling down the volumes of the *Encyclopedia Britannica,* Pop's pride and joy—finding the article or picture of pirate gear or piece of equipment that was not familiar to him, and pinpointing its use. The three pored over the pages and volumes, looking for the uses and names of the items they saw. Each time the bookmobile came to school from Manteo, the town on the mainland that was the county seat, they searched for new pirate books. As a direct result, Blake became a reader beyond his grade level, fueled by his strong desire to keep up with the older kids.

Ellie's interests were broader, as she memorized what she saw in the pictures scattered around on the many bookshelves in the various rooms. She looked up costumes, the clothing of the period, hats, jewelry, and gloves. She was fascinated with gloves. The plumes of the pirate hats reminded her of the feathers she noticed in the fashionable attire of the Croatoan Indians. She had followed Sooleawa around, watching and listening as the proud Indian maiden directed the mixing of exact colors she desired for her wedding. She saw evidence of all the colonial woman's style in the picture frames on the walls.

In one of the bedrooms, Ellie carefully rummaged through the closets full of period dress and even discovered a ladder leading to a room above, which turned out to be an attic where they found trunks that they opened gingerly to view the contents. They just knew that Grandpop did not know about this secret space. The house itself was a treasure chest of history and mystery. Each new discovery sent them closer to their dreamlike adventure, but the adventure did not yet come. The saints were not ready. What the saints had in mind was a small adventure, one to introduce a much larger and slightly dangerous escapade that would rival the one embarked on when they learned of their Indian heritage. Even their whip practice was a design of the saints in anticipation of a skill they would later use.

The children began to interact with their wolves, as they continued to guard the large house. The horses and wolves did not become friends, as such, but they tolerated and respected the role each would eventually play in the grand scheme. Blake and Ellie were shocked at the docile reaction Blue displayed when he came in contact with Ellie's wolf, Twylah. He did not make a sound, did not nervously paw the ground, nor did he snort and show fear. It was as if he had been in Twylah's company all his life. Maybe he had. The wolves covered a lot of territory and must have known every inch of the island. Their size and stealth made it easy for them to roam undetected from village to village. Surely they had introduced themselves to the young foal in Mr. Burrus's pasture on some dark night.

The raven that flew with the pack knew everything. He could have easily seen the birth and, knowing the future, led the pack to the corral for an introduction. Ellie had a feeling of comfort around both Twylah and Blue that filled her heart with harmony when she was close to the creatures that complemented her life. She even became aware of the presence of the raven as he moved from venue to venue following the wolves. He was a sign in the sky that the pack was near, and she paid attention. She felt that if she held out her hand, he would land and look her straight in the eye. But she had never held out her hand, and she did not know if she could take that kind of closeness yet.

One day the children gathered together their special deer hide of Indian gifts and transported them to the old house. Here they could easily hide the gifts and pull them out when they wanted to without fear of an adult sneaking up on them. Luke practiced on his bow skills, and they all searched the woods for the special limbs that would fashion two more similar weapons suitable for the strength and size of Blake and Ellie. Ellie searched the woods for the feathers that Luke would need to fasten to the shaft and guide the arrow. She studied the ones Manteo had fashioned to Luke's arrows and for weeks tried to duplicate them. Sometimes she wondered if the birds were cooperating, knowing of the need that would eventually arise from their use. Just when she thought that the day was gone and it was time to head home, she sometimes discovered the feather she sought. This was Indian land, and the kids had walked here before, in a dream.

Blake, having moved his special knife from the compound to a new area in the old barn at the house on the hill, allowed Luke to use the knife to whittle off the unnecessary wood from what would be either a bow or an arrow. They were busy times, and the children were getting ready for something they did not know. They found they were driven internally to complete certain tasks.

They began to stock the old house each weekend with things from their stash at home that they thought they might need. They never took anything they thought that Grandpop or Grandmom would ever use, but there was never an empty saddle bag or empty rolled-up blanket. When they ran into a problem, they purposefully solved it with things from home. They acquired matches, a little oil for the lanterns, and flashlights—all of which they returned. They saved food, usually light bread and something to go in between, and once, an old shovel that had been discarded for trash. What they did not know was the smile Grandmom displayed when she missed some food. She knew, and sometimes she even "accidentally" left out something she wanted them to have. On certain days, she would catch them in the barn and offer a bag of sandwiches for the day, knowing where they were going. Those kids were so clever, but did they not realize what Grandpop could see from the top of the lighthouse? But nobody said anything, and the three adventurers sneaked away down the beach, on the ruse of just exploring.

They were not privileged to the quiet conversations Grandmom had with Grandpop about all things mysterious. Captain Charlie at first was astonished that the children were so connected to Odessa's mental advancement, but after a while he just paid attention and considered himself a lucky man.

Ellie was mindful to take things to cover her delicate skin and hair from whatever abnormality sticking out from the trees or caves would serve to scratch her. They had figured out how to get into the little cottage, and some things were stored there. They had complete run of the property, and at times, when they knew they were going to visit with Grandpop, they even learned to brush away the tracks of the horses with an especially bushy tree limb, something they had also seen the Indians do when tracks needed to be covered.

Luke was caught more than once daydreaming in school, but so many things were racing through his mind. Still, he kept his studies beyond reproach and learned everything he could about the world around him. He wanted to be just like Grandpop. He studied and asked questions about the sky, and his teachers gave him special books to read. He exhibited the same interest in both the sea and the land. His study of the creatures that occupied both he did on his own, and unbeknownst to him, his dreams (with his personal saint, Micah) were filled with the answers he sought and the ones he would need to know later.

The children chattered and laughed and shared their feelings as they went about their secret life. Their adventures were smoothed by the information Grandmom was given in her dreams. She was quite intuitive, knowing their thoughts and deeds, and what she did not see she was told in her dreams. Weroansqua was a constant night visitor, and Grandmom loved it. It kept her young. She was excited for the kids to discover the house. It had been in her family for two hundred years, and now she was sharing it.

Odessa was in her sixties, of slight build and with long, dark hair, not yet graying, gathered at the nape of her neck and held together with wide pins and beautiful combs that Grandpop loved to give as presents. Her eyes were brown. With her failing eyesight, she covered them with tiny wire-rimmed spectacles. She did not wear trousers, nor did any of the ladies of the island. Their attire was dresses. Odessa's complexion was flawless, and she used no makeup, not even lipstick as some others did. There was a natural blush to her cheeks. Most of the time she wore a small string of real pearls, which rested at the bottom of her throat, and single pearl earrings, but never any jewelry more elaborate than this.

Her dresses all seemed to be of the same style but with different fabric, the quality differing only for church, when the cloth was softer and more special. The style of dress was always with a flat round collar, buttoned down the front, most with special buttons. She was quite excited to find buttons that were different from the ordinary. When she felt that a dress had seen better days she discarded it, but kept the buttons. She wore flat shoes and thick stockings, except for church when there was a slight heel to the shoe and thinner stockings. Stockings were a luxury on the island, and most women had only one good pair, which they kept for special occasions. The dresses usually had a matching thin belt, and sometimes, Odessa wore a beautiful lace collar, which either she or someone more talented in the village had crocheted.

Odessa always smelled of lilac or powder, except when cooking. On those occasions, when the smell of food carried on her clothes, she changed before supper. She had wonderful aprons equally as fancy as her dresses. They covered the whole of the dress, without sleeves, pockets in the front, and tied in the back of the neck. There was also a seamstress in the village who made things for her when she felt there was no time for her to make her own. This seamstress was also talented in embroidery and would make a special surprise design for "Miss Odie." Odessa moved quietly through the day, only sitting down in the rocking chair after the dishes were done, and at night to read aloud, and then, silently, her Bible. She must have read it one hundred times through and through before she died.

Grandmom smiled slightly, laughed quietly, and was even-tempered. The children never saw her upset, and she never raised her voice. She could control Grandpop with the smallest look, maybe even an eyebrow, but it was obvious to everyone where she stood and how firm she stood there. She was a mind reader, a secret keeper, a healer, and a decision maker—all with only the fewest of words. Somehow she drew everyone in to her and her wishes, and they were totally unaware that she had done so. It was hard to tell if Odessa was beautiful on the outside or the inside, but it appeared to be both.

Captain Charlie was still a handsome man, even as he entered his mid-sixties. He kept himself fit, though the thickness that comes with age was creeping up on him. He was of medium height, with thick black wavy hair and blue eyes. His eyes always were alive behind his glasses, and smiling, but they darkened when his dander was up. He did not carry facial hair as did some others on the island. He thought being clean shaven enhanced his appearance when carrying out his political duties with the Lighthouse Service and for his stature in the community. His walk was brisk and purposeful. Ellie was usually standing at the door to hand him his hat as he hurried out the door for a meeting or church. He depended on that. She had learned long ago that Grandpop could never find his hat, so she made it her business to provide him that additional time and relieve him of the worry and scurry of looking for it. She could tell by his clothing exactly which hat he would require: there was the uniform hat when he wore his khakis, his official hat that went with the dress uniform, on church days he wore his Sunday best—a civilian suit and the most special hat. On county commissioner days his hat was a little more subtle, so as not to upstage his constituents. Yep, Mr. Charlie was a hat man, and Ellie was his hat girl. Keeping up with Charlie's hats was a chore that Grandmom gladly ceded to Ellie. Her job was keeping peace in the house.

Captain Charlie was not only a man who wore many hats (as long as they were brown) but also a man of many talents. He was stern with his peers and with his children and grandchildren. It worked with his business but did not fool his descendants. He imparted learning and knowledge at all times. He was driven to excellence and displayed it in all of his undertakings.

As a deeply religious man he was heavily involved in the church. His was an outlook of optimism that was forever shaped by the Bible readings he listened to every night as Odessa took to the great book to read aloud. Sometimes he would stop her in order to explain something to Ellie's confused little face.

He was so well respected that he was often detained after church by some member of the congregation to help solve a problem that needed an outside review or an assessment from someone whose opinion they held in great respect. More than one time Grandmom sent Ellie scurrying up the lighthouse steps to "fetch Charlie," because Miz Austin or someone else was at the house and needed to enlist his help with a problem.

He was also one of the few notary publics for handling legal matters. This side of him was most impressive to his son Wallace, who later studied law at the University of North Carolina and was eventually conferred a chair in the law school there. He was a teacher, also a profession eventually for his son Jack, who in the course of time went on to get his master's in education and become a principal at a large high school outside of Washington, DC. Captain Charlie was also a politician, serving as representative for the island as county commissioner, a path his son Tommy would follow. He also handled many properties that Grandmom inherited over the years from her affluent family, their son Curtis became a prominent figure in real estate. Grandpop's love of ships and the sea was passed on to his son Fatio, a merchant marine.

Captain Charlie was a Renaissance man who married one of the talented Jennette women. Miss Odessa was the love of his life, and it was a complementary union.

★ 2 ★

The Attic

The children spent their days in school, and their evenings, after homework, upstairs in their rooms near the windows, looking at the stars and talking in hushed tones. Nett, the boys' mother, was in her private quarters on the second floor just a hall and a doorway away. Grandpop and Grandmom were in the living quarters on the first floor. Grandmom would read silently from the Bible or knit while Grandpop smoked one of his Camel cigarettes and listened to the radio, mostly news, while also reading the day-old newspaper. Occasionally he would turn to one of his programs. He loved listening to *The Lone Ranger*, and *Edgar Bergen & Charlie McCarthy* (a man talking to his child-size wooden puppet, who had a sarcastic wit and always said funny things). On the radio it sounded like a man and his smart-mouthed little boy, but mostly the captain was concerned with the troubling affairs of the world. H. V. Kaltenborn was his favorite commentator. The family worried about Nett's husband Bill and knew it was only a matter of time before Jack, Wallace, and Curtis would follow suit (Jack, Tommy, and Curtis in the Coast Guard; Wallace in the navy; and Fatio in the merchant marines). These were busy times for grown-ups, but the children were not yet affected.

17

The anticipated trips to the old house on the hill captured all of their imagination. They pored over the books they read and added to that knowledge with other books they were discovering on the shelves, in addition to the volumes placed on top of chests of drawers and in boxes in the closets of the magical rooms. The books had been collected by a family of readers—from Uncle Jabez's time, Rhetta's, Sabra's, and all who had ever occupied the house.

As they planned their weekends, they were transported to a world they had only read about. They could hardly wait for Friday afternoon, when they rushed home, groomed their horses, and packed for the trip back to the woods.

One particular weekend, before the scheduled Pirate's Jamboree and while exploring Uncle Jabez's house, they were busying themselves in the three bedrooms located between the large apartmentlike bedrooms at either end of the second floor. Ellie claimed the bedroom next to the apartment she visited when Weroansqua introduced her to Rhetta, Sabra, and Annie, her mother. Luke claimed the room in the middle, and Blake was on the other end. These were to be their own special hiding places for treasures. Little did they know how close to reality they actually were. In the future they would all physically occupy these rooms when the family was forced to move away from the beach as the anticipation of the advancing war began to occupy the minds of the military, now both navy and Coast Guard.

Ellie was fascinated by the vintage clothing that hung in the musty closet of the room she had chosen. The walls of this closet were covered with neatly arranged shelves, and multiple dresses on hangers lined the spacious storage room. Along another wall were dressers full of old items: handbags, hats, stockings, and one whole drawer full of very special gloves. As she carefully moved aside what looked like an antique military officer's jacket—with its shiny buttons, large and ornately brocaded cuffed sleeves, and gold epaulettes on the shoulders—she also noted a beautiful gown hanging near it. As she moved forward to investigate the gown, she inadvertently stepped on a small floorboard that, further scrutiny showed, was different from the others. She heard the creak in the floor, and to her surprise, the wall behind the antique clothing moved back and then aside, revealing a ladder up against the exposed second back wall of the closet. She climbed the ladder to investigate and saw that it led to an obvious door in the roof of the room. Excitedly she called to Luke and Blake to hurry up and have a look.

Blake was busy staring at the pirate artifacts on one of the shelves in Uncle Jabez's office on the third floor, and Luke was in the anteroom that was Uncle Jabez's bedchamber adjoining the office. He had taken down a book to look at as he searched for a possible journal from Uncle Jabez. He did not know if such a thing existed, but it occurred to Luke that just as his grandfather kept records of his various jobs, maybe all businessmen did the same. He was determined to find out just how a dealer in pirate booty was able to pull off such a thing on an island where everyone was aware of everyone else's business.

Luke found Blake after just coming in from the yard, where he had been practicing with a rope he found in the barn. Having listened to so many cowboy adventures on Pop's radio, he had been enthralled by the accuracy of a lariat. His arm was tired. He had yet to lasso anything successfully, but in true Luke fashion, he would not quit until he mastered the skill. He had not seen the others for quite a while, so he moseyed upstairs to see what mischief Blake had gotten into.

They previously discussed going into the cavern but thought this was not the day, as they had forgotten to bring the second pair of shoes to change into in order to scour the damp, slippery floor of the caves. Also they were all a little hesitant, as it had been quite a while since they had been down there. They did not know the conditions they would find with the dormant winter growth beginning to respond to the coming of spring. What if there were new branches or bats or creatures beginning to crawl about? They had talked themselves out of it, with the promise that they would be sure to explore after the Pirates Jamboree.

Ellie's excited voice broke their own intense concentration on the treasures they were probing, and both boys hurried to see what she had uncovered. Sure enough, there was something there. On the back wall hidden behind the clothes, the wall had moved aside, exposing a ladder flat against the wall and leading up to what looked like a hatch that could be pushed up. The hatch was not framed up so as not to be obvious. On closer scrutiny, a square of wood was showing a slight crack along the edges where it fit snugly into the ceiling. It could easily have been missed.

Luke went first, but as he tried to jolt the hatch open, it did not budge. Years and years of not being moved had jammed the trapdoor firmly in its place. On this precarious perch, it was not easy for a small boy to muster enough strength to push without losing his balance. He pushed up as hard as he could, with one hand holding on to the ladder and the other above his head. As hard as he tried, it did not budge. He climbed down and stood at the bottom of the ladder staring upward, trying to figure out how to get that thing unstuck.

They all had ideas, but all of them would make obvious to others that someone had been messing around in that room. They had hammers, but striking the wood would surely leave a mark, if not totally destroy what was very old wood.

The ladder was not wide enough for two of them to climb to the top and push. They sat in a semicircle on the floor of the bedroom and tried to figure how to get into that attic. They decided that it would be necessary to have a sturdier and wider platform on which to stand. Possibly a footplate would serve to support Luke, allowing him to use something like an andiron from the fireplace to wedge into the crack of the trapdoor and unstick the stubborn hatch.

They began to walk through the rooms to see if they could find such a platform. They split up and each took a floor to explore in anticipation of finding a piece of furniture that could be moved to the area by the brawn the three children could muster. Luke found just such a thing in the kitchen. There was a narrow cabinet, filled with decorative bowls and dishes that would fit through all the doors located between the kitchen and the second floor. If emptied, it was light enough for all three of them to move.

By the time all of this had been accomplished, it was too late to embark on such a project. They had to leave it, knowing that right after Sunday school, they could ready the horses and pack them down once again for the trip south. This time, they needed to ignore the kids and adults practicing whatever skill they intended to display at the festival and find a way to get around the contestants who were also using their yard and walk their horses toward the beach undetected. Among all the cars and horses, this was to be a mighty task. Maybe there was so much commotion they could go unnoticed.

It was proving more than exciting to come up with ideas to get that hatch open and discover whatever was beyond it. They speculated on what they would find, and each time the suggestions became more and more outlandish.

On the way home, it was all they talked about.

"What if there is nothing up there?" Blake asked. "Wouldn't we be fooled?" He giggled at the thought.

"I *know* there is something there," Ellie said adamantly. "Why would the ladder be behind a secret panel and not out in the open?" She had a strong feeling, but not being sure of her telepathic intuitions, she did not trust herself. She then was struck with a thought! "What if I could *think* it loose?" she said. "Weroansqua taught me how to think fire. Why could I not loosen an old hatch?"

"Wow!" Luke exclaimed. "Why didn't we think of that before? We seem to have forgotten our powers. I think it's because we never use them." He also began thinking out loud. "That's a great idea, and I'll bet it will work! I think if we all thought hard and concentrated, we could do it! Let's practice tonight. We will try to move something!" He was so excited at the thought, it was catching, and without knowing it he moved Gus along a little faster. Ellie did the same to Blue, and they fell into a trot along the wash in a hurry to get home and put their plan into action. Blake would have been excited also had he not been holding onto Ellie for dear life as the horses moved along faster. The only thing he could really concentrate on was not falling off. He was definitely not worried about the hatch.

As they neared the compound, they saw the boys racing their ponies and horses on the beach and realized they needed to cross over the dunes soon to get out of sight, and then sneak them back to the barn. At this point, the children could not be trusted to come up with any explanation of where they had been or why their horses were panting. They slowed down and moved toward the dune line and over the sandhill, which would take them behind the lighthouse and away from all the action taking place. Even so, they were not sure what other activities were being practiced in their yard. They began to try to find a path through the woods to completely avoid the area and come home from, what would seem to an observer, a trip to the village rather than one from the south beach.

They successfully maneuvered through the woods and almost came within sight of the Coast Guard station, but that would also enlist questions. This was getting complicated. They dismounted and began to walk the horses through the holly and yaupon trees and bushes. They came upon the path the navy had used to build the concrete structure that was hidden in the woods. Finally they saw a break in the trees that allowed them to catch the two-track road leading to the compound from the village. Nonchalantly they walked the horses back to the barn without anyone being the wiser.

"Whew!" Luke said when they were finally inside the barn. "That was close!"

"I was a little scared," said Blake. "It looked like we were gonna be caught. I forgot about those guys practicing for the Jamboree. Glad the Coast Guard didn't see us. They would surely tell Pop."

"I was trying to think of someplace we had been, but I couldn't think of anything. We couldn't have come from Mr. Hollivey's store, because they would have wanted to see the comic books. Besides, we don't have any money. I was just sure we wouldn't get to go back to the house anymore. We better be more careful."

All this chatter took place while they rubbed down the horses, got them water, and filled the oat bags hanging on the stall doors. Ellie looked at Blue, and she thought she saw him smile. *Naw, that wasn't possible.* She continued to brush him while Blake busied himself with cleaning the saddle they had hooked to the pulleys and swung it over to rest on the fence.

Exhausted from worry and excessive thinking, and excited to get started on their new plan, they came into the back door only to face Grandmom, who was busy fixing supper.

"Well, if you three don't look like the cat that swallowed the canary! What have you young-uns been up to today? Mr. Stocky, Mr. Anderson, and Mr. Leon were trying out their souped-up cars today on the beach. It was so exciting that your mother and I had to go out and look. Grandpop was trying to find you to get you to watch everything from the top of the lighthouse railing. Hope you didn't get into any mischief today. Don't want your grandpop to take away those horses just to keep you home."

Grandmom looked at the three guilty faces, and they could swear from her look that she knew exactly what was going on. She gave a sly smile and said, "Go wash up, now. It's time for supper, and Grandpop will be coming in any minute. Go upstairs and get your story straight, and come on back down."

The kids filled buckets of water and started up the stairs. Grandmom knew! And better than that, she didn't say anything. Grandmom was just the best!

They went to their rooms, filled the basins on their washstands with water, and washed off the obvious grime. Blake slicked back his hair, which, of course, didn't look *too* obvious, and they all marched downstairs, but only after planning that the two youngsters would keep their mouths shut and let Luke do all the talking. Usually when they were caught, they all tried to explain at the same time, and it made their problems even more obvious. This time they were prepared, thanks to Grandmom. They looked more casual as they descended the stairs, hoping Grandpop was not curious. Deep down, they all wanted to tell so-o-o-o badly.

Grandpop was so enthusiastic about watching the car races that he got lost in his description and didn't really press the issue. When asked where they were, Luke just said that they took the horses on the south beach, which was true.

Seems the Midgett boys were challenging all comers to race their good cars during the low tide of the wash. There was no match for the boys who operated the Blue Bus, as no one could match their skills in the sand in any vehicle, with one small exception. A boy from Buxton had his mother's fancy new car and was determined to compete. Since this was exactly what would happen on the day of the Jamboree, the kids figured they would still get to see the races, just not from the top of the lighthouse, which would be closed for climbing on the day of the festivities. With so many people, and children especially, it would be hard to control the crowd.

The privilege of climbing the lighthouse came with rules, and everyone complied. The entire island was proud of that huge tower, and all took part in seeing that it was cared for. The rules included no bare feet (that let most of the children out), only so many people at a time, and someone needed to be near the lens area to protect against curious greasy fingers, and so on, and so on....

Grandmom had made delicious biscuits to go with a pot of navy beans, and she had strawberry Jell-o for dessert, topped with heavy cream from Twinkle's milk. How she did this was a mystery to the kids, but Grandmom was talented. They knew that.

Pop loved Jell-o, as did the kids. Nett and Grandmom kept talking about the races from the afternoon, and Grandmom looked slyly at the kids, knowing they were up to something but she had yet to put her finger on it. She did know, however, that it involved the old house.

As soon as they were excused from the table, they rushed upstairs to start working on their thinking plan.

They went to Ellie's room, which was the farthest away from Nett's apartment, and sat on the bed cross-legged, trying to figure out how to go about moving something they couldn't touch. Finally they decided to close the door and attempt to think it open. They settled themselves on the rug in Ellie's room. Believing they needed to be touching each other in order to give more strength to their minds, they figured they would concentrate on the word, "open." They linked arms, with Ellie in the middle, and closed their eyes as they put as much concentration as they could muster into the word. It seemed like an awful lot of effort, as they all thought so hard and their sending was so intense they began to get light-headed. After more time than they had anticipated, they loosened their grip and opened their eyes. Before they had time to speak, the doorknob slowly began to turn. All three felt their hearts pound, and Ellie put her hand over her mouth. Luke was drained of color, and Blake's eyes were so wide they looked twice their size. As they watched with suspended breath, the door creaked open, and Nett stuck her head in.

"Everything okay in here?" she asked, without seeming to notice anything. She continued, "Grandpop said to come on back downstairs in a few minutes. He is going to find *Charlie McCarthy* on the radio."

Nett looked at the three on the floor and was a bit puzzled at the shocked expressions on their faces, to the point she actually became a little concerned. "You three okay?" she asked again.

"We're fine, Mom," said Luke. "We were getting ready to play a game." He swallowed hard, surprising even himself at the quickness of the reply.

"All right, but don't let it be too long. Pop will be waiting. The show starts at eight o'clock, and he thought you would get a kick out of it. I'm going to the room to write Daddy. Anything you want to say to him?" She was completely unaware of what she had interrupted.

"Mom, tell Daddy we miss him," Blake said sincerely, "and we love him."

"Me, too, Mom. Tell him we say his name first in our prayers, and we like it when he tells us about his adventures on the ship." Luke also was giving a truly sincere answer, as both he and Blake sadly began thinking about their dad. They did miss him, they did love him, and they felt like his sea stories were just like being with him.

"I love him, too," said Ellie, "and he is always first in my prayers, too." At that point, all thoughts of opening hatches and doors disappeared as they put all their commitment into thinking about Bill.

Nett closed the door, and for a minute, all was quiet. Then the three children doubled over with laughter at how shocked and scared they had been when that handle moved. All three felt like they had had small heart attacks when the door opened. It had shocked them so much, they could not get back to the feeling they had before it happened. So they decided to go downstairs with Grandpop and leave opening things telepathically for another time.

Charlie McCarthy was so funny, and the relief of laughing so hard with Grandpop was welcomed, as the three had worn themselves slam out with their experiment. They still did not know exactly who opened the door. Did they *get* Nett to do it? Or was that a coincidence?

Charlie McCarthy, the puppet, was a character—kind of a kid in the things he said and did—and was always getting in trouble, while his "Master" or "Father," Edgar Bergen the puppeteer, tried to cover up his antics to those around them. Ol' Charlie reminded them of themselves, with all the ducking and dodging he did to have fun, and not let the grown-ups know about it. Wonder if Charlie could open doors?

After Sunday school the children only tolerated the beautiful Sunday dinner Grandmom and Nett had prepared, and they quickly excused themselves from the grown-up conversation that seemed to linger on.

Inconspicuously they sauntered out to the barn for the horses. They had decided to attempt to open the hatch telepathically while staring at the trap in the ceiling. Getting away and being by themselves in the old house guaranteed them that there would be no interruption. Grandmom met them as they rounded the keeper's quarters' long porch.

"You young-uns be careful now, and keep a watch on the time. Supper is at six o'clock sharp, and I will expect you to be home at that time," she said with a wink and a suspiciously sly smile. I'll be thinking about you." With that, she turned her back and went to rejoin the others.

As Grandmom was returning to the dining table, her son Tommy and his wife Winnie's car rounded the corner of the compound for a visit. The cars that would occupy the compound for viewing the practice races had not yet begun to arrive, and the kids knew that everyone was coming over to watch the fun. They were leaving just in time to avoid questions as they crossed over to the hard wash of the ocean. It was low tide, which meant they would be returning at the incoming tide, and would need to anticipate the soft sand and be careful with the horses.

They discussed all of this as they traveled down the south beach to get to the Trent Woods. It was a pretty day with blue skies and billowing white clouds that formed special shapes. The sandpipers and smaller, plumper sanderlings along with the plovers ran in companies along the wash, searching out mole crabs and chasing each other away from the best pockets. Shells, both whole and broken, tumbled onto the beach, only to tumble back again. The sand near the wash was hard, and the horses enjoyed the romp. Gus and Blue struck a striking contrast as they picked up the spring sunlight on their manes. The weather was still a bit chilly, but the kids were prepared with their jackets. The salt air was refreshingly pure. At one point a school of dolphins swam along with them, playing beside the travelers as they also moved south along the beach.

The kids were quite familiar with the dolphins. The cacophony of sounds, as well as the individual sound of a particular dolphin, comforted them. In their minds, the mammals were talking to them. They realized that the beautiful creatures had chosen to spend time with them, because the dolphins so often followed them down the beach. As some of the most advanced nonhuman intelligences on the planet, the dolphins were recognizable as the kids heard the modulated whistles and clicks that came from the sac below their blowholes. They were interesting to watch as they touched each other and played in the surf, jumping in unison, tail walking and spinning. Their short, distant squawks were almost synchronized, like the chant of a huddle.

Watching the dolphins also provided the children with knowledge of impending danger, whether from sharks or the approach of a squall. It was fun to see the dolphins swim upside down in order to catch something. They were familiar with the kids' weekly appearance, and they followed along, showing off at intervals. Their whistles indicated different things and were recognizable to each other as belonging to a particular individual. As each human had a particular voice, so did the dolphins. An excited whistle brought on the troops. Today, they were in a playful mood and only swam along until they instinctively moved out to sea when they knew the horses would leave the beach for the woods.

Tying up at the house, the excitement built as the three anticipated their next move. They easily accessed the house and hurried to the second-floor bedroom off the hall to the closet, where the ladder and hatch awaited their concentration.

They moved away anything they thought would distract them, quieted down, and began their even breathing, which would calm them enough to focus on the task at hand. Sitting on the floor, touching each other as they had seen the dolphins do, they bowed their heads and began to concentrate on moving that hatch. After some minutes and a slight headache, they realized that they had become so absorbed with the mental picture of the hatch that they were actually leaning heavily on each other. At that realization, they opened their eyes and slowly turned their heads toward each other in a quizzical look of fulfillment. Without hesitation or conversation, Luke rose from his position on the floor and slowly climbed the ladder to where his hand could reach the hatch. He pushed up.

The trapdoor opened with only the slightest of pressure, and Blake and Ellie uttered an audible gasp. Probably the most surprised was Luke. Without pushing it all the way open, he turned and looked down at his companions. Almost embarrassed, he slowly began to smile. Blake, of course, laughed out loud, and then all of them began to laugh. Luke pushed the tip of the hatch until it moved to the side and rested on the floor of the room above. He climbed the last steps of the ladder and looked around in the dim light. The only available light was coming from a small, round-framed window that faced the sea.

"Ellie, you and Blake go back down to the kitchen and get a couple of lanterns. It's dark up here. Be sure not to forget the matches. There isn't enough light to look around!" His shout was a mixture of purpose and excitement. He did not move from where he was standing. He just turned slowly, straining to see what was in that room. The closed room gave off a heavy, musty smell, and he pulled his shirt up over his nose to keep out the dust. There was much to do up there if they were to explore any at all. This was a long attic, and it looked to be on the back side of the third-floor quarters that Uncle Jabez occupied.

Blake and Ellie, lanterns in hand, climbed the ladder. As Luke extended a hand, they both were hoisted on to the floor. Immediately, each also covered their noses. In the dim light, Luke lit first one then the other of the two lanterns. Finally, each mustered the nerve to move.

The large room was not in disarray but neatly packed with trunks, chests, and wooden boxes. The trunks were of different styles: round topped, with metal strappings, and some totally flat, with either corroded leather closures or lashed with tarnished metal around the sides and tops. All were closed. Some had clothes, others had books, and the children carefully opened the ones that had latches. None seemed locked. The trunks backing up to the wall had to be moved away from the wall to open them and display the treasures. They were careful with the side handles in moving them, as one leather one was so old and corroded that the strap had disintegrated and dangled down on one side.

There must have been nine or ten trunks, and several short bookcases against the wall. Statues were placed in various places, depicting the busts of pirates, kings, or ships. Some appeared to be of Poseidon or some other Greek figure. It was a strange collection. There were ornately framed paintings of people and scenes stacked against each other, the trunks, or a wall. They decided that since everything was so old and undisturbed, they needed to be careful in how and what they touched. Their plan was to do one at a time and not run around opening everything at once, scattering things as they searched.

"I never noticed that window before," said Blake. "Do you think we can see it from the oceanside?"

"From the ground, I think it is overshadowed by the third floor, but look, it is just beside that part of the house that faces the beach." Luke stood looking out the small round opening, and he could see the trees and a little of the ocean through them.

Then they noticed that the attic ran all across the entire area of the second floor. Upon further observation, they noticed a door at the far left end from where they were standing. When they opened that small door, they saw another complementary round window in that room. The windows appeared not really to be for viewing anything, but only to let light into the attic. Both round openings were on the back side of the house, obscured from anyone who might notice there was any room or attic above the second floor. The ceilings of the rooms on the second floor were high, so the attic had to be above them, and it appeared that the third floor was just above this. So the house really had four stories, the third being secret, like the inside walls.

As they opened first one, then another of the trunks, they carefully took out the things they found, then deliberately put each piece back as they found them. There were hats and small boxes of jewelry—maybe good stuff, maybe just ornamental things. The children were not expert enough to distinguish the real from copies. There was a box of trinkets, the kind a seafaring man would collect, parts of a compass, a trumpet horn, ship's charts, rolled-up maps, a sexton, a telescope, and other brass paraphernalia from a ship's captain's quarters.

Another chest was filled with women's fancy clothing, and hidden in the lower part they touched another, smaller box that had been carefully placed in the middle near the bottom and under mounds of cloth. Luke reached in and put his hand around something hard, wrapped in red cloth. It was a rather thick book. As he pulled it out, Blake and Ellie moved from their knees to a sitting position, bringing all the lanterns in for a closer look. The book was fine leather, bordered on all sides with gold piping, and with a substantial clasp of leather binding. The ends of the two-piece leather strap that kept the book closed were covered in a brass two-piece plate, and one part slid into the other. In the middle was a keyhole. Luke tried to separate the leather from the two pieces, but it was locked. On the cover, in the middle under the locked leather strap, they could distinguish a medallion that appeared to be etched in the rendering of a skull and, below, crossed cutlasses. That was clearly what it was, even though the leather binding that locked the book covered most of the middle. It was marvelous. The red cloth that had wrapped the book appeared to be a flag, with the same rendering of a skull and crossed cutlasses stitched into the front. Ellie put her hand to her mouth, and Blake collapsed flat out on the floor in one of his fake faints, stretched out on the floor, with both arms splayed out.

The Book

The discovery of the magnificent book stopped the search for anything else. No other trunk was opened, and there were so many. The children just stared at the book, with its expensive leather and brass binding. When they finally gained their composure, Ellie got back on her knees and began carefully feeling around in the pile of antique clothing for something hard that might hold a key to open the book. She found nothing. She brought up several items that might have been the size of a key, but she located only a purse, a piece of brocade, or epaulets and other trappings attached to one or the other of the dresses. Finally, with no successful result, she stopped and sat down beside the boys, who were still running their hands over the outside of the book.

"I'll bet it is Uncle Jabez's journal. Or maybe his accounting book, or maybe a very famous book on pirates," Luke guessed.

Blake had his turn at guessing, but they did not know what they had found, and until they uncovered the key's hiding place, they would never know.

Ellie sat quietly, just looking at the trunk and its carefully packed fancy dresses. Her mind wandered away from the book to the clothing she saw. *Who wore these,* she thought to herself. *Were they stolen from a king's ship? Or did they belong to Aunt Rhetta, Jabez's sister? She also lived in the house. Maybe Uncle Jabez was married, and these belonged to his wife, or maybe to Sabra, Rhetta's daughter, who also occupied the house with her mother and uncle, after her husband died. And, after all, Sabra's son ran a business in Hatteras and had lived for only a time in the house.* Preferring to be near his shipping business, Soloman Jennette Austin had moved his family to the village of Hatteras. There he lived in a canal next to the sound, which emptied into the shipping docks he owned. His life was away from the old house, but he saw to the upkeep. His son Jesse Meads Austin did not survive the Civil War. At his death, the house went to William Bateman Jennette, who never lived there. He kept the house repaired until he died, even fending off the Yankee Civil War officers who tried to make it a headquarters, but one night of wolves fixed that, and they believed the house to be haunted. William subsequently left this property to his granddaughter Odessa. His holdings in the village were divided among his other children. He had been left two Jennette tracts of land: the one on the hillside in Trent Woods, and his own estate in Buxton. Odessa Scarborough Jennette was not the oldest, nor even the only girl. She had brothers and sisters, but according to her grandfather, she was the joy of his life and the one he preferred. She kept company with him as he grew into his later years. His gift to her was like a magic castle, almost untouchable, that she dared to visit as a child. Had she discovered its secrets? Her memories were of dreams. The magnificent mansion stood empty for more than fifty years.

The ladder was well hidden, the house held its secrets close, and the hidden passageways were not discovered after Sabra. Nothing was obvious to the casual observer except the heavy canvas coverings over antique furniture, and other items that were so old nobody wanted them. The wolves had taken it all over: porch, barn, surrounding woods, and the property. The protective pack only allowed a few to visit. William Bateman

Jennette was one of the few, and with nine children and a store to run, he did not want to move to the woods. It would have been quite a hardship to travel over unforgiving sand trails to run a general store. He lived in the village in a house he built next to the store. He kept his fishing gear in the boat barn and his cows and horses in the larger barn. He only needed the property, not the house. Neither of his wives ever wanted to be that far away from the village. Living there was fit only for a reclusive person, like Uncle Jabez, one who wanted neither friends nor company.

Having built the house of stone from the quarries in the mountains, the house was set to stand for hundreds of years, similar to European castles. Located away from the ocean and sound—and surrounded by heavy woods with only a small wagon track in the beginning leading to the main road—nature had little effect on the deterioration, especially since the house was subject to constant caretaking by the Jennette family. When Charlie Gray married Odessa, and as a young couple they toured the property, Charlie fell in love. Being first a merchant in town, then in the service, then with his keeper's job, all he could do was to fix what he could. To Charlie, it was amazing that none of the Jennettes seemed interested. The hardship of its location allowed the magical house with the web of secrets to perfect itself as the Jennette blood began to come to strength while waiting for Ellie. The very stones were enchanted by Rhetta. She first guided Jabez, then Sabra.

In the beginning, the kids had not chosen to explore any of the trunks nearest the trapdoor, but decided to open trunks not in such a prominent position. What they came to think of as The Book was hidden in one of the more elaborate trunks. Instead of the metal strappings that decorated many of the trunks, this trunk displayed beautiful slats of a peculiar wood along the sides, unlike the plainness of the others. It did not have a fancy domed top, but a flat one. It was inconspicuous and prominent all at the same time, but not one that someone would pick as the most ornamental. Others were truly finely appointed, and after this find, the kids could only conjecture what was in the fancy trunks. So what made them choose this chest? The puzzling questions rattled around in Ellie's mind until she was so intrigued that she could not move from in front of the trunk.

The boys had given up trying to find a key. Not being able to figure out how to open The Book, they placed it back on the red flag, folded as best they could to match its original state, and placed it on top of the other articles in the trunk. Then they closed the lid. The trio then moved around to briefly open other chests and explore their contents. Some were filled with old books—so many that they did not attempt to go through them. They pulled out several unlocked diaries. Some had exquisite writing paper, filled with sketches of everything from the sky to a frog, and some were yet to be filled. Ellie imagined herself entering her thoughts in one of the special books.

Satisfied that none of these journals were the particular one he hoped to find from Uncle Jabez, Luke decided they were something to read for another day. Actually, it would require several other days. This project looked like it would last them a long time. Puzzled, they all agreed they could do nothing more that day in the attic. The light was running low, the dust choking, and they felt the need for fresh air.

Ellie opened the special trunk, decided that The Book was safely wrapped in its red flag, replaced it under the top layer of clothing, and closed the lid. They all climbed down the ladder, closing the hatch behind them. Carefully they rearranged the clothes back in their position in the closet and left the room for another day. They were mentally exhausted as they returned the kerosene lamps to the kitchen. After they closed up the house, they headed toward the horses, failing to see the yellow eyes peering at them from behind the brush next to the little house.

The ride back home was refreshing. They breathed deeply the salt air of the sea, eliminating the musty feeling in their nostrils. The boys chattered about the pirate artifacts and the things they had uncovered, but Ellie was strangely quiet. The pounding of the waves, the squeaking of seagulls, and fresh ocean air filled her lungs as she breathed deeply, lost in thought about the key.

When they rode up to the lighthouse compound, they could hear the shouts of excitement coming from the various teams practicing their entrance into the sea with their dories. Ol' Tony and Big Roy were patiently standing on the beach, freed of the harness they had pulled to launch the boat, and the village boys were just rounding the anchored buoy used to mark the turnaround. The Coast Guard dory was lagging behind, as the sailors pulled hard to overtake the dory in front of them, whoever that was. It looked like the Jamboree had already started, but this was only a rehearsal.

In the compound were several jalopies that had been practicing on the beach, which was now coming into high tide, leaving the sand too soft and thick to race anything, not even a horse. Men and boys were milling around in the compound, holding the reins of their ponies or horses and talking excitedly about the possibilities of the Jamboree. There was a lot of friendly ribbing about the abilities of this one or that one, and nobody noticed Gus and Blue as they were led to the barn. The official Pirates Jamboree was to take place in two weeks. This weekend had been the first time for practice. Everyone had one more weekend to perfect their strategy and obtain whatever they thought they needed, or whatever they had found lacking, on this weekend.

The children went around to the barn and groomed their horses. Presently Grandpop and a couple of other men walked Ol' Tony and Big Roy into their stalls and began grooming and feeding them. They, too, had experienced an exciting day. The kids were glad, as the two older horses did not get the same amount of exercise as before the new horses came, and it seemed to make them happy to get out. The kids had considered taking one of them every time they left the compound on Gus and Blue, so that each child would have his own ride. But after discussing it, they did not want one of the horses to be left behind, so they never discussed it again. It had occurred to Luke that they should make sure to ride them around the compound once in a while, and that became a plan. None of the kids wanted the animals to be neglected.

Grandmom was happy to see that the children had returned in plenty of time for supper, and she was also happy when Ellie came into the kitchen to help her. Of course, Ellie spilled everything to Grandmom. Ellie told her grandmother that they had seen where Pop placed the key, and using it, they had gone into the house to look around. She apologized for not having told her before, but she explained that the house held some meaning for her. She reminded Grandmom about the dream she had of seeing Weroansqua and meeting her mother, Annie. The child in her had wanted to return ever since she had those thoughts, to see the rooms again and experience any familiar feelings she could pick up from her mother. She told her grandmother of the beautiful dresses in the closets, but she did not reveal their secret discovery of the attic or what they found there.

Odessa listened, knowing she would ask Weroansqua in her dreams tonight and get answers. Also, she smiled as she remembered how many times she talked her more adventurous older brother, Alaska, to go with her as she had explored. She did not judge the kids for their curiosity. She was glad. She knew there were secrets in the old house, but she had never found anything out in the ordinary old stuff, so she had no idea what these three had uncovered. Odessa and Alaska had found the place interesting, but not so much that they spent much time there. These kids were one hundred times more curious than she had been, but Odessa was the only one in her family at that time with extra perception. She had found Alaska not nearly as energized as she was, and therefore she spent time with her other sisters, leaving the ancestral property alone.

The house had been left to Odessa, as Grandpa Benjamin saw her as his favorite, and the Jennette will that accompanied the house through the years had specifically stated that the house would be left to a female of the family, not the male. Nobody understood the request, but it was made through Rhetta, and Rhetta knew what she was doing. There would be another, like herself, who was expected, and she counted on intuition to choose the correct lineage.

When Odessa married Charlie, he had graduated from college and volunteered to serve in the military for a while, as did all the men of his family. His father, Amelick Thomas Gray, won medals for lifesaving while in the service of the surfmen, while stationed out of the Big Kinnakeet Station south of what is now Avon. He instilled his love of country in all the boys. On the island, and especially in the Gray family, all males felt the need to serve—some out of patriotism, some to see the world, and some, like Charlie, to please their father.

After his military service, Charlie and Odessa settled in Buxton village, where Charlie ran a general store, involving himself in construction, which had been his concentration in college, and politics. Then he was offered the position of keeper of the Hatteras Light. His connections in the service were strong, and his brothers-in-law were certainly well thought of in the Lightkeeping Service. So Charlie moved his growing family to the lighthouse compound and found that there was little time to deal with that huge mansion on the hill. They tried to keep it in good repair, visiting it at least monthly, but with eight children and the store, Odessa had little time for the project. Now they were even farther away. Tommy took over the store in the village, but he also had a growing family. He and his cousin Mahlon had met two pretty schoolteachers, and both got married. It was up to Charlie and the sons left at home to see to it that the old place did not end up a pile of stones.

When Bill married Nett, he was delighted to help with the place. Thomas O'Finnegan had moved his young family from Ireland to New York City. His wife Kathleen and three young children, John, Bill and Margaret. He made a veiled attempt to "Americanize" his name by dropping the "O", and settled in the Irish section of Brooklyn. Bill was only 14 when his father died, leaving John as the head of the family. By now there were other siblings, and Bill realized the hardship of his brother John to support his mother, his sister and younger brother Thomas. Bill lied about his age, joined the Navy and began to learn a trade. Not only did he keep it in good condition, he rigged up a system of wires and sounds, using the pipe organ that Uncle Jabez had bought for Rhetta, thus discouraging any vandals who had designs on the old place. The wolves did the rest.

Grandmom loved the old house, and many times she wished she could live there. Knowing that was impossible, though, she never expressed her desire to Charlie. She did not want to appear disappointed with her lot in life, and as her days were filled trying to raise the children, there was little time. To her knowledge, only Jack had expressed interest. He and Lindy spent time there, and he kept her informed of the condition. Otherwise, she did not ask.

That night as Ellie snuggled down in bed, she fell into a deep sleep and dreamed of the elaborate wooden trunk and its contents. Somewhere in that sleep, she found herself

in front of the trunk, on her knees, rubbing the wood that decorated the piece. She ran her hand across the side on one of the ornate wooden slats that wrapped horizontal on the outside. When she slipped her hand from back to front of the third slat adorning the right side, it moved. Repeating the motion, a little more forcefully, the wooden piece moved aside and exposed a hollow compartment behind the slat. As the wood moved, a small velvet bag dropped to the floor from the obviously hollowed-out slat. She picked it up, emptied it, and out dropped a key. She retrieved the key and turned it around in her hand. It looked to be gold. She lifted the lid to the trunk and rummaged around until she found The Book, securely wrapped in the red flag. She uncovered The Book from the cloth and turned it so the locked leather pieces were on top. She tried the key in the keyhole of the brass closures, and the two brass pieces fell away.

She awakened in a cold sweat and immediately got out of bed and tiptoed into the boys' room. Quietly, trying not to startle, she gently nudged Luke until he groggily responded.

"Whatsa matter?" he said sleepily.

"I found the key," she whispered. "I know where the key is."

Luke sleepily turned over and squinted into the darkness at his little cousin's pretty face so close to his own. He was not sure what she had said.

"What?" he asked.

Ellie whispered again. "I think I found the key to the pirate book," she quietly repeated.

Luke almost knocked her off the edge of the bed as he sat straight up. Even in the dimly lit room, when the lighthouse made its sweep into the window, she could see his startled face.

"How?" he said.

"I think I dreamed it. I had this dream. . . ."

By this time Blake was moving around, saying, "What are you guys doing? Are we going somewhere? Don't forget about me. I want to go, too."

"Blake, be quiet, and come over here," Luke said. "Ellie had a dream about the key."

"I think I dreamed," Ellie continued, "where the key is hidden. I had this dream that I was sitting in front of the trunk and rubbing the pretty wood on the side, and one of the slats of the wood moved back, and the key dropped out the hollow part of the wood. When I tried the key in the lock of the book, the book opened."

"What was in it?" questioned Luke.

"I don't know. I woke up right then, so I decided to come in and tell you about it." Ellie was trying to be quiet, but they were all sitting cross-legged on Luke's bed, just staring at each other in the dark. The lighthouse illuminated their faces every seven seconds, and their sleepy little eyes were glowing.

"We can't do anything about it until next weekend. But I can't wait to try it!" Luke was so excited, he thought he might not sleep for a whole week thinking about that book and its key.

It was the slowest week that ever crept across the calendar. Every day they made Ellie tell her dream again. They almost forced her to go to bed early each night in hopes that she would have another dream. It did not happen. But what did happen was that the three saints—Travis, Micah, and Brendan—were sitting on their silver-blue cloud, holding their sides, laughing at the anticipation of the three charges in their care. They loved the games the children provided them. They had to control Brendan, or he would be in a perpetually silly mood and probably drive Blake crazy. They loved the kids and tried to fill their lives to overflowing with adventure and knowledge of the lives around them and the ones who had gone before them. They were in constant communication with the wolves who protected the children. The saints were also in total control of the horses the children rode. Even the dolphins were pawns the saints used to fascinate the three young ones and shield them from harm. The adventure the angels had in store for them was their most elaborate yet, but not the most elaborate *ever*!

Everyone has been given a guardian angel, and the three saints that were in constant communication with these charges found that their assignment involved children who had been given special powers. The duty of these three saints was to allow the three children to uncover their family history. It was their mission to give the children experiences that would unveil the mysteries of the special place where they were born, and the people in their family who had contributed to the island as it progressed in history, isolated from the mainland. They allowed the children to travel through time, to observe their ancestors and how they lived. It was the saints' idea to enlist other spiritual beings to help them know the ocean and the creatures that inhabited it. The saints were to pass on the talents and strengths of the island in order for it to take its relevant place in the world. It was the task of the saints to have the progress of these island people continue to contribute to the advancement of the world, guiding them and allowing them to relay the past, insuring that it would not be forgotten.

The children would later learn the journal was special to Jabez. It was purchased from an old bookshop in Boston, and immediately on seeing it, he had to have it. He had never seen anything quite so marvelous. As a young man, he had the feeling it would be a special part of his life, and as he kept it, he only wanted to fill its empty pages with important information. To him, the journal held secrets that he felt should be guarded, as the names entered in it were to be protected. Because it contained the names of people with whom he had clandestine dealings, he was both preserving and protecting the information within it.

Jabez felt it necessary to chronicle the life and times in which he found himself. In his private diary, he did not want repercussions for the people whose names he entered. He freely entered his thoughts and business, taking steps to keep existence of the book secret.

To ensure that the private diary would stay classified, Rhetta put a charm on the book after her brother's death. This incantation would not allow the book to be read by anyone not chosen. Therefore, she revealed only to Ellie, in her dream, how to access the book.

In it were the names of heroes and villains—local people who had defied the government to provide for their neighbors and adventures that at that time people were forbidden to have. Under the spell, the book would provide colors that formed pictures disguised as words, and as the children read, the pictures would be revealed to them through colors. The children would see the pictures as they read, and the colors that radiated from the pages formed in their unsuspecting minds the vision of what was taking place. Rhetta had designed the book so that the kids would go on an adventure every time they read it.

What the children did not know was that after the book had been read, it would lock forever. They were to be the only ones, besides Jabez and Rhetta, who would ever have knowledge of what the book contained.

The Family Business

The thick, puffy fog of early spring was heavy on this Saturday morning, and the weight of it rained down from the black, dark blue, and silver-laced cloud that hung densely over the beach. It was hard to see Blue. He seemed to disappear when he got even a little beyond Gus. But there were times that Gus also vanished in the fog of silver-dusted droplets of dew that wet whatever solid object they hit. It was a little exciting for the kids, although if Ellie and Blake had not been together on Blue, they might have panicked in the thickness of the morning.

Luke kept a level head. He was sticking out his tongue to see if he could capture some of the silver droplets that were falling from the sky. His mind was filled with thoughts of The Book. He just knew it was the journal he had so been seeking. *What else could it be, except money transactions, the kind that were always kept secret?* He had read enough books to know that a man should keep his business to himself.

He hardly noticed as the big dark mass passed him near the wash of shoreline, splashing up foam and stark, cold water. Shivering brought him back to consciousness, and he realized that they could be nearer the turnoff than he expected.

He yelled to the others to slow down, and he saw a dark shadow coming closer until the pretty face of a young horse filled the fog in front of him. His black face was framed in mushy clouds around his neck like a fur collar. The thick billows of white fog suspended his face in midair. His dark eyes sparkled in clouds of an endless opaque mist. Luke could not see his legs, nor his feet, nor the two probably grinning faces behind him—just those blue-black eyes, with ears erect, and a nose snorting out little puffs, as Blue waited for a greeting from horse and rider.

"Hey, buddy!" Luke said to the inquisitive young horse. He looked like he thoroughly loved these adventures. Well, by golly, Gus did! He couldn't wait to get next to the fence for mounting, then he and Luke waited patiently for the others to mount Blue. Gus would look like maybe he forgot, moving away, shaking his head and golden mane. Luke was getting used to jumping on him full on. First he had used maybe a run, hitting the bottom pole of the fence, and a sideways jump method he had perfected (after many skinned knees) in order to give him the height he couldn't get on his own. Now he was beginning to skip the bottom rail of the fence, as it was awkward. He kept one of Grandpop's crates near the fence and slid it behind Gus, who had learned to stand still. With that boost, hands landing on Gus's rump, on he went. This had taken him quite some time to perfect, but determination ruled his life, and this was no exception. Blake complained all during this process, as he, Ellie, and Blue had to wait for Luke to do his thing.

Luke landed on Gus's back—solid sometimes, most times taking more than one try, struggling to hold on—but he was getting better. This was one time that Blake's cry, "I big enough!" did not cause either of the other two to let him do anything but mount from the fence. Blake, it seemed, would never get used to being the smallest. What he didn't realize was that he was so talented in other ways, he had saved the day for everybody more than once. He just could not get over not being Luke.

As the fog lifted with the morning, the saints settled in to watch the children discover The Book. They had planned everything just right. Ellie was beginning to respond and respect her inner thoughts as they were sent to her in dreams. The three silver-clothed deities reclined on their bellies with arms crossed under their chins, hanging over their perch, thinking about leading the kids into discovering the secrets of the mansion. Now it was only a matter of time and patience, as the children were progressing right on track.

Tied to trees, Blue and Gus nuzzled each other as their rope allowed them leeway to roam. They were content to wait. The kids could have put them in the barn, but cleaning it would be obvious. They could not fashion a corral, as that, too, would be noticed, so the trees were the answer and the horses were satisfied. The wolves showed up at the edge of the woods, and all acknowledged the others' presence, proceeding with whatever they were doing before: watching and waiting.

The children closed all doors behind them. They felt comfortable that they would not be disturbed, especially after seeing the wolves, and hurried through the kitchen to the middle stairs. They moved the clothes in the closet aside, and placed a possible catch, a nearby chest, just in case someone should misjudge a step. They found the loose board that revealed the ladder, and as they climbed up and opened the hatch, they were glad to see the sun coming through the morning clouds and streaming through the tiny window, like it might have been trained to do that very thing. It lit the entire room, even some corners newly revealed, for just that special amount of time.

The kids very carefully moved the trunk and slipped it to a more accessible place, near where the tiny window would light it for most of the morning. This time they were prepared, as they had earlier placed the lanterns nearby to grab as they rushed through the kitchen. They were now armed with light to survey whatever they imagined they might find.

They opened the lid of the extraordinary trunk. The sun bounced off the wood of the top, so it was hard to distinguish the rich wood from the brass trappings that anchored the corners, as the practically windowless attic still was a little dark. Ellie rubbed the wood, which felt smooth. She sat back and looked long at the trunk. The front was wood planks, highly polished. There were wooden rounded slats that ran twice across the front and sides of the outside, like straps to keep the sides of the chest in place. They were also highly polished. The corners of the trunk had brass plates bolted in place. The loose piece of wood seen in Ellie's dream was one of the slats on the right side. She put her hand on the piece, like in the dream, and as she pushed, the slat slid back, exactly as she dreamed it would. Out of the cavity behind the slat dropped a velvet bag.

"Oh my!" she gasped, as if not realizing that she had experienced what later would be defined as a *vision*. It seemed that anything she could think of, she could solve, if she wanted to. She had thought of nothing else but that book since she unwrapped it the first time. The feeling of the beautiful red silk cloth alone stayed in the memory of her fingertips. Her heart pounded just a little faster as she poised to lift a key from the pouch.

"Wow!" Luke was equally astounded, even though he believed Ellie on the first night she told him about finding the key. He had long been convinced that they were beginning to connect with things. He depended on Ellie's dream to set the path, and he knew, with the state of mind Powwaw had given him, he was also intuitive, even if it was only the ability to determine what was right or what was wrong. His sense of bearing in life was strong. He possessed great hope and the confidence to lean toward what was meant to be.

He felt sure that something was getting ready to happen, when he saw the trunk and recalled how Ellie had described everything exactly as he was now seeing it. He simply could not wait to uncover the secrets The Book held. He actually had more faith in Ellie than she had in herself.

Blake thought that neither one of them could do any wrong. He worshiped both of them. They were his idols, and he looked up to them as his role models. He was not gullible. Even though he believed every word he heard from anybody, he still always checked it out. He only counted on those he found he could trust, and Luke and Ellie had never let him down. He seemed to be smart beyond his years. Maybe *savvy* would be a better word for Blake.

Ellie opened the purple pouch by the shiny gold braid that also pulled it closed. She dropped out a golden key in her upturned hand. As she closed her fingers around the smooth metal, she raised it to her head, touched her forehead between her eyes, and then handed it to Luke.

Luke scooted over on his knees to a position in front of the open trunk with the book resting inside of it. Wrapped in a red flag undisturbed from the week before was the huge and rather heavy volume. He placed it on the floor in front of all of them. As he unfolded the flag, the brass trappings around the leather binder gleamed and winked as if to be glad for some sunshine. There it was, its brass corners, which also ran along the edges of the cover, shining. The strap that seemed to hold The Book together was finished off with brass ornamental edgings. Even the keyhole in the middle of the strap was carved from metal. Also visible underneath part of the strap, embedded in the top cover of the book, was a fancy medallion, like the stamp of a king, but larger. The red waxlike material, making the insignia of a skull with crossed cutlasses under it, was tipped in gold. Layers of wax and metal had both hardened over two hundred years to a seemingly indestructible finish.

Luke put the key into the keyhole and immediately was thrown back. They all were. The force had been so great, they found themselves all resting on their backs and elbows. They had been knocked at least two feet backward.

Each sat up, all looking around, first at each other and then scanning the room for something to explain what happened. They waved away the sparkles in the air to gain visual access to the scene. The Book was glowing! They straightened upright and looked at The Book and its halo, like a rainbow in front of them, all over the floor and ceiling. But The

Book was not only still closed, but the brass edges of the binder had come together on all four corners to lock it down on the sides. Still, at least the flap was off, and both pieces were resting at the side.

Ellie examined The Book, the new brass corners, the flap, and the key still in it. They saw the open lock and the closed corners. She felt around, in and out of the translucent rainbow of glowing colors that emanated from the cover. If one was trying to sneak around and open The Book, it would surely not be possible as the highly visible glow was rising upward from the cover. She kept looking, and Blake reached over and touched the skull on the red insignia.

They all felt like the room had moved, but it was only the top of the book as it opened and displayed the text on the floor in front of them:

> This book belongs to Jabez Benjamin Jennette
> late of Buxton, on the Island of Cape Hatteras
> all contents of like script will become record

The first page was written in really rich-looking gold script. Maybe Uncle Jabez was a rich man? They just looked at each other and turned the page, which revealed in bold type.

RECORDS OF TRANSFER

Under each column of the pages and pages of transfer of goods and money was an amount, the date, a description, the seller, the buyer, the price, the final transaction, and the line for witnesses. Everything.

Usually the witness was Rhetta, Jabez, or both. Later records showed Sabra's signature. The amounts and numbers of goods were astronomical.

They turned the pages, as there seemed to be a second half of the ledger separated by a thin leather sheet, maybe deer hide or some other skin.

Part 2 was most unusual. It was, from beginning to end, story after story of the pirates who touched Cape Hatteras soil: a record of their tales of each other, or tales observed by Jabez, or rumors told in dimly lit meeting houses. Added to the stories were observances of those in attendance. The pages were filled with a pirate's day, week, month, and year, before he hung like a dog on some public gallows, on some public dock, in some public display of justice—all over the Caribbean Islands, plus all the colonies from Florida through Rhode Island.

The children were astonished with the treasure they had found: true stories of the pirates. They knew nothing was better than a good book, one that would set readers down in some magical space and take them on an adventure. They laughed at how wonderful it was going to be to read even one story. The colors streaming up from each separate tale were different. It was evil, adventurous, scary, and dangerous all at the same time. The pirates were bold, not as cruel as former books had described. They were younger than the other books revealed, riddled with disease, hungry, mostly drunk, rich and poor in the folly of the moment. They were not allowed to play cards below deck, as wagering could lead to killing, and conflict among thieves was to be avoided at all cost. Some captains did not allow card playing at all, and some did not allow wagers, but that was hard to determine. Thieves knew the art of deceit.

The first story was of the privateer: Most came to the trade of piracy by way of Her Majesty's Navy. As a young man, the future privateer usually worked on his father's trading ships, ones he would someday own. He was usually a gentleman in training, someone with a great future. Then his country went to war, first with Spain, then with France. They were beginning to colonize the New World—the entire two continents, the islands, and the strip connecting both large land masses—as they were yet to officially belong to anyone. The countries were robbing each other, all in the name of war. England sent out as many ships as possible, so it was natural for them to offer a wealth of riches to a trader and his family in exchange for the use of their vessels, especially if they owned a ship large enough to participate in plundering the trade coming or going to the enemy.

Graham Johns was just such a captain. He rigged his barquentine with twenty guns, and had his own trading crew with him, all ready for new adventures on the high seas. They carried with them Letters of Marque from England. Captain Johns and his crew became privateers. They were allowed to sail in a particularly designated area of the world, and to pillage or capture—or both—any ship flying the colors of either Spain or France. Captain Johns had added to that list the Dutch, as he had mistakenly boarded one of their vessels and unloaded—stolen—their cargo of sugar, cinnamon, silks, and gold bullion. He released the ship and crew much the poorer.

Johns needed to unload his illegal gains somewhere away from English law. He was in danger of losing his right to plunder, as he had chosen the wrong country from which to steal. the captain met a young man while drinking at a cliff bar on the island of Jamaica. This bar was on the outskirts of the nearest town, high up on a cliff with water pouring into the sea from the blue mountain above. Only the bravest of men frequented this establishment, as it was a known pirate hangout. Johns felt sure he would find a way to unload his illegally confiscated cargo at this place. The young man he met owned a dock on an island off the coast of the American colonies. After a few drafts of ale, they struck a bargain for unloading his merchandise.

This young man was Jabez Jennette. Both men recognized they were young and inexperienced, so they decided they might as well trust each other. They surveyed their surroundings, each quite cautious and being there for the very first time. Jabez was a fraternity brother to the son of a prominent elected leader in the Virginia colony, Charles Henry Jarvis Jr. Together, they decided to deal in black-market trade that came into the ports of Ocracoke and Hatteras. This was the time of Pirates, lawless robbers and Privateers, who carried *Letters of Marque* from the King, to confiscate valuables of their enemies.

Pirates and privateers both had more than they could use for themselves and needed to trade goods that were useless to them for an agreed-upon value of money. They frequented the drinking holes of tolerant island nations to meet up with those willing to sell items legitimately for them, thus converting the contraband to gold. Jabez and Charles Jr. considered themselves businessmen with a marketable service. Sometimes stolen items were hard to sell and were simply thrown in with the bargain to get rid of the evidence, as they were practically without value to either party. The buyer was always the winner in that respect.

This night was Jabez's first entry into the clandestine world of pirates and businessmen. Jabez was as wealthy as his friend and partner, Charles Jr. from Williamsburg, and they were about to make their first purchase.

Jabez was in a delicate dilemma, his parents having died of illnesses that swept the island in the early 1700s, which also took most of what was left of the Indian population, since they had no immunities to the white man's diseases. Jabez and his baby sister, Rhetta, survived and were raised by his grandfather. Then the untimely death of his grandfather left him to care for his sister and himself. The huge Jennette estate was left to Jabez to manage. He hired caregivers from off the island to help him raise his sister. Jabez had little experience in anything. He was freshly graduated from the fancy college on the mainland and had only worked in his grandfather's shipping business office during school breaks. Here he studied for his degree in shipping. He thought he would be building ships, not handling a trading business using vessels that someone else built. He did have his school project of a modern ship on his drawing board, and now he needed money to help him bring the project to life. This Englishman sitting in Jamaica seemed to be legitimate, after a fashion, as Graham Johns showed Jabez his *Letter of Marque* and relayed his own dilemma. Both young men were amateurs in this worldly trade, both from respectable families, both sons of shipping magnates, and both left to run the family business with little experience. Captain John's father was dying and had turned the operation over to his son, who had signed on to sail for his king and now was at war without the proper number of ships to compete.

Jabez's grandfather had sent him off island to a military school, more for convenience than a need for education. The older man, Cyrus Jennette, was devastated at the family losses to the severe sickness that swept the island. Jabez did so well in boarding school that he won a grant for the only college around: Harvard. There he advanced his studies and met others from affluent families.

The Jennette family was prominent on the island of Cape Hatteras, holders of great tracts of land. Their property, where it was deeded, stretched across the island from sound to sea. Several adjoining tracts had been given to Jabez, who was his grandfather's favorite. After military school and Harvard, Jabez came home to learn the business. While at Harvard, he befriended Charles Henry Jarvis Jr. from the Virginia colony. Charles Jr.'s father was a prominent politician and close friends with the governor, with an eye to succeeding him in office. Together, both boys did a short term at the University of Oxford in England, as both families wanted their boys to be familiar with the world. They were both southern boys, and with that background, they formed a lasting friendship. Now they were in business together.

On a nearly moonless night, Jabez waited with his wagon and horses at the edge of the Ocracoke slough where he and Johns had agreed to meet. Jabez had it well lit, and he could plainly see the bobbing lights of the three-masted barq silhouetted against the faint sliver of moonlight. Both having studied the heavens, they picked a date with only the thought of a moon, as they were nervous about detection. Streaks of blue edged through the dark clouds hanging over the spars. The ship could be seen riding a slight swell. Two longboats, each with an eight-man crew, rowed toward the makeshift dock in the rushes of the inlet. They found their way in, and the men began unloading the boats to Jabez's wagons. The transaction took surprisingly little time, and Captain Johns, who looked only slightly older than his counterpart, was willing to strike a "generous bargain," as Jabez recorded the night.

Captain Graham Johns had just gotten his first taste of piracy, and this was the way it started with most pirates. Edward Teach, Captain Kidd, Charles Vane, Stede Bonnet, Israel Hands, Edmund Tew, Charles Hornigold, Woodes Rogers, Sir Francis Drake, and Sir Walter Raleigh all started their careers on the seas as privateers. When that was no longer available, some continued on as pirates, raising a flag of their own design, robbing any ship they chose, and keeping all the spoils.

The *Joli Rouge* ("pretty red," in French) was a flag used by many to signal, "No quarter given" or "Fight to the death." Pirates actually used any symbol they chose to mean "death." Usually the flag was black or red. Most pirates also carried the flags of the many nations that roamed the sea. They would hoist the same flag displayed by the oncoming ship, or another one friendly to that ship, to fool the approaching captain of their real intentions. When they got close, the pirates ran up their flag of death. The pirates did not always kill their conquests. Usually the victim ship was outmanned and outgunned, and therefore the prey gave up willingly, in exchange for their lives. Sometimes, if the vessel was one of great desire, far superior to the pirate ship, the pirate confiscated the vessel also and sent the unwanted passengers away in the inferior ship, after having stripped it of its guns, other weapons, instruments, and charts.

For pirates working down the east of the northern Atlantic seaboard, the only gold and precious gems they pilfered came from passengers of the conquered ships, who were relieved of anything they carried that was worthy: gold and silver in any form, rings, necklaces, fancy waistcoats, belts, pistols (especially French-made with ornate handles or grips), knives and swords of the finest steel with fancy cross guards and hilts, the ladies' daggers, and hats. They always took the fancy hats.

Either way, the pirate or the privateer took what they wanted from their victims. Both were on missions to pillage, one with permission of a king, the other with permission of a ruthless captain. These men of the sea were fancily dressed, as they outfitted themselves from the trunks of the wealthy. Their cabins were well appointed with the finest dinnerware and silver table services available at the time. Even the decor on the walls of the captain's quarters reflected the finest paintings of Europe, often destined to adorn a Caribbean mansion. The loot was endless and the pirates were wealthy, but it did not last.

Captain Johns was well fitted as he stood erect, making a deal with his new business partner. There was something about Jabez that the captain liked, and he figured he had found a new friend. Jabez was comfortable also. The dealings were more generous for him than he could ever have imagined. These transactions were the only method used to make this cargo worth taking. Not everyone could dispose of these items. But Jabez with his dock, and Charles Jr. with his political connections, easily sold the stolen goods to legitimate customers in North Carolina and Virginia. Items not having gone through customhouses of the colony—black-market items—were considerably less expensive than any other cargo. The quality was better, and the price was definitely lower. Jabez had found a business he could cultivate.

Luke looked around at the other two. "Looks like we got some good days ahead, I think Uncle Jabez probably knew everybody. Look, it has a page here about the connection of this house. Look! These are the drawings for the little cottage. No wonder the cottage looks so solid. I'll bet it has been bricked over, it shows it was constructed of wood here. It must have been the first building on this property. Man, this is great!"

Luke's enthusiasm was catching with his cohorts. Ellie was leaning over his shoulder, and Blake had his head *in* the book, until Luke had to nudge him aside.

"Get over there, me hardy, or I'll run ya thru w' me pen here."

Blake knew if he didn't get his head out of there and stop blocking the page, nobody could read it to him. But he just had to see if the lights from the book would show on his face. Nobody said anything, so he guessed they didn't.

"Let's read a whole story every time we come," said Ellie "Wonder if Uncle Jabez saw anything that was bad?" She looked at the book and turned another page. It looked normal enough, just that pretty writing at the top, and the handwritten script that related the story.

here in tells the story told to me of the great Blackbeard.

"The handwriting is bold and readable. I know I can read it." Ellie was looking at Luke.

"I know I can, too," Luke said. "We'll take turns. This should be fun."

"No Luke, I'd rather you read," Ellie said.

They carefully wrapped up The Book again and were gently putting it back in its place. Then they began to reconstruct the other items so that everything was left looking undisturbed. They closed the trunk and slid it back in its place. Taking the lanterns, they explored a little more, but it was just too overwhelming. They carefully made their way back down to the lower floor. They stepped off the ladder and to on the floorboard to close the wall that hid everything, moved the second chest back in place, and began looking for an area to have their lunch. They decided to go to the little house. After all, it was here before anything else was. They intended to inspect the walls and explore how many times this house had been rebuilt. It was more special than they had previously realized.

Luke found the key on a hook inside the rafters of the barn, where Grandpop had shown him. They went inside and looked around the dusty little cottage. It had a huge stone fireplace in the center of the north wall. Behind that wall was also a bedchamber that shared the same huge fireplace on the other side. On the south side was another whole room. Ellie opened the door and was staring at the most beautiful four-poster canopied bed she had ever seen. The fact that it was also covered in canvas gave it an even more ghostly, heavenly, spiritual look. On the far wall of that room was a smaller, more personal stone fireplace, with a mantel that was flanked on either side—from the mantel to either wall and stretching within two feet of the floor—by golden, ornately carved, framed mirrors. The mirrors on both sides made the tiny room take on an endless depth. Over the mantel was a portrait of a mountain man. The furniture was rustic. There were few chests, one straightbacked chair, and one rocking chair. In between the two outer rooms was a common area with a fireplace, a table, several chairs, and a couple of tall, skinny chests.

These rooms had for several years been the home of Jabez and his little sister, Rhetta, while they built the fabulous mansion. Here, everything— all windows, doors, and furniture—was simply adequate, nothing fancy, which was quite unlike the trappings of the mansion. There was a kitchen area in conjunction with the living quarters and dining area at the east end of the cabin. Here again, there was a woodstove oven for baking. This house had more chimneys than the big house.

They settled down at the round table with the four chairs positioned in the middle of the room. The chairs were surprisingly comfortable. Blake opened the saddlebags, and they tore into the wrapped sandwiches Grandmom had laid out for them. There were also lots of cookies in a smaller bag inside. Snooping around made them hungry. The little cabin was so quiet that they could hear the many forest birds coming out for their song of spring. The musty smell of the closed-up rooms was tolerable with the door open, allowing the breeze to waft through.

Ellie had seen the first cardinal of the year as she tromped through the graveyard located near the Methodist church after church one day, on her way to visit Nancy. He was beautiful and bright and fat. As he plopped on a branch, she was thinking that he made those dead people smile. She noticed that people still put flowers on their family graves. *Everybody must talk to the spirits like I do*, she thought.

The wolves were around back of the cabin, resting against the north wall, with the breeze from the sound slightly ruffling their long fur. They seemed to be dozing. The kids filled the rest of the afternoon with talk of what might be in the pages of The Book. They had just cracked the surface, they knew. They had been too busy to look carefully through the journal. If they had, they might have recognized names of families with whom they were acquainted. They were so excited to get to the pirate stories that they did not even finish the account of how Jabez had come to occupy himself with such a dangerous business.

They were impressed that Jabez had traveled, and they wondered, *What kind of ship? Whose was it? What was he looking for?* As they recounted what they knew, they began to wonder many things about their great-great-, and maybe even more great, Uncle Jabez. They had heard that other families had arrived on the island through someone who had been shipwrecked and had decided to stay. They had heard of people misplaced from one colony or another and others who had decided to settle, but they never heard anyone say that someone in their family was a pirate!

★ 5 ★

The Pirates Jamboree

The weekend of the festivities finally arrived. The Coast Guard, Grandpop and his crew of new keepers and several others, vendors and cooks—all persons with a vested interest in making this community effort a success—were all on the grounds at daybreak. They were stringing a banner of weather and warning flags from the tip of the lighthouse down to a stake in the ground. The flags were colorful, the wind blowing them to face the sea. It was a glorious sight ... a string of pennants from the tip of the railing of the lighthouse, all the way down, more than 270 feet long down to the ground. Everyone stayed out of the other's way, as each moved in his own sphere to make everything run smoothly. Someone from a local radio station, which normally broadcast from the mainland, was there to relay his show from the island festivities. Those building the staging were making sure it supported the equipment needed to both broadcast and announce to the crowd. The hammering alone was noisy enough to drown out any instructions given for other endeavors.

These celebrations were the brainchild of photographer-journalist-author Ben Dixon MacNeill. He wrote a book called *The Hatterasman*.

Some say it's not accurate, as he was truly a man interested in promoting the island, but with all its exaggerations and stories, it is a thoroughly intriguing read. MacNeill was also a historian, community organizer, and local promoter of anything and everything having to do with tourism. The kids knew him as the old guy who was always posing someone, usually pretty girls, on the lighthouse steps. He was always around. He got his training as a newspaperman working for several papers across the state. Finally he was given a grant to freelance. MacNeill fell in love with the island and settled in a small cottage on a knoll near the Buxton Coast Guard Station. Most locals thought of him as just an old man carrying a camera or two around his neck. His desire was to preserve the way of life he and others had found here. He shot thousands of pictures and was the self-appointed representative responsible for keeping this island in the minds of tourists looking for a pleasant vacation.

MacNeill promoted sport fishing, seafood, and activities around the island, and was quite popular with newspapers off island, as their patronage of his work always provided a great story and guaranteed sale of their papers.

He was especially interested in the Pirates Jamboree, a celebration he could use to promote the life on this island. Here, he had what he called, in various prints sent around the United States, "the world's largest fish fry," and he thought it would make the island famous.

However, Billy Mitchell, Reginald Fessenden, Guglielmo Marconi, Lee deForest, and the sinking of the ironclad *Monitor* off Diamond Shoals all served to make the island famous as well. Everybody knew old man Ben Dixon. He was everywhere, and he belonged to everyone. He was always taking pictures of Ellie—the boys, not so much—but he thought that the little lighthouse waif was adorable.

At least 80 percent of the people were dressed in some sort of pirate attire. Most of the men had full beards. Ellie was dressed in a fancy dress with a silk vest edged in gold braid. Her hair was covered with a red bandana like a pirate girl would wear. Luke and Blake both sported eye patches, which they had pulled up on their heads in order to see what was happening. Both boys had the typical three-cornered hat worn by pirates, and coolest of all, their pants were held up by a rope. Nett and Grandmom had really gussied them up. Had there been a winner for children's costumes, Grandmom was sure they would win. They all had been so excited to get dressed and strut around. Looking for the proper fish vendor allowed them to observe everybody else's costume, and if they needed more or less fancy, they could go home and change.

Tables were set up, and risers placed in strategic places. Squares laid out for games were marked off in various ways to designate an area. All spaces were indicated with painted wooden signs sticking near the center pole of each individual space. Sailcloth was raised and anchored to make a tent or central area. There was even a covered stage for the many contests. Of course, there was a prettiest-girl contest, a handsomest-man contest, and crowning of the king and queen, which was announced at dusk. *What a shame that they announce the king and queen last*, Ellie thought. Ellie did not approve, as the winners missed the chance to enjoy being special until just before the day ended. She kept nagging Captain Charlie to promote the announcement early. She begged and, but he just smiled and went on about his business.

The winners would reign over the dance that night at the school, the only building large enough for a crowd. When the chairs were folded up and placed against the wall, the room was ready for dancing. Tables and chairs were moved around for socializing, and the cafeteria wall was open, displaying sweets and drinks. The bands took the stage, and the communities let loose, pirate style.

There were areas for horseshoes, croquet, darts, bow and arrow, and foot races. Before 9:00 a.m., the horses began to arrive. Their owners wanted to make sure their steeds were used to the surroundings and the sights and smells of the new environment. Many of the island boys were hanging around each temporary stall of the racehorses from their village. Every horse from every community had a fan club—those who were friends of the owner or the rider, or just for village pride.

Then the beach buggies, jalopies, and modified cars began to assemble to try out the sand for firmness. As no two days were alike, the drivers needed to test that day's conditions. Luke, Blake, and Ellie sat quietly at the breakfast table, almost hesitant to go outside. They had thought how great all of this activity would be on the day of the festival, but somehow, now that it was here, it seemed a little overwhelming to look out and see the entire grounds covered with people. The festival attendees respected the privacy of the family that lived there and did not go into the yard of either the assistant or the keeper's quarters. They were quite considerate about that, but the beach was covered with blankets, onlookers, oarsmen, horsemen, and auto racers. It was crazy. There was a parade of floats from the local organizations down the sandy road, crab races for the kids, and some had in mind to show off the tricks they had taught their banker ponies. They knew their ponies were not fast enough to beat the horses, but they intended to show that these animals were smart.

On the other side of the yard, the smell of fried fish cooking filled the morning air, and at once, hunger set in. As the fish started cooking, people started moving around. There was even a band located at the bottom of the lighthouse steps tuning up their strings. Music was the preferred pastime of the island. Nights were customarily social gatherings at stores or people's houses. Most knew how to play a musical instrument. The island was always rocking out on a piano somewhere.

Inside, Grandmom handed Luke some money and said, "You young-uns go over to the stands where they are frying fish and bring back half a dozen dinners. Can you do that?'

"Sure can, Grandmom!" To the others, the kids said, "C'mon, we got to go over to the fairground and get something for Grandmom. Let's get goin'." Luke was putting the rush on the other two. He was so curious, and now he had a reason for not just scuffling around looking, but walking by on a mission, with a studying gaze of purpose, as he made his way to the portion of the compound where barrels of burning wood were topped with wire, making a stove on which to fry the fish.

The kids skipped along the alleys made between vendors and groups of families that were making themselves a compound from which to come and go during the day. There were people everywhere: eating fried chicken, shucked oysters and clams, a variety of fried fish, (Spanish mackerel, sea trout, bluefish, spot sea mullet, flounder), cornbread and pan cornbread (pie bread), all kinds of soups, and all fashion of cakes and pies. There were plates of candy, cookies, stacked-up cupcakes, and sweet bars. It was like the Milky Way had landed on the lawn of the lighthouse.

Grandmom loved to hear all that the children had seen, so that she could make her plans, and she had her mouth set for a "good piece of fish." They all dug into the plates as the kids gave Grandpop, Nett, and Grandmom the lay of the land. They did feel a little special, having all this in the yard of their own house. They finished their fish breakfast and got ready to meet the day. They decided to check in with each other by going round to the back door and reporting to the kitchen at noon. They were given money to buy what they saw to eat, and everybody went their separate ways.

There were radio stations broadcasting from a raised table. Or one may have been the Coast Guard, since the equipment was fancy. Mr. MacNeill was busy doing what he did, taking posed pictures of the comely island beauties on the beach, standing on a piece of driftwood on the steps of the lighthouse, and once in a while he snapped one of a particularly handsome beard. These he would send to newspapers around the country, and if coming from him, they were printed. No newspaper would refuse a photo from Ben Dixon MacNeill.

Every venue had a crowd around it, and every place had people waiting in line. The crowd wanted to do almost everything. It was hard to decide what to do, as there was so much going on.

The kids decided they would see what was taking place near the water. They went over the low dune to a sight they had never seen. The beach was full of cars: old cars, ones with mostly rusted-out bodies, cars like the oldest one Grandpop had ever had, what appeared to be a few new cars, and all the descriptions in between. Some had been hacked up so much they looked like nothing more than a seat, a motor, enough floorboard for the pedals, and rails. The new cars would be old cars within the hour. They all had their tires slacked down to their lowest air, making them look like pancakes rather than circles. The racers were practically running on rims.

Rules were established, and names of drivers were divided into heats. Consideration was given to the timing for low tide. It was necessary to run at the lowest tide and hope the beach wasn't torn up before a winner could be decided. When the water got too high, the races were suspended. With a six-hour window, it was a rush to beat the night. Most drivers didn't care what the tide was doing. They were going to race in the wash or the dunes, but they were going to race!

The beach leading from the lighthouse to the ocean wash was at least 100 feet. This wide beach was, at the time, covered with anxious people. When the kids took their perch on the dune, they could see the area for racing cars and also the dory races getting ready to start.

The first contest of the morning, taking advantage of a higher tide and allowing the boats a better seamark, was the dory races. The boats were in line—the larger dories helped to the surf by horses, and smaller ones carried as far forward as possible by a truck. The boats raced according to size and numbers of men. A few small skiffs, manned by only one person, waited behind the bigger boats. Those that had to be pushed to the wash had no problem, as island boys were ready to help lift a boat, even if they were not in the contest. The larger dories of the three Coast Guard stations and the largest fishing dories were first. All day, men struggled against the surf, whether as a team, single-man, or two-by-two. It was an island man's duty not to refuse the sea, and this day was as good a chance as any to prove it. The water races lasted almost the entire day.

The men rowing in the first race were getting ready for their heat. Ol' Tony and Big Roy were pulling Captain Barnett's heavy fishing dory. Eight of the biggest island boys around were four down the sides, stripped to the waist, pant legs rolled up, oars at the ready, sticking straight up, in anticipation of pushing out and hopping in to man the oars. Each had a coxswain already in position in the back in anticipation of counting cadence and keeping an eye on the competition.

Captain Andrews from the USCC was ready with his sailors in line. Captain Midgett, from Rodanthe, was a favorite with his seamen, mostly local guardsmen who had grown up on the island. Captain Foster from Hatteras Coast Guard's boys were ready. They had a bone to pick, as their softball season the previous year had come to an early end.

The kids settled in where they could easily see down the line and the anchored buoys out to sea. They were careful not to be either downwind nor in the sight of their own horses. It wouldn't do for Ol' Tony or Big Roy to spook, or be distracted by familiar smells, when they needed to pay attention to their handlers. The local boys using Grandpop's horses knew them, as they had borrowed the two for launching in choppy waters before, during fishing season. These two had also been used for fishing with Jack and Lindy on several occasions. Use of the horses was a reason to allow Jack and Lindy to fish with the more experienced lads. Two local boys held the reins for Ol' Tony and Big Roy. The Coast Guard sailors had Jackson and Beauregard, two of the government horses, and the team from Rodanthe had Apollo and Zeus. They all looked evenly matched and anxious. They would get the boat to the waves, and be unhitched and pulled away.

The crowd listened for the gun. When it cracked, the sets of boys yanked the bridle of the lead horse, and the mighty steeds pulled, as men in the back pushed. The horses got the heavy dory out almost to the first breaker, while the handlers quickly unbridled them and led the wet horses away from the smashing breakers. The horses shook off the waves and water, and went to watch the rest of the contest from the beach. The rowers were fast and strong. Even though they had gotten a boost from the animals, it would not do for the heavy boat to sit there too long, as the weight of it could bury in the sand of the soft bottom of the ocean, becoming impossible to get unstuck. If that happened, the race was over for that team. So, at the gun, the teams pushed to take advantage of the position the horses had given them. All needed a fast break and a huge effort to climb into the boat quickly, grab the oars they had thrown in at the start, and hit that first breaker. The men boarded the boats, took to the oars, and with a coxswain at the rear, you could see them strain on the oars as the loud rhythm count began, each adjusting the count to beat the other team. It reminded the kids of the coxswain at the back of the thirty-man Croatoan canoes, as they silently rowed in the night to rescue the colonials stranded on Roanoke Island.

The first breaker saw the bow of the huge dory rise skyward, and at that point, though a little disoriented at the angle, the men put their backs into the pull. So visible were their bodies that the kids could see the ripple of hard muscle straining against the rise. The local boys matched the effort the sailors made. The boats rose, with the extra motion of the oars, and all made the first and hardest breaker. The boats slid down the back side of the rising sea and prepared for the next strong effort. Waves came in sets of threes and sevens, so it took a bit of muscle and skill to settle into steady rowing for gaining ground. The first heat of big boats were remarkably accurate in their judgment of the marker and rounded them with ease. This was Coast Guard vs. local in every heat.

The trip back was a study in strength and determination, each coxswain doing his best count to win, calling for faster pulls as his boat reached and then passed the other crew. He paid attention to the opposing count and knew how fast to push his own men. The local coxswain proved worthy and shouted his men to victory against the Buxton Coast Guard. He had kept up a ridiculously fast count for about three fourths of the race, and with a surprised look each man matched the rhythm with his pull, never thinking they could handle that much energy and strain, but as they fell into the count, the strength came. All efforts that day were timed, and as each two dories mastered the race, in the final heat, Hatteras Coast Guard lost to Rodanthe, the time placed by the local team besting the military men.

Every man aboard was exhausted when the final time was announced. It was the most miraculous event of the day, and the day had only started. The Coast Guard boys were a little let down, but they knew the strength of these locals. They had played baseball against them, so it was determined they would all meet again—first, a baseball game. There was so much backslapping, it seemed as though exhaustion was put aside. The oarsmen checked their blistered and bleeding hands and were glad it was over.

Around noontime, just before the heat had a chance to set in—and with the tide going out, yielding firm ground and more beach—the first rounds of time trials for the horses began. With four horses abreast and a flagman at the end, winners and losers were decided. The children just knew that either of their horses could have entered these races, and they would be walking away with ribbons.

But Grandpop said it was too soon. They were too young, and their legs not strong enough for the sand. He was glad of the training he knew they were getting, he liked that the kids walked them in the sand, so maybe next year, truthfully, Grandpop was also thinking, next year, and felt the kids were getting them ready. Grandpop, from the top of the lighthouse, saw the horses as they went down to the south beach. Over 250 feet high was an excellent vantage point for seeing things from a distance. Grandmom might have had the *knowing*, but Grandpop had the sight. Neither one of them talked about it. Grandpop thought Grandmom didn't know, and she felt the same about him.

Mr. Burrus's horses were the winners every time anyone who owned one entered. Grandpop really knew from whom to buy his steeds. The kids knew them all. They had cleaned their stables when Gus and Blue were there, and had made friends with the herd. They even knew to whom they were sold, as they had pumped Mr. Burrus the whole time they were helping. His horses were the prettiest and the fastest of all the ones on the island. Some people had even gone off island to get a better choice, but they found there was no better choice. This knowledge always came too late.

One beautiful cream-colored horse reminded them of Gus. His name was Ivey, and he was Miss Tinker's horse. It was Luke's choice because of color, but Ellie's choice because of Miss Tinker. Racer was another. His owner was Colby's dad, and Thomas's dad owned the two very best horses on the island. Luke and Colby were planning on asking if they could go for a ride some Saturday, but neither had yet worked up the courage to ask.

The races continued, with some boys riding bareback and all boys riding barefooted. A lot of dust and sand got kicked up that day as the horses tore up the shoreline. The expected riders won with their horses in categories. After the horse races, some of the contestants simply reviewed the rest of the day from the back of a horse, being careful not to get in the middle of crowds. Others wandered over to the area where the banker ponies were doing their tricks. As the numbers of horses milling around proved to be a little dangerous, all the horses were tied securely to a post, limb, or truck rail, for the rest of the day. Only the proud kids riding their small banker ponies were left to wander, and that too became a hindrance as the owners wanted to play, and the novelty of the horse had worn off. They were satisfied that others had admired their pets, so they, too, ended up being tied to a bush, and it was back to the food again—until really low tide and the automobile races began.

Never had anyone ever seen so many vats of grease frying fish. There were more than thirty just around the base of the lighthouse. The food was hot, and there was lots of it. Blake ate almost an entire chocolate pie, piece by piece. This lady from Hatteras made the best, and Blake had heard so much about it that it was the first vendor he hit, even before his chicken legs. Ellie and Luke had to give the crown to him, as they could not keep up. Where was that little body storing all this pie? Strawberry pie was obviously Luke's favorite, and he had some all along his cheek. He wiped it off and smacked it in his mouth for the last taste. He knew that gesture would bring disgust from Ellie, and he was right.

"Eeeeeeewwwwww!" She squinted her eyes in offense.

They watched the horseshoe throw, but decided it was too slow. The buoy throw was good, and some of the younger boys tried that. The heavy buoy was tied to a line, and the toss went round and round, and they let it fly. It was cool. Then they went to check out the kid races. They needed to run off some of the sugar they had just consumed. The men were beginning to set up for the knife throwing, and marksmanship with a rifle. The bull's-eyes were waiting at the end of a long track, the very same track the boys would run on. They all found a spot on a knoll to watch the men compete. Blake was disappointed at not joining the knife throw, but Luke would not allow him to ask.

"Blake, you would give everything away! For sure they wouldn't let you, and if you did it anyway, where would you learn such a skill? Back off, buddy! Bet I beat-cha in the races," and Luke laughed it off. However, he knew his little brother could slice these items in half. He knew he would have won. They were content to wait and get their stomachs straight for the run.

The kids knew when the races were getting ready to start, as they saw Grandmom, Grandpop, Nett, Uncle Tommy and Aunt Winnie, Uncle Curt and Aunt Pete, and Uncle Jack and Lindy coming from all over the Jamboree area to the one spot where the kids were to watch them run. The Coast Guard boys were making up the back row. The boys were under pressure now!

Blake was literally pawing the ground. He had Uncle Jack at the end of the line, and Blake had him in his sights (just like Wematin). He knew how these things were to be done, and he had already proven himself a champion. He locked in on Uncle Jack as the whistle blew for his heat to get ready. Blake was the first off the line and the first on the line. He just left everybody else in the sand. He was the fastest kid!

When time came for Luke's age and size, he started confidently, saw over his shoulder that a boy from Kinnakeet was gaining on him, and then put 'er in second gear. Even though he had to lean in, they took it home for the Finnegan boys. Lindy swung him around until they both were dizzy—or until Lindy realized that Luke was going to compete in bow and arrow in a few minutes. Lindy started limbering Luke up for pulling back the bow. This was to be a surprise to his family. They did not know how good he was, or even that he had skills at all with this instrument. Lindy and Uncle Jack, plus the kids, were the only ones who knew how good he was. In the woods, Jack and Lindy couldn't believe their eyes, as he knocked off any item they pointed out. He shot an arrow, then shot again, and aiming at his first arrow, split the original one in half.

The family and friends moved over to the bull's-eye set up for shooting the bow and arrow. No young boys were entered. Jack and Lindy looked at each other and shrugged, and with their customary smirk, they marched Luke up to the line after the last man shot. His arrow had not yet been pulled out, and better yet, was not even centered. Lindy shoved Luke in the spot and gave him a wink. Luke readied his bow, dropped it down, stuck up a finger to test the wind, looked around for shadows, and steadied his feet—all while the last man just stood stupefied, looking at this skinny kid do some kind of ritual. He stopped smirking when Luke raised his bow, took an arrow from his quiver, smoothed and licked the feathers, and pulled back—to let it fly right between the feathers of the previous arrow, splitting it in half, with just the right angle to follow the lean of the previous one.

The Coast Guard boys lost their minds. Nett and Grandmom had to cover their ears, Aunt Winnie and Aunt Pete were hugging each other and jumping straight up and down. Uncle Tommy grabbed Uncle Curt for a hefty handshake, and as they went to slap Captain Charlie on the back, he was already wrapped around his boy Luke.

Blake kept screaming, "But it isn't over yet. Wait! Let me get my twig. Watch this! C'mon, Luke, let's really show them something." He was jumping in and out of the crowds around Luke, and Luke, seeing his excitement, just couldn't resist.

Ellie stepped up to the crowd: "DRUMROLL, PLEASE!" she shouted.

This time Luke reached for the waistband at the back of his pants. He withdrew the whip he had curled up under his shirt. Only he and Blake knew of this, as they knew there would not be a contest for a whip. Blake was ready with a slender twig, also stuck in the waistband of his trousers. Blake stepped off a measured distance, turned sideways, stuck the twig in his mouth, turned and looked at his brother. Luke began his ritual, this time, unfurling the whip and cracking it, then cracking it again, this time louder. At the sound, a crowd began to gather. He set his feet, turned to the side, and looked at his little brother who, with his hands behind his back, stood about six feet away, with a long twig sticking out from between his teeth. Luke leaned forward, judging the length of the whip, and side stepped to the spot that he knew his whip would reach. With one smooth steady motion, he lowered the whip and quickly jerked it up and down again with a snap. The startled crowd gasped in awe as half of the twig in Blake's mouth fell to the ground.

With all the commotion, the crowd around the youngsters had grown. The faces of family and those in the crowd stood for a minute in stunned silence, then burst into a loud noise of cheering and clapping, as both Jack and Lindy, equally surprised, rushed forward, each grabbing a boy and hoisting him to their shoulders. Luke and Blake just laughed, and rode all the way over to the venue for buggy races on the shoulders of the two order boys. Ellie skipping along beside them, also basking in the pride of her cousins. Capt'n Charlie's face was split in a wide grin, Grandmom and Nett were arm in arm, nodding to the approving neighbors, but most obviously was the stride the Coast Guard boys took as they acknowledged among themselves, "their family, their kids."

The announcer yelled through the microphone that the buggy races were about to begin. The kids, almost sick from making their own choices on what to eat, opted to stop eating and raced to the previously chosen dune to get in position to see the start and finish. Their plan for being fully stocked with food was no longer a problem. They finally got to relax, and both boys couldn't stop talking about their performances. Among the grown-ups, they were embarrassed, but alone they were giggling.

"Ellie, did you help us?" Luke just had to ask.

"Of course not! I didn't even think about it. But wouldn't it be funny if I had? But no, they said not to play with our powers." she snickered, and they all smiled, and said, "Yeh."

They had experienced all the contests they could stomach, literally!

The buggy racers had drawn lots, cars four in a line. They knew the course. It went around a dune that stuck out by itself, round again, and back. There were five laps. Those who went first had the better track, but by the time all had raced, the loose sand was an equal problem to everyone, so no previous winner had an advantage at the final race. One thing nobody did was to scratch off, like one sees on a hard-track race. Gunning the motor or bearing down on the gas pedal is not the way to start a beach race. That type of action could get the vehicle stuck at the starting line. They had to get the feel of the sand, then they could put on the gas. Those who tried to get the jump found that they did not know how to win this style of race. Those boys who knew the sand were the ones with the best advantage. There was a perpetual dust cloud hanging all over the beach during the race. The Midgett brothers, with all the experience driving the Blue Bus, were always the winners, but racing against them was fun. It was also worth some bragging rights to talk about how close one came to beating Stocky or Andy, but nobody could beat them. One kid from Buxton, Leon, came close, but close was not winning.

The cars were stripped down. Some had no fenders, and others, no doors. The kids felt sorry for those with no doors. The sand was spewing over the cars like water sprays up alongside a boat. Sometimes so much sand was in the air, it was impossible to see who was winning. People could recognize some cars by their color alone. Other cars one could tell who owned it by how old it was, since dirt-track racing was a hobby some boys left the island to pursue. While there were experienced amateurs racing against novices, nobody has the advantage in sand. A few of the drivers had painted a huge lucky number on the car's side. Some got stuck solid in the flying sand, and everybody had to race around them until that heat was over, when the guys rushed out to dig out the car and send it off. One fella took a corner too fast, and while up on two wheels the car decided it had had enough. It just rolled over. Nobody was hurt. After all, it was just sand. Even with that cloud in the air, it was amusing to look around and see sand hills covered with pirates.

About thirty cars started the race, but only seven finished. So many things happened in the dust that it was hard to see what was happening to whom. The motor of the "family car" entered without the family's permission burned up and spewed black, stinky smoke from under the hood. It was so bad, the kid had to stop after the third lap. He sat there in the way of the racers until some of his friends had a chance to push it far enough to the side that it was no longer a hindrance. The continuing racers were able to avoid it safely. One of the older jalopies—or, at this point, dune buggy—lost a wheel and had to quit. Two cars smoked so badly that those behind them had trouble seeing. More than one ran into the surf trying to pass other cars, and one went slam into the breakers. Those watching just shook their heads. The cars in the ocean water might continue for a while, but they were ruined by the salt and everybody knew it. In three or six months, their floorboards would be gone, and probably most of their engine would have to be replaced, piece by piece. Some just quit!

Finishing first was the youngest of the Midgett brothers, whose grin when he got out of the car was as bright as the sun.

Serious beach racing was not for amateurs. At the end of the races, those cars that could no longer run were either towed away by others or left at half speed, chugging down the sandy road on their last cough before becoming yard art.

The crowds had a big laugh at the children and their crab races. The viewing audience was mostly made up of parents, and they all had a great time. Luke and Blake had previously planned to enter this one until, in practice, Luke pushed Blake so hard he shoved his face in the sand and Blake refused to compete. He knew Luke's desire to win would probably end up with him eating dirt.

In early afternoon, the races and contests finished, and the musicians took to the stage. Mr. MacNeill should have billed this one as the world's largest sing-along. The songs were familiar, and the musicians colorful in their costumes. As it was well known that pirates loved music, all the revelers got into the spirit of their clothing, and the singing was lively. In certain spots, dancing broke out in little clumps.

Blake ran up and grabbed Luke's shirt.

"Momma's dancing! She's dancing with another pirate, but I can't tell who it is! Come watch!"

He was so excited he could hardly wait to get the others to the spot in time to see Nett being slung around by a big pirate, and keeping up.

The kids ran over to the area, and when Nett saw them, she let go of that pirate's hand and grabbed Blake. Off they went, dancing around in the crowd. Luke grabbed Ellie, and they too danced around, mostly in a circle and joined the group. Sand was flying again, but nobody cared. The singers went from song to song, and finally the kids and Nett were worn out. They all moved to the lighthouse steps, found a spot on one of the higher tiers, and sat down. Nett sent Luke and Blake for a bottled drink, and she and Ellie picked out the prettiest girl. Ellie, of course, chose Miss Tinker, and Nett, since Tinker was taken, settled on Betty Ann, Uncle Baxter's daughter, and a cousin of hers.

The day went long, and the kids were glad that they would not have to go to the dance afterward. They could not imagine how anyone could go, because everyone was so tired and a little grimy. The ones planning to attend the dance left early and went home to freshen up and change. Grandpop announced the king and queen, early enough for them to hear congratulations and gain some attention during the day. Ellie was extremely proud of that. She squelched the urge to run up and tell them that an early announcement was her idea. But she did let Pop know that she had noticed he took her advice. He smiled.

The dance at the school was a grown-up affair, and here again, the costumes were spectacular. There were excellent seamstresses on the island—ones who could look at a picture and tell exactly how to make a garment. It did appear that some of the ladies had made several costumes—one for day and one for evening. It was a funny-looking room, as all the men sported full beards, earrings, bandanas, jewelry, fake cutlasses, and toy pistols, and only talked in the pirate way. There was a lot of "Ahoy matey," some "shivering of timbers" (referring to the state of mind that a one-legged man, with a wood stump for a leg, used to express surprise or just indicating his stump was shivering), and everybody was either a "lad," a "lubber" (a land lover), or "matey."

There, of course, were dances—some in square-dance style and some slow dances. During intermission, the band broke for food and drink while everybody cleared the floor, and one of the men wrote down numbers in chalk on the floor, running in a wide circle, as the group got ready for a cake walk. Women of all the communities made special cakes, their most elaborate, and they were all lined out on several straight end-to-end cafeteria tables, with a little piece of paper in front telling who made it. The caller got into position, a fiddler took the stage, and everybody walked around the interior of the numbers. When the fiddler stopped, a number was called, and whoever was nearest that number got to go to the table and pick out their favorite cake. After a while, the dancers were many, but the cakes were few. The music continued until all the cakes were gone. Usually the person choosing a cake left some money in its place. Hard times were hard times, and the islanders were always looking out for each other. The cake makers usually left the room or lost themselves in the crowd as they were not interested in their cake being picked last.

Grandpop came home with a cake made by Miss Nita, whose cakes were known all over the island. The kids woke up to a sliver of wonderful cake before they went to Sunday school. When they got home, they couldn't finish dinner fast enough to get another piece. They then joined with the others in the community who came back to help clean up the grounds. Lots of children came with their parents, so Luke, Blake, Colby, Thomas, and Ellie had a full contingency of pirates to play in their fort. It had been a great weekend, and Luke decided that Gus was going to win in Pirates Jamboree the following year. He was a little older than Blue, and maybe Grandpop would allow him to be trained and raced. Luke could picture himself in full pirate regalia, on back of the cream-colored horse whose namesake raced across the sky. Luke did not know just how close that pirate adventure was to happening.

Uncle Jabez

The week of school went by fast. Jamboree stories were passed around, and beards were shaved off. Now, all the clean-shaven men looked strange. People had gotten used to all that hair—those looking at it and those wearing it. Having their faces covered in a beard actually improved the appearance of some men. Even Mr. Austin, the principal, had shaved off his beard. His face looked so very white! Some men had shaved in the morning before church just a day after the celebration. Maybe those beards were not as comfortable as they looked.

Finally another weekend arrived. On Friday afternoon the kids took to the beach to plan their attack of The Book and its stories. They had to come up with a yarn that would allow them to be absent from their duties for an entire day. They thought and thought, because trying to sprinkle deceit into a story without an out-and-out lie was tricky, and they never wanted to *really* lie. Instead, they wanted to sprinkle truth into a story that was a secret. They came up with nothing, so they got busy getting chores out of the way as soon as possible. First they found Grandpop and sincerely offered to do any task he might think up. Right away, they were sent out to clean the barn. That was no problem. They kept it pretty tidy all the time anyway, as they were always hanging out there. Grandmom even threatened to put beds in one of the vacant stalls, because she was always looking for them, only to find them hanging out with the horses.

Grandmom was easy. She only needed help with supper dishes. Nett was off for the weekend, practicing the piano at church, in anticipation of playing for a wedding the following weekend. One of the Barnett boys was the soloist, so they were practicing down at the church, picking out songs and going over them. Things were shaping up for the kids to spend all day at the house.

Grandmom was getting used to making sandwiches for the kids on Saturday. It was easier than planning a huge meal for the family. Grandmom kept the store shelves empty of "light bread." This way, too, she was free to indulge Grandpop in his favorite foods, usually dishes the kids did not like to eat. They were not fond of snap beans, and there were a lot of them growing on sticks and strings in the garden. Even after growing season, Grandmom would can them, so there was always a threat they would show up on the table. Also, the kids were not big oyster eaters either, but the time for those was almost over, as oysters were best in cold weather. It seemed there were only a few weeks left to enjoy a solid mess of fried oysters, so that threat was not going to be a problem anytime soon.

They had awakened early and surprised Grandmom as they huddled around the breakfast table earlier than usual. They all ate heartily and were so polite. Grandmom smiled to herself and planted a zinger.

"Going over to the old house again today?" she asked.

Blake almost snorted milk out of his nose. Luke, Mr. Cool, gave his most devilish grin, and rolled his eyes at the other two. Ellie swallowed hard, and true to form, never disappointing

Grandmom, answered the question.

"Yes, ma'am, is that okay?" she said, almost in a whisper, and with much pleading in her voice.

"Of course. I haven't been in quite some time, but your Grandpop and I spent a lot of time there when we were first married. Grandpop had never seen such a house, and I was proud to show it to him. He thinks that we will eventually have to move there, if the navy takes over the beach during this war." Grandmom was so cool about everything, and they kept forgetting that she was in touch with everyone who was in touch with them.

Did they hear her correctly? Did she say they might move over there? What about the lighthouse? Who would take care of it? They loved the old house, but not nearly as much as they loved the lighthouse. It was a shock, one that left them speechless. The kids had so many things running around in their heads.

Grandmom recognized the information she had given was probably coming too soon, so she quickly removed the worry from their minds and went for a lighter subject.

"The house has been in our family for over 200 years. They say in the village that it is haunted. Aren't you afraid to go there?"

Boy, did she open a can of worms. All the children began speaking at once, defending the house, debunking the haunted theory, just spilling love and curiosity all over the breakfast table. Their response made Odessa relax and feel comfortable about being able to talk to the children about their adventures. She had been waiting for just such a moment. She needed to let them know that they were never sneaking around when it came to her. She either knew instinctively or was told by those who visited her in her dreams, advising her of what the children were doing. At all times their guardian angels were in touch with their grandmother, making her comfortable to steer the kids in the direction designed by their spirits. She needed to let them know that. What she didn't know was that she had made them feel a lot better about rummaging around the old house. They were very good kids, so full of energy and curiosity. It was good to know that when Grandpop found out about their visits to the house—and that was a when, not an if—they would have Grandmom on their side. They would have all given one of Blake's fake faints if they knew that Grandpop was fully aware of their trips, too.

They gave their grandmother an especially big hug when they left the table with their bags of sandwiches. On the ride over to the house, they promised to make sure Grandmom did not get in trouble because of them. They had new resolve to be careful with the things they found, always putting them back in place and making sure the house was taken care of. Grandmom had just given them the job of caretakers to the old house, and they might prove to be the best ones yet. It was a light and spirited trip down the beach. They felt carefree, trusted, and responsible, and they would carry that feeling with them every time they visited.

They settled in front of the open trunk and gently lifted out The Book. Each had secured a pillow from one of the rooms to make their long morning more comfortable, after taking the pillows outside and beating the dust out of them, that is. Naturally Blake had more than one, as he was stretched out on his belly waiting to be read to. He didn't have to worry about where to sit, because they weren't going to let him read, so he would not be expected to do anything but be entertained. Luke took more of an in-charge attitude, carefully going through the steps it took to open The Book.

The reaction to the colors spewing out on the ceiling, walls, and floor was the same as before. Magic always made everybody's eyes light up, and as The Book took on a glow, the kids became more quiet and respectful of what was in it. They couldn't help but wonder who put all the spells on The Book? Uncle Jabez was not known to have powers. Was it Rhetta? After all, Weroansqua had said that Rhetta was talented in the spirit world, and one could tell that Jabez respected that. Possibly he had enlisted her help in making sure The Book was a secret from prying eyes. It named many people, and all were deeply involved in clandestine activities. These were things he did not want anyone to know, and his friends and neighbors doing business with him trusted that he would keep their secrets, along with his own. However, he kept no secrets from Rhetta. He knew that it was useless to try, because, like Grandmom, Rhetta knew everything. She just did not speak of it, or did she? Ellie's mind started to wander as she looked around at all the other trunks, thinking that maybe Rhetta also kept a journal. But Ellie quickly put those thoughts aside, because this journal was all she could handle at this time.

Jabez and his little sister were close. Even though cousins, uncles, and aunts in the Jennette family lived in the nearby village, he and Rhetta seemed to consider themselves a family of two. They did not venture far from each other or home. He had made her a special room in the tiny cottage. Her bedroom in the little house was the closest to the door, allowing her to come and go at all hours without being detected or disturbing anyone. He was also aware of an unusual power she had. He did not know where it came from, so just in case it was from nature, or creatures of nature, he wanted her to develop it to the fullest, unencumbered from any restrictions he might be tempted to impose on her. He was a practical man, but he respected the spirit that lived in his sister and felt lucky to be around such a gifted person.

Rhetta knew her powers. She knew where they came from and the condition of her having them, and she had dreams. In her dreams, she was told many things. Weroansqua visited her in visions. She also met Powwaw in the same way. She never time-traveled. She was only whisked away in vivid thoughts. She saw rather than experienced the past. It was not known if she had the same access to the future. Though she did not recognize it, her intuition, was a path to the future. With Jabez, her intuition seemed to be what drove her. Not until she was a teen did Jabez begin to confide in her. After the first time he allowed her to enter his world, he knew they worked better as a team.

He introduced her to his partner, Charles Jr., and they both decided that Rhetta needed to be educated off island. Through Charles Jr. and his lofty connections, they found the perfect finishing school, whose young ladies were boarded in several dormitories located on the property, one that was between Williamsburg and Richmond. It was situated where he could keep a close-enough eye on her. Jabez visited often, and Rhetta always knew before he came and the reason for his being there. With premonitions of a visit, she was prepared to answer his questions and give as much guidance as possible. Other than that, she enjoyed the life of a wealthy young woman in a prestigious school. She was quite popular and had many girlfriends, all of whom were "in love" with either Jabez or Charles Jr. They were both quite handsome, in entirely different ways.

Jabez used the land his grandfather left him to build a private compound for his little family of two. First, of course, he had the small cottage constructed. He was trained in construction and was fascinated with it, whether it be ship or house. Since his teens he aspired to be a shipbuilder, but he found that building was his love. It didn't make any difference what form it took. His mind worked best when he was involved in creating. He also had a gift for architecture, designing elaborate and unusual things that suited him. He never could have built for someone else, because he had too many ideas that were not yet conforming to the world around him. It was what led him to do what he did. It was exciting to experience adventures, to test his mettle, and to make the things no one else did. Normal was boring to him.

Luke found the place in the script where they had decided to put The Book away and began to read again. Jabez continued,

as a light frosty ship loomed on the ceiling of the attic, water splaying out on the walls and floor:

> I met Captain Johns, and he proved to be as good as his word. I took with me two trusted friends, Charles Henry Jarvis Jr., my friend from school, whose connections off the island are as good as my connections

on the island. He is politically connected in the parliament in Williamsburg, his father in line to be the future governor. And, I brought with me a man from my grandfather's docks, William, who oversees all the loading and unloading of goods to be traded. Charles Jr. and I met the Captain, while William stayed with the wagons and horses. William is paid well, and being older, not really interested in having the adventure that both Charles Jr. and I crave. He is a freeman, who has been my rock since my grandfather died. He is family.

Charles Jr. and I inventoried the cargo, and agreed upon the price. The exchange was agreeable to both my partner and myself. We were surprised at how generous the exchange was. Captain Johns, satisfied that I too was trustworthy, inquired if we might be interested in moving cargo for him again.

After discussions among the three of us, it was decided that we would continue our correspondence, and I would meet him again at the bar in Jamaica where first we met, in three months. If one of us does not show up, we would consider the partnership terminated. I am willing. Charles Jr. has a family, and a respected position, he will not always be as available to rendezvous with possible non-law-abiding individuals as I am, therefore the risk is mine alone. I am satisfied with that.

William drove one wagon, and Charles Jr. and I drove the other. Both wagons were tightly covered, and we brought them back here. William took one of my horses, and went back to the village, having been well compensated for both his help and his silence. He was more afraid than either Charles Jr. or myself. Having worked most of his life for my grandfather on the docks, he is a trusted friend, and a fine man to know. I will make sure he is well taken care of.

William advises me to build a barn on the property. He is right. He will begin immediately. I think William is beginning to take to this adventure. Charles Jr. is staying with Rhetta and me in the little cottage, and tomorrow night, we will meet William at the docks, and oversee the loading of cargo on ships bound for Richmond. They will travel to the Chesapeake Bay up the James where Charles Jr.'s men will take it to warehouses in Richmond. From there, he already has contacts among the wealthy to deliver to buyers in both Williamsburg and Richmond. They are happy to get such fine goods at a price that is much lower than market price, with the English taxes attached. If we are selective, and most careful with whom we deal, we two can work out a very good business. As Charles Jr. takes a portion of goods to the colony north of us, I will sail up the Pamlico to points of trade near New Bern. These are merchants that I have had dealings with over the years, with both my grandfather and myself. We know them and they are trustworthy. Charles Jr. and I feel we have no need of further contacts than the ones we have.

Luke finished reading Jabez's first entry into the logbook. In looking back at the beginning half of The Book, to the pages of records, he found the entries of the cargo unloaded that first night at the slough on the end of Ocracoke. It appeared to be barrels of sugar, barrels of cinnamon, more than 100 bolts of silk from China, and chests of gold bullion. Luke turned back to The Book and read the final portion of this story.

Johns agreed to our keeping one chest, in exchange for secrecy, and for me to keep his share in the other chest, safe for when he returns. There were two chests of treasure. Maybe there had been more, but Captain Johns only sold to us what he and his crew could not use, or hide from the English government. He gave both chests of valuables to us and we struck an agreement on the understanding that for our negotiation to hide the chosen one for him, he would share the treasure. Should he not return, all treasure would belong to me. When I opened the trunk I was given, it was full of gold bullion. I halved it with Charles Jr., each of us holding out a share for William. We did not open the chest we were responsible for saving. I had an excellent idea where it would go. Charles Jr. and I both realized this one transaction would start the foundation of this business. I feel the three of us have become friends, we have no fear of betrayal, to betray one would betray all, this first transaction has been a good bargain. Charles Jr. and I agree this is lucky. We are so green and unschooled in the way of this world, we could have been in much trouble had it not gone as it did. We are fortunate.

The next entry was the second time Jabez visited Jamaica. It also included the details of his trip to New Bern, and how he disposed of the cargo from Captain Johns. There was silence as the three children closed the big book, the colors disappeared, and light returned to normal.

Ellie took The Book and wrapped it exactly as they had found it, in the red flag, and placed it gently back into the trunk. When it was again in its proper place, Luke just laid back flat on his back and stretched, looking up at the ceiling of the attic. He was tired and drained of emotion. He had been tense and sitting in the same position for so long, and there was much to think about. He wished he could have been there on that dark night when Jabez met Captain Johns at the Ocracoke slough. *Why Ocracoke?* he thought. *Did they have to row across Hatteras Inlet to get there? Why did they not tell the privateers to meet them at the Hatteras docks?*

Ellie began to look in other trunks in the attic. She was ooohhhing and aaahhhing at the amazing clothes and the beautifully bound leather books that were stored there. She also found an entire set of silver knives and forks, but she thought they were just trash, as the tarnish made the silver service look dark and unimportant. She actually did not know what she had found, but she was still careful with it anyway. In one trunk she found a fancy porcelain doll that looked too fragile to play with. It probably was something that was for decoration, because it was too delicate to touch. It reminded her of her precious bride doll, but the clothes were more elaborate than the gown her doll wore. It was nice to know it was there. She would keep it there and know she had a friend in the new house.

Blake was rummaging around in a separate trunk, one that had weapons. He picked out an old long-barreled pistol, sort of unusual looking, and not what he was used to seeing. The pistol had special grips that were sort of green, with fancy scroll work on the side plates of the handle. Also etched into the metal were renderings of dragons and sea serpents. Even the hammer was fashioned as the head of a cobra. It was heavy, and therefore hard for Blake to imagine how a man could fire such a piece. It did remind him of the style of pistol he had seen in pictures as the sort that pirates stuck on their baldrics and had stuffed in their vests. *Wow*, he thought. *They were so heavy. How did a man stand up straight when carrying them? Oh well, they must have all been big men.* He rummaged around and found another, sort of a twin to the first one. It was heavy, too, and he held them both next to his chest, imagining how it might have been to carry around weight like this. Carrying this kind of thing around was a job all in itself.

Luke, still stretched out, drifted into a nap. The attic was hot, the window was not the kind that would open, and the air from the hatch was not nearly enough to make the attic comfortable. Also, the heat from the lanterns was beginning to make the place stuffy, and he realized the smell of kerosene was getting to him. As he drifted away, he found himself on the wagon seat beside Uncle Jabez, whose visage was obscured and dark, so he couldn't really tell who this dark figure was, but he *thought* it was his uncle. They were on the sandy road leading out of Hatteras village. In his dream,

when they got to the inlet at the end of the village, there was no water. The two-track road kept on going, and he could smell the salt air on either side, coming from the sound and the ocean, but they did not get to the inlet. As they continued down the road, he saw a house and a garden. There were large live oak trees in the yard, and beyond the house was another. Yet they did get to the inlet. As they traveled on, he came to a part of the road that looked like they would be nearing a stand of trees, maybe a forest. He did not remember these woods at the end of Hatteras village.

The wagon rumbled on for a long, long time, and it was like they were never going to get anywhere. He saw himself looking around for the ocean, but there was more land, and he lost sight of the sound completely.

He began to smell oil, like there was a fire somewhere, or a shipwreck, he couldn't figure out what the smell was,

and suddenly he was awake.

What he was smelling was the oil from the kerosene lamp beside him. As he sat up, he realized the others had not even known he was asleep. They were over near the open hatch, so engrossed in looking through the chests and drawers of some of the upright trunks that they never even looked over his way. Luke's nap had been short—in reality, only a moment. People only dream just before awakening, in the few seconds before consciousness. Most dreams feel longer. Some feel like they last all night and sometimes there are several, but they are only moments, and just before the dreamer's eyes open to reality.

When he moved, Blake crawled over and was chattering on about the pistols he had found. Luke realized the air in the attic was becoming unhealthy.

"Hey, don't you guys smell the lamps? Look, they are almost empty. Maybe it is too stuffy up here for spending a long time. I think I have a headache from the burning oil. I'm going back down the ladder. I need to go outside and clear my head." Luke got up and started toward the hatch.

"Me, too," said Ellie. "I was feeling a little sick, too. Coming, Blake?" she asked.

"Yeh. I need to go look at some of those books in Uncle Jabez's office. I'll bet there are some pictures there that look like the things we are finding." Blake was not about to be left behind.

"Don't you have a headache?" Luke asked Blake.

"Maybe, but I'm going with you," he said.

The three gathered their pillows and threw them down the hole and began to make their way down the ladder after they were sure that nothing in the attic appeared to be disturbed. Luke went first with his lantern, and he watched as the other two managed their own lanterns and descended the ladder. They replaced everything at the bottom and made sure the wall was closed, with the clothes rearranged to their original position—all to obscure the entrance to the attic. Then they hurried downstairs to the kitchen. Replacing their lanterns, they decided they would eat lunch in the little cottage again. That seemed to be their special place, as it was small and comfortable, and they were together.

Luke took huge breaths when he reached the fresh air. He advised the others to do the same. Fresh air was a problem he was going to have to solve.

As they ate lunch around the table in the little cottage, they began discussing where they were going to get more oil for the lamps. They decided they would spend the rest of the day looking around for supplies. Surely there was a container of oil somewhere on the property. They also had the cavern and caves to explore.

Ellie told them about her vision of something in the grotto, near where the stream made a waterfall, in the deepest part of the cave. It had happened when she had been watching Luke and Blake with their wolves the day they first found the hidden stairs. As she watched them in her mind, she saw something in the water behind them. She had been concentrating so much on the boys that she did not know what she was looking at, and so much had happened since then, she had not remembered the vision until they mentioned they needed light for the caves. It was the first time they had talked about it. She thought she had mentioned it, but the excitement of trying to find out how to open and close the door to the stairs hidden between the walls was so intense that it caused talking about the caves to take a backseat to all else that was happening.

There was so much to do with this mansion and its secrets. It was hard to figure which thing was most important to find or investigate. That pirate book was going to take a long time, and it was too interesting to leave. They were curious to find out about Uncle Jabez, but also to stop reading and go down into the caves. Maybe they would leave the caves until summer. It would be cooler down there then, and maybe the attic would be too hot.

"Look out the window. It's Rafe," Luke said. "I'm going out to try to get next to him. I really want him to know my scent."

"Maybe they are all here," said Ellie. "I'm going, too. I wonder if Twylah has her pups with her." She was out the door right behind Luke.

"Wait for me!" Blake grabbed the rest of his sandwich and followed the other two out the door.

Luke went near the wolf, and the wolf did not shy away. Luke began to talk softly to the animal as he walked around the yard, just to see if Rafe would follow. He did. It appeared maybe the wolf also wanted to be friends. Blake tried to walk with Luke, but Luke shooed him away. He wanted the alone time with his wolf and didn't want to be distracted.

Disgruntled, Blake went to the front yard to complete a task he had wanted to do since they first saw the huge mansion. He was determined to climb one particular tree. The huge live oak's twisted limbs were almost a foot thick everywhere, an indication of how long this old tree had been growing. As Blake climbed, higher and higher, he periodically glanced down to see how high he was. Everything kept getting smaller. As he looked straight ahead, he realized he was even with the second story, yet the tree went higher still. Nearing the top, he sat down in a crook of the mighty limbs and looked out in the direction of the ocean. He could see the breakers, the pattern of the woods where they made their path, and the thickness of the trees in the entire area. The tall trees gradually led to smaller, windswept ones, their branches leaning in to the land and almost growing sideways, their tops looking like someone was blowing them over. Then the view went to bushes, then sand dunes and sea grass. Anyone sitting in that tree could see movement in all directions.

Toward the sound, the pines obscured the way. This tree was one of the largest he could see anywhere. Mostly toward the sound were tall pine trees, what looked like millions of them. He realized how truly isolated this place was. From the tree he was in, looking over the property and taking a look in all directions, he could see the covered path they took from the ocean, and on the other side the sandy road they took to get here from the village. Things were beginning to get green again, and he thought maybe in another month, he wouldn't be able to see anything. In the northern direction, he couldn't see past the house. To the south, it was total forest, with only treetops, no houses. He wondered how far this property went. East was the ocean and the small path leading to the house and a portion of the huge barn. It occurred to him that the barn was originally built to store cargo from the wagons that met the ships. West, only green trees and a portion of the road, but the trees were too thick to see any civilization.

As he sat on his perch, totally protected and cradled by the huge limbs that supported him, it reminded him of his view of the world from Wematin's shoulders that first evening when they were taken to the home of the Croatoan. Finally he looked down and saw Theo, his wolf, seemingly asleep at the trunk of the tree. His heart skipped. Theo had found him and was waiting to see if he was all right way up there. He began his descent down the crooked limbs, carefully finding the right steps, and quietly, so as not to disturb Theo. He wanted him to be there when he stepped to the ground.

Meanwhile, Luke and Rafe were no longer just walking around. They were searching for the supplies the children were beginning to need. They first opened wide the barn doors, to let in light so that they could see to search. Luke suppressed the urge to treat Rafe like a dog, so they did not touch, but Rafe lumbered a short distance behind Luke as he began to scour the area for more kerosene. He found a couple of cans and picked up two of them to move to the kitchen area. They were a little heavy, but he balanced them out and the exercise made him feel strong. He was thinking how he was becoming a man, like his dad and Grandpop. He thought of himself as the master of the place, and he figured he needed to get more responsible in preparing each adventure. He also thought about how he could get more ventilation to that attic room. The fumes of the lamps had made him drowsy, and he needed to think how to solve that problem. After all, he was responsible for the other two. Maybe they had not been as sleepy as him because they were closer to the opening of the hatch. He was a problem solver.

As he walked toward the house carrying the cans, he remembered his strange dream. He had forgotten to tell the others while they were all in the small cottage. He would tell them tonight. Maybe Ellie could help him figure out what it meant. At least he could start her thinking about it. All the while, he was aware that the wolf was following him, like a companion. He didn't think he had ever felt so safe. He was also thinking how lucky he was to have both Gus and Rafe. Maybe someday they would all ride together.

Ellie didn't get far out of the house before she heard the whimpering of the pups near the wooded side of the cottage. She went back, and there they were, just sort of hanging around in the small brush before the tree line began. She did not see Twylah, but she knew, or rather she felt, her presence nearby. Ellie sat down on the ground, and the four pups rushed up to her, licking her on her face and crawling all over her.

This day of bonding was the entire conversation on the ride back home. Everybody was talking at once, each telling what to them was the most exciting tale of friendship. This had been such a special day. Their grandmother had given them her blessing, they had "met" Uncle Jabez, and their wolves had finally gotten close to them all. How could things get any better?

★ 7 ★

The Confession

After Sunday dinner, Grandpop decided to take Grandmom for a ride.
She did not leave the compound often, with all the work she set for
herself to do, and it being a pretty spring day on the island, Grandpop
suggested that everyone go on a Sunday afternoon drive. Nett stayed
home to do schoolwork and write to Bill.

Luke started out, "Grandpop, I had a dream the other night that I was
riding in a wagon through Hatteras village, and when we got to the inlet
at the end, it was not there. We rode and rode, and never did have to stop
because of water. Also, Pop, there were houses down there, ones past the
village. In my dream, there was no Ocracoke, just Hatteras. What do you
think that means? Do you think that Ocracoke is going to sink?" Luke
was leaning over the seat, right beside Grandpop's ear.

Ellie and Blake were giggling about something and not paying
attention. After all, Luke had not yet told the others about his dream,
since they hadn't even noticed that he was napping while they were going
through the other trunks.

Grandpop was silent as he saw an approaching car. They were into the
Trent Woods by now, where there was only a single dirt road. He knew

95

someone would have to stop or pull over to relinquish the right-of-way. He looked for a suitable clearing on his side of the road.

"Just a minute, son," he said. "This is Mr. Farrow, and one of us has to give way. Let me see if there is a shoulder where I can pull over."

Grandpop maneuvered the car over as far to the right as the trees would allow and was completely off the road to the side on a pine-straw-covered shoulder. Mr. Farrow, also wanting to be polite and give way, pulled his car over until he only had two wheels in the track. He moved forward slowly as each man gave a greeting to the other. Normally in that situation, both drivers would stop and talk, share the news, and move on. Today they each had a car full of people, so this was not the right time. Mr. Farrow was from Trent and had family in Buxton, so Sunday visiting was customary.

"Now let me get this straight," started Grandpop as he regained the road. "You were in a wagon, and you were down at the south end of the village. That right?"

"Yessir, and Pop, we went and went, but there was no Ocracoke." Luke now had his chin on the back of the front seat, and out of the corner of his eye he saw Grandmom smile.

"Well, son, it sounds like a strange dream, but I'll tell you the truth. The islands of Hatteras and Ocracoke used to be connected, with no inlet between them, and there were people living on that strip of land. It sort of looked like the sandy area leading from the end of Trent Woods to the beginning of Hatteras village, the way it looks now. There were a few houses on that spot, and there was no inlet separating what we now know as two islands. Then it was just one island. An extremely powerful storm came through, so strong and so intense that it took out houses, washing them right into the sound, and left a huge inlet there. The cut was so big and so deep that it separated Hatteras from Ocracoke, and it's been two islands ever since. At that time, what we now call 'hurricanes' were just referred to as 'storms.' But, son, that was near 100 years ago, 'round 1850, I think. Where would you get a notion in your head like that? You couldn't have seen or heard of it. Did you read something in a book about it, and just have one of your dreams?"

Grandpop was curious as to how Luke would know a thing like that. He didn't remember ever telling him, and it was even before his time.

"I think I read something like that, Pop. I've been reading a lot about pirates in Blake's books, and maybe it was in one of those. Anyway, I was just curious." Luke was now trying to wriggle out of the discussion before he got so far in that he would get caught and not be able to explain how he knew. He quickly changed the subject. "On the way home, can we stop by the old house? Bet Grandmom hasn't been there for a while."

The kids heard that one and started a chant in the back.

"Old house, old house!" and their silly giggling and tickling started up again.

"I think I would like that, Charlie," said Odessa. "Maybe instead of going to Hatteras, we can do that. I haven't been there for some time now. I would love to see it. We're almost to the place in the woods where we turn off, aren't we?"

"Well, Dessa, if you want to. I just wanted to get you out of the kitchen. Seems like you've been working so much, you never get to go anywhere but church." Charlie was determined not to let this be a kid trip, as he really wanted to give his wife a break from her daily routine.

"Grandmom, say, 'Yes.'" Blake and Ellie were now leaning over the front seat, one in each of Odessa's ears, and then there was Luke, leaning over in Grandpop's ear. There was just no peace with these three. But Charlie and Odessa were entertained, giving each other that *I give up* look. They both agreed it would be fun to take the children to the house.

Since talk of the impending war, they had discussed with Nett, and Bill before he left, that they probably would have to move there from the lighthouse, since the navy was beginning to have more and more of a presence on the grounds. They could not move back to their old house

in the village, because Tommy was living there and running the store. If
the Germans with their submarines (U-boats) started sinking ships off
the coast again, like the end of the previous war, it would not be safe to
stay there. Odessa was curious as to how much it would take to get the
old place in living condition. In her lifetime, nobody had lived there. They
only just kept the place up and did repairs when needed. She remembered
it as a beautiful old house, with lots of things that were fancy, and it was
full of antiques. Yes, she was curious.

Grandpop turned the car left into the side track leading up the hill
to the old mansion. Spring was making things grow rapidly now, and he
hoped that the limbs from bushes did not scratch what he considered his
new car. He had not yet been able to cut down the side bushes. He was
sort of waiting until one of his sons, "the boys," could help him. It would
be an all-day, maybe two-day job.

They rumbled up the hill toward the house, and even Grandpop was
excited. He didn't get to have adventures with the kids enough, and he
could envision what this was going to be like. He just hoped he could keep
control of the situation. He glanced over at Odessa, and she was smiling.

Luke was sitting back now, looking out the window at the trees they
passed. He was remembering his dream. On the wagon with Uncle Jabez,
at that time in history, the islands of Hatteras and Ocracoke were joined,
and that's why Jabez had to meet his privateer at the slough in Ocracoke,
not at the docks in Hatteras. Captain Johns did not want to be noticed
going 'round into the area of Hatteras docks, because for one, he did not
know the shoals on the back side of the island, nor where it was shallow
or deep. He was more comfortable anchoring out at sea and coming in by
longboat. His ship, being a three-masted barquentine, drew a deep draft
and needed the depth of either a true harbor or the sea. There would be
no way to float him off a shoal, should that happen, much less explain his
cargo. The dream now made sense. Uncle Jabez had taken the risk away
from Captain Johns by meeting him in a secret spot, where they both

could get in and out without any trouble. After all, in the log book, it did say the meeting happened on a dark night.

The car pulled up to the front of the stone mansion. Ellie and Blake waited with Grandmom, not patiently, for Grandpop and Luke to go around back and turn off the security system. Bill and Captain Charlie had put in the second diesel engine before Bill left for war, and had wired the house for electricity, a fact the kids had not taken advantage of. They saw the big engine in the barn but were not sure what was going on with it, so they never tried to figure it out. They would have been in huge trouble if they messed it up, so they just let things be until someone else could show them how to do it.

Odessa got out of the car and walked up the familiar stone steps to the porch. Immediately she began looking around, surveying the porch, the shutters—all in disrepair. Even the steps needed scraping. They were so slick with debris, they were dangerous. She was taking inventory of all the things that needed to be fixed before it was "fittin'" to move there.

Charlie came back to the front and unlocked the door, letting it stay wide open to allow in much welcomed fresh air. Both he and Odessa began moving aside the huge curtains and opening the windows on the first floor. The dust from the curtains was a little bit daunting, but the light and fresh air gave the place a totally different feel. It was like the children were seeing it for the first time.

Bill and a crew from the Coast Guard had spent at least the last two weeks before he was deployed repairing, fixing anything broken, and updating the house. The kitchen was fine, but the structure of the old house made it difficult to hide some of the wires, so they were sort of running along the baseboards of the rooms and up the corners to the overhead fixtures. It didn't look bad, but it could have looked a lot better. Surely when real electricity came to the island, other homes would have the same problems, and that was just the way it had to be. Bill had done a marvelous job and used some extra wood to cover some of the more unsightly areas. The new wood had yet to be painted, and Odessa took note of still another project.

She realized right away that the whole place was full of dust, and that could be a problem needing to be addressed before anyone could live there. She was thinking of having Charlie construct several clotheslines outside, because all of the curtains and rugs needed to be removed, hung over the line, and the dust *gently* beaten out of them, then reinstalled. There was a worry about the age of the fabric, and that would come into play once they tried to restore the cloth to its former condition. Maybe it was not possible, maybe everything had to be replaced. Time would tell. Since the island was not privileged to any type of dry cleaning, the clothesline method was the only way to remove dust from heavy brocade and velvet. Heaven sakes, they did not yet have washing machines. She and Nett always took their washing on the back porch to a huge galvanized tub and scrubbed clothes with a metal washboard, much like the Croatoan women did on the rocks that the men provided for them. They would go to the opening near the end of the freshwater stream that ran out of the caves.

Odessa was doing some old-fashioned pondering about how to move into a 200-year-old house. Charlie also was thinking about dust as he struggled to breathe in some areas. He had his mind set on a newfangled washing machine he had seen in a store window in Norfolk. Everything was beautiful when it was new, but times had changed, and this would be a major project.

"Grandpop," Luke began, "we have been riding the horses over here some weekends, and coming in through the kitchen door, and reading some of Uncle Jabez's books."

There, it was out! Luke's conscious was finally clear. He was not normally one to be deceitful, but somehow, he never could find the way to tell on himself, so he just blurted it out.

"I hope you aren't mad. We didn't do any damage, and we didn't disturb anything, but it was like a big playhouse, and we love the place so much. Maybe we could start helping to get things cleaned up. If we need to be punished, we are ready for that, but I just had to tell you."

Luke turned to see the relieved faces of both Blake and Ellie. They, too, were glad that Grandpop knew.

"I know, son. Grandmom told me about two months ago, and I watched you ride out each Saturday and most Sundays. I was wondering when you were going to tell me, and I'm glad you finally did. No need to keep things from me. I'm a reasonable man, and I want you to confide in me. Sometimes when you get in trouble, you'll need to tell a grown-up, and I want to be the one you trust enough to do that. Yes, it was wrong to sneak, but from now on, ask my permission, not my forgiveness." Grandpop put his arm around his truly wonderful grandson and gave him a squeeze. Blake, who had not confessed anything, moved in for a hug also. Grandpop laughed and grabbed both he and Ellie and gave them a squeeze, too.

"Grandpop, now that you know, can we keep on coming?" It was the obvious question, and wouldn't you know, Blake was the one asking.

"I would like for you to tell me before you do it," Grandpop said. "I wouldn't want anything to happen, and me not know where you are. Also, I don't want you bringing your friends here, not unless I'm here also. Have you been bringing friends over?" Captain Charlie was almost afraid of the answer, but he had to know.

"Nope, not one time," said Blake. "We haven't even told anybody about it."

"Good, let's keep it that way for the time being." Grandpop turned around and smiled. He had been hurt they had not told him, as he had seen a lot from the top of the lighthouse. What they didn't seem to realize was that from that vantage point, he watched them ride south almost all the way to the turnoff. With his telescope, he could keep an eye out. He knew where they were going. He also had so much faith in Luke that he felt comfortable in his ability to handle most things. Also, with two horses and three wolves, they were pretty well taken care of, as far as being safe. He and Odessa spent endless hours talking about it, but they did not tell Nett, for fear she had enough on her mind with Bill gone, so this little secret was one they all felt glad was out.

Odessa walked around, taking mental inventory of what had to go and what could stay, and Ellie was right at her elbow the whole while. At the same time, Luke and Blake were on the job with Grandpop, listening to what he thought needed to be done to make the place livable. The most important thing for the day was the light flooding the rooms from the open windows. Now they could see things, rather than guess what was there. The windows were also cool. They were like doors, and swung out, not like windows that pushed up. The whole place was magical.

It was truly the most fun they all had experienced as a family for a long time. They felt closer to each other, and Grandpop was starting to realize that maybe moving away from the lighthouse would not be such a traumatic situation for the kids after all. He and the boys went out to the barn and discussed where the horses would stay, and just walked around talking about grown-up things. When they came back in, Ellie and Grandmom were ready to go home. There was going to be a lot to talk about over the next couple of months. The navy had hinted to Grandpop that he would have to vacate the compound sometime during the summer. No specific date yet, but he knew it was coming. Grandpop was an avid listener to the news on the radio, and he knew how serious the world was getting, with Bill's letters to him indicating the same. Even Bill had suggested the old house.

The government was anticipating shutting down the lighthouse. Because of the certainty of war coming to their shores, there was no doubt the shipping lanes would be attacked. The Germans had already learned of the banquet of supplies anticipated coming up the coast from South America to New York, and then on to the Allies in Europe. At the end of World War I, the Germans had successfully destroyed a British tanker, the *Mirlo*, with their newest invention: the underwater fighting machine they called the U-boat. The Allies knew that with the amount of time that had passed between 1918 and 1942, they would have perfected the stealth of the submarine and would be headed to the shores of North Carolina once again. This time, they knew the area and the lighthouse that guarded it.

They had turned water to fire when they sank the *Mirlo*, and the surfmen on duty in Rodanthe had rowed through fire to rescue the British from the inferno that had been their ship.

The navy needed to turn off the light and watch the quiet sea for the underwater threat that was now on their shores. The captain had seen the increased number of cargo ships going up the coast in front of the lighthouse, and even a skeptic could see that this was a perfect target for the enemy. One ship had already been hit nearby, and the kids could see the fire from their bedroom windows. This was serious! The navy worried about civilians in harm's way, and the Gray family was in desperate need of protection. They did not have time to worry about the family living on the beach. They had to go. Grandpop did not tell the kids that. He would in due time, and it was fast drawing nearer.

Supper that night was interesting, Grandpop spilled the beans to Nett about the visits to the house and did his best to keep the boys out of trouble. She was shocked, but her father was such a practical man, one whom others came to for advice, and he didn't seem upset. So Nett just made up her mind that she had to be more aware the kids were growing up. This kind of thing was bound to happen to kids like these with this much curiosity.

Luke took advantage of his confession and the leverage it gave him to ask, again, if they could continue visiting the old house. This time he asked in front of both his grandfather and his mother. If all this information was out, they might as well get totally comfortable, or they would be right back in sneakyville because they knew they were going to read that book. He spent fifteen minutes or longer building his case. When he finished, they agreed on certain rules, asking permission being one of them, and it was agreed that they could do some chores while they were there. Care of the yard was paramount to getting the place livable, and it was something they could do. Cleaning the barn was another. Grandpop wanted the horses to get used to being in a stall when they were there, and it seemed like a good idea. Gus and Blue probably were tired of fighting the flies and mosquitoes in the woods. The horses went through the dipping vat regularly, so the tick problem was taken care of by the state's Department of Health.

Saturday rolled around. Grandmom made sandwiches, Grandpop waved good-bye from the top of the lighthouse, and the kids and their horses struck out down the beach to the Point and south to their own special crossover. This time seemed more carefree than any other time, and they felt good about everything. They had mapped out their time for chores and planned to get a short look at the pirate log again. With new purpose, they began to clear their path from the beach as they went along. No longer was there a need to let things get overgrown. They kept the path obscured from the beach, but began clearing just inside the wall of bushes and trees. They also planned to clear the sandy track that veered off from the village, so Grandpop would not worry about scratching the car.

It took them a while to get to the house this time, as they led the horses through the path from the beach and hacked away at overgrowth that had always hindered them before. It was a mighty job, and it would take them several times to get it right, as Ellie stayed on the beach side to keep them from revealing anything to passersby. They left the entry as secret as possible, making sure it was hidden from anyone who might want to explore where it led. They were not the only kids to explore on the weekends, and they did not want strangers finding their house, not until they were actually living there. Everything was fun for them, even work.

Grandpop gave them instructions on using the new electricity, and he was pleased they knew what to do. It was decided they would leave the curtains alone, Grandmom left them open, and the only open windows were on the first floor. It was still important to be careful to clean up after themselves. On some days, Grandpop would be going with them. Even Grandmom was anticipating more frequent visits, Nett expressed an interest also. She couldn't wait to get the old upright piano tuned and have the pipe organ repaired and in working order.

This was a little disappointing to Nett, thinking about another move. She had just gotten comfortable in her new quarters at the main keeper's quarters and had her space just as she wanted it. Now she was looking at starting all over again. To her, this was only a maybe, not a given, and there was no need to stress over something that was not a sure thing, she had enough on her mind with Bill in harm's way. She did like the old house, so fixing it up would be a challenge. Maybe they would not have to live there. No matter, it needed to be done anyway. She brushed the thoughts aside and continued with her projects.

This time the horses were loaded down with kids and tools. They had chores to do, places to clean, and bushes to chop, and they needed equipment to aid them. They wanted to help Grandmom and Grandpop, and if this was going to be theirs, well, there were things to fix and they just better get at it. Grandpop had given them a job to do, and they planned to carry it out in the best way they could. They would make their grandparents proud. As if they weren't already.

Blackbeard and Charles Vane

N ow that the kids had permission to go to the old house, it was easy to talk to Grandpop about things they found there, and they, as usual, had many questions. Grandpop was a historian of sorts, and he loved the rather grown-up banter that went on between him and the kids, especially on those nights right after they had experienced one of their adventures. Grandmom quietly sat by, knitting, embroidering, crocheting, or planning the next meal. She also loved to hear the conversation, but she did not enter in, unless her husband asked her opinion, her remembrance, or verification of a particular thing. This was Charlie's time to bond. Grandmom enjoyed knowing the kids were now confiding in their grandfather. She had always been impressed with Charlie's education and knowledge, and did not feel threatened at all.

Grandmom was privileged with the children's confidence from the beginning. She was the one they went to with all their questions, and she was always ready to interpret one of Ellie's dreams. She did not feel out of the loop when it came to helping this trio of curious children. It was she in whom they confided. Sometimes she wished she could discuss their stories and adventures with her husband, but she did not want to betray their trust. That would no longer be a problem. Educating these three was the most entertaining job either of these old people had ever had. It was turning into a new life for them, watching and exploring through the minds of their grandchildren. She sat silently in the comfy rocking chair, next to her sewing box brimming over with yarns and threads of her chosen task. Charlie had fashioned the box with legs so that she would not have to bend over, making it convenient to reach her threads and needles or crochet picks. So she listened. Once in a while she nodded her approval.

She was amazed at what the children had learned already from the books made available from the bookmobile, which came to the island from the Dare County School Board in Manteo. Hatteras School was the stepchild of the county, with little money put into desks or new books. This was their only library. She also recognized that they had been perusing through Charlie's *Encyclopedia Britannica*. His set was the ninth edition, published in 1911, and was his most prized possession. This set was at least twenty years old, and Charlie Gray considered it the best, as following editions were simplified to broaden their appeal to the American market. Grandpop's was leather bound and quite handsome.

Now, with the approval of their grandparents, the children hastily readied themselves for another Saturday adventure. They had very little school year left. It was nearing summer break, and it was almost scary what they had planned for their daily jaunts. But that was in the future, and this was now. They had only had one chance, so far, to really get into Uncle Jabez's log about his Pirate adventures, and today there would be few chores. At this visit, they planned to read what appeared to be their first encounter with Uncle Jabez meeting a true pirate.

Captain Johns was a privateer, and only once so far, by accident, had he ventured into the world of piracy. This incident happened when, while searching the African coast for ships flying either the Spanish or French flag, he had mistakenly attacked a Dutch ship. As the Dutch were not at war with England, this was not in line with the orders he was given by his *Letter of Marque*, and he feared government reprisal. Should King George learn of his indiscretion, he was liable to lose his position with the monarchy.

Queen Anne had recently died, and the throne went to the closest Protestant, George, Prince Elector of Hanover. George was already fighting for his throne with those who found fault with his German heritage, and England was in constant turmoil as they tried to dethrone him in favor of James Stuart, a Roman Catholic and son of James II. These Jacobites, as they were called, proved quite a force as George, being German, spoke little English, mostly German and French. The Scottish clans banded together to foster their claim for James III. With all this maneuvering on the side, Captain Johns felt he and his crew might be overlooked, if only they could hide their treasure. He was sure the Dutch claim would go unanswered. There was such an internal war that took precedent over mistaking the Dutch for an enemy.

With the unpopular George needing more and more money to fight his battles at home, he both depended on stealing from the spoils of the New World through shipping, and mounting stiff taxes on the colonies of North America. Plunder from the pirates was a way for the colonies to buy goods at cheaper prices, without purchasing the taxed goods from England. The Navigation Acts, passed in previous years, had prevented the colonials from trading with anyone but England. This made pirate cargo even more acceptable. Jabez had chosen a dangerous and lucrative business, and he and Charles Jr. were excited to participate.

In the next entrance of the log, Uncle Jabez made another trip to Jamaica. Anticipating this next story, the kids were so excited they almost put their horses in a trot, rather than a leisurely stroll. They kept realizing their speed—and then slowing down. A lot of planning went into this trip. The horses now had a decent place to spend the day, as the kids had previously cleaned out the stalls that the horses would use, and had worked hard on organizing the barn. They were regularly accompanied by the wolves, who lazily hung around the open double doors, although so far, the horses were not introduced formally into that circle. Maybe, today, that would also happen.

There was plenty of oil for the lamps. Luke had done research on how to better ventilate the attic. Being able to open the front door, even though far from the attic, drew down the draft from the open hatch on the third floor. Grandmom made sandwiches and threw in a few treats. Grandpop waved from the top of the lighthouse. The kids were off to enjoy another adventure.

The panel to the wall of the closet was moving easier. Luke did to the panel what he had seen Daddy do on things to make them slide. He took the meat of an open walnut, and rubbed it on the edges of the tracks on which the wall panel moved. The oil from the nut lubricated the rail quite well.

He was first up the ladder, followed by Blake, then Ellie. They hauled with them a bag of old rags to clean the area, allowing them to breathe easier. Now their presence here at the old house was not a problem, although they were not *really* sure if they had indicated *exactly* where they would be reading. By the time either Grandpop or Grandmom climbed that ladder, the kids would be gone to college, or on second thought, that time would be…never! So for their own comfort, the kids cleaned the attic. Today was going to be all about enjoying The Book.

Luke retrieved The Book, and as he unlocked it and pushed the skull,

the colors raced up to form a tavern scene, with rough men drinking and smoking long skinny white bone pipes at makeshift tables of barrels, and some chairs, some stumps for seats. The figures swirled around the room fading in and out:

By the time I sat down with my friend Capt'n Johns the room was beginning to fill up. A surly group, not a gentleman to be found, except Charles Jr. I might have need to apologize....but, ah, we are in this thing together. Alas, Charles Jr. needs to learn the jib of the group, but I have no reservations of Charles Jr. He is quite equipped to take care of himself.

The room was lit by candles along the craggy walls. Boards thrown together to fashion walls, and to hold off the rain, the roof being the same cover, with extra thatch. Through the candles and the smoke, I saw tables of rough-looking men. I recognized Blackbeard, and another man, more handsomely dressed, sitting across from him at his table. Charles Jr. and I were glad it was dark to hide our reaction.

Blackbeard was dressed as an English officer, w/ waistcoat of much pomp and flourish. He wore a red silk scarf tied tightly around his unruly hair, topped by the most impressively displayed gold braided black tri-cornered gentleman's hat in the room. There were other Pirates, of whom we had heard, as only from drinking and listening, and not calling attention to ourselves, could we quietly observe this culture. We needed to learn of them, in order to earn their trust.

Capt'n Johns relayed the reputation of each man in the room, he being the wiser. He said of their history, the man at the table with Blackbeard, and, there was no mistaking who he was, even though Johns pointed him out, was Captain Benjamin Hornigold. He, being Blackbeard's mentor. (The very same Hornigold who "founded Pirate's Republic," located at New Providence, on the island of Nassau, also known as the sanctuary for "The Brethren of the Coast.") Blackbeard started as mate to the man at his table. Hornigold gave Blackbeard his first ship, "Revenge." As this tavern was a known safe haven for those following the creed, Johns named: Charles Vane, Israel Hand, Stede Bonnet, Jack Rackham, they called him Calico Jack, a social type, and his fellow associates, the lady Pirates, Mary Read and Anne Bonney, both sitting alone in a dark corner of the place, where the light was so low, one did not readily notice their sex. They were known by their reputation as being strong and willing fighters. No man dared encroach in their direction, for fear of instant reprisal.

We did our trade with Graham Johns. Before we parted, he formed an introduction for us with those who needed to trade without inquisition. Charles Jr. and I consider ourselves merchants who can satisfy a need discreetly. They unload their goods, we find a buyer. We are involved in the exchange of services. Capt'n Johns vouched for our honesty, and competence to complete the job, without fanfare.

Another visit to Jamaica. Our business flourishes.

I have built a house, my sister Rhetta and I. It is a small cottage, beside the barn I am also constructing, suitable for our needs until the Mansion I envision can also be built.

We are now finished with the barn located on the property. The horses are used at night and need to be close. We are comfortable in the little cottage. William stays close to Rhetta, in the barn, while I am away. She no longer is in need of staying at William's home, although she has formed quite a bond. Finally I am comfortable that she is well taken care of. She is invaluable to me in this business. Something in her mind makes her different. Her counsel is correct, and I have learned to take it. Sometimes it is not what I want to do, but mistakes have made me know, she has a vision for both the future and the past. Charles Jr. and I marvel at her accuracy. What a strange world surrounds me.

Meanwhile cargo sits in the barn in wagonloads waiting to discreetly place at the docks.

Teach visited the village dock tonight. He is anchored down the deep part of the sound, and came by long-boat to make the way through shallow water. He is now anchored at the south end of the island. He admires where he is. He is curious of the land, and finds southern village of Ocracoke much to his liking. He has risked peril, coming this far around and into the sound as it presents too much of a hazard for him to take, he runs into the perfect trap, should he be recognized. He is a feared man. He is checking me out. He has the assurance of Capt'n Johns, but while survey-ing my abilities to sell his product, he has found the perfect spot to careen his ships, and become invisible. I find him intimidating though I should not be, as he begs a favor of me. Hornigold, he says, told him to instill fear in all he meets, therefore, he would have to kill no one. He always tells fearless tales of his tangled long black hair which he plaits into stray braids, adorned with silk ribbon, and, under his hat, he's known to stick footlong rope-type fuses which he allows to smolder around his face as he steps forward to challenge an impending victim. Teach does not realize, he instills fear with his mighty stature alone. As Blackbeard the Pirate, he is a thunder of a man.

As all other Captains, Blackbeard, Edward Teach, is a follower of the code called "Articles of Agreement." His reputation does not insure longevity as a Captain. His men do. With all his bluster, he walks a line between fair and cruel. There is a tale that he once challenged his men to see who could breathe smoking water and limestone the longest in a closed room. They took the dare but ran out choking desperately as Blackbeard chastised them with curses of "coward."

I hear lately that Edward Teach (Thatch, Drummond...he seems to have several last names, there is no assurance that any of them are true) separated partnership from Benjamin Hornigold. These days Hornigold is long a reformed Pirate, who has taken to being a hunter of his former friends who are still Pirates. He has accepted a commission from Woods Rogers, appointed Governor of the Bahamas, the very same islands where Hornigold is known to have enjoyed power. Now he settles on a plantation with occasional hunts to track down an old friend or foe.

This new encounter to Ocracoke for delivery of goods comes from Charles Vane, last seen by me in Jamaica. He is doing business with me on the advice of Blackbeard, whose confidence he keeps. Vane also got his start, and first ship, from Hornigold. He is reputed to be the cruelest of the lot. His own men had him in chains at one point, and eventually he was marooned by his crew on a deserted island, there left to die, save a storm did remedy his fate. The storm pushed a vessel near the island where Vane was marooned, and he was thus rescued.

Vane being indirectly responsible for the capture and thus hanging of his counterpart Stede Bonnet. Vane was hunted vigorously by Colonel William Rhett under the authority of the Governor of South Carolina, Robert Johnson. Governor Johnson received word Vane would be traveling south to Florida, when in actuality he was headed north to meet with Blackbeard for a Pirate collective in Ocracoke.

The Naval assault from the Governor of South Carolina caught Stede Bonnet instead. On their hunt for Charles Vane, they spotted masts in a cove, which they assumed belonged to Vane. Instead, they discovered Bonnet, who was careened on an island near Cape Fear, and as the Naval assault knew it had cornered ships, they mistakenly thought the ships belonged to Charles Vane.

Careening of ships is an important part of this trade. Even at my harbor, we must lift our vessels out of the water at least twice a year, to clean off the barnacles, burn off seaweed, caulk and tar the bottom, or the wood will rot or be eaten by worms. The teredo worm, to be exact. This practice of careening also makes the ship faster, as debris collecting on the bottom slows down a heavy barque.

Vane, I hear, was recently hanged on the docks of Charlestown. Not a surprise.

Pirates do not last long. Some only two or three years. What a reputation they amass in such a short amount of time. There are many stories about Charles Vane. He once fired on the Governor of the Bahamas as the official was entering the harbor of Nassau. Vane set a ship moored in the harbor and belonging to the governor on fire, and sailed it into the ship carrying Woods Rogers, the new Governor. The flames of the moving ship darkened the sky and obscured vision as the moving ship threw fire into the sky. Rogers was struck, but managed to put out his own ship set afire by Vane's vengeance. Vane immediately evaded capture by sailing away in the smoke of night to rendezvous with others on the island of Jamaica.

I remember him to be a burly man, small of stature with skin burnt brown by the sun. He was too young to have wrinkles, so the marks on his face had to be scars. One scar split the growth of hair on his lip and chin as it streaked across his face. His eyes were piercing and ice blue, shining in the dark of the tavern where I first saw him.

In remembrance of Vane, he only came to the island to enjoy his friendship with the Pirate Blackbeard. They sailed and raided together, and also along with Hornigold, thus, the friendship was strong. Vane played the devil in the Caribbean and in the area around Charlestown. He was successful in halting the trade of ships coming and going from that important harbor, thus peaking the ire of the Governor of that colony. He even struck ports leading into and out of the harbor of New York. He did not pirate around Ocracoke, he rested there.

Today's log is of the spoils of Pirate trade. I am building a larger house. One with no equal. My training in shipbuilding transfers nicely to the mansion I intend to construct. I find myself in need of a tower that overlooks the sea, and gives me an indication of when and where my ships are. I also need to watch the sea for trade, and also for my own protection. My business demands the tower. On this hill which overlooks the sea, I am surrounded by tall trees and thick brush. It is not easy to get to this place and I intend to make it even more difficult. William has the men. He demands secrecy, as do I. I have seen the mansions of the Caribbean, and aspire to re-create such a fortress. I first got the idea from a load of stone stolen by Ben Roberts, a man who employed himself in the Pirate trade on the rivers. He had heard of me, and contacted me through the docks, inquiring if I could use loads of stone from the mountains west of here. He says he can deliver enough to build the massive structure I need, and it is easier to deliver here then all the way to the Caribbean. The house will be three or four levels high, strong enough to weather the mighty storms that hit this island every summer. Rhetta needs more space, and elegant trappings like the friends she visits from school. She is back and forth in finishing school even though she continues to advise me on matters in which our family of two is involved. Where does she get her inspiration? She is never wrong. I would not think of sailing without her approval. She keeps me safe, even Charles Jr. has commented on her perception.

We are still in the cottage, only a few more months. I hoard bolts of fabric from China for Rhetta to choose her favorite. They are so handsome they will never go out of style, ladies of Richmond and Williamsburg would pay top dollar to have even one bolt. Rhetta can take her time choosing. Charles Jr. can always sell what she discards. I too, can unload them, as the governors of the colonies are rich as well. I keep the bolts of cloth in the loft of the barn. The loft above the barn keeps the hay from rotting, and allows the bolts of fabric to be well stored. The loft gives me an idea for my own mansion, as the hay is easily dropped for feeding the horses. I am beginning to understand the value of storage. I allow few people up here to work my property, I pay well for secrecy, and William and I move men in and out of here at will, mostly strangers, ones who do not traffic with the village. I hire on condition, and my skills in construction allow only me to see the plans.

Rhetta is home for the summer. The house will climb fast now. She spends time outside with old friends, the creatures of the woods, who have missed her. I know they are here. I do believe they like me also. She sees clear skies for a few months, and I am relieved. I have a meeting in Bath, up the Pamlico Sound to the river, then on to the Bath River, and on into Bath Creek to Front Street. This is an open town, tolerant of questionable people. I have business with Teach, who seems to have settled there. I hear he married someone who was well connected. He has a cargo to distribute before he accepts a pardon from Governor Eden, of that city. It seems to be a fashion for Pirates to accept pieces of paper, that absolve them of past deeds, with only their sign. The paper declares they will abstain from lawless ways. A pledge they have no intention of keeping.

A Pirate's Demise

Luke continued to read, beginning to become stiff from such a long story. As he looked at the next few lines he realized he needed to go on, as Jabez's world continued.

Luke finally had to take a break. The last small pause was not long enough, and Blake's loud sigh was reason to know they all needed a break. He sat up and stretched again. They had been sitting in the attic far past morning, and they were all tired and hungry. Long past lunch, they were all sore from shifting around on the hard floor trying to take in all that they had heard. As he closed The Book, the colors were sucked into the leather-bound cover, and the room was dark and dusty in an instant. It did appear that the visions coming from The Book lit the room in order for the children to read. They decided to try and finish the part on Blackbeard, then rest for a while. Blake retrieved the package of food Grandmom had packed, and they ate where they were—walking around, eating and stretching, getting ready for the next part of Blackbeard's story.

After climbing back down the ladder and bringing up more pillows from the living quarters, they positioned themselves once again to listen to Luke read. They were tired but curious, and they did not think they could leave this part for another day.

When Luke opened The Book again, colors splayed all over the room

this time of a village, rather, a town on the river. The waterfront looked like a forest there were so many masts from ships.

Blackbeard unloaded barrels of rum, sugar, bales of silk (stolen from a ship coming from the Red Sea), and linen from Egypt. Also, I was presented with a chest of jewels, collected and stolen from wealthy passengers unlucky enough to be traveling on the targeted ship of a Pirate. These I would go through with Rhetta, she can have what she wants, there is enough profit here for a decent gain in trade. The ladies of Richmond and Williamsburg, through Charles Jr., will be highly adorned at their next ball.

I do not want to forget what I have seen. Here I take note of the crew on Blackbeard's ship. Before in the dark of the taverns of Jamaica, I cannot discern the appearance of the many patrons. They are shadows of men who are obscured with smoke which curls thickly from the long bone pipes. In that setting they are all no doubt disheveled, no matter their dress. In daylight, in Bath, with no cause to worry, I saw they dressed in the spoils of their trade. The unlawful sailors donned fine waistcoats, vests with gold buttons, jewels not unlike the chest given to me, pinned to their clothing and hats. Most wore proudly the striped shirt normally worn as Navy uniform. Obviously stolen from a dead sailor's body, or worn themselves before jumping naval vessels to join the Pirates, where treatment was fair. They wore rings, and had them in their ears as well as on their fingers. They were young men who had started on a path that had only one end. The gallows. Did they not know? I question, but stay silent on the matter.

Most of the Pirates I know were formerly Privateers. Blackbeard, Kidd, Avery, Hornigold, Vane, Roberts, I hope not Johns, his intrusion into that area the fault of him being overzealous in his job. He seems to have strong family ties in England. His honor is most important. Johns is not greedy. As a Privateer, he and his crew confiscate enough booty from their legally appointed assignment. But, for others, when the countries cease conflict, they no longer issue "Letters of Marque" for robbing the enemy's trade. With no job, and knowing the thieving trade well, most turned to perfecting what they had learned, by continuing their profession, but as a business for themselves. Being a young boy who goes to sea, joining the Navy ensures hardship. The hours are long, the pay is poor, menial labor demanded at all times, strict treatment, no time off, it made being a Pirate sound like a good choice.

To their credit, they all signed a code of contract called "Articles of Agreement" as follows:

1 - every man has a vote when decisions are to be made
2 - equal share of spoils—those w/extra share: captain, quartermaster, first mate

3 - no game of cards or dice for money on ship

4 - lights out 8:00 continue after that above decks in the air (fear of fire)

5 - all weapons, pistols, cutlass, cleaned

6 - no women on board ship, on suffering of death or maroon

7- punishment for desertion ship or quarters in battle draws maroon

8 - no strike randomly on ship .. settle quarrels on land with pistol or knives

9 - musicians rest on Sabbath

Signing on as a Pirate, which was encouraged when men were on a captured ship, it got a young man out of the rigors of the government's rigid Navy, and into the same life, half the work, twice the pay, adventure, danger, but usually came to a quick end. Most do not survive the frequency of battle more than two or three years. It does not take much time before the Pirates become the hunted, rather than the hunter. There's a hanging tree on every dock these days. Some have a cage, or gibbet where the body is displayed for all to see, and beware.

We have a hanging tree in Trent, not for Pirates but for local island thieves, this one is located in the woods near where the Indians had lodgings at Kings Point.

Most of the mates on board Pirate vessels spend their money at the first port available. Here there is a make-shift bar on Beacon Island, near Portsmouth Island where boats are unloaded to vessels which carry a lighter draft, in order to get cargo through the sound to the inner cities. Heavy vessels cannot manage the shallow waters which appear from nowhere to ground a ship. There is even a jewelry store nearby. It is just a hole in the wall, but run by an old Pirate, calls himself Captain LaPlume, a former French nobleman running from the French Revolution. He deals only in jewelry, as Pirates give him gems in exchange for money to purchase grog in the adjoining tavern. LaPlume's shop is popular among the Pirates. His is a lucrative business. I must cater to him, as I could sell the gems he collects for a handsome profit on the mainland.

LaPlume began his career at the gaming tables of New York. Here he won a ship and its crew. His reputation is well known by the Pirates, as he was completely inept at being a Captain. He knew nothing about navigation, nothing about the type of man he was commanding, and did not have the skills to take control. He ran his ship and crew aground three times. He never accosted a ship, of any nation, did not produce a single prize, and therefore his crew spent their time at sea, broke and without decent provisions. They voted him out as Captain, stole his ship and threw him overboard near what they considered a deserted island.

LaPlume is one of the characters for whom Charles Jr. and I have great affection. He found others on the tiny island and escaped with them to the Pirate's haven. His name, among the thieves is LaPhew. His personal hygiene, being so foul, even the worst of the Pirates steered clear of him. Having been set to sea, and finally washed up on an island, his fear of water included the bath. His person and attire so offensive he was made to sit at the back of the boat, as the company rowed to the larger island. He was saved by his families' wealth, which allowed him to open his jewelry business, as he was familiar with Pirate spoils. Phew's customers lingered in his shop only a short time, and accepted his first offer of payment for even the finest gems, they were so bent on staying upwind of him.

Blackbeard himself is early thirty years old, he talks of marriage to a young girl of Bath, named Mary Ormond. At the tavern, he brags of having married near thirteen other wives. He speaks not of children. He dresses as a gentleman, and is well loved by the local merchants as they are quite pleased to garner a profit from the inexpensive goods he provides them. Blackbeard needs to deal with me when his cargo is larger, or consists of more quantity than a single town can consume. Also, some things are too obvious to conceal, therefore, they need to be disposed of elsewhere. Goods like the fine woods that pass through here, extraordinary spices, cinnamon, from India, brass fixtures, iron, sometimes finely tanned animal skins, rare fur, sugar, dyes, cocoa, rice, flour, and casks of wine and rum. These are items both Charles Jr. and I have buyers for.

Just returned from meeting Blackbeard on a quick trip to Jamaica. We met at a long bar right on the water's edge, set high on a rocky cliff overlooking the dock. We made our exchange and as we shared a dram of ale, we observed a confrontation between two men near the end of our meeting. The young men had been there, by appearance, all day, maybe waiting to crew for a ship out. They were fighting on the narrow walkway that bordered the rocks. Apparently they had just unloaded a cargo from the ship in the harbor, and were spending their wages. Their aggression caused one man to pitch head fo-mus into the ocean below, which was heavily beating up against the rocks. The mates went back to the bar without concern for their fallen comrade.

Teach was at the bar, as his men secured provisions. We finished our business and parted straight away. Me, to load my ship for returning to my company ports. On this occasion, Blackbeard looked to battle, he was braced with pistols, his waistcoat was topped by crossing silk bands each with three pistols sticking out. They were primed and ready. His pouch of gunpowder plugs for refill fell at his side in a velvet bag. He brandied a cutlass of fine quality and ornate cuff, to protect his wrist, and add leverage for chopping, the action for which that blade was famous. At his back, stuck in a silk wrapping of cloth, were several daggers of varying sizes. He was unloading his cargo in anticipation of chasing a known vessel from the Spanish islands which was passing through an area familiar to him. He had expectation of a meeting which would afford him a grand prize. He carries so many pistols because a flintlock only fires one time. This is not desirable in a fight. His men were getting drunk in anticipation of becoming totally intoxicated so they would not feel the pain of battle, should one ensue. Blackbeard alone, in his garb and smoking hair would serve to buckle the knees of any merchant Captain. The pirates carried sometimes three hundred fifty men, and traveled several ships together. Should a pirate desire to take or trade up to a better ship, he simply crewed any ship he fancied, and put it to sail with him. A practice he learned from Hornigold. Word traveled fast among sailors. They knew from stopping at other ports, who was sailing, with what cargo, and where she was headed. This is the network of these days.

Luke looked up from The Book and sat up with his legs crossed in front of him in a crouch. He stretched out his shoulders and back. Blake was lying flat on the floor, looking up, with his elbows crooked and his head resting on his hands. He rubbed his eyes. Ellie was lying on her side on several pillows from downstairs, with her head propped up on her hand. She too straightened up, legs tucked under her on the beautiful purple velvet pillow.

"Gosh, I didn't know pirates lived like that," said Blake.

"They didn't know all that stuff would happen when they joined up. Wonder if Uncle Jabez was scared when he met them?" Ellie was thinking about being by yourself and meeting someone like that. "He must have been a brave man."

Uncle Jabez was a brave man, and a smart man. He never traveled alone, he and Charles Jr. always were armed and had a bodyguard traveling with them, one who rendered himself incognito. It was a dangerous occupation, therefore one went prepared. The overhead scene *changed to a deserted beach and a bonfire around which men staggered and danced.*

I have heard of Blackbeard. He has met his final battle at his beloved Ocracoke. It is well known that Blackbeard's connection with the Governor of North Carolina, by the name of Charles Eden, is known to deal with Pirates. Governor Spotswood of the colony of Virginia, is long interested in deposing Eden to steal the North Carolina governorship for one of his circle, thus to combine the wealth of both colonies. He has no love for Blackbeard, and acts upon a tip, given by his prisoner, one William Howard, late a first mate of Blackbeard. Howard was incarcerated in Virginia, jailed on piracy charges, and scheduled to hang for his crimes. In exchange for a pardon, he gave up the location of Teach to Governor Spotswood, who sent ships, under the charge of Robert Maynard of His Majesties' Navy, to a rendezvous with the Pirate near the mouth of Ocracoke Inlet, between Ocracoke peninsula and Portsmouth Island.

Blackbeard stove up on Ocracoke with his pirate friends drinking the barrels of rum confiscated on his last venture. Known to be on the island during that fateful week was Charles Vane, Israel Hands, Black Caesar, Jack Rackham and his associates, Anne Bonney and Mary Read. All assembled in camaraderie, maybe taking the opportunity to careen their vessels, in friendly waters and shores near Portsmouth and Ocracoke. Would that Governor Spotswood could have only gotten the news earlier, he might have cleaned up the whole lot, and saved the entire east coast much heartache and loss of livelihood, from that band. Instead, Blackbeard was alone on his ship "Adventure." His fellow pirates long gone. The ships from Virginia arrived, after a week's voyage from their port located inland to Virginia.

The Navy waited off the mouth of the inlet of Ocracoke, seeing masts looming on the other side of the dunes. They needed high tide. Blackbeard was confronted on his awakening from a drunken week, by cannon shot across his bow. He mustered his men, also in poor condition, and it is said that Blackbeard took the helm of the "Adventure," himself and steered her toward shore, where he alone could make the sea, knowing the sandbars as he did. He slipped through a deep drop-off between the shore and a sandbar, and avoided the Naval vessels. Unfortunately, firing his own mighty cannon, drove his vessel backward with the force of the blast, against the shore, grounding him in the shallow water, crippling his efforts until the tide got him free. Maynard, totally ignorant of the shoals, had both ships held tight on sandbars close by. All participants fired at will at the other as they waited for the tide to float them free.

At the peak of the fight, Maynard, wounded and suffering heavy casualties, ordered his men below, leaving only the dead and wounded visible on the deck. Blackbeard bombarded the deck with his grenades made from old rum bottles stuffed with rags and gunpowder, until even he could not see through the smoke. He thought that Maynard and his men were finished, and with the tide, moved the "Adventure" near the "Jane," Maynard's sloop, and proceeded to board. Maynard and his men gained the deck from below and the melee began with close range pistol shots, cutlasses, knives and hatchets, hacking at each other till the deck was red with blood and standing was difficult. In the end, Blackbeard and Maynard faced each other, each vowing no quarter taken, and as the wily Pirate faced his foe, several of Maynard's men began hacking away at the Pirate, eventually cutting his throat. Blackbeard received more than twenty deadly blows, and finally fell to the bloody deck. They say, had it been an even fight, and Blackbeard had not been hacked apart by the Navy sailors, he would have bested the young officer. They say that the Lieutenant severed Blackbeard's head and hung it from the bow-sprit in display. On returning to Virginia, he presented the carefully wrapped head to the Governor.

In Jamaica again, I hear stories of Blackbeard told in taverns. Once he played a game of cards in his cabin with men of his company. Quartermaster Israel Hands among them. After smoking, and drinking heavily, he leaned back in his chair, and with a pistol cocked under the table, aimed it across the way and shot Israel Hands in the knee. Crippling the poor lout. Hands meant a great deal to Blackbeard, but Hands, they say had been talking about bringing a vote against his mentor for Captain, hoping to win over his boss and take command. Blackbeard was questioned about shooting Hands, and replied that it was what a good

Captain did when those under him doubted his resolve. He is reported to have said that a Captain needed to shoot someone once in a while just for sport.

The house is near finished. I cannot quit. Some treasures given in trade of services we now are free to enjoy. We have pulled from the barn those pieces of furniture I have been saving from items "thrown-in" as not in demand for sale, but too valuable to be discarded. Chests made from the finest wood, mirrors ornately framed, beautifully upholstered chairs of silk or velvet, lamps and small elaborate figurines. I have now begun to explore underground. It is necessary to be safe, and I have installed double walls with walkways in between each, and secret entrances for safely leaving the house undetected. The stairs lead down to even more safety. Rhetta and I can access the caves from underground and reach the sound should the need arise.

We moved in today. Rhetta is pleased with her quarters. She is a great help here, she eliminates my fear. Her perception is never wrong. I am in her debt. She spends her time with nature and the books I have collected for her. I see wolves on the edge of the clearing. I think they protect her. It is comforting to see them. But, when I leave, they are always gone. I am used to them.

"I think we have finished with the section on Blackbeard," Luke said, as he paused for another stretch. "This next part looks like logs of another pirate, Stede Bonnet. What about doing this next time? I want to think about what I read already."

Ellie agreed. "There is so much, I want to look around and see what we can find. Uncle Jabez said one time he got a jewelry chest. Do you think he still has it?"

"Maybe, but let's go eat lunch. All this has made me hungry. Want to eat in the big kitchen?"

Luke sounded excited about being able to wander around the floors of the house and be comfortable enough to use the rooms.

They all agreed and, extinguishing their lanterns, put all things away and climbed down the ladder, rearranged the room as before, and headed for the main kitchen. Food never tasted so good. They drank from the water canteen their father had gotten from the ship's store and talked about what they had learned about the pirates. Luke hopped up on the long butcher-block table which stretched down the center of the kitchen. As he sat there he was silent, and he seemed to be affected by what he read. It seemed like he was sort of going there with the people in The Book. He and the others did not realize just how real the stories were to them, as the colors made the figures and pictures rise from the page and drift around their heads. This was Rhetta's intention, her spell on the magic book. Luke, as the reader, was more affected than the others. He was actually there in the story as he read, and it took him a while to regain reality. After a while, still not involved with the silly conversations between Blake and Ellie, and the laughing and playing they were doing with their food, he snapped back from his dream state and joined in.

The rest of the afternoon was spent continuing to clean the barn. Ellie left that to Luke and Blake, while she shined up the little cabin. Some of Rhetta's clothes were still there, or maybe they were Sabra's. They were old, and they could have belonged to anyone. Anyhow, they were interesting. They were sort of prairie-looking, maybe they were for walking around in the woods. Rhetta had some moccasins like the ones Weroansqua had given Ellie. Could it be she also went back? Ellie wished that there was a journal from Rhetta, that would be cool. Maybe there was, maybe Rhetta kept her stuff somewhere else. Or maybe in one of those trunks. After all, Rhetta had lots of time to sit down and write. As intelligent as they say she was, surely she wrote something also— things she saw, things she did. Ellie decided two things: she would ask Weroansqua, and she would begin a search.

★ 10 ★

Stede Bonnet and Calico Jack

All the way home, two of the adventurers were mostly silent. Their thoughts were often fractured by Blake, who spoke right in Ellie's ear. Luke could sort of drift in front, or back along the wash, or even give Gus his head and saunter into the slightly chilly water of the incoming surf. The horse was also having fun. He knew his rider was daydreaming by the slack reins and loose legs, so Gus did the same. No doubt his mind was with Poseidon. Maybe Gus was racing across the sky or pawing at the surf with his five other companions. But horse and rider were one, sharing feelings and understanding. It was so easy to be friends. They were going along and definitely getting along. Luke became aware of a splash, which was so inconsequential that he did not bother Gus by moving him. He simply continued his previous thought.

The Book was still in Luke's mind. He, more than the other two, lived the colors. His eyes saw them dancing across the page, as well as the floor and ceiling, but for him, the picture had more detail, and he was beginning to get a look at the characters. His familiarity with the look of his uncle was beginning to develop sharply, and he was puzzled because it was something he had already seen.

Tomorrow he would look.

Luke had stared and stared at the painting on the bookshelf in Uncle Jabez's office. He knew this man. It was Manteo. Not as dark complected, hair not as long, but the color as black as Manteo's hair. His eyes were the same. He looked to be the same height. He was dressed in a long, tan canvas duster. It was styled in the fashion of the day, with leather buttons and long slit up the back, an expensive riding coat. He wore a wide-brimmed, brown felt hat, unstructured, not like Luke was used to on Pop, but rather like those in comics. It was cocked and pulled down over one eye. In his posture he stood with one hand opening his coat to display a pearl-handled pistol, in a worn leather holster, devoid of design, slung down on his hip. It was balanced on his trousers by the weight of the other twin, higher on the other side. Behind the low-hanging pistol was another leather sheath, and showing just at his back was the leather handle of a large knife. It was poised to be snatched to the ready by a left-handed combatant. Most who swung a sword were equally as talented with one hand as the other. Usually those with skills used two swords anyway.

He was a handsome man—rugged, straight nose, high Indian cheekbones, and there was that Jennette smirk, which was known to serve as a smile. Dark, smoky eyes were portrayed as noncommittal. A family disguise of *knowing* that was passed down from the Native American side of the family tree showed in this painting. He appeared noble, strong, decisive. Where had he seen this very portrait? He only glanced at it before, skipping by it as his eyes searched out the pirate renderings. His subconscious had memorized it. Here it was again. Was this somebody important?

A strong thunderbolt struck Luke in the head, and he slapped the side of his noggin. It's *Uncle Jabez! It's Uncle Jabez! I know it!* He was alone in the room, but he wanted to scream to the others. This was the same man whose portrait was hung in Aunt Rhetta's bedroom in the little house. He knew who it was. Luke was so excited he began running, sliding through the rooms, and checking out pictures in cabinets and bookcases, and on the dressers and the walls. He was excited to find more than enough to fill his vision of his Uncle Jabez. Luke had such an inner connection, he knew that it was not Manteo. But the look of his mentor was also in the countenance displayed by his Uncle Jabez. It could have been the stare. Maybe it was the hair, and the way he looked a little Croatoan. After all, he *was* a Jennette. Maybe the boots?

He had it! It was the way Uncle Jabez stood. Totally in charge, not afraid, confident, ready for anything, and most of all, calm. These were all the things he knew in Manteo. Pop was like that, and in lots of ways Daddy. He realized that his great uncle was a good man, like the other good men in his life. He smiled as he went from one likeness to the other. People had sketched and painted him, so he must have been respected, or at the very least, known. The art showed the same kind of confidence in his face. Boy! Uncle Jabez dressed almost the same in all the renderings. His long coat, rakish hat, deerskin pants, knee-high boots, and those pistols. Should anyone doubt, the man of the house was ready.

Luke also began to recognize Charles Jr., Uncle Jabez's business partner—in pictures together, some back to back, some with boot on a stool, or stair, sometimes with one or two pistols displayed in the air. Charles Jr. did not dress like Uncle Jabez. He carried the look of a country gentleman. He dressed in black, with a black string tie, black shirt, black pants, black shiny boots, and a tailored long waistcoat, also black. His dark sandy hair was slicked back and tied with a ribbon in back. His hat was black and cocked; these two looked like trouble. As Charles Jr. was poised with two pistols raised, it was noticeable that across the foot rest leaned a beautiful shiny cane, with a silver knob shaped like a lion's head. It appeared to be a gentleman's cane, one with no particular need except to look smart. No wonder they did business with robbers and thieves. They looked to be pretty slick themselves, and it did appear they were primed and ready for business. Luke was almost ashamed he had not fully understood the "jib" of his Uncle Jabez, and why wouldn't he have chosen a friend like Charles Jr.?

He stared at the pictures and tried to imagine the life these two led. He knew he would take more notice of what he was reading and the pictures on the page that only he, so far, could see. He tried to know them.

His daydreaming was interrupted by Ellie and Blake. They had refilled all the lanterns and stood against the chest ready for him to join them at the sliding wall behind the closet. They were patiently waiting for him to go first. Today they would read another story, and the kids had anxiously prepared in case the light did not last. They also had opened the windows for a draft to flow through, and from the looks of the room, as Luke entered the bedroom, these two were taking half the house up there with them. This looked like the makings of sleeping quarters. Ellie had already started up with an armful of pillows, and Blake was standing at the bottom with an armful of his own.

"Ellie, get on back here. I'll go first to open the hatch. You know you can't do it with all that stuff you are carrying up. Come back, drop your stuff, and go 'round and collect something for me to sit on. Remember, I can't shift around like you can, so think about that. Where did you get all that stuff? I don't know where anything is, so do that please, and I'll come back down and help bring it all up. I have to come back for the lanterns anyway."

Ellie slowly descended the ladder and went off to search for something comfortable for Luke. Meanwhile, right behind Luke waited Blake, carrying at least four pillows. As always, you never could tell what Blake was carrying. The obvious was only a drop in the bucket. He was going to be pulling things out all day.

Luke went down the ladder for lanterns. That was a self-appointed job in the beginning. They were full, and he didn't trust anyone but himself to navigate the ladder with them. It was okay for them to carry down an empty one. So it was established: they couldn't go up there without him.

As they all finally had their nests made, they actually laughed when the colors splayed up from the magic book. Each individually wondered which of the many spiritual beings they all knew would want to put a spell on this book. And what was the spell? Hopefully it was a good one. They knew their intentions were good.

The saints hovered in the attic in what seemed to be a dark, shadowy place. They decided they needed to bring in some light, so they blew around a little sparkle dust to make the children's eyes see more clearly. They were having to lie down over the edge of the soft, gray cloud that blended in with the wall and ceiling around them. The only visible sign of the three saints was a broken silver outline thread of the reclining, curious angels. Their robes only sparkled when the rays of the sun landed right on them, but the children did not notice, as their dreams and visions were playing out as they faced the floor, and listened to Luke read the journal

as the form of Uncle Jabez slowly rose from the colors of The Book…

I met Charles Jr. once again in Jamaica. We do not stand out there, we are not bothered by the natives, nor the Pirates with whom we do not deal. I smile, we deal with everyone.

We have learned that we are a day behind the hanging of Charles Vane at Gallows Point near where we are drinking. Charles Jr. and I recounted the stories of the rogue, as we drank and smoked. We waited to rendezvous with Capt'n Daniels, of the islands north of us. He has asked to meet us here in the islands. Strange, we wonder why he did not contact us for this meeting closer to home. We have heard he is a local Pirate, but we have never done business with him. He left a message at the boarding house desk, for us to meet him here. He must be avoiding pursuit.

Charles Jr. recounted that Vane had been instrumental in the hanging of the Pirate and former associate, Stede Bonnet. Vane was reported careened on a small island south of the Carolinas, and reveling in pursuit of celebrating his newest prize, a schooner taken with a quantity of Spanish pieces aboard. He took the ships, manned them with a crew under Yeats, a man of his quartermaster, and sailing with several ships, set about plundering vessels off the Carolinas. He caught the attention and wrath of the Governor of South Carolina, who sent Colonel Rett to end the rampage. The Colonel, having encountered Yeats alone, without the protection of Vane, successfully talked him into abandoning his mentor and giving up his position. Yeats was certain to hang, as they had him outnumbered. On Rett's orders, Yeats surrendered his charge of Vane's captured ship, with crew and cargo intact, on promise of a pardon from Vane's determined enemy, Governor Johnson. Charles Jr. had heard that Vane was blindly furious at losing his possessions. When Vane got wind of the capture, he left word in Charlestown of his intention to sail south. The Navy followed him south, and when they saw masts, they fired on the ships only to find the masts they blasted did not belong to Vane. His ruse had worked. He had instead sailed north to Ocracoke, where he met Blackbeard. He departed company from their feasting on the beach, less than three weeks from that fateful day when Blackbeard was killed. At Ocracoke, there were several Pirate Captains, on the invitation of Blackbeard, who enjoyed a meeting, complete with music and strong drink. Some careened their ships near one of the small islands south of Portsmouth Island, and rowed up the shoreline in longboats to join the others in revelry all at Blackbeard's invitation. The other Pirates and Vane left before the conflict with Maynard started.

I had occasion to meet Stede Bonnet. A more unlikely man never sought out the trade of a pirate. He and I had many late night conversations of the arts. He being an educated man. When I introduced him to Charles Jr. there were nights of drinking and artistic discussions not unlike the talks we had as fellows at Harvard. Stede was quite the scholar. He was the son and grandson of a wealthy plantation owner, overseeing forty or so square miles, on the island of Bimini. On that island he was known as Major Stede Bonnet, having served time as a gentleman soldier. When he was not thirty years old, he left his plantation, plus his wife and children, on a ship purchased and outfitted with questionable sailors bound to his orders by payment. He was no sailor, but relied on the help he had purchased. Bonnet was a successful Pirate, his ship was sound, and he had hired a large number of men to crew. Conquests were fast and many. Bonnet collected three vessels. Then he met Blackbeard.

Charles Jr. just made a good trade with a man named Roberts. He has the wares to finish my house. He is a river Pirate, and has knowledge of a barge of stones coming down into the harbor of Charlestown from the rivers of North Carolina. These are stones from the mountains. They will wall the sides of my hilltop manor. I will make this a fortress. My life's work is about to be realized. I have worked for this. These walls will be outside the exact brick replica on the inside. I have enough bricks to enclose the cottage also. I have walls built between all partitions of this house. They are not accessed any in the same way. Rhetta and I will be safe from any retribution of my trade. I feel I am supplying hard working people with goods that the government will not provide.

Charles Jr. and I are well received in polite society for the service we provide. Although most do not know our profession, they guess, but say nothing. Seems they admire us for our ingenuity, and the merchandise we provide, at a price they can afford.

I write to say that I am sorry I ever did business with the late Charles Vane. I have found from others he was a cruel man. He was a man without respect. He was hated by his men, and voted marooned at one point in his piracy. He was rescued by a passing vessel, after he killed the man who bore his punishment with him, to ensure his silence. The Captain of the ship recognized the rogue as the notorious Charles Vane, and took him straight to Jamaica to meet his fate on the hanging dock. It was to the gibbet he went.

I hear that Jack Rackham has taken over the vessels formerly belonging to Vane. I never did business with Calico Jack, as those who knew Rackham labeled him a coward, and referred to him in that manner. I found him to be a dandy in pirating, who dressed in unusual fashion, more like a woman than a man. His demeanor was effeminate, however, he struck great store in the ladies. Jack, as took over command of Vane's last ship, was the one that set him adrift to maroon or die.

I have given in to Rhetta's wish to connect to the stream which runs underground this property. Rhetta is a creature of the wild. I went with her on horseback to the mouth of a stream of water which flows to the sound. There is a cave which follows from the sound up the hill to an underground freshwater waterfall. I am aware of the stream by the well dug on this land. We walled up the sides of the well, and in doing so discovered it to be bottomless, and let it be. We did not explore the area further. Now I see we have a more substantial connection to the underground stream than we first knew. I now see the advantage of connecting to the caverns underground. Rhetta says the Indians used it also. She says they lived in the caves. I do not doubt she knows.

Luke sat erect and stretched. His position has been much improved by the pillows that allowed him to extend. No longer having to read in a cramped position, he had a renewed temperament. Everybody was beginning to make this place their home. Blake walked around and twirled as he listened, with his hands and arms extended like a top. Ellie rummaged through the trunks quietly and only gave a soft sigh at one point or another. Luke began again. He was wanting to get close to "Calico Jack." He had already read about him in other books. He also had read about Blackbeard, but somehow it didn't feel the same as reading firsthand accounts. In ways he questioned his previous accounts. He imagined the books were guesswork, but Uncle Jabez knew.

soft island colors splayed across the ceiling, swaying palm trees moved with the slight breeze, and Luke could swear he heard the rush of a waterfall coming from the blue mountain in the distance. Large tropical flowers stretched up the walls, adding more color. On another wall, on a hillside were mango trees, their green fruit hanging in abundance.

Luke saw the waterfall, but he did not hear it. He only imagined what it might sound like. He was so engrossed in the words and pictures, he found it hard to tell reality from the words on the page.

Jack Rackham was reported hanged of late. He met his noose at Gallows Point on the island of Jamaica.... Strange...so did Vane...whom Rackham disposed. Charles Jr. and I no longer frequent Jamaica. Our trade now comes to us. But we hear tales. Calico Jack was brave enough to get voted in as Captain of Charles Vane's crew. Many say he was a coward. His reputation disputes that. At one point, he hired on two female Pirates. Anne Bonney was his close companion, and Mary Read, a deceiver who hired on as a man. Read was a pirate on Charles Vane's ship,

STEDE BONNET AND CALICO JACK ★ 145

and when Rackham took over, she was given a choice to be marooned with Vane, or join the new crew. As a Pirate for Vane, there was no equal. She found him to be cruel beyond necessity. Those who disagreed with a change of Captain were free to pursue another course, or be marooned with the fallen. Read chose to stay with Rackham, preferring to sail under his flag. She was happy to be rid of the monster Vane. At some point she later befriended Bonney after having revealed her true gender. Both women dressed as men on ship, only a few were aware of the ruse, and on pain of the sword, did not reveal the secret. Both women were fearsome in battle. Rackham was drunk when he was captured and jailed. Anne blamed Rackham's cowardness as the cause, and cursed her lover. The fate of both she and Mary Read I have not yet heard.

I only dealt with Rackham one time. He needed medicine. He had illness on his ship he could not cure. I get this request the most. Blackbeard found he could not wait to sail to Ocrakoke for the medicine which he ordered from me, so in haste, he hijacked the harbor at Charlestown. This time he took hostages, including women. He stopped a merchant ship bound for England, and took on board the wealthy. He threatened the docks of Charlestown harbor with cannonade, unless they send him a chest of medicine. They complied. Illnesses on Pirate ships were paramount in deaths, more so than battle. They encountered wounds from battles that did not heal. Amputations more often than not were performed by the ship's carpenter, with primitive

methods of sterilization, mostly liquor of some sort.
Doctors were often referred to as "sawbones," coming
from the manner in which limbs were removed. The
same man who whittled out a replacement, especially
for a missing leg, was the very same man who took the
limb off in the first place. Uncleanliness and association with filth was also deadly. Calico Jack was in
just such a predicament. He feared he would lose his
crew to sickness, and maybe himself in the process, so
he needed to obtain medicines from the society he
pillaged, in order to save himself. He was a popinjay,
one who wore silk breeches, with white silk socks to
the knee. His shoes were of fine leather or velvet,
and had shiny large buckles. His waistcoat was just
as elaborate, made of damask cloth, which must have
come from a very wealthy gentleman. He had rings
and jewelry that rivaled any finely dressed woman
of the colonies. Under his waistcoat was a silk shirt.
His baldric was fashioned as a wide thickness of silk,
which held gold-handled pistols. The handles were
ornately carved, and gleamed from their nest of fine
fabric. Most wore a wide leather baldric across the
chest, which held a fighting sword or cutlass. Some
fitted it out with several pistols.

I finished the connection to the caves underground,
sailors from a transit ship did the job. This precaution
I took to ensure the secrecy of any escape I might need
to implement. It took less time than I imagined, but
they are fortified now. The entrance is dug deep and
again I have used rocks and stones to hold back the

walls. I take great care going down there, it is a resting place for animals on the island. Rhetta has given them names. It is damp there, and as I spend much time at sea, I prefer the fire of above ground living.

"Okay, I'm quittin'. I think the next story is about another pirate. This looks like an ending of some sort. I'm putting everything away, 'cause there is something I want to check out. Are you guys staying here, or going down with me? I can help take some stuff down." Luke was thinking about all those pictures of Jabez, and he had just read about walls behind walls. He wondered just who was in those pictures, for sure, and were the people he read about in those likenesses? While it was all fresh in his mind, Luke intended to have another, closer look.

They all decided they had other areas to explore, and The Book and these chests were not going away. Ellie was bound to look for Rhetta's diary or journal. Or even her schoolwork. Anything she could find to connect to Rhetta was Ellie's goal.

Blake was headed up to the top floor to begin looking at the types of weapons displayed on the shelves and walls of the tower room. He had paid attention to Luke's warning about not being allowed to come back if he touched anything, so he was content to look. He would wait for Luke to handle them. He compromised in his mind. He would not pick up the pistols or guns of any kind, but he might touch the knives. He had been trained by Wematin to respect knives, and he was a worshiper of the shiny blade. Blake had learned to gingerly handle knives, especially good ones. He had never seen ones quite as handsome as the ones in this house.

Luke went from room to room studying the pictures scattered about. They were mostly pencil drawings, one in particular of Jabez and Charles Jr., sitting at a small, dimly lit table in a rustic tavern. The artist had caught the casualness and manner of observance the two displayed, as each leaned back against his chair, one arm back displaying the hilt of a pistol.

One leg was bent, and the other stretched out in a casual manner. Always they both were depicted as dressing in similar style at every turn—Jabez in long oilcloth duster, Charles Jr. in black. They too, could have worn the spoils of the trade, but apparently they chose not to.

He sat down in one of the generous plush chairs of the main living room and stared at the large painting on the wall of a camel-colored duster, fine boots, a felt hat rakishly cocked on his head almost covering one eye, and brandishing to one side an ivory-handled pistol. The other side of his waistcoat appeared to bulge with a holstered pistol also, and there was the blade. This time it appeared to be a sword, rather than a cutlass. It was longer and thinner, and the cuff around the handle was different. It flourished up and over the hand, protecting the wrist. He stared at the face, the breeze from the open windows allowing his mind to dream away as he imagined the life led by his dashing Uncle Jabez.

He and Uncle Jabez entered the darkened hall of the rooming house on the island. Uncle Jabez had both his guns in his holsters, and lazily carried a musket over his shoulder as we crossed the threshold.

"This is my boy," he announced to the desk, looking from under the brim of his wide hat. The clerk handed Uncle Jabez the key, and we wandered down the weathered hall, painted a washed out turquoise blue, we passed down the hall to the door at the end. It opened to a large sitting room with big windows, and two overhead paddle fans, lazily turning, finally allowing us some relief from the heat of this tropical island day.

As Luke's mind drifted to the afternoon scene,

he is sitting beside Uncle Jabez at a table in a large room with chairs of all descriptions, some wood, others upholstered in fine fabric, in total contrast with each other, tables set in various corners, unkempt men scattered about. This looked like a common meeting room for the guests of the inn. Luke is taken aback by Blackbeard, who is sitting across the table from himself. Across from Uncle Jabez was Calico Jack, and beside him was Stede Bonnet, who was dressed like a military man from some imaginary island.

They seemed to all get along. A dark man stands behind Uncle Jabez, and they both have a hand resting on Luke, the dark man's hand on his shoulder, and Uncle Jabez with his hand on Luke's knee. Blackbeard looks like a storm! He is interrupted by an angry Stede Bonnet, and Blackbeard dismisses him with a flourish of the hand, stands up and turns his back. Calico Jack looks on approvingly as Stede Bonnet glares at Blackbeard behind his back. He looks capable of strong retaliation for Blackbeard's dismissive treatment of him.

Luke is snapped back by Blake's shouting at him to meet him on the third floor. He is yelling, "Uncle Jabez's office! C'mere! Hurry!" Blake was having one of his dramatic moments.

Luke got to the top room, and in the bedchambers next to the sitting room he saw a big hole where the fireplace used to be. Even from where he was standing, he could see a stone walkway between the outside wall and the inside wall. The opening was accessed by moving a stone in the back wall of the fireplace in the anteroom to Uncle Jabez's study. There was a stone protruding outward on the right wall of the structure. When the stone was pressed, the opening appeared. His uncle could come and go from the ground floor to the tower without anyone knowing. He was absolutely impressed with the mind of his uncle. He was beginning to be Luke's hero. Breaking his shock, he stepped into the fireplace and followed the walkway for a bit, long enough to know that the stairs were cemented to each wall. There was a house within a house. Uncle Jabez had built a stone house with stone steps and walkways throughout, and inside that frame, he built his house, simply covering the infrastructure, and allowing access to the walkways between the house at various points. They realized they would be in need of torches, and along the walls there were places that protruded to hold the flames upright. They saw the very same while exploring the caves with Mingen. He used thick wooden logs wrapped on the end with deer hide, and soaked in whale oil. He wondered if either Jabez or Rhetta had seen them, or maybe Rhetta devised these torch sconces from dreams of the past.

The discussion on the ride home was centered around what should come first. Should they finish the stories first and put The Book away? Or, now that they had discovered a part of the house that was quite unusual, should they explore that? It would be hard to search between the walls when there were other people in the house. Now they were there alone. Should they suspend the reading and go exploring to learn the secret passages? Jabez and Rhetta, and probably Sabra and maybe her children, knew them all.

They decided that the next time they went for the day, they needed to touch every item on a wall to see if it was a passageway to some part of the house yet undiscovered. They could not believe how exciting the house was becoming. It seemed to beckon them to explore its secrets. The house acted like it wanted to tell all. There probably were spirits of the departed that loved this house and all the security it provided. Here after dangerous work, one could rest easy and relax. In this area Rhetta had perfected her mental connections to family and creatures. Both she and Sabra had moved back after heartache, and the house had welcomed them.

The kids needed to understand where they were. There was more than two hundred years of family connection within these walls. They were just beginning to read the stories. Ellie was sure that Rhetta had left journals also. There were desks in all the bedchambers. The journals would have to wait. They needed to understand the layout of the building. It was now their responsibility to study where they would live. The house was open to their exploration, even welcomed it. After all, why not? There would certainly never be any other more curious and careful potential caretakers than these three.

The hilltop manor was speaking to them.

★ 11 ★

Yer Ladyship

oaded down with tools, extra clothes, and flashlights, the horses were transporting all the works for an archaeological dig on this trip today. Grandpop thought as he watched them from the rail of the lighthouse, *Those young-uns must be manicuring the yard. I should have thought to tell them not to burn anything. Hope Luke is smart enough for that. I'll tell him first thing... maybe ride over there this afternoon. Yup, I'll ride over there this afternoon.* And Captain Charlie turned, walked inside the windowed room where the lens glistened in the sun, and began his day.

Putting the horses in the stall and making sure they were watered, the kids unpacked and stored things in a proper place. They had been taught not to leave a barn in clutter. The tools were easy to find, each having a designated storage spot, and Luke could send for a needed item, simply by saying the name. The others knew where to look. There were perks to being the oldest. It felt heavy to be responsible, thinking and planning, keeping the little band together. Their help allowed him to lighten his load. They both loved helping and were just glad to be included in the plan.

The first thing they did was divide up the floors to look for objects that would allow entrance to the walkways and stairs between walls. Blake would take the top, Luke the middle, and Ellie the main floor. They would take a rag and begin to explore the areas of the walls that could hide a button, lever, or panel that moved aside to reveal the area behind the walls.

"It's almost like dusting, and Grandmom will *love* that. Don't forget to touch each book, maybe move it out, use the rag, so's not to leave messy fingerprints. That would really tell we were looking for something, and that would appear odd. Grandmom *knows*! Be careful, don't force anything, or break anything." Luke saw the excitement in the eyes of the two, and he was also beside himself with curiosity. They all began their quest.

Blake opened the fireplace on the top floor and shined his flashlight all around the area. When it lit up to the right, there was a wall a few feet past the corner of the house. Where it stopped must have been the windows. He knew this, because the wall did not go to the floor of the passageway. It stopped, and one could crawl through, under the window to again stand erect beyond that structure. He went, standing and crouching all the way around the turret until he ended back close to where he could see the fireplace. He had encountered stairs going down to the second floor. Along the way, he tested the walls for loose bricks and found none. Instead of going downstairs, he returned to the opening of the fireplace and began to touch items that might hide a chamber of some sort.

He found just such a book, on the study side of the wall that separated the office from the bedchamber. The volume revealed a hole for Blake's hand, and as he felt around, part of the bookcase became a door. The walls between the rooms were thick, but not this thick. He examined the new chamber and found many log books and record-keeping journals, mostly business dealings. Not stories like The Book. He also found a jewelry chest, but it was locked. Maybe it was the one Ellie wondered about. That would be another day. He could not get over how deep it was. The walls did not look that deep. He went around through the door leading to the bedchamber with the fireplace, and just opposite the bookcase on the other side was a standing wall-type clothes chest, and he went through that. He found a part of the drawer part, and the drawers only pulled out a little bit. Then solid wall behind. He was yelling like crazy when he ran out the study door, into the small foyer leading down the stairs to the second floor, when he stopped and realized he could have used the inside stairs, but what the heck? He was in too much of a hurry.

Luke stepped out of the passageway just in time to meet Blake at the bottom of the third-floor stairway. He was in the doorway they first discovered when Blake pushed the knob of the carving in the center of one of the wooden framed panels located on each side of the ornate stairs leading up to Uncle Jabez's quarters. He had just come from the master bedroom to the left of the middle stairs, but he had come through the inside wall. He followed until the light of the open panel they had first discovered led him to encounter Blake as he faced him, his face flushed with color. Each told the other of his find.

Luke had found another small side panel beside the fireplace in the west apartment on the second floor. It just moved aside like a barn door. All you had to do was push. He headed toward the stairs and met Blake. Both ducked back inside and went back left near the area Luke had discovered, because he had also found stairs at both ends. He now knew the stairs he saw going up led to the fireplace above, but where did the descending stairs end up? They headed toward the downstairs, and at the bottom he pushed open a door to the kitchen. But there was another door, to the left of the kitchen door. The kitchen door was straight ahead, going into the mud room beside the back door in the anteroom that led to the kitchen.

They saw where the door facing them went, and both turned to the side to examine the crack in the wall they had become accustomed to as the way the house was constructed. Still talking to them, the house was becoming a familiar pattern. They pushed, and the stairs going down to the caves opened up to them. Someone could go from the sound to the tower, or vice versa, and never be detected by anyone else on the property.

"Wow!" Luke said, "This place is great!" He pushed his way back, and stepping into the mud room he met Ellie, who had come from a room under the hallway that ran across the second floor, between the bedrooms. She had been wiping books near the main stair, which had beautifully carved bookcases on both sides, and one of the law volumes triggered the case to slide back. It revealed a chamber with high ceilings, narrower than a regular room, very long, with easy chairs and sofas and desks. Beautiful oil lamps attached to the walls, as it was windowless, were yet to be hooked up to the generator. It was just a long, richly decorated room for study, according to the looks. The end door that led to the kitchen was on the right of the kitchen door the boys had come through, but they just didn't turn in that direction. They were looking for stairs, not another room.

She turned them around and showed them her find. "Bet it will make a nice office for Grandpop when we move here. He can sit by his radio, read his paper, and sneak into the kitchen for a snack without Grandmom knowing."

This suggestion lightened the mood of all they were seeing, and they began to be surprised at nothing. "Look, here is a panel, like the bookcase, it slides to the side when this section of three books is pressed. It goes all the way behind the main dining room, under the stairs, down walkways that go between the kitchen walls and all the way down to the living quarters." Luke was beginning to understand the intricacies to the mansion, and the reasons for them. Next to the kitchen door, the stairs went underground until they met the walkways and stairs below ground level. It was almost a maze. In time, it was fun and fast.

They followed each other's light back to the kitchen, and trying hard to take turns, but not succeeding so well, they talked and drew designs with their air pencils and agreed that they might have found most, if not all, the secret openings. Just in case, one of these days, they would scour the inside and push all the buttons they found, and they might even amaze themselves. It appeared Uncle Jabez was a crafty and humorous genius, who designed and implemented his passion for building. This might not have been a model ship, but it had the same intricacies. The grotto could be accessed from every floor, most every room, except the dining room, and they actually did not look there. And it appeared from the levers that hung from the inside ceiling above the stairway entrance that pushing a panel let you back in, and pulling the overhead lever locked down that door.

They walked back through, making sure everybody knew how to get in and out. All the panels and hidden doors were examined. It was far past lunchtime, so the kids headed for the cottage to eat and make a plan. Luke showed Ellie and Blake the painting in Aunt Rhetta's old bedroom sitting area in the cottage, and indicated he thought it was Uncle Jabez. As they all stared, they were snapped back by the sound of a car coming up the road from the village.

They looked at each other, and Luke immediately said, "Let me do the talking. You two stay right here. Don't help me. Stay here!"

He walked confidently across the yard to the sound of the car at the front of the mansion. Ellie and Blake closed the door to the cottage and sneaked out the back Dutch door, sort of standing in the forest edge of the house. They could see, but not be seen. They didn't want to box themselves in, so they needed a way out and to protect Luke's back. They had learned quite a bit from the tutelage of Manteo, Weroansqua, Wematin, and Powwaw, knowing the wolf tribe, and its rules. Strange, they did not see the wolves. What they did see was Luke coming around the house under Grandpop's arm, just laughing and sort of skipping ahead, so excited that Grandpop was here.

Ellie and Blake came from around the cottage and rushed up to Captain Charlie. They grabbed his arm and pulled him inside the little cabin to show him how much they had cleaned up. Grandpop was so happy about the brush trimmed back on the dirt-track road leading from the village. He was quite pleased, and said so. He actually felt the car had plenty of room, for a couple of months anyway. Then the spring will have repeated itself double. *These boys do a good job*, Charlie thought. He flipped them all a coin. Comic-book money at last! It was almost like ring around the roses, the way they were showing him everything. They even took him to the secret ladder. They did not tell him about The Book, but they told him about books. Captain Charlie was pleased, surprised, hesitant, and confident all at the same time. He cautioned them about locking up. He cautioned them about secrecy. He could tell that they understood both and were way ahead of him.

Actually, Captain Charlie thought they were way ahead of him anyway. He thought it so much, he sat and had a talk with Odessa. She assured him that he was right. He got it. Sometimes you just had to let things be. He knew what he was getting into when he married into the Jennettes. She, at that time, explained Ellie's gifts, and the accompanying gifts of the boys. She also told him they had not yet developed fully.

"They don't quite know they've got it yet, but its coming." Odessa just kept her head down, afraid to look at his reaction.

She asked him if he wanted to know everything. The captain thought of all he knew of the kids, and decided to wait until they came to him. He thought that maybe he should get used to what he was finding out, and how he felt about it. They hugged. He gave her a peck on the forehead. *It's just us*, he thought. He felt lucky to have the opportunity to watch, as Odessa reminded him about the protectors the kids had: the saints, the wolves, and that raven that was always hanging around.

There is a big difference between a raven and a crow. There were plenty of crows on the island, in every huge live oak tree in anybody's yard, and there were more than enough in the woods between the lighthouse and the Coast Guard station. The hill behind the Coast Guard station is covered with trees, and some of the officers who live in houses back there are always complaining about the constant chatter of the crows.

Wallace, Capt'n Charlie and Miss Odessa's oldest son, was known by his brothers as a great "killer of crows," and hearing the boys ragging Wallace about his war on crows, Grandmom knew the difference between looking at a crow and seeing a raven. Funny, Wallace's war began when he got his first shotgun. He did make quite a hunter, and crows were probably not the only target.

The Indians believed the raven escaped from darkness and was responsible for the delivery of light to the world. It was associated with the creation myth that said that the raven brought light where there was darkness. They believed the raven carried messages to and from the spirit world. To the Indians, it meant change and transformation. The raven meant prosperity for the family. It was said to be a protector and a teacher of seers and clairvoyants. The raven was known to draw energy toward itself and release it back in a new form. Its shocking coverage of black plumes being iridescent, giving off the blue and green of black, represented constant change. The raven fed Elijah and Paul in the desert, according to the Bible.

The color black symbolized void (or absence of light). Odin, God of the Norse, had a raven who represented powers of telepathy and clairvoyance. Considered one of the oldest and wisest of creatures, it is also associated with wisdom and prophecy. Ravens were always kept in the Tower of London, even now, as symbolic protectors against possible invasion.

The raven is noted by a pointed tail, with his wings resembling pointed fingers. To Native Americans, ravens meant a sign of healing, as they circled above the smoke signal sent up to inform them of one thing or another. To see a healing sign meant all was well.

Odessa was surprised that Wallace had not shot him. But she guessed even he knew. The crow was smaller, with a flared-out tail. The raven had a larger, pointed tail. The crow flaps its wings, while the raven soars. The raven is rather silent, the low call more *kraa* and not constant. The crow is quite boisterous, with its constant high-pitched and shrill *caww ... caww caww*. The raven acted as a watcher. Odessa saw, as she sat on the porch waiting for the kids to come home, that they were friends.

Ravens went back two million years. Distinguished by their dark brown iris, wedge-shaped tail, and soaring rather than flapping, their ceasing sound likened to the rustle of silk, a deep croaking sound. They were associated in history with the wolf—cunning and problem solving. This one once dropped stones on a snake in the garden near the chickens. Grandmom could attest to that. She never missed a shiny button that she did not suspect that sneaky raven. He even looked guiltily at her when she rested in the long porch swing. He was known to do aerial loops to attract attention. He forecast bad weather or storms. Grandpop paid attention to that. Yessir! They had themselves a raven.

She hoped Charlie could make sense of all of it, because he had seen most of it, but their conversation just didn't go far enough. Charlie had heard about Odessa's family, so he knew.

Having the kids show him so much of the house was just what he needed to make his day better. He had not known what to expect, but he shouldn't have worried. Blake took him to the third floor and talked about the books and portraits he was seeing. Grandpop took a mental note and decided to look up all of it in the *Britannica*. Over just this amount of time, the kids had excited Grandpop about the house also. There were certainly enough old things here to pique the interest of the most curious of men. He looked around, agreeing they should do their reading here, not take things home. Closing up the house was most important. He was impressed with the cleanliness around the grounds, the trails, and the road, as well as around the little cottage. The barn was the biggest surprise. The horses were quiet and well taken care of in their own stalls.

Grandpop left after sharing lunch and getting a tour. They did not show him their idea of his potential study, as that would have revealed the secret bookcases, and they needed time to approach that subject. He was totally satisfied the house was in safe hands. He was exactly correct. The house had never been in such good hands, not since Jabez anyway. The kids had gained respect for both while reading Jabez's thoughts. They were also going to honor it. They were happy to be a part of all of this history.

The three hurried up the ladder to read just one short pirate story from Jabez's journal. He was telling about the ones who worked off this coast. The ones in The Book were the ones he knew, if only for one meeting.

Everyone settled down in front of The Book, as it opened,

displaying a likeness of Rhetta, she was young, and as Luke began reading, the carriages of Richmond loomed overhead ... the cobblestone streets ... the row houses ... beautiful horses....

> I think Rhetta has met a young man from Richmond. He is well connected, Charles Jr. approves of him. She wants me to come to Richmond to meet him. I will need to polish my appearance. Charles Jr. will supply my attire. It almost seems like one of our college pranks.
>
> ---
>
> I like the young man. He is near my height, a lawyer, a potential politician I believe. He speaks of the times, and agrees with Charles Jr. on most things. I listened, offered little, but knowing our circumstances, it is wise to see what this young man is about. Charles Jr. admonishes me to stay my judgement, if there is a cause for concern, he assures me he will bring me there again, and we will sort things out. I have great faith in Rhetta. She of all people will know the right thing to do. I trust she is more than knowledgable of

the young man she is taking into her confidence. I have never seen her in this circle of wealthy socialites. She shines above others. I find her beauty above those of her peers, no wonder this fellow is smitten. I don't know. I do not know how she will leave this life, but she is the best judge. Are the wolves left to me? I am curious, but Rhetta's smile assures me my fears are unfounded. This is our first meeting, and there is time.

This house has survived its first visitors. The beauty of it is magnificent, thanks to Rhetta, and William's contacts in the village who have stitched the items using expensive cloths. Rhetta and Royster were here. He was taken with the docks, liked the horses, and asked for Rhetta's hand in marriage, as a fine gentleman would. He will now ask Rhetta. I have given my blessings. I am glad to see Rhetta so happy.

The wedding ceremony was in Richmond, at the Governor's mansion. Charles Henry Jarvis Sr. gave the toast. Rhetta was a most stunning bride. She is dark, and against all that white, magnificent. I fear I shall miss her more than I now know. When at boarding school, I always looked forward to her vacations here, now, I do not know. I cannot help thinking about the forest creatures she leaves behind. I will manage, but it will be lonely. Should I marry?

Charles Jr. and I visited Savannah for the first time to speak with a Captain there. He is in need of moving fine articles of prize from a convoy taken off the coast of Africa. He is a Privateer, and needs to unload his bounty to this side of the Atlantic, so as not to break the bonds of his agreement as the King's Privateer. Capt'n Johns gave the introduction and assurance of my discretion. The cargo includes marble, items of ivory, some gems, ladies' diamonds, fine china, bolts of cloth, spices, and a case of the finest made rifles and pistols in the Orient. Charles Jr. and I are amazed at the size and worth of this transaction. Maybe this is the one we have worked for. Without Rhetta, we both are not as comfortable as before.

I am finished with this business.

When Luke read this passage, Blake sat up and gave out a huge sigh. "Ohh, no more pirates? I guess I didn't want him to take so many chances. It would mean he got in trouble, but I wish there were more stories," he said quietly.

"Don't worry, there is more here. Just let me keep going." Luke continued,

Charles Jr. and I have learned the fate of two ladies we are well acquainted with. One Anne Bonney, and one Mary Read. Both of Rackham's crew. They both lie in a Jamaican prison well-guarded. Taken along with Rackham, they were not hanged along with him. I cannot imagine hanging a lady.

I find their stories need to be told. I do not know all of it, but this is what I do know:

Anne Bonney was a handsome woman. She was born into wealth and lived with her father and his mistress, her mother. Her father fled England and marriage with his child and his mistress, and found work in the practice of law in Charlestown. Her father gone so much, Anne befriended her father's gamekeeper, Charlie Fourfeathers, and it was he who schooled her in weaponry, guns, knives, hatchet, and fencing. It seems she was always headstrong, and willful. At sixteen she ran away to marry a sailor named James Bonney. They traveled to the "Pirate's Nest," of New Providence, in the Bahamas, where he became an informant on Pirates, and she became a Pirate. Disguised as a man, she joined the crew of "Calico Jack." Anne was always dressed as a man, even in the tavern where first we met her. It was obvious she was not, but she kept her disguise. Anne Bonney was reputed to fight better than any crew on board. I do know the story of the final fight. The governor was on the hunt for Pirates who had struck four times in his harbor in a two-week period, and he sent young Captain Barnet after them. Barnet found Rackham off the coast of Jamaica. They overtook the pirate's ship while they sheltered, and as the Navy men boarded the vessel, with surprisingly little resistance, they found the deck void of Pirates, save two women. At the time, these two, in disguise, were not given any quarter, and were forced to fight to defend the ship. Anne watched as a drunken Jack walked past her on deck and went below with the other drunkards, paying little attention to the fight about to begin. The crew, now under attack, were too drunk to fight. Anne stood her ground, killing eight men on her own, and along with Mary Read, and

YER LADYSHIP ★ 163

another unnamed sailor, the three made good work of the Governor's men. All were captured. I hear that some danced the rope, including Jack.

Anne was truly a striking women, maybe only nineteen years old, maybe twenty, but young. She was tall, broad shouldered, dressed in a black waistcoat to her knees. This in order to conceal her slim hips and lack of bulk, thus allowing her to appear to be a young man. It was of military style with double rows of brass buttons down the front. No doubt having belonged to some young officer, from the cut of it. She had dark reddish hair, thick and unruly, needing a hat. Her hat, wide brimmed, covered her crooked smile, or sneer, one could never tell. I would hate to come up against her. Her weapons were of the finest. She had a whip rolled at her side, that I hear was as deadly as a pistol. She could snatch the knife right out of a man's hand. I had often felt to challenge her, as my whip is also true. So far, she prefers to be invisible. Her ruthlessness in battle is legendary. She now lies in prison claiming to bear Jack Rackham's child. That is what has saved her from the gallows.

I have heard of late that she died, no mention of the child. I remember well this colt of a girl from Ireland, shipped to the Carolinas with her father, a wealthy lawyer. Leaving an inheritance, she ran away with a sailor. Then, to Jack Rackham. Talk is of another child, earlier, who now lives with a family in Cuba. She saw Jack hanged, and there has been no more word

of her. We have inquired of them, and some say that
Anne's father secured her release before the Jamaicans
could hang her.

"Boy, she really was a pirate. She sounded angry," Ellie said while looking up at the ceiling with her fingers making circles in the air above her head, following, no doubt, the figures dancing in the colors. She rolled over on her stomach, and wondered out loud, "Is there more? What about Mary Read? I read of another lady pirate, Grace O'Malley. See what he says about them."

"Okay," Luke sighed, and shifted his position, glad for the interruption, as he began to get tired sooner, and could not seem to find the right way to rest, hunched over the beautiful book. He continued to read as

Pirate ladies danced around the room, some clothed in fancy dresses, and always with knives, pistols, and whips near their side.

I also need to mention Mary Read. If I am to write
my thinking about all the Pirates I have known, Mary
Read stands out as a phenomenon. There are others, as
thousands of pirates operated the seas, rivers, wher-
ever a ship sailed with cargo. They are as determined
in their craft as any stagecoach robber out west. Just
as there were always gangs of robbers, outnumbering
any stage, or bank, so there are ships full of pirates,
that far outnumbered any merchant ship they encountered. That's why Hornigold advised Blackbeard that
his size alone would allow him to gain the advantage,
and save the lives of his victims. So outnumbered was
the prey, there was no reason to get in harm's way, as
the Pirates wanted their wealth, not their lives. Some

Pirate stories are humorous. They tell of Hornigold chasing down a merchant ship only to gather their hats. His crew had recently taken a lucrative prize, and they all threw up their hats in celebration, and the sun was letting them know what a foolish act they had done. Covering one's head is a most important part of dress. Hats keep out the baking sun, the bone-chilling cold, and in the drafts of halls everywhere. There being the polite custom of not wearing a hat inside, men resorted to wigs. Even the barristers of London wore long warm wigs in the drafty courts of law. Kings in castles cold as the outdoors warmed themselves by wearing a wig. Heat and cold, both escape a man through the top of his head. Hats were important.

Here I only speak of what I know, the sea scavengers I met in the Caribbean, in ports along the coast, and here, on my island. These are Carolina Pirates I write of, some strayed into Virginia, but the government there was strict, and they marked the rivers around, as well as the coast.

Mary Read, an "Englishman," was a North Carolina Pirate by way of Charles Vane and Jack Rackham. They say she lived the life of a boy since birth, in order to claim a birthright that could only be bequeathed to a male child. So her father dressed her so, allowing his wealthy parents to think she was male. She even entered the French Army and served in the Cavalry. All while posing as a male. An unhappy marriage, set upon while she was in the Army, proved to be a disaster, thus she sought the sea. She ended up on Charles Vane's ship, just before his crew deposed him as Captain, marooning him and any who sided with him, so Mary chose to stay with the new Captain, Rackham. All the while, successfully disguised as a man. After a time sailing with Rackham, she revealed her ruse to Anne, who she recognized as in the same mind as she. Bonney took her straight away to Jack, who accepted her because of Anne, and the three became inseparable. They fought as one, they parlayed, they manned the ship as one, the ladies were excellent seamen. It is said Mary would have fought to the death, had she not been so outnumbered. She later died in the Jamaican prison, after delivering a child. I am not even sure of that, as there seems to be no record, of either her or Bonney. There were rumors that Bonney's father was able to save them both. But Charles Jr. and I are suckers for a happy ending.

I see these men gone, I always knew it would happen, but maybe we were all in it for a short burst of time. Charles Jr. and I have moved on, we no longer do business in Island taverns, or on a moonless night. We have business in the city. These men and adventures are in the past, but I need to remember, while I still have the mind of youth, in age, all that disappears. The only thing left is the written word. There will be nothing but ashes of my body in the end, and all will be forgotten. On their account, it must have been uncomfortable to have lived a life never being truly dry of clothing. Everything about a ship be wet, water sprays everywhere all the time. I have met with them when the entire bar was infected with some illness or the other. Their carpenter was also their surgeon. Some have lost limbs since first we laid eyes. They compensate with hooks, pegs, crutches, clubs, patches, slings, padded stumps. It is amazing what happens to the men who have chosen the sea. Most depended on strong drink to get them through the hours, and the fight. I must be quick-witted, and they dim-witted, or they would surely talk themselves out of it. The women were another kind, they were the best fighters, invaluable when careening the vessel, they could fit into small spaces, and had no trouble filling in for the doctor when it was time to "operate" on a future amputee. They fired up the axe and cauterized the wound in a manner that would seal it, from eventual loss of blood. Mary Read could also read the heavens. She memorized the names of the clusters of stars and knew where she was in reference to land. Charles Jr. and I listened to her one night at a tavern in Jamaica. The roof had been torn off in a storm, and had yet to be repaired. We all sat under the stars, through open thatches, and Mary recited the stars to the entire bar. She did not falter in her descriptions. Charles Jr. and I are educated in the finest schools, and we also know the heavens, as we have made many a voyage on the open sea, not trusting the navigator. We knew her listings to be accurate. I know not of her schooling, but the knowledge of the heavens was in her mind. Most seamen know the heavens, maybe not the proper names, but the position, as they sail by it. When instruments fail, the heavens never falter.

It appears that our last venture accepting plunder was lucrative. We have enough. It is to a man's credit when he realizes that. Most, Pirates especially, do not recognize when they have enough. There is a difference in men. We are now in possession of Navigational charts, ship's instruments, cutlasses of a fine quality, 35 hogs, brass dividers, rulers, sounding leads, sounding lead ropes, ivory and indigo, not much to unload, but necessary to choose a variety of places. From another ship, furs. The satisfied Pirates are now in search of a small secluded island to careen their ships. And surely to get drunk. Maybe to New Providence Island, in the Bahamas to "Pirates Nest."

Luke stretched again, as did they all.

"Time to go," he said.

"Yup, time to go." Blake echoed.

"It was cool to hear about the women. I don't think they were around Uncle Jabez, I don't think he ever did business with them. They were sort of soldiers, or fighters, or bodyguards, or something like that. It seemed like they were angry inside, and just wanted to strike out." Ellie was deep thinking now, trying to figure out why anyone, man or woman, would just want to strike at something. She was picturing the girls all broken and bloody, and it was disturbing to her.

Her mind was further along anyway, she was letting the boys straighten up while she checked one more trunk of articles belonging to a woman, looking for something hard, like a journal.

★ 12 ★

The Chase

Ellie was deeply immersed in the treasures she was uncovering from the trunk. There were several journals, one belonging to Uncle Jabez. Ellie picked up the first one, and the writing was young. Blake was also examining the trunks on the far side of the room. He needed his lantern.

"Be careful of the light near those old papers!" Luke cautioned, and that was the last thing any of them heard of him for the rest of the afternoon. They were all drawn into the project in front of them, allowing Luke to think on the adventures with Uncle Jabez. He quietly crawled down the ladder to the second story. Then he opened the door to the tower and went up the stairs and entered what he now knew to be the fourth-floor rooms from there. He wondered why, when he climbed the stairs before, he did not notice they went beyond the ceiling of the second floor. Why did he not realize there must be a floor in between? No matter, he knew it now. Hopefully, it would be their secret. But even if Grandpop figured it out, he could not access the third floor except from the ladder, and that would not happen.

Luke looked around the foyer of the landing, the chest with the bust of a pirate and over that, an ornate gold-stained mirror and the beautiful door in front of him. He searched the door for some hidden button, but this door was legitimately just a thick, old Spanish door, unusual in appearance, as were all the doors. They all came from someplace different. Not one alike, but all massive beautiful exotic wood. He entered the study belonging to this man he was beginning to admire. He sat down cross-legged on the daybed in the office. He studied the desk, across the room, and even from his position he could see the sky and a little of the ocean. The door to the anteroom was open, revealing the fireplace, now closed, and appearing as just a fireplace. In the room that served as a workroom or study, there were bookcases on either side of the door. Scanning both rooms, he saw through the open door a portion of a painting beside the fireplace. Blake had also told him of the fake wall of books that hid an opening, and among other things, a jewelry chest with no key. No need to pursue that further. He arose and went into the bedchamber to study the painting in full.

It was another painting of the man he suspected was Uncle Jabez, but in this one, he was painted with his left hand cupped around his musket—exactly as in his dream, when he and Jabez were in Jamaica. His subconscious must have recalled this picture, even though he was not aware at the time. In the painting, his right hand pulled his coat slightly to the side, still showing one of the ivory-handled pistols, and the back of the sword, which was sheathed and hanging behind the hip. His copper-colored coat had its collar turned up, and the dark wide-brimmed hat showed only his eyes. And that smirk. His boots were knee high, his breeches of deer hide stuffed down into them. His shirt in this picture was ruffled at the neck and sleeves and, it seemed, down the front. He wore a vest of black plaid watch material, like an English or Irish lord. Posed in his long coat and knee breeches, he was a striking figure. His musket barrel rested on a chest with wooden slats, the chest that housed The Book. Luke sat on the bed, next to the inside wall. The window on the front of the tower held out the rain, but not the sound of the ocean.

With the faint roar of the sea, crashing on the beach, in his head, he drifted again still staring at the picture. . . .

The Pirate Stede Bonnet, stands, to storm out of the lobby of the dirty board-
inghouse where he and Uncle Jabez are staying. Blackbeard begins to curse
and stomp around. Uncle Jabez puts his hand on my arm and glides me to a
corner table. We sit down, away from the trouble brewing in the other corner,
as Calico Jack excuses himself from the table. Ever the coward, he wants no
part of a quarrel between Blackbeard and Bonnet. He moves to the other end
of the tavern, much like us, he turns his back to the smoldering storm.

The tavern is roughly walled in stucco work, made from shells coarsely
ground and mixed with limestone, dyed with green patina made from plants.
Most of the color was the same whitewashed wood or stucco tinted with some
plant hue. All the furniture is either totally hand cut and unpolished, or totally
the opposite, finely made with expensive material. The paradox of a thief.

We can hear Bonnet accusing Blackbeard of taking his ship, his command,
and his respect. Blackbeard leans back and laughs a roaring sound, further
insulting his fancy friend.

"I took yer ship because ye were worthless in a fight," he growled at Bonnet.
"Me and Hornigold, we's men who acts fast when in pursuit. Ye fell behind,
and it almost cost us our prize. Learn yer trade, Major," and he spit out the
title like it was a joke. "Ye be a lubber not fit fer the sea. Keep to the land, fer
it's what ye know! It's a farmer ye are."

Stede Bonnet kicks aside the chair where he is sitting in his haste to rise,
knocking it over. He motions for his quartermaster to follow. The members
of Bonnet's ships, those who were still loyal, left also. It looked like the quarrel
was over. Uncle Jabez leans down to me, "We'll not be staying around. This is
a nasty quarrel, and not over yet. We'll not get caught in it."

The afternoon goes well for us after the turbulent morning. We roam the
docks, looking at what the wharf has to offer. More taverns, some boatbuilding
sheds, showing all manner of repairs, and a stable, where Uncle Jabez rents

two horses. We ride down the beach. This is not like our beach. It is calm, with foam only at the edge, which washes in quietly, in ripples, not waves. It is clear and a greenish color, not blue like ours. It looks shallow for quite a way out. Our horses walk slowly down the beach on the white hard sand. Once in a while they might step into the water, but mostly we travel the shore. After a bit, we leave the taverns and docks far behind and come into an area where only palm trees and yucca plants are growing. The forest of palms is blanketed on the floor with huge ferns and small tropical underbrush. We continue, and Uncle Jabez and I see a tent far down the beach. We head for it. Uncle Jabez is not without his musket, the saddle having a cover for a long gun, also his short sword (cutlass) and pistols, so we are not afraid. Maybe he knows who lives in the tent. When we near the shelter, it is an old sail, covering an area for cooking, and tables strewn with papers, charts, and kitchenware. On the ground around everywhere are buckets of tar, scraping irons, and vats of something boiling. The men around are ill kept, but they seem to recognize and welcome Uncle Jabez. This is not a living space. This is a space for repairing and possibly shaping materials for careening a ship. I do not see a ship, but it is probably beyond the curve of the land. I switch my interest from finding a ship to listening to Uncle Jabez talk to these men. He is gaining much interesting information about future and present ship arrivals and departures. I meet a boy there, my age, his name is Nathan. He is accompanied by his father who is also doing business with the pirates. He talks, I listen. That much I have learned from my uncle.

We leave tomorrow to sail back to Hatteras.

Luke's head falls forward a little, and he gets more comfortable on the pillows, putting a couple to his back...and is lost again.

He is now in a cabin below deck of a rather large ship. Charles Jr. and Uncle Jabez are talking to the captain. They are all worried. This is one of the privateering vessels that my uncle deals with. The captain's name is Johns. He has heard that one of the pirates off Jamaica has stopped a ship near the coast of the Carolina colonies, and they have taken hostages. The pirate needs a chest of medicine and stores of food, rum, and water. He means to make a trade. Captain Johns says they sound like a desperate lot, as the hostages are of political importance and include children and at least one very important English Lord. Captain Johns is in the area because of this affront. While doing business in the islands, the local governor gives him the message from a small ship just docked. The messenger is ill equipped to help. It was only his speed of size and vessel that allows him to track Johns to the island. This message must be weeks old. Johns is unsure if his ship can even find the offending pirate. He has no name of captain nor ship. His orders from the king are to intercept the pirate, remove the hostages, and if possible cripple the pirate vessel. He is discussing the problem with my uncle and his friend, who are already on the ship. My uncle's grin shows me he is up for an adventure. Charles Jr. is reacting the same. They both look at me, and my uncle hands me his whip. I feel like I did with Manteo—safe and ready to learn. I stand, just as the rogue wave crashes on the side of the brigantine, sending us all flying and sliding into the opposite wall of the cabin. Capt'n Johns scrambles to his feet.

"Tie that boy up!" he yells to Uncle Jabez, who is also gaining his feet. He reaches down to give a hand to Charles Jr. They both check their weapons and find a rope. Uncle Jabez tethers me to him, and keeping close, we both head to the upper deck.

"SECURE THE SAILS!" Johns yells. "Take the strain off that hull!" He is shouting orders to save the ship from being beaten to timber as the monstrous waves strike smashing blows broadside of her. "Git 'er turned 'round! Head 'er into the wave! Git 'er outta this side hit! We'll break up in this pounding!"

Sailors were rushing around, sliding in the water on deck, holding on to any of the hundreds of miles of ropes both rolled up for extra and crisscrossing the upper deck. Uncle Jabez was leaping up the steps, dragging me with him. He reached the wheel deck and grabbed the wheel along with the helmsman, and pulled with all his might to turn out the bow of the boat, which had twisted itself sideways, allowing the huge waves to strike broadside of the vessel. A few more of these, and the ship will roll. My tether was long enough for me to also hold on to a post in front of the mighty wheel and keep clear of Uncle Jabez as he worked the wheel. His shipbuilding knowledge was on display, as he also shouted orders to the men around him on the upper deck. Captain Johns looked up once, as he managed the men and sails, and I thought he grinned at his friend's expertise. They needed to head the bow straight into the waves to keep from being beaten to splinters by the relentless pushing of the mighty onslaught.

The sky was dark and howling, with streaks of lightning crisscrossing the skies. The noise of the ocean being pushed by the roaring wind was deafening. The waves were beginning to show themselves above the ship. Huge plots of foam were everywhere. It was beginning to cover the deck of the ship. This was a flash storm of the worst kind. It came from nowhere. You could hear the cannon loose below deck, crashing into anything in their way. Men were drenched, hanging onto ropes that were there for just such a debacle. One man fell into the sea from the rigging, as Charles Jr. appeared at my side, followed my tether to Uncle Jabez, and loosed me. He strapped me to the short mast that held up one of the ship's instruments leading down to the deck below. Finally my uncle was free to work his magic. Charles grabbed one of the spokes of the wheel, and the three men pulled the ship into position to crash its bow into the oncoming wave. We rode this storm for an hour. All of us were drenched, and as far as I could tell, there was fear in everyone's eyes, except Johns, Charles Jr., and my uncle. I might have been blinded by the salt water in my eyes, but I thought Charles Jr. was smiling as he shed his fancy coat and fought the wheel of the ship.

The water was coming so fast, as each salty wave hit our faces, causing every man to choke. It was getting hard to breathe without taking in water. I kept my head down and turned away, but it was useless. I felt I might drown on the topside of this ship.

Finally water splayed over the bow of the ship, as it lurched skyward straight into an oncoming wall of water. Glad to be heading into the huge curtain of water heading my way. I grabbed onto the rope and post where I was tied, and did my best not to go backward, for fear I would be washed over. The breakers ate up the sides and settled into the middle, only to spill out the bow on the way down the back side of each huge angry wave. Going up and through the wall was saving us, but plunging down the back side to meet the monster again made my stomach drop, it was such a plunge. Anyone in the way of that action was sent scrambling and reaching for a hold on anything that would prevent them from going over the side with the water. The ship continued to fight to mount another monster, this time keeping the raging winds behind the sails for forward motion. The men at the ship's wheel were doing an impossible job. Even they were surprised the rudder did not splinter in two.

We battled the ocean, wave after wave. The ocean roared, a deafening sound, with spray so dense it was impossible to see. Driven by strong wind, the combination was whipping away the sails, shredding the ones that hung on, and now were only controlled by the ropes attached. Men were hanging from the yardarms of the masts, standing on roping, trying to pull up the sails to keep what was left of them from shredding also. Lightning streaked across the skies, and the dark blue of the sky turned to black. My feet got swept out on every wave. I righted myself, only to get knocked down again. I was trying to stay upright, but each time I hit my butt on the deck and scrambled to keep my feet. Most of the time, all I could see was a blue mountain of water laced in white as the waves washed toward me. Uncle Jabez was wet from his bandana, which wrapped his hair, all the way down. It was pouring in a steady stream from the sleeves of his coat, down to his boots, but he still had control of his short sword, and his coat protected his firearms. The men were bailing, strengthening the ropes on the cannon. Wet ropes dry tight as they shrink, therefore this was a good time to ensure the protection of the ship's guns. Below, the cook and his crew were pounding anything they could find in the holes beaten in by the strength of the hammering the sides of the ship was taking. . One of the masts had wrenched loose and was dangerously sweeping the deck. Men were trying to chop away at the strip of roping holding the rogue mast on its stump, all the while trying hold their stance and stay upright enough to not get swept overboard by the next wave. For a while, the danger was either the water or the mast. Meanwhile, mixed with the deafening thunder was the sound of the ship's bell, still in its place. I thought my mind would burst. I was too involved to be afraid.

"Keep your loft!" "Hold 'er to!" "Grab holt!" There were shouts of fear and warning all over the ship. There must be a flood below, as the water freely washed down the honeycomb hatch leading below. Luke wondered if the parrot swinging in the fancy cage in the captain's cabin was still safe, and thought of the chickens contained in cages in the kitchen. The storm lasted until finally we ran out the other end. We headed for clear skies, and now that the bow headed into the breakers, the ship presented a smaller target. I could see everyone relax as the sun broke through the clouds and we left the black behind us. Taking deep breaths of salty air, my lips were parched and swollen, and I longed for fresh water. We could still see a curtain of rain obscuring anything on the other side, as we steered toward brighter skies.

We headed back to the coast of the Carolinas. Uncle Jabez promised to supply Capt'n Johns with a strong straight cedar tree from the Trent Woods. This would replace the broken mast with a better one, which, because of its kind, the worms and varmints that eat wood would be discouraged. Cedar's ability to repel insects made it valuable. Many ships needed cedar from Hatteras Island for their ships. That, too, was a lucrative business for some.

Luke then was walking the dirt roads through the village of Hatteras. Johns had repaired his ship and was getting ready to leave. Luke kept close contact with Charles Jr. and his uncle as they roamed the docks jumping from one boat or the other while they carried on their business—all taking in the fresh air along with the fish stink and blood-stained boards of the dock. Luke wandered across the sandy road to the small general store located near the docks. He spied Nathan, the boy from the island, the one whose father was dealing with the pirates. He only got a glimpse of him as he was heading in the direction Luke had just come from. He yelled out to him, and when Nathan turned at the sound of his name, Luke thought he saw fear in the boy's eyes as he quickly got away from sight by ducking out the door of the small merchant's store. Luke ran to catch up with him, and to his surprise, Nathan made great effort to avoid him. There was definitely fear in his eyes, and as Luke reached out to touch his arm, Nathan pulled away from his grasp. At that same time, a rough-looking character grabbed both boys by the back of the collar, lifting them off their feet. In his strong grasp, they were dragged along at his side, unable to get a grip on a gait to keep up. Their feet seldom touched, as they struggled to get free of the burly, dirty, cursing sailor. Just as he threw them over the side of a moored ship, the captain shouted to loosen the ropes, and leaving the dock Luke got a glimpse of Uncle Jabez. He heard himself yell, "HELP UNC—!" before the dirty sailor clapped his hand over Luke's mouth, cutting off the last word. Jabez looked up as he recognized the familiar voice, only to see a raven land on the yardarm of a ship. Before he could blink, a wolf cleared the railing of the departing ship and disappeared below, unnoticed in the commotion of casting off in a hurry. Jabez grabbed Charles Jr., and they both searched out Captain Johns.

Luke and Nathan were thrown below the third tiered deck to the bottom of the ship, tumbling down on to the ballast of the sloop. The floor was covered in huge boulders meant to keep the ship weighted to counter the massive structure of decks above. When they gained their senses, they began to crawl around on the slippery rocks and look for some relief from the musty, damp smell that was choking them in the dark hole.

Luke had gotten accustomed to carrying the whip Uncle Jabez had handed him. He wondered at the time, did Uncle Jabez know he knew how to use it? He had it rolled up with a small rope tied through holding it to his belt loop. As they were tossed in the dark of the ship, they could hear the ship groaning as it slowly, clearly made the sound that could only indicate they were headed to the open sea. The boys strained against the dim light. As they moved around, they heard another small voice.

Nathan said, "Mills?"

"Yes," whispered back the voice. And another boy crawled forward to sit beside them. He extended his dirty hand to Luke. "Mills McAden," he said most politely.

"Luke," he said as he reached out and shook the new boy's hand, in answer back. Nathan moved closer to Luke, and in a quiet voice, he attempted to explain. He could not see the shock on Luke's face, but he imagined it must be there. "He was taken also, his father is a wealthy landowner in North Carolina colony, and they are holding both of us for ransom. There are others also. We know the pirates have sent word to our parents that we would be killed if they reach the harbor and there are no chests of gold."

"They have others in another part of the ship. The younger ones, and the girls." Mills was pleading. One of the girls was his sister.

"We are going to escape," assured Luke. "Trust me, we will get outta here. My uncle and his friends are following us. But even so, we have to help them. Ready?"

He listened as Nathan told him of his capture. The pirates took him to control his father. His father was unused to dealing with pirates, and as soon as they realized how much of a prize they could get from this unsuspecting gentleman, they rustled the kids on ship in the middle of the night. Nathan had overheard the pirate captain as he demanded an amount of ransom expected from his family in order to get his children back.

"My uncle and his friends will not let these pirates take me away. They will give chase. We must be ready to help them. They need for us to take advantage of any escape they begin for us." Luke decided he must live up to the example of his uncle. Luke and Nathan began to work on the hatch that kept them below the boards of the deck.

Topside, after the pirates had eaten and they went on the open deck for drinking, cards, and a smoke, the trio struggled to lift the heavy wood and hide among the sacks of rotting foodstuffs. The smell of the rank potatoes was dusty and foul, and caused them to attempt to wipe away the aroma if they could. Nothing was clean. They thought to put a rag over their mouth and nose, but that was foul smelling, too. They needed to get to the first deck if they could.

There would be chests, cannon, sail, and rope, many things to hide under for such small bodies. If they could help, the swifter the rescue, the less likely their rescuers would get hurt.

Meanwhile, the sailors of the pirate sloop were unaware that anyone followed them and had no idea anyone would be hunting them. They considered that their only pursuers were the ones they left behind when they, too, entered the storm. They did not raise all sail, nor did they hurry.

Rafe's soft nose nudged Luke from a small opening in the wall, his big furry head sticking through behind the sacks thrown up against the side. Nathan and Mills grabbed each other in total fear at the sight of him.

"Shhhhh... he is my friend. He is here to help," Luke whispered as he hugged as much of the massive head as he could touch. "He's mine."

The two strangers looked quizzically at each other and thought they might be mistaken. This must be that boy's dog. But it looked like a wolf, and a mighty big one at that!

With a great deal of caution the three boys followed the burly animal through the skeleton of the ship to another opening, near the captain's cabin. This opening found them behind the cases of wine and barrels of rum stored in the room beside the main cabin. This room was locked from the outside. They had to wait until someone came to open the storage for wine or rum. As the boys looked around, they discovered they were also located in the closet where the captain and his quartermaster kept their finer weapons. They first found the ammunition. As they tried to figure out how to blow the lock, they discovered the pistols. Each boy armed himself with something he was familiar with, and waited. Nathan looked scared. Surely it was his first adventure, but so far, he was being very brave. Luke thought of how scared he was when Manteo raided Roanoke colony, looking for the stranded colonials, but he had survived it. He hoped that Nathan could have as much faith in him as he had in Manteo. As it turned out, Nathan was more worried about his two little brothers than himself. He was being brave for them, much the same way Luke tried to show Blake and Ellie they were going to be okay.

Luke tried to comfort Nathan and get his mind off the waiting. He knew they were in a much better position to be rescued than when they were below ship, and Luke had his trust, not only in his uncle and Charles Jr., he had faith in Rafe. "What are their names?" he asked.

"Gavin and Liam," Nathan said, trying to look nonchalant, and trying also not to show his worry. He actually did have faith in Luke, and from the looks of his dog, he was beginning to think maybe the pirates should be afraid.

"I got Maggie and Sara Rose," Mills said quietly.

"We'll be okay. You don't know the two men tracking us. One is my Uncle Jabez. He is smart and can handle all kinds of people. If he has to, he will destroy the pirates. And he can!" Luke spoke with such conviction that both the other boys sort of sat a little more comfortably.

Mills knew how to load a pistol, but it was long, and he was holding it with both hands. Nathan was looking through the firearms for one he could feel comfortable with. All the boys had been hunting. It was the way of the South in those days. If they knew how to kill a rattlesnake, they could surely get the attention of some pirate who wanted to harm them. They weren't interested in killing anybody but the pirates didn't know that, and the sea raiders hadn't counted on three little southern boys and what they could do. Luke touched his whip.

He had seen the calm reaction to crisis that Jabez displayed. Every time, he knew what to do. He would know what to do now. Luke could feel Jabez coming for him.

Captain Johns pulled out of the fog almost right on top of the pirate ship carrying the boys. They were completely taken by surprise. The fog had been left from the mighty storm, as the sea was still settling down from the pull of the gale. The fog meant that they were again going into the storm, as it was still raging somewhere away from them. Capt'n Johns headed straight for the ship of thieves, with the intent of ramming her. He meant to ram her broadside, and he was angling the bow of his ship toward the unprotected and least fortified part of the pirate ship. His bow to them made a small target for any cannon fire, and before they could fire, Johns was pulling around and throwing grappling hooks to board her. On the crow's nest of the Mary Anne, Captain Johns's ship, sat the best bow man available. His job was to kill the helmsman, so that the ship would have no direction. He did not use a musket, but bow and arrow. Johns did not take the chance of the unsteady flintlock of a pistol or musket to spark a sail and cause a fire. He wanted those children, and the rest could fend for themselves. He was only counting on two boys. He knew nothing of the other five. The arrow found its mark, the wheel began spinning out of control, and the ship was sent into utter turmoil.

Jabez was on the ship first, working his way down to the captain's cabin. It was in his mind the children were worth much money to the pirates and would be stored there. As Jabez passed the small closet, he heard the single bark of a wolf. Wolves are not prone to bark like a dog. Their sound, if short of a howl, is distinguishable from other animals in that it sounded like a yelp. Jabez broke the lock on the door with his ax.

Luke felt the strong hands of his uncle grab him from behind the casks of wine. The boys had stowed themselves behind the wine, not knowing who was going to come through the door. A raven sat on the sill of the open closet door. Watching Luke, the boys knew this man was coming for them, and they acted quickly to make sure he, too, was safe. Behind him was another man, dressed all in black, and to Mills this man was not a pirate. He had the manner of a gentleman, and Mills decided he would follow him. As they all struggled to extract themselves from behind the kegs and get to their rescuers, the pirates charged Jabez and Charles Jr. from behind on the narrow stair that led down to the closet. The pirates were shocked to be facing the teeth of a very angry wolf, and Rafe began to back those pirates up the stairs. They wanted to shoot, but when the first man did not, the others would have been shooting each other, and in this short amount of time, the wolf had the advantage. He stealthily growled his way to the first man, who fell backward, giving Jabez and Charles Jr. the advantage they needed. The wolf disappeared just as he had appeared, and the fight was on. Luke got Nathan's attention and motioned for him and Mills to follow. They crawled out of the way of the heated fight between

Jabez, Charles Jr., and the pirates. As the boys reached the top deck, they were confronted by a melee of action as Captain Johns's crew was taking care of the rest of the pirates. Spying the boys, several pirates began to go for them, thinking they could bargain their way out of the deadly mess they found themselves facing. Once again, Rafe landed in front of the children and bravely faced the angry pirates, his teeth bared, and a low guttural sound coming from deep inside, with that sound getting louder and the wolf advancing toward them. Rafe lunged and caught the first pirate by the throat and weighted him down to the deck, spewing blood from his torn throat.

The other pirates advanced. As one whipped out his pistol and tried to aim at the wolf, Mills quickly popped the rope holding Luke's whip and within a wink Luke reacted with one huge snap that wrapped around the pirate's wrist, causing the pistol to fall away. The pirate cried out as Luke did even more damage by snapping the whip back and tearing open the man's arm. He, too, was pumping blood from his wrist, and he grabbed his arm, with no other thought than trying not to bleed to death. The gun went sprawling along the deck and slipped through the honeycombed hatch cover into the decking below.

Nathan saw another pirate lunge into a pile of roping on the deck. He grabbed the coil and upended the thug with a mighty pull. Mills grabbed a club and rendered the fallen pirate unconscious. Rafe now faced down the others, with all three boys at his back, all brandishing the pistols they had taken from the wine closet.

Suddenly the three boys were snatched from behind, as Jabez, Charles Jr., and Graham Johns had them while Rafe and the crew of the Mary Anne held back the pirates. The men and their baggage leapt to the rope netting hanging down the ship and disappeared behind the thick railing. Rafe cleared their heads and landed on the deck of the Mary Anne.

Luke smiled as he saw Rafe jump from behind Uncle Jabez, across the open space and clear the railing between the ships. He come down on all fours safely on Captain Johns's deck. From the screams of shock and terror issuing from the sailors aboard Johns's ship, he assumed Rafe to be safe. Charles Jr.

grabbed Nathan, and the four began to make their way across the deck. Johns had Mills by the jacket, and Mills was keeping the pace.

As soon as the boys were safe, Jabez and Charles Jr. went back to the pirate ship for the other children. Meanwhile the crew of the Mary Anne was handily whipping the pirates, who seemed to be unsure of where the next barrage was coming from, man or animal. Maggie, Sara Rose, Liam, and Gavin were locked in the captain's cabin and tied together with rope—the four of them all together.

Charles Jr. and Jabez grabbed the bundle of children and rope, while cautioning them to pay attention and keep their feet. And to help when they could ... and hurry!

The men and their bundle gained the stairs as Captain Johns and his crew fought back the pirates. They tossed their bundle toward the Mary Anne. The roping binding the children together caught on the railing of the rescue ship, resulting in the children dangling over the water until Johns's cook and cabin boy drew them up and out of danger. They were a little banged up, but so happy to be in friendly hands.

Graham Johns shouted for the ships to uncouple, and his sailors complied. The crew was throwing grandees all the while, leaving the rabble of the pirate ship in a confusion of smoke, gunpowder, and fallen men. Finally the Mary Anne was in position to fire, and they aimed for the main mast.

The cannon struck its mark, and the mast crashed down on the crew below, covering them with wood and sails. The scene was one of black smoke and fire, wood chips raining down on the pirates like snow Ash covered he deck as things began to blow up under the constant pounding from the cannon on the Mary Anne. As she pulled away, the pirate ship was beginning to list toward them, as the cannon blew out the one side. Water was pouring into the belly of the vessel, and men were grabbing anything they could hold on to as they met the sea.

Luke awakened to Rafe licking him on the hand. He lay crumpled down on the floor in front of Luke's feet, with his head down to eye the room. Blake's yelling up the stairs startled both boy and wolf, and Rafe sprang up, lightly nudged the fireplace, and disappeared behind it as the fireplace resettled in its old position. The wolf knew the workings of the house better than anyone. He had come all the way to the tower from the interior stairs to hang out with Luke and Jabez's spirit. He used the fireplace like it was something familiar to him. Because it was.

Luke turned to see Blake in the doorway.

"Whacha doin'?" he asked, casually leaning against the door sill. He looked around to see if there was someone else in the room. Somehow he had the feeling he had just missed something.

"Just daydreaming," Luke admitted. "I like reading about Uncle Jabez. He is such a courageous man."

"I kinda like Charles Jr.," said Blake. "He is a snappy dresser, and like a gentleman soldier."

"They really were quite a duo. It seemed that they thought alike. They must have been good partners." Luke admired the friendship and the camaraderie one must feel when aware that there is someone on whom you could count to have your back.

"I've been looking through the chests up here," Blake began. "There's lots of stuff in them. Stuff that maybe I don't know what it is. He has a book on insects, and it says that Aunt Rhetta drew the pictures of the insects. She is a good drawer. There is another book, with drawings of birds, and the names, telling the kind of them. This book has Aunt Rhetta's signature in it. I found lots of things she drew. Did you know she could draw?"

Luke sort of smiled and got up to look at the portrait he had been staring at all afternoon. Way down in the bottom of the right-hand corner were the initials *RJ*. She painted all these portraits of Uncle Jabez and his friend Charles Jr. No wonder there were so many. On another look through, Luke eventually realized that Rhetta had painted Uncle Jabez at various times of his life. He started to look at other paintings. Some he identified as possibly being Rhetta herself. It looked like one was painted from the reflection in a mirror. But the biggest giveaway was the huge portrait of Rhetta in her wedding gown, which was over the fireplace in the main dining room. It had someone else's signature at the bottom. It looked like a queen was getting married. The dress was huge, and the stairway against which she stood was the grandest Luke had ever dreamed. He had always felt these stairs, here in the big mansion, were the finest in the world. He had not bothered to study the ones against which Rhetta rested, as she displayed her wedding gown.

The afternoon was wearing on, and the adventure Luke had dreamed had actually made him hungry. He and Blake went to find Ellie, to see if she, too, was ready for lunch. She was still in the attic, rummaging through the old trunks. She gladly stopped and began to put things away. She had no success in finding Rhetta's journal but was encouraged by the things she found that Rhetta did write. She had shown Blake the books of artwork and knowledge that Rhetta had been collecting. Both were impressed with her skills with a pen, in script and picture.

What they were learning was that the Jennettes must have always been lovers of nature. Rhetta appeared to be as familiar as Ellie was with the creatures of her surroundings. Ellie wondered aloud if Rhetta could talk to all these animals she knew. She was beginning to become as close to Rhetta's memory as Luke was with Uncle Jabez.

When Ellie joined the boys, Luke took her around and pointed out the paintings he had seen, those that now he figured must have been painted by Rhetta. In the corner of each he found *RJ*.

The knowledge that Rhetta painted touched Ellie. She swallowed hard at the pictures she knew her ancestor painted, thinking of her in her billowing dress with all those underskirts, sitting in the woods, painting what she saw. Lunch had to be delayed while the youngsters wandered about becoming familiar with the look of the two people who had occupied such a magical house. They even picked out the paintings of what must have been Rhetta's daughter, Sabra. Ellie recognized her from the dream she had before, when she met all four ladies of her past.

Ellie was more determined than ever to find Rhetta's journal. There must have been a lot to tell of life from Rhetta's viewpoint. Did Uncle Jabez marry after Rhetta left? Did his friend Charles Jr. marry? What went on at home while the pirate business was in its heyday?

At the table in the little cottage, the kids began to piece together what they could of the life that had taken place in the house. Luke told the two of his dream. He didn't know what to make of it, except maybe he had wanted to meet Uncle Jabez, and maybe Uncle Jabez was happy to meet Luke. In the dream, Luke felt close to his uncle, like they really did know each other.

They wrapped up their lunch, and Blake went to find Theo. He was putting up a good argument for going down into the caves, and he really wanted Theo to go with them, or, him. If the others did not go with him, Blake was thinking of going down with his wolf.

When Luke discovered Blake's plan, he quickly turned into an older brother.

"No!" he said. "There is no way you are going to wander around this property by yourself. Whatever gave you the idea you could go off on your own? None of us will do that!"

He was adamant about sticking together. He kind of thought maybe he shouldn't have left them earlier in the day. Yes, he had taken some alone time and dreamed an adventurous dream. But he also realized that he could be in trouble, going off by himself, and he needed to be more careful. They all did. Luke was the responsible one, and he had two following him who were capable of almost anything.

They agreed that both boys would go on a hunt for the wolves, maybe to go into the caves with them. Meanwhile, Ellie would search Rhetta's bedroom in the little cottage for her journal. When she finished, they would all get back together and possibly check out the big sitting room on the first floor. They had always passed it by for more interesting places.

They went their separate ways, Ellie to the bedchamber, the boys to the woods, with the promise not to explore the caves without her.

Ellie studied the chests of drawers in the bedroom and found nothing but a few drawings, and some half-finished ones. These scraps of paper were worth a fortune to Ellie. Imagine having the workings of drawings that were maybe 200 years old. She flattened out what she had, spread the papers on the table in the little cottage, and continued to look. At one point she stopped long enough to stare at the wonderful painting of Uncle Jabez. He almost looked alive. He was a handsome man, maybe he looked a little like Manteo. He stood straight, hands on hips, legs spread apart, pistols showing, sword sheathed on the left. But she thought that was because he looked so rugged. She stared at his smoky brown eyes and the large hat that lay on the floor beside him as he looked full face to the painter. She had not noticed before the slight scar that went across his cheek. Maybe that was why he always turned, looking out one eye, and wearing that hat. Maybe he didn't like the scar. Ellie thought the scar made him more handsome.

As she looked closer, not only did she notice the scar, but a bulge of sorts under his pistol. The more she looked, the more she realized that the bulge was really a bulge. It was something behind the painting that made a lump in the canvas. Quickly Ellie ran to the door, and yelled for the boys to come back.

"Look, Luke. See that place behind the pistol's butt? What is that?" she outlined in the air, a bulge that caused the pistol to protrude. "And see, he has a scar!"

"Come here, Blake. You help me, and Ellie, you make sure nothing falls." Luke grabbed one of the chairs from the table and moved it to the side of the ornately framed painting. He moved the picture aside, thinking to lift it off the wall. He had to get to the side to see how the picture was hung. As he lifted the picture a little away from the wall and to the right, something dropped, hit the mantle of the fireplace, and fell to the hearth below.

He turned, looked down, and saw a leather binder, a book. Luke carefully moved the painting back to its original position as Ellie and

Blake knelt down to the floor to examine what had been hiding behind the painting.

Ellie screamed in delight. She found it! She held it up triumphantly and without worrying about getting the huge portrait back in its place, she hurried to one of the other chairs at the table. Here, on the top of scraps of paintings she had been collecting, she opened Aunt Rhetta's journal.

★ 13 ★

Aunt Rhetta's Journal

Ellie removed the covering from the big chair in the sitting area of the cottage. The dust trickled to her nose, causing her to sneeze. She took the heavy cloth to the door, turning her head away. She shook it violently to remove the years of dust that had settled on it. Dust was the enemy. The kids had not spent enough time in this area to be bothered. With the door open, they had only cleaned the table and chairs. Now the dusty covers had to be aired out. Luke and Blake carried as many cloth items as they could outside. Everything needed to be aired out. It was the same drill as the attic. They could not stay in this little cottage until it was breathable. All began to take turns, as the dust, now being stirred up from moving, was making all of them sneeze. Ellie seemed to be affected the most, so the boys took over the chore completely. Ellie was left inside to wipe off everything: walls, dressers, chairs, kitchen pots and pans, dishes, and more. She pumped up some water from the hand pump at the sink and got busy.

Meanwhile, outside, the boys got into it as they spread the bedclothes, chair coverings, and draperies on trees, bushes, and across the sticks still standing where a clothesline used to be. They played hide-and-seek, they

189

wrapped themselves in items and pretended to be pirates. They looked around for the wolves. All the while, Ellie was up to her elbows washing down everything in the little cottage. She suggested to the boys they beat the dust out of the items, as that is what she saw Grandmom do. But the boys were afraid to wallop away at the material as it was so old, it might disintegrate before their eyes. So they spread everything out and decided to let the wind do their job for them.

When everything was finished, Ellie had thoroughly washed down the cottage, and the boys had wasted enough time outside for her to finish knowing that if they showed their faces inside, she would put them to work. Real work. She did manage to sit while they replaced the now freshly smelling linens back inside, where they folded each and placed them on the floor to be dealt with later. All of this took away the day, and Ellie had not read one word of the book she cherished. It was now time to go home. She would have to wait now until the weekend, but there was just no time today. The boys actually felt sorry that they had not helped more when they looked at the disappointment on their cousin's face.

Luke was especially feeling guilty, as he realized this book meant as much or more to her than the pirate book meant to him. But it was already done, time was gone, and Ellie would have to wait. He convinced Blake to ride back with him, knowing that Ellie probably needed to be alone with her thoughts, and that Blake would probably drive her crazy on the ride back. Blake was more than excited to ride behind Luke. He had a lot to talk about. Luke prepared himself for the million-question game he was going to be subjected to. It almost made the guilt go away, knowing what he was now getting himself into.

On the way down the beach, Ellie dreamily watched the soft, floating tufts and long streaks of billowing clouds slowly moving across the water. Scanning the heavens, she made out an owl, only his fat little head and eyes. She could imagine the rest. As that cloud reshaped itself, it began to resemble a raven, and next to him, a dolphin, smiling, his whisky body and tail trailing off into obscurity. She twice allowed Blue to get his feet wet, but before he got too excited, she reined him back. She was so glad to be alone.

"Look, Ellie!" Blake was sitting backward behind Luke, hanging on to Gus's tail. She laughed, he was so silly, and Gus didn't seem to mind. "Let's play I Spy. I see the fin of a dolphin," Blake declared. Ellie first looked at the sky, for her imaginative cloud dolphin, then realized he meant one in the ocean. Sure enough, the boys were swimming along beside them, and she had not even noticed. Could Blue have wanted to go swimming with them? Could Blue swim? And she was off on another daydream.

Ellie was sitting in the same room where she had met her mother, except the only person there was Aunt Rhetta. She was dressed in all black, some kind of lace at her neck, and a jeweled necklace at the throat. She had on the same kind of shoes Ellie wore, high-top lace-up boots. Maybe she was also not very strong and needed to be careful, lest she stumble while walking in the forest.

"Aunt Rhetta, what did you do while Uncle Jabez was on his trips? Did you stay in the cottage? And were you afraid?"

"Well, child, when I was younger, Mr. William's sister, Phoebe, stayed with me. She was not old enough to marry, and we played a lot. Phoebe was afraid to go into the woods, she was scared of the wolf, and that is why she stayed with me. She felt protected, because as she told me, if others are as scared of that animal as I am, they ain't gonna come on this hill anyway. We played all day. Mr. William would bring his wife up in the wagon to bring us food, and at night, I read to Phoebe. When she went to bed, I would go outside and play with my friends in the woods.

"Aunt Rhetta, did you ever get married?"

"Now, sweetheart, you will have to read my journal."

Ellie drifted in and out of imaginary conversations with Rhetta all the way home. When she walked into the house, the look on Grandmom's face let Ellie know that she *knew,* and if Ellie wanted to talk, her grand-mom was there to listen.

To Ellie, this was the slowest week ever. Even the boys picked up on the melancholy mood she was in. They talked about needing to hurry back and let Ellie read the journal, so they could have their playmate back.

When they returned on Saturday, it was to a clean cottage. Immediately they opened the windows and doors to let in the fresh air, and proceeded to put the cottage back together. The boys left her alone while they explored the cave.

"Ellie, we're going down into the caves, maybe get rid of some of those cobwebs and loose sticks so that when you come down, you won't get hurt," Luke said. "Can you sort of keep an eye on us? Sort of like you did before, you need the practice, don'cha think?" Luke was serious and made sure Ellie did not think he was poking fun. He, more than Ellie, had faith in her powers.

She agreed, on both counts. Yes, she should practice, and yes, she would keep them in her mind's eye. They left, and she settled in the oversized chair with the book on her lap. Just to be sure, she sat quietly before opening the book, and thought hard, with her eyes closed. She could see the boys slapping at the walls as they descended into the caves, and she was satisfied she had the power to find them. She settled back and opened the book. There was something about the book she liked. It carried a light, sweet scent. As she leafed through the pages, the odor intensified. Finally, she thumbed to the middle where the pages looked rumpled. Here she found the crushed, brown, crumbled dust of an outline, both dusty sprinkles and oil stains of a flower, crushed into the pages of the book. Beautiful! As she held the remnants of the dust to her nose, she recognized it as formerly being a gardenia.

> I sit to write of the things I see. I am the sister of Jabez Jennette. We live in the Trent Woods, on Hatteras Island, in a small house on the grounds which can only be accessed by the trail that leads from the village of Trent. My parents died

when I was young, and I was taken in by my grandfather, Joseph Jennette. Unfortunately, my grandfather has died, and I now live with my brother Jabez. My brother owns a business at the docks in Hatteras, my grandfather's business. I sometimes think maybe my brother would rather follow his wandering soul, to lands unknown, and feels me a burden which holds him fast to this duty, of occupation, and having me as a charge. I try to be helpful so as not to be a bother. There are others who would take me, but Jabez will not see of it. I have another sister and another brother, who are both married and also have children. I am thankful he has decided he will shoulder the responsibility. As I grow older, I wish to gain my keep.

Jabez puts his trust in me, as I have learned to take advantage of an active mind. I am in school in the nearby village of Buxton, at Miss Clara's house, but Jabez wants me to be educated in a similar manner as he. I will be going away to school in two years. I am not looking forward to it. I wish to stay here. I had a strange dream four nights ago, leading me to pen things that I do not want to forget. Jabez has given me one of his journals for my thoughts. He says that our lives are important and will be needed by those who come after us. My dream was of the indians. I met a chief, a woman, named Weroansqua. She is connected to me. She sometimes has talked to me.

This is the first time I have seen her. She reminds me of Uncle Jabez, she gives off a powerful aura. I find that I can do things that others cannot do when she is in my mind. I will follow the chief's instruction, as she says she can help my brother.

Jabez and I are often visited by Jabez's friend from the mainland, Charles Henry Jarvis Jr. They delight in asking me strange questions, they say I will know the answer. And usually I do. Jabez asked after a man whose name is Gibbs. He and Charles Jr. are thinking of doing business with him. I said no. I felt a shiver in the room when his name was mentioned. I also saw the color red around him. I did not see him. I felt his aura. I see colors around people, and I know them by their colors. The aura surrounding this man named Gibbs was dark murky red, indicating dishonesty and anger. My brother strides inside an orange hue, giving off a creative, adventurous, and detail-oriented nature. Charles Jr gives off a slight blue tint, indicating thoughtfulness, calm, and great intuition. I am glad Charles Jr is in Jabez's life, he brings balance to my restless brother. I feel safe when they are both here. Together, they cast a pure green light, indicating camaraderie. I do not know my own aura. I have tried to see it in a mirror.

I listen as Jabez and Charles Jr drink wine and talk about school. They make it sound so fun, maybe it will not be such an unhappy experience for me. I hope I meet a friend like Charles Jr is to Jabez.

They make me giggle when they speak of girlfriends. They make a handsome pair, and from their tales, they have made many women swoon. Charles Jr is talking about marriage. My brother scoffs. He fears he will lose his companion. Charles Jr asks Jabez about Stella. At inquiry, Stella is sweet on Jabez and would marry him at will. He says he is still looking, and winks at me. I think to tell them of my crush on a boy from Hatteras village, but I hesitate, as they will tease me.

I got a horse today, I have named her Star. She has a perfect star between her eyes. She is otherwise black. She does have four perfect "socks." I could have named her that, but I like Star better. There is a lady from the village who comes in to help me with my dresses. She also washes my hair, cleans and irons my clothes. I wish she was not here. She likes Jabez and is not happy when it is just she and I. When she washes my hair, she digs her nails to my head, and it hurts. I have told her, but it makes it worse. I want to tell Jabez, but I have not yet. Today, she hurt me, I need to tell Jabez.

———

The girl who hurts me is no longer coming. I could feel she did not like me. Wonder what she did? For surely I did not tell. There is a new woman, much older, and very kind. She feels sorry for me, not having a mother. I do like her. Star and I have been followed by a wolf when we walk through the woods. The wolf does not scare me or my horse. We three make a good team. We have been friends since I can remember, but it never follows me. Maybe the wolf is also a friend of Star. Maybe I will find a friend at the new school. The girls at the Buxton school do not find me a suitable companion. They do not know that their colors are not compatible to mine. I am not unhappy to stay away from them. My days are spent wandering around the woods with Star and my wolf. I am good at books, and Jabez brings them home to me. Sometimes I take Star and Wolf and read at my favorite spot on the hill overlooking the ocean.

———

I slept in the woods tonight. Jabez and Charles Jr are not here, but William is. He is asleep inside the cottage, and I

will return before the daylight. Jabez should be back from
his trip soon. He has been delayed, I see both of them in a
tavern of sorts, not a place around here, that I have seen.
They are laughing, so they must be all right. I will not
worry William. I feel safe in the woods.

I slept in a nest of grass made by the deer. Wolf slept
nearby, and Star stayed near. The animals get along fine
together. I am happy in the forest, and safe. The deer put me
with their fawn, and we all sleep together. Jabez on a night
I slept outside, he returned late, and found me, as he knows
my favorite spots. He carried me to my bed. He is so understanding of me and my animal friends. I know William
slept in the barn last night. Wolf told me. Poor Jabez, I fear
I worry him.

School today was a waste of my time. I drew insects on my
tablet. I have read all the books. Charles Jr teaches me math,
I have no friends, I am ready to go away. I have told Jabez.
He understands, and will get Charles Jr to find a suitable
Academy. Academy, that sounds exciting. I will not go
back to the Buxton school. There are only girls in my age,
all the boys have stopped. There are a few little boys there,
but only on some days. The lady the villagers pay to teach
is going to have a baby. They will have to collect money for
someone else, in a different house. It is time for me to go.

There were pages and pages of how Rhetta felt about school. She
wrote about the books she read, her birthday when she turned twelve,
with Jabez and Charles Jr. Mr. William and his wife, Mozell, came with
a cake Mozell had baked. Evidently Rhetta didn't get very much cake,
because she raved and raved about the taste later. She chronicled the

building of the big house. The first stones were placed that would enclose the brick shell. The interior walls that led down to the grotto were fast becoming a house. She wrote of the comings and goings of Jabez, and sometimes he took her to their sister Beulah's house, if it was just a night. He wanted her to play with Beulah's children, but they were always so unruly she didn't want to stay. Rhetta always wanted to come back home to the growing house and the two-bedroom cottage.

Charles Jr. got married, and Jabez took Rhetta to Richmond. She was outfitted in the finest dresses of the city. Everyone made her feel special, and she and Jabez visited a nearby academy. Miss Sophie's Finishing Academy. They toured the school, Rhetta was enrolled for the coming year. Over the next few days, she took tests to determine her skills. She was graded higher than her age. She felt that Jabez's books and Charles Jr.'s teaching of numbers put her ahead. She would be in this school for the next three years. She lived in the dormitory with other girls from the East Coast, and came home on holidays.

As I come back for holiday I find the house on the hill is closer to being finished. It is grand. I shall be able to bring my friends home. I have visited their families. I do not like to spend holiday with other families. I like my own. I know Jabez and Charles Jr worry about me making friends, but I spend all my time with my girlfriends during the school year, and want to come home when I can. Even though I only have Jabez, I am happy. Star and Wolf miss me. I can tell. I developed a love of painting and sketching. I have decided I will be an artist. I can draw Jabez from memory. I see him as if he were standing in front of me. I have been having weird dreams of seeing things that Jabez and Charles Jr are doing. I told Jabez one, and he was so interested, he has asked that I tell him all of my dreams. Sometimes I see Jabez as he works, it seems I am connected to him with my mind. I told him of my visions. He seemed very interested, but puzzled. In my night dreams, Weroansqua tells me that my gifts are unusual, and she will guide me. Charles Jr visits sometimes and we sit in the salon of the dormitory, and he asks me questions that he and Jabez want me to comment on. Mostly, they inquire about what I see when a certain name is mentioned. He says that the things I say help with the business, and that I am a partner for them. The girls in the dormitory like to sneak downstairs to hide behind the door and look at him. He is handsome. But, they should see my brother. They would swoon, just like the other girls.

More and more pages of new friends and vacations as Ellie pored over the journal. Finally, the boys came back and began packing up for home. They had thoroughly gone through the main sitting room. Luke had even tried the piano. Ellie felt she had been so involved in the journal, she did not hear the music coming from the big house. She excitedly put the book in a safe place and readied herself for home. The trip down the beach was full of her description of her new connection to Rhetta. Luke liked all the parts that told about Uncle Jabez, and Blake liked the parts of her story that dealt with Charles Jr. Seemed they all were having personal connections to the relatives who had come before them. They began living two lives each.

Ellie became so involved in her mind with the little redheaded girl in the woods that she began to dream about her.

Ellie and Rhetta were friends, and they rode their horses everywhere. In one dream, Rhetta, Star, Ellie, and Blue went through the woods, crossed the main road ambling through the villages, and through the woods on the other side, to the sound. Both horses being black, it looked like shadows moving through a dream. This was all familiar to Ellie as she was now in very recognizable territory. She remembered when she went with Sooleawa to the area where the women washed. Rhetta showed her the exit of the water runoff from the grotto. They could not take the horses all the way, but they went as far as they could. Then the girls dismounted and went into the beautiful caves that ran all the way from the sound to the water running down in the underground stream, whose mouth was located outside the house. As they neared the water-fall, the color of the water turned from dark to beautiful sparkles of blue, as the sky above reacted against the dark. They stopped before they got back to the waterfall, and the dream ended with the sighting of Rhetta's wolf, who indicated they should turn back.

Ellie awakened as Christo crowed at the first morning light.

The school year was ending, and the children were excited to know that they would have more time to pursue their adventurous souls. The Navy was everywhere on the grounds of the Lighthouse. It had been decided that they would move to the big house over the summer. Grandpop had permission to take Ol' Tony and Big Roy. They were beginning not to be needed by the modern Coast Guard, and they were old. The kids were happy to keep them, and had been feeling sad thinking they might not see them again. They promised to continue to take care of them so that Pop could do other things. The village had approached him to serve as principal of the school.

Each time the kids returned to the house, Ellie went straight away to the cottage and Rhetta's journal.

> I am learning to speak to animals. We seem to communicate with thought. I know I can see Jabez when he is away. Some-times I warn him, if I have a dream he needs to hear. Yesterday I moved a pine cone from one place on the ground to another. Wolf was with me. She sat beside me, and it seemed like she

was thinking also. It is fun being home for the summer. I do miss the girls at school, but I miss here also. Star and Wolf were glad to see me. I was invited to go home with Catherine Anne, from New York City. It was tempting, but I wanted to come home. I have many friends at school. As I watch them, I am learning how one should dress and talk. Jabez says I am learning to be a lady. I would rather be a deer. Even the deer on the property are glad to see me. I suspect some of them I slept with when I was a child. But they are now grown, and twitching their little white tails when they smell me.

Jabez and Mr. William were home when I awakened this morning. They were unloading wagons, and moving some large chests, burlap bags of something, and barrels of other things into the barn. Tonight Jabez and I will search through the cargo for things for the house. While I was away, Jabez bought me a piano. There is a music teacher at the school, and some of the girls take lessons. I will also. Maybe I mentioned to Jabez before that the girls took lessons, and it seems he wants me to have everything everyone else had. I don't need it, but he is always so happy to give. He is constantly looking for ways to make me proper. He doesn't realize, I Am! There were men with wagons this afternoon taking away the containers from the barn. We are beginning to furnish the house. The bolts of cloth are beautiful, not like any I have ever seen. Jabez knows a lady in the village who will make window coverings from the bolts of fabric we have saved. This trip, he came home with rugs from China. I wonder if Catherine Anne's house is this grand.

I awakened to the strong feeling that Jabez and Charles Jr were in trouble. Star and I went straight-way to the docks. I needed to tell Mr. William. Mr. William always takes care of Jabez. Sometimes he accompanies Jabez as a bodyguard. He knows where Jabez is, and will figure a way to help him. I know that Jabez is always in danger. He deals with such unscrupulous men. I also know Jabez can take care of himself. I have seen him practice swords with Charles Jr, and I would not want to parry with him. Jabez carries two pearl-handled pistols at all times. He either also wears a cutlass or a sword at this side. On occasion he carries a musket, that he calls Bess, on the seat of the wagon. It has a bayonet that would be fixed to the end. Jabez did not take that with him. He said that if he needed that, he was probably not going to prevail. My brother is an excellent shot, as am I. We practice on the property. Charles Jr is also a good shot. He also wears two expensive French pistols. However, Charles Jr is never without his walking stick. For Charles Jr it is a weapon. I have seen him practice with Jabez, and he can disarm him with that cane. The cane acts as the sheaf for a sword, with which he is also talented. He is so quick, it makes me laugh. William thinks the two can take care of themselves, he laughs at whoever wants to confront these two. He always says they might not look like much, but they are deadly.

Mr. William has sent me home, assuring me he would mount a search for Jabez and Charles Jr. I am going to the woods, back to the deer hollow, and maybe I can see where they are.

I have had my vision. I saw Jabez and Charles Jr. They were being challenged in a tavern. The place was dirty, and the bandits wretched and disheveled, they were demanding money. Jabez was smiling. Charles Jr was twirling his cane. A fight ensued, Jabez drew his sword, and ran through the man who drew a flintlock, just as the weapon fired. He does not appear to be hit. Charles Jr knocked down two men with artful flourishes of his cane. They are now, back to back, as the others of the tavern circle them. I see Jabez and Charles Jr draw pistols, the men quickly flee. I am anxious for them to return. I will stop now, and find Mr. William. I cannot tell him what I dreamed. My brother wants me to hold secrets for only he and Charles Jr to hear.

Ellie has been no good to the boys because she only wants to read the journal. This day, the boys have convinced her to scour the walls of the house. The three, armed with lanterns, begin their exploration at the tower. With lanterns showing the way, the hallways and stairs become less fearful. At the beginning of the secret passage from the fireplace, Luke discovers another crack in the wall, just past the stairs that have been built to avoid the window. When he pushed on the section, the wall moved to display another false door. This door has taken them to the attic. The attic! The place of the trunks. This discovery has made it easier to enter that area of the house, and has eliminated the need to climb the ladder. It must have been how they moved the trunks of memories and secret information into that room. They always knew the attic was just below the tower. Collectively they decided the hidden door was much more convenient than the ladder as an entrance to the room of treasures.

As the three roamed around, they explored every passageway. At last, they found themselves on the first floor ready to go down to the caves. As they descended, they could feel the dampness of the walls and smell the freshness of the water. The musk of dampness took over.

Then they heard the silence broken by the soft sound of something moving and knew they were near the stream. The water stretched both ways at the opening of their stair-cave. They decided to do the short distance first. Blake was anxious to see the grotto again. They all wondered if it looked the same. Did it get smaller? They could tell, that over the years, it had gotten a higher ceiling, or maybe the floor was lower, but there was a huge cavern ahead of them. The water seemed to be wider and deeper than before. After a short walk going uphill, they found an old canoe rotting near the edge of the stream. It gave them an idea. Luke and Blake talked about building a canoe, one that would stay in the caves. Now, all they had to do was find an old tree, downed by one of the mighty storms that went across the island every summer, one that could be hollowed out to make a boat.

As they moved up toward the sloop, they heard the rush of water and the sound of the waterfall. When they got there, they discovered that the grotto had gotten bigger. The water was coming down with more force, and the waterfall was wider. The rush of moving water had burrowed out a much deeper trench through the underground passageway than they remembered. Time and active water had carved out the solid rock even more.

Ellie began to remember when she had followed Luke and Blake with her thoughts, when they had first discovered the entrance to the caves from the second-floor hallway. Vaguely she recalled seeing something in the pool that formed at the bottom of the waterfall.

"Luke, remember when I saw you and Blake with the wolves the first time you came down here? Well, didn't I tell you I saw a chest or crate or something in the water?" Ellie looked over the edge of the pool as she talked to Luke.

"Yeh, I remember you saying something like that." Luke got down on his knees beside the pool and strained to see.

"I remember that!" chimed in Blake. "Maybe it was a treasure chest. Maybe it is full of Blackbeard's treasure!"

"Don't be silly, Blake. Blackbeard didn't have any treasure. He spent all his money on that house and plantation he built in Bath. You know, when he got married." Luke remembered the accounting in the first half of Jabez's book. It had the name of the cargo, from whom it was taken, and to whom it went. There were no entries of Blackbeard giving any treasure of gold or gems or silver bars. Most of the cargo Jabez moved for Blackbeard consisted of cocoa, rice, bolts of cloth, sometimes iron, wheat, molasses, sugar, spices, and sometimes valuable wood, like mahogany or cherrywood, even bamboo from the Caribbean. The things Blackbeard stole were not of the Spanish Main, but from shipping along the East Coast. What gems, gold, and silver he had, he spent.

Blackbeard's lack of treasure to bury might have been because he had moved his base of operation from the Caribbean Islands to the mainland. While he was in the Caribbean, he pillaged the ships loaded with Spanish gold and netted much gold and silver. Blackbeard had worked that area when he was with Hornigold, but it appeared in the journal of accounts that he began to attack merchant ships off the Atlantic coast, and the goods he robbed made him popular with the wealthy businessmen. Possibly Blackbeard longed to be a gentleman rather than a pirate. He enjoyed both worlds. Luke had read that Blackbeard's plantation up the river in Bath was the grandest in the area.

Wasn't it ironic that men usually want what they see others having? Stede Bonnet was a wealthy plantation owner, and wanted to be a pirate. Blackbeard was a successful and feared pirate and dreamed of being a plantation owner.

The kids peered into the deep pool at the bottom of the waterfall. Ellie was not sure where exactly she envisioned the chest. They decided that they would fashion a canoe and probe the water with a long stick. They continued their exploration of the stream, this time moving toward the far end. Ellie told the boys about Rhetta meeting Weroansqua in a dream that led to them to the caves.

As they continued to follow the stream, they all had fond memories of the wooden bridge crossings the Croatoan used to move from place to place along the vine-covered passageway. They encountered several caves, ones too deep to explore on this day. There was to be much time for them to examine every opening they saw. At a slight turn of the stream, they saw Twylah lying at the mouth of one of the caves. It seemed she was waiting for them. When Blake turned to look back, he saw Theo, head lowered, eyes straight on him, poised for any trouble Blake might encounter.

It appeared that Twylah was lying in front of her own cave, as four tiny black noses and eight golden eyes peeped from behind her. The pups. They each made a single yelp, and at the cocking of their mother's ears, they scooted around her and went to Ellie. The boys had not seen the pups up close before, and the kids all sat on the damp ledge of the stream and spent the rest of their time, until their lanterns appeared to be low on fuel, playing with the pups. The small balls of fur crawled all over them, licking them, biting them with their little sharp pointy teeth, and crouching to challenge them. One fell into the stream, and Luke quickly picked him straight up and tried to wipe him dry with his shirt. They were all rolling around on the damp floor.

Twylah and Theo maintained their original positions, only keeping watch, and as Luke looked around, he saw the shadow of Rafe downstream of them, as a sentinel. It seemed the wolves were never very far away.

Back at the house, the children quickly put the house and cottage back in order and mounted their horses for the trip back home. There was much to talk about. Ellie related the journal, Blake and Luke described the house, and they all wondered about all the strange things that the caves offered. They could not wait to end the school year.

★14★

The Network

Luke pored over Uncle Jabez's journals. He was fascinated with the logistics of how he did his business. As he was busy in the attic, Blake was occupied roaming the forest with Theo. It was strange. Theo was always around when Blake was near. Not being able to read as well as the others, he left the journals to the older two and spent his time playing. He never went to the beach, as he heeded Luke's warning never to go near the water without either him or Ellie. That also included the sound. So Blake and Theo entertained themselves. It was never clear whether Blake made discoveries or Theo showed him the way, but knowing he would be in the woods, Ellie tied his pant legs and sleeves to keep out the ticks. She camped out in the cottage as she continued reading Rhetta's journal.

Blake did not stay away for long. He was just too curious, so he came upstairs, through the hidden door to the attic, and settled down to pester Luke.

"Why don'cha go over there and find some more stuff in the trunk?" Luke begged.

There were so many, and they were stacked up against each other to the extent they were several deep. Now that Grandpop knew they were at the house, it was acceptable to move things around, so Blake started from the back row of trunks, ones that had yet to be opened. It took him all morning to position himself in a comfortable kneeling position in front of the chests, and to ferret out a place to kneel or sit. All the commotion was an irritation to Luke, as he was busy deciphering what he was reading. He was now into the business part of the journal. What Blake could not see was the colorful theater of characters that were fading in and out on the ceiling, over The Book. The same vision was in Luke's head as he read. Blake made a discovery. Luke looked away and lost his concentration as he was drawn away to Blake.

"Look, Luke, there are some more drawing books from Aunt Rhetta." Blake had indeed made a fine discovery. "Here is a book of knives and guns, and one on ships."

Luke crawled over to Blake's cleared-out section and examined the leather-bound sketchbooks.

"These might be Aunt Rhetta's drawings, but this is Uncle Jabez's handwriting. Save these, we will read them with Ellie tomorrow."

They looked interesting, but Luke already had his mind set on what he was doing and did not want to stop. The books were not going anywhere, so tomorrow would be as good a day as any other. He left Blake to look at all the pages, and suffered his ooohhs and aaahhs as he found something he either recognized, or might have a question about. Luke tried to concentrate. Blake was a bother, but it was better to have him in the room with him than to have him roaming all over the land with a wolf. Luke felt that if he could see Blake, he didn't have to waste time worrying about him.

Uncle Jabez had carefully kept a log of all his activities. It appeared he did business from the Caribbean to the ports of New York. He met and dealt with pirates with cargo to dispose of, and privateers who needed a secret outlet for ill-gotten gains.

Jabez listed the town where he first made contact with someone who needed a vendor. He listed the date, place, seller, delivery, and drop-off port, and in another column the name of the company or gentlemen who would purchase, how much for the seller and how much for the vendor. If some of the cargo was scheduled for Jabez, he listed that also. The seller took into consideration the risk Jabez was taking, and whether the goods would be marked as a gift or a sale to Jabez.

The items for Jabez's personal use were usually put down as a gift: chairs, tables, lounging couches, sconces, rugs, bolts of cloth, chests, and so on. All these items were stolen from wealthy captain's cabins from various ships, plus their cargo, and the cargo carried by the passengers. The stone and woods he was given were purchased by him, as they could also be easily sold elsewhere. There must have been a goodly exchange of money, as the wood inside the house was among the finest—even the rich dark woods of Africa and delicate woods of the Orient. There were multiple shipments of brick and stone. The supplies were always delivered on dark moonless nights, with wagons pulled up to some predetermined slough, unloaded, and delivered to the hill in the forest of the Trent Woods.

The accounting also gave names of clients. That was more interesting than the sellers. Names of the sellers were usually pirates, but the names of the buyers were prominent men of the colonies. Some were governors, like Charles Eden of North Carolina. There were entries attributed to Lord Proprietors, lawyers, councilmen, and every elected official, including governors. There was no official separation between lands at that time, and everyone had a perceived claim on certain plots. English dukes, barons, and other self-appointed noblemen asserted ownership of unoccupied land in the new colonies. On one page, there was an entry of sale to a militia, and labeled Indian Wars. Luke was more and more impressed with the danger of Uncle Jabez's business, and he had a clear picture in his mind of the rugged colonial who was his ancestor.

Apparently, some of the cargo went to merchants in Hatteras village. Those names listed were Austin, Gray, O'Neal, Willis, Burrus, and a merchant from Kinnakeet, Williams. This was probably the reason for secrecy, as the people of the island generally frowned on anyone dealing with the unscrupulous pirates who sometimes landed on their docks. The pirates were loud, mostly in need of a bath, and ill-mannered. The islanders did not have to worry, as there was nothing to keep the pirates on the island. It was thought that most of the time spent on the island was in their attempt to avoid capture at sea. The inlets and coves were good places to hide, and the unoccupied smaller capes were good places to careen a ship. Most of the visits to the island were for supplies, freely sold, as the pirates paid well.

Jabez also traded in trees logged for shipment to England or other ports where ships were made. The forests of the island were thick with tall cedar and pine trees, which were much desired by those who worked in construction. Those on the island who dealt in the culling of trees knew to contact Jabez for a market. Sometimes his entry was labeled, "Cape Hatteras Banks," which Luke figured to be the section now known as Ocracoke.

Some of the meeting places for pirates looking to trade was Beacon Island, the 1,000-year-old stretch of grassy dune that had been built up to serve as an island by freeholders of the mainland. It was located at the south end of Ocracoke, off Hatteras Island. They took advantage of the need for a supply drop for ships that drew a lighter draft to take on the cargo and travel to the inland cities with it. They had decked over a portion of the tiny knoll and carried on quite a trade with the pirates, no questions asked. It was also here that the pirates knew they could contact Jabez. As his business grew, he and Charles Jr. traveled less and less, with the business now coming to them, usually by word of mouth. Pirates leaving the Caribbean knew what ship they were looking for, when it sailed, what it carried, if it was armed and how well, and where they could unload the cargo for a pretty profit. The earnings were decided equally among the crew, with a larger share going to the captain, quartermaster, first mate, and sometimes the surgeon or cook. If that profit should be paid at Beacon Island, there was an enterprising, smelly old pirate who had spent his share of earnings on a tavern and jewelry exchange, located near the warehouse on the mound that took in the cargo.

Jabez used his ships and docks to great advantage. Charles Jr. made a good partner, as he moved cargo inland and discreetly sold to prominent Richmond merchants, thus avoiding the taxes—placed on them by their English proprietors—that were beginning to plague colonials.

Jabez showed in his ledger that much expense went to the building and furnishing of the huge mansion he was constructing. Some of the ledger was earmarked with terms like "the tower" or "the new kitchen." It appeared the house was built in stages.

Jabez was a collector of fine pistols and elaborately fashioned swords. As Luke read the many purchases, he began to wonder where all that stuff was. Of course, not all of the trunks had been opened, and he actually had found a set of golden-handled French pistols in the first trunk they opened. Studying further, he saw where Rhetta had evidently been the recipient of many chests of fashionable dresses, probably headed for the prominent ladies of the Caribbean from the fashion houses of Europe. He knew Ellie would leave the reading of the journal for a little piece of information he found here in this book. He also stumbled on an entry that was labeled "Rhetta's Wedding." He sat back with his hands behind him on the floor and stretched out his legs. In his mind, and overhead, was playing a misty wisp of a white wedding scene. As he read, he had a feeling about the room. There was life here in this old house. He wondered if the former occupants minded him reading what was personal and secret to them.

Luke thought that the Jennette family was an interesting group, from their very beginnings on this island to now. It seemed they had been assigned as protectors of the Cape Hatteras lighthouse. He knew from Grandpop that eight men from this family had held that job. The fact that he, Blake, and Ellie were descendants of innovative, adventurous people was not lost on him. Equally his pride extended to other families on the island—those who lived off the mainland, on their own, with their own inventions, their own entertainment, their own distinct language, and their shared experiences with nature. He could not think of anyone in any large city with whom he would change places. He and his barefoot friends had as many adventures at their fingertips as any child about whom he had read in any book. Even in his book *The Adventures of Horatio Hornblower*, he could not find a page that shocked him. He had been on the ocean and seen the ships in storms, maybe only in his imagination and daydreams, but these strange thoughts came to him from his connections with the past, through the gifts Powwaw had given him, and from his inner voices.

Tired of reading, and hungry, Luke closed up his precious book, with the colors it emitted, and convinced Blake to come to the yard for a demonstration of his skill with a lariat. It was a new skill he was teaching himself, like he had seen Mr. Burrus do, when he was wanting to corral a horse. He had learned a lot from Mr. Burrus, and always went with his Pop when he visited the horses.

Blake put the sketchbooks on top of the trunk for easy access and closed the lid. He also was in need of a good stretch. They made their way down to the kitchen and out to the little cottage. This time they made the trip solely from the inside passageways and stairs. That was beginning to be the most fun, as they became more and more familiar with the structure.

Ellie had learned much in her reading of Rhetta's journal. Rhetta traveled the island on her horse, Star. She was a familiar figure at the docks and spent more time in the village of Hatteras than either Trent or Buxton. Jabez had given her a small two-wheeled wagon that she could hook to Star allowing them to wander down the sandy roads of Hatteras village, sometimes watching the villagers put up their fish on the docks. At various houses there were nets drying in the yard and strung up on poles for mending done by young boys, old men, and even women talented in keeping the nets ready for a good catch. Rhetta had at one time thought to be a schoolteacher. She admired one of her island teachers (the young lady who was newly married and left to have a baby). The small community had taken up money to pay someone else to teach reading, writing, and numbers to local children. Most of the time, school was someone's home or in the small church building in the center of the village.

As Ellie read, Rhetta described the look of the village as it stacked up to the look of the city. She missed the appearance of the island. She would sometimes sketch it in her journal, trying not to be homesick: the sandy roads, the clapboard houses void of paint, the porches and the gardens. Horses—banker ponies included—cows, goats, and pigs roamed the island at will. They fed off the small tree saplings, the acorns that dropped from mighty oaks, and the small, tender young sprouts from vegetation trying to replenish itself. She had heard Grandpop complain about how the animals who roamed free in the early civilization of the island had damaged the land. They had eaten up the new growth of the island by not being contained, and now, in barren areas where the trees and plants had not replenished themselves, the blowing sand took over, and ruined the land for any future production. She had heard these stories, and now she was reading about it in Aunt Rhetta's journal. Innocently Rhetta had described and drawn the area she so loved, not knowing that the things she was remembering about the land would be gone as time went on, and the huge forests she drew were no longer around.

Ellie felt sad reading Aunt Rhetta's memories, as she could see in her a kindred spirit for the land and its inhabitants, and she wished she could see what Rhetta saw. Then she remembered the trip she took with her aunt on the horses, when, in a dream, they traveled to the mouth of the stream located on the shore of the Pamlico. Except for the many years separating them, Ellie felt like they were friends.

"Do you remember the forest we lived in when we were with the Croatoan tribe?" she asked the boys when they came for lunch.

"What about it?" Luke said, but Blake wasn't listening. He was in

Uncle Jabez's bedchamber thinking that was a place he had not explored.

"Well, don't you think things have changed? Remember when we would stand under the trees and they were so thick that the rain would not even hit us?" she said sadly to Luke.

"Yeah," Luke hesitated in thought. "I remember the houses in the trees where the Indians hid if there was trouble. And the places, I think, near here, where they showed the colonists how to ride out storms, it was so thick there. Why? What are you thinking?"

"I've been reading Aunt Rhetta's journal, and she is writing at the school in Richmond, about how much she misses the island. She describes the village, and she talks about the animals running free. She was happy they had enough to eat, with all the sprouts and nuts from trees located here. Remember hearing Grandpop complain about people not locking up their livestock? He said that those people were doing damage to the island, by allowing their goats and stuff to eat all the new sprouts that grew the forests. He said that's why we have so much sand, cause there are fewer trees and bushes to stop it. Rhetta talks about that."

Luke answered, "Jabez talked about selling the trees to build ships. It's interesting to learn about how this island grew, and sometimes how it was not allowed to grow. People then, I guess, just didn't know any better. Makes me sad to think about it. When I get rich, I'm going to plant trees, and everything we lost, and make the island green again. Maybe here, on our land, it is like it used to be, 'cause no livestock lived here, and I'm sure the loggers did not go on Uncle Jabez's property. He would not allow it. Uncle Jabez said the loggers came from the mainland and bought up people's property just so they could cut down trees."

Luke and Ellie were having a grown-up moment as they talked about the island they loved. Maybe it was good to learn the history, and also bad to know it.

Blake walked into the room where they were talking, and in true Blake fashion, switched on the silly button. "Aren't we ever going to eat?

I'm hungry. Looks like I'm gonna have to eat trees and nuts like a goat." He had heard a portion of the conversation and totally missed the point.

The older two doubled over in laughter, sort of a needed laughter, and sat down at the table for their bag of sandwiches and surprises from Grandmom.

After lunch, they struck out across the yard, following Blake as he insisted they see the places he and Theo had found as they explored. He took them to a pine-needle-covered hill. The needles were so thick, there was no sign of the solid ground they covered. The kids stepped over the broken limbs from the strong gust of severe storms that regularly swept the island. Limbs were covered in green moss and made beautiful patterns on the floor of the forest. At the top of the hill was a huge live oak tree, much like the one that was in front of the house. Its twisted limbs stretched out and up almost as tall as the pines. The bald spot under the tree attested as to the thickness of the foliage, which did not allow sun to hit that spot, therefore letting nothing grow. From the huge tree hung a very thick vine—the kind of vine they saw crisscrossing the woods, in the Croatoan adventure, and from which they knitted roofs and made rope bridges, and had used as a tool for hauling during that time. This was the first one they had seen since then. Where did the vine come from, what kind was it, and were there more?

They began to trace the vine to its origin and found a huge trunk that sprouted at least two more, going in different directions.

"Lemme show you something," Blake said.

He took hold of the vine and began to climb, hand over hand, moving his feet up the trunk of the tree, until he got to a thick limb.

"Watch me!" he yelled down, and he grabbed the vine and jumped. Nearing the ground, he let go, landed on what appeared to be a pushed-up pile of pine straw, and with the slickness of the needles, slid all the way down the hill. He got up laughing and brushing off debris, with the biggest grin ever.

"Try it, Luke!" he yelled to the top of the hill, but he was late in his suggestion. Luke was already halfway up the tree to the limb and was poised to swing down.

"Land on the pile of straw. I put it there so's we'd have a soft landing." Blake was supremely proud of the game he had invented and was smart enough to make safe. But what they didn't know was that he had first tried it without the pile of pine needles at the bottom, and had hurt himself. It had taken him quite a while to recover, but having done so, it was too much fun to leave alone, so he managed to figure out how to have a soft landing. Luke was ecstatic. It was more fun than anything, and he was racing Blake back up the hill to try again. As they both neared the top, Luke let Blake go by him as he stopped in front of Ellie.

"Ellie, you can't do this. This is for boys, and you know you cannot get any scratches, so just watch. I don't want you to get hurt, okay?" He was sorry to say that, but he did realize there were some things she was not allowed to do. Skate on the sidewalk, and this. Hopefully she wouldn't mind. She didn't. She knew the dangers of a cut, and she didn't want that either. She knew also, that she could easily bleed to death in the forest before any help could come. Grandmom and Weroansqua had warned her sufficiently of her illness, and she knew to be smart and protect herself.

Ellie cheered on the boys as they jumped until their hands could take no more. Blake had found a special place, "the rope swing." Here in the green forest, with beautiful green moss growing on the fallen branches, and gray moss hanging down from the mighty oaks in the area, Ellie wished she could sketch like Aunt Rhetta.

⋆ 15 ⋆

Living Off the Land

It was springtime. Grandpop had so much help around the grounds—with all the new assistants, the navy and Coast Guard thinking to close down the light, working underfoot, as Grandpop said, in preparation for shutting it down on short notice—he decided to take a day off. It had to be unsettling to be in charge of so many people with their own agenda, most of them outranking him, at least in their minds. Their plans were totally different from his daily routine.

The first full moon of May, named the flower moon, brought soft-shelled crabs to the island, and everybody was on the marshy shore of the Pamlico Sound at night, with a dip net and a flashlight. The flower moon was the month the locals waited for. This was the moon that caused blue crabs, which have recently molted their old exoskeleton, to nest in the grass near the shoreline while they grew another, slightly larger, hard protective shell. This molting process happened many times during the lifetime of a crab. The numerous times gradually decreased as the crab got older. Just before molting the crab had grown the basic template of a new shell underneath the old shell, the calcium absorbed from the old shell becoming flexible. The old shell split down the back of the crab and allowed the crab to literally back out of the old skeleton, leaving behind even the eye stalk and gill coverings.

At that point, crabs would find a place to hide in the mud and grass as their shells were soft and easily damaged. The crab stayed hidden for the next two, maybe three months in order to grow the hardened shell again. This soft-shell period, with their lack of movement, allowed the capture by simply dipping them up, the entire crab at this stage being edible. But most people cleaned them before frying. The only parts of the crab not safe to eat were the mouthparts, the gills, and the abdomen. It was a delicacy most islanders relished. The next stage of the edible crab was the paper-shell crab, also eaten fried. After the cleaning, they were battered and deep-fried.

Grandpop decided to haul the little boat from the pond down to the sound in the late evening, just before dark, and we talked and waited. At that time, he manned the push pole and poled around the edges of the sound, while the kids shined the flashlight in the wet, wilted-down grass, looking for the shiny eyes or the body of a motionless crab. The kids were more than excited, and Grandmom had her mouth set for a mess of crabs. She had the kitchen primed for the meal: frying pan, flour, seasonings, plus hungry people. She fried the crabs up crisp for the kids, with the claws crunchy like a cracker, and the meat and shell so tender that it appeared there would be several more trips for this delicious treat. (All of the crab is edible after the underside is cleaned.)

This was a new experience for the children. Blake was just old enough. The kids loved crabs. All summer long, islanders with boats crabbed for the community. At this point in time, crabs were not yet a commercial business but a specialty for the locals. The men made crab pots from chicken wire, with a tease stuffed in the middle, like a piece of raw chicken. This was put in a hole for the crab to crawl into to get the meat of the chicken. Their pots were made so that leading from the hole was a wire tunnel, which prevented the crab from crawling back out once it was in. The men had an understanding as to who crabbed where, and as they sunk their pots below the water, they attached a long string with a distinctly personalized, painted buoy to float on the waterline and let harvesters know which pots belonged to whom. Of course, teens looking to have a crab feast on the beach usually snuck out in the sound and pilfered a few crabs from each pot, throwing the pot back in to catch more crabs. Usually no one was the wiser. If they were, they only had to think back to their own years growing up "island."

On those occasions when the family was going to eat a mess of hard crabs, Grandmom covered the table with an oilcloth tablecloth, and the steamed crabs were dumped in the middle for anyone to grab, pick apart, and eat the tasty meat. Crabs were good no matter what their growing stage was. The kids all knew how to clean a crab. Even Blake didn't need any help. He stealthily broke off the apron, then claws, put his finger under the shell and popped it off, then with the crab skeleton showing, he snapped the body in half, cleaned out the stuff that was not meat, and was eating and eyeing the next one as he did it. Those times around the table eating hard blue crabs lasted all summer long. Crabs meant summertime, and here it was: time for the soft shells, then came the hard shells. What a feast!

Luke remembered his trips around the edges of the sound with Powwaw, looking for types of grass and foliage that would make a dye or a medicine or a useful brew. He wondered if Powwaw found soft-shells. Surely he did. The Croatoan ate most everything that was good.

When Uncle Jack and Lindy were around, they had their own crab pots, and there were plenty of crabs then. But Capt'n Charlie had to rely on neighbors for crabs, as his time was taken up with the grand lighthouse. There was never a shortage of crabs, though. The summer was full of them. It was not unusual for Miss Odessa to get up in the morning and find a huge red drum fish, or black drum fish, or mess of blues (bluefish, which Ellie hated, as their taste was so strong. Maybe because the fish was strong, it was a hard fight for the angler to bring it in, and all those fish muscles were not tasty, according to Ellie), Sometimes there were a few flounder, or sea mullet, trout, spot, croaker, ducks, geese, or a side of venison. The islanders looked after each other, and many took advantage of Capt'n Charlie's talents to help them get a job or turn in papers to the government or sign anything that needed notarized. It was a barter system. The best find, however, were the channel bass. When they hit the beach, the anglers must have smelled it, because they filled the shore at The Point within an hour. How they knew is anybody's guess, but they all knew and they all came. The old-timers said that Captain Bernice hand-lined the huge and delicious fish before they had access to spinning reels.

When Uncle Jack took them fishing in the sound, they loved to catch croaker. They made the funniest noise, just like a frog croaking. Their second favorite was the blowfish, which was not edible, but it was so much fun watching it puff up, then deflate, then blow up again. Finally, they threw them back for fear they would die. Islanders lived off the water, land, and sky. Many mornings the kids had fish for breakfast, with cornbread fried in a skillet, looking just like a pancake. Often in the winter, Grandpop shucked oysters standing on the back porch, handing the body of the oyster to one of the kids from the end of the shucking knife, and they slurped it up. Raw oysters were the best. It was a way of life they found normal. Sometimes inside the oyster shell, along with the oyster muscle, was a tiny little bubble of pink, the beginning of a crab. Small and crunchy, these were called "crab-slew" oysters. They were not easily obtained and were the best bushel. They only were harvested in certain areas of the sound, under certain conditions. Men in the oyster farming business knew where they were and how to seed them when they made their own oyster beds at the given spots in the sound.

Another fun thing was to go clamming. The tool to use was a normal garden rake. The kids went with an adult, an uncle or cousin usually, to a known clam bed, and raked up the clams that lay slammed shut on the bottom, buried in the mud. The smaller clams were the best, and Grandmom's clam chowder was even better. Sometimes she made clam fritters. These were chopped-up clams mixed with meal and fried like a pancake. Island cuisine was fit for a king. The *Odessa W*, the boat constructed in Uncle Baxter's backyard, was built to be seaworthy enough to go into the Atlantic and drag for shrimp.

For a while, shrimping was a good living for locals. That also provided a source of delicacy to the island, as many locals bought them straight from the docks by the crateful. So many were pulled up in nets that it became a lucrative business on the island, until those same boats became useful and more profitable being used for party fishing or deep-sea fishing—not catching a lot, but one very special fish. Wealthy men from the mainland hired out a captain, his boat, and a mate for doing all the dirty work, like putting bait on the hook and taking the fish off the hook after it was reeled in, and sometimes the mate did that also. But the sportsmen were having fun, as they went to sea for one of the huge monsters that occupied deep water. These were the days of the blue marlin or the delicate sailfish, neither of which was eaten. The men took their prize to the mainland and had a taxidermist make it into a wall adornment, showing neighbors and friends the big fish he reeled in. Most of the time the mate was the one who brought in the fish, scooped it out of the ocean, and stowed it away in the fish box of the boat. These days, since these fish are not for consumption, it has become a custom to tag and release the mighty fish to live and fight another day, and leave the fisherman with a picture of his prize.

After the soft-shelling excursion, Grandpop loaded up the little boat on the wagon, hitched it to Ol' Tony and Big Roy, and hauled it to the boathouse near the big house on the hill. They were beginning to move more and more stuff to that area—little moves, nothing that would allow anybody to get upset about moving. The kids were beginning to realize they might have to leave their beloved lighthouse. They began spending more of their afternoon school day on the top deck, just outside the light, while their grandfather worked. The view was magnificent. They felt they could see the world. They had the spyglass and were privileged to see huge ships go by, with their smokestacks puffing away as they maneuvered around the shoals. The kids did not know that once the war escalated, these were the very ships that would sink, leaving the crew and cargo washing up on the shores. These ships would be the target of submarines (U-boats) belonging to the German Navy, but that's a later story.

Several times the kids persuaded Grandpop to go with them after supper up the steps and on to the walkway that encircled the light, and watch the stars. On those nights Grandpop would begin to tell about the stars and was shocked at the knowledge Luke had about the heavens. He listened as his grandfather pointed out a meteor shower or told about the pictures some Greeks saw in the constellations. The stories these people told allowed them to remember the shape of a star cluster they needed for navigation, and therefore one could pick out the Archer or the Hunter or the upside-down head of a horse.

But to Charlie, this was natural, as he was a man of the heavens also. It was never hard to get Grandpop to go back to his place of work at night. He, too, was going to miss the duty he and so many others had loved for every minute they had it. There was something about that tall structure. It was a friend and a playground. It separated life from death as it warned ships at sea that they were getting too close to land, and needed to adjust their course. Others had said that passing it on the way up or down the coast was a comfortable, friendly, and warm feeling. It was a sentinel of power that watched over the sea and spoke to all who were in sight of it. Their dad, Bill Finnegan, having painted it by hand, felt as though it belonged to him, and he asked about it often as he faced danger and longed for home.

The kids had so many things to occupy their time. School, the lighthouse, the huge mansion, their friends, the wolves, the horses, and the dolphins. They were determined to contact the dolphins sometime during the summer, to let them know that they had moved. They hadn't quite figured out how to do that yet, but they would. They accomplished every task they set their minds to, and without realizing it, all they had to do was *think* on it, but they were still not used to all the power they had among them.

It would not be an exaggeration to say that every household had a personal garden. Everything was available. Pop's was full, and so was Uncle Tommy's. Between the two of them, there were fresh vegetables all year round. Grandmom spent the summer fixing food for the winter in jars. Even though she tried to get the children to eat the "canned" food, the only thing they liked done in that fashion was figs. The folks called it "canning" but more properly, it was preserving things in jars, not cans. Another thing they liked done that way were the jams Grandmom made from blueberries and strawberries. There was no shortage of food. The gardens on the island were stocked with collards, various other greens, string beans, squash, pumpkin, watermelon, tomatoes (a fruit when raw, and a vegetable with bragging rights when cooked), zucchini, onions, sweet potatoes, carrots, and peppers of all kinds. If it grew anywhere, the islanders would coax it to grow in the sandy soil of the island. The refuse from the livestock enriched the soil. Cultivating the soil was important. Some people even grew their own corn. There was a windmill in Kinnakeet where islanders could take corn for grinding into flour. Cultivating the soil was important, and islanders had learned over the years how to grow plants almost in sand.

One problem that the islanders solved, to a certain extent, was the influx of mosquitoes. There was a fine carver in Trent who made the most remarkable martin boxes. That is the name of a bird that eats thousands of mosquitoes a day. Everybody had several martin boxes. These birdhouses sometimes reminded the kids of the hotels in Nags Head, they had so many holes for birds to crawl into and build a nest. Also they cultivated the citronella plant, whose odor was offensive to the irritating insect, so they planted it all around the porches and yard. Screened-in porches were a must. Most homes had one or two, or built them all around the house, usually with a swing to while away the hours.

The food product not readily available was beef. Pork was plentiful, with all the pigs, but cows were usually for milk, and there were not enough on the island for slaughter. Some had dozens of head of cattle, and those did sell beef. Most had only one, and it usually had a name. Of course, chicken was plentiful, and island cooks invented hundreds of ways to prepare it. Some had smokehouses on the property for preserving meat and pork, and also used in the art of salting down the fish to give them a longer period before spoilage. However, most months of the year provided a school of fish for catching in either nets or by hand casting.

Early in the life of the island, subsistence on the land was paramount. For many years people made their living from the water, including being specialists in maneuvering the many shoals and sandbars of the Pamlico. Some men were hired to pilot ships through the shifting sands of the inland waterway. Boats were a necessary part of the island way of life. On a pretty day, going from one village to another was best down the back side of the island, or "sound side" as everyone referred to it, making the journey less stressful by a small boat called a spritsail skiff. This style of transportation was flat-bottomed, with a sprit-rigged main, and jib. They were about thirteen to twenty feet in length, and easily handled by one man with a sail or pole. Poling was easier than rowing, and it was an activity that was easy on the back, but hard on the walking. Like Powwaw, the traveler put the twelve- to sixteen-foot-pole in the water near the bow and just walked it back, moving the boat forward. The shallow water was not a factor in this mode of travel, for with a flat bottom, the spritsail skiff just slid over the top with ease.

The depression did not hit the island as hard as it did the mainland. The barter and trade system had been in operation since the colonial days. The price of food was high, but the islanders adjusted. Some store owners voluntarily went bankrupt to keep the community fed, as they did not demand payment from those who were without a job.

Then came the Works Progress Administration. President Roosevelt tried to create a system so that anyone could get a job. The WPA, to a man who otherwise had no job, provided a small paycheck for doing odd jobs for the community. It entailed, among other things, distributing government food, dairy, flour, apples, oranges, rice, raisins, and some sugar. Also, they drained ditches to combat mosquitoes, fixed roads, gathered seaweed for sale off island, and even built a baseball diamond and repaired small bridges that were scattered over inlets across the island.

The Civilian Conservation Corps was another organization enhancing the community for a small paycheck. They built sand dunes to combat beach erosion. During that time, the theory was that the high dune line would keep the sea at bay during a storm. That has now been disputed as a problem in not allowing the water to run off, but rather stay and damage the villages due to lack of a place to go. The thing never considered was the water from the sound that came ashore and had no access to the sea, creating flooding in the villages. The CCC planted bushes to hold the sand, and sea oats were planted for the same purpose. The sea oat has been such a help that it has made it necessary to exact a fine to those who would pick them. The erosion of the island has been a problem since the beginning. The battle continues.

Books and music made life on the island even more pleasant. Even the lightkeeper was included in the rotation of books from the service. One lightkeeper off island once took a boatload of books with him as he was stationed in the middle of a surrounding body of water.

Medical books were also a part of the rotation. The island had spent long periods of time without doctors. Sometimes it was necessary to improvise. There have always been women on the island who studied the effect of plants to heal, either by making a salve, or brewing a tea, in order to cure certain ailments. They shared their knowledge willingly and accepted whatever the patient could pay. Sometimes pay was just a fat chicken. Once the Coast Guard became an official part of the island, the medical corpsman was also generous with his talents. Of course, there were stories of people dying or being permanently damaged from lack of medical attention. However, it was not from lack of care or concern. Locals did what they could with what they had and did not complain. The trade-off of living here was worth it.

Medical attention has always been a wagon ride away. The midwives and those who had medical talents never refused to attend to the sick. Community has always been a comfortable feeling. Illnesses among the islanders might have had to be tolerated for a longer period of time than if one lived on the mainland, yet even though modern medicine was in short supply, the cure was available from the land, and it worked.

Music was an important part of the island both then and now. There was hardly a family who did not have someone who had the ear for the piano, guitar, banjo, or fiddle. Grandpop's specialty was the harmonica. He rocked out on "Red winged Blackbird", stamping his foot to the rhythm. Singing around the piano was a way to get through a bad storm. There has never been a shortage of tutelage for any instrument. People of the island love music so much, they joyfully taught each other. Most learned by ear, but some could read sheet music. The guitar was a natural instrument for some. There was never a time not suitable for music. Hard times were made easier with the sound of music. Even the Indians of the various tribes on the island made their own instruments and enjoyed the melodious tones they emitted.

Captain Charlie's great love of civil engineering continued no matter what job he held. He constructed buildings for both private and community use. His main concern for many years was obtaining an electric co-op. He truly wanted everyone to have electricity. After Bill installed the huge ship generators in the big house, the main keeper's quarters, and Uncle Baxter's house, he wanted everyone to have the same conveniences as he had. For several years he petitioned the federal government for a loan to do just that. He and his son Curtis wrote hundreds of letters (now on file in the Library of Congress) to state and federal representatives and senators on the subject. Finally, when the government agreed to a loan, the bids they received were all too high. Possibly they really did not want to give that money to such an out-of-the-way island as ours. Charlie Gray went to Washington, DC, and stood in front of the committee. As a graduate in civil engineering he said, "I'll get it built for that," and he did.

The Cape Hatteras Electrical Co-Op still sends checks—small, but cashable—to the members when there has been an excess. His petition to the Rural Electric Association was successful, and eventually every home on the island was wired for electricity. By 1930, 90 percent of the country had electricity. Only the rural areas did not. Private utility companies that supplied electric power to most of the nation's consumers argued for years that it was too expensive to string electric lines to isolated rural areas. The private companies also said that most were too poor to be able to afford to pay. By 1939 the Rural Electrification Administration—created because private enterprise did not supply electric power to the people—opened the door by helping to establish rural electric cooperatives. Captain Charlie, chairman of the Dare County Board of Commissioners, worked tirelessly and finally got the grant for the island.

Along with E. S. White, and his wife, Maude, both avid community workers, and Charlie Gray, Clarence Brady, the Midgetts of Rodanthe, the Burruses of Hatteras, and Charlie Williams of Kinnakeet took on another project, one that took more than twenty years. It was to bring the communities together for a consolidated school. Before consolidation of the community schools into one island school, young people had to go away for a couple of years to a high school on the mainland to obtain certification from an accredited school in order to apply to college. The citizens of all communities worked to get the Hatteras schools consolidated for state accreditation, allowing island children to qualify for advanced education.

Growing up "island" seemed to always be a plus rather than a minus. Once children from the island went to school on the mainland, whether to boarding academies, college, or just mainland high schools, they were never behind. More than likely they were ahead. The amount of private reading in the home was excessive, as was the attention given to children by various teachers. Also, with other students they could work in teams, and the parents were always involved.

Shipwrecks were prominent off the Diamond Shoals. Added to the problems of captains not knowing where the shoals were, was the frequency of violent storms, which played havoc with shipping. Because it became such a problem, especially with shipping government supplies, the government established the National Lifesaving Service. Since there were seven stations on the island, and the local talent had knowledge of managing the ocean, an abundance of qualified applicants were available. This work provided a government paycheck to those who were not involved in fishing. Many men, as a result, received paychecks and pensions helping with the ability of the island to survive the economic depression plaguing the mainland.

One such ship in trouble during a storm dumped a portion of its cargo overboard. That was the day the beaches were full of bananas. Everybody ate bananas in every way a person could prepare them. Those not near the beaches came to collect from those who did, and bananas were distributed through all seven villages. The necessity of word of mouth was paramount, as the bananas spoiled so rapidly, nobody wanted a single person to go without. It has always been a funny story for islanders to tell.

Revival time on the island was almost a celebration for the entire community. There were no tents. The event took place in the church and did not happen every year. Revival was a weeklong nightly church activity that invited all inhabitants of the village to come hear a particular preacher give a special religious talk. It was a community event, even for the children. A traveling minister booked the church for a week and held nightly sermons for the folks to enjoy. At the end of the week, those who heard sermons and wanted to be baptized into the Christian faith dressed in a white robe and met at what is now Canadian Hole, the long stretch of beach between Kinnakeet and Buxton. The area was always a haul over for small craft and a place with a sandy beach on the sound side of the island.

Dressed in white choir robes, the new converts to the church met with their families and friends to participate in an official baptism ceremony. The local minister, along with two men who were deacons of the church, waded out in the water, accompanying each new Christian. With the special subject between them, they cautioned people to hold their nose, and quickly the two deacons held on to the convert and dipped him or her quickly backward in the water, fully submerging as they were blessing, and immediately pulling the newly baptized person up—sometimes sputtering, but always well and happy.

The islanders looked to a higher power for guidance. They had experienced too many miracles not to do so. The hardship of living isolated from the rest of the world was so much better tolerated if one was given hope—hope that even though there was a problem, and it seemed impossible to solve, there existed the possibility that a higher power would intervene and help. People also called that inner feeling, "faith." Sometimes it came in the form of a neighbor, sometimes what some would call a stroke of good luck, but the believers felt better with the knowledge that they were not alone. The communities have forever been tightly connected to each other, and that closeness has been the glue that kept life moving forward. The churches of all denominations have worked together since their formation and were a positive fact of living on a barrier island. It was the island way of life.

Someone said about Winston Churchill, "Cometh the hour, cometh the man." This was true of the island. When the need appeared, so did the man to fill that need, whether it was the Midgett brothers, Frazier Peele, Charlie Gray, E.S. White, Charles Williams, Captain Lavene Midgett, or countless others. The men to build the sets for a play, the women to make the costumes, the person writing letters for electricity, the men and women who built the seven communities—they all rose to all the challenges. The island produced people with vision, intelligence, fortitude, and the stubbornness to carry out their plans.

Sailing Ships

On the next trip to the old house, just before the school year came to a close, the kids were in the attic again, Luke pouring over Uncle Jabez's ledgers, Ellie with her nose in Rhetta's journal, and Blake left on his own. Not wanting to be alone, he usually stayed around one or the other of the kids. Usually it was Luke, his subject being more interesting than Ellie's. Plus, he was in the room where all the chests and trunks were stowed away.

Blake, rummaging through one of the trunks, pulled out the most interesting of all the books: the one on ships. Uncle Jabez, using Rhetta's artistic skills, had created a compilation of the types of sailing ships they saw passing the island from the tower window. Jabez was conscious of all ships using the area, and he had his business at the docks where those vessels that drew a lesser draft came in to pick up or drop off supplies. He was also knowledgeable of ships not usual to the area, which usually sailed into deeper harbors with larger docks. At the larger ports Jabez did his scouting for captains who wanted to sell cargo in a more discreet manner. Here he would manage to contact someone who would vouch for his ability to distribute cargo that was questionably obtained. His first love was ships. He had studied to construct them, and now all he could do was hang around them. It was better than working a land job or an office position.

Luke became so excited to look at that book, and for the rest of the afternoon, he and Blake read. Blake could see the pictures, but Luke was needed to read the name, how they differed from each other in use, who used them, and what they normally carried. Jabez had chronicled it all. No one knows if he kept a running journal or spent his later days remembering the life he led, but the particulars were written down for future generations to see what he saw and understand his love of the adventurous life. Rhetta's journal also talked about the women in his life. But his love was the sea, and the excitement of being in a clandestine occupation.

Each entry had a sketch of the description. He must have described them to Rhetta.

The ships that sailed by this Island were of every kind. I have tried to tell about them here. I knew them by heart, they were all beautiful, small, medium and large. They conquered the mighty ocean.
Sails: Either square sails or fore and aft rigged.
Fore: towards the bow.
Aft: towards the stern.
Bow: front of ship.
Stern: back of ship.
Mizzen mast: the third mast from forward in a vessel having three or more main masts.
Quarterdeck: the part of a weather deck that runs aft from the midship area or the mainmast to the stern.
Poop: a superstructure at the stern of a vessel.
Main mast: middle of a three masted or front on a two masted or only one mast.

Yard: a long spar (stout pole) supported more or less at its center, to which the head of a square sail, lateen sail, or lugsail is bent.

Yardarm: either of the outer portions of the yard of a square sail.

Square Masted: sails hung from yardarm carried right angles to the mast.

Advantage: catch wind from behind.

Spar: a stout pole such as those used for masts.

Gaff: a spar rising aft from a mast to support the head of a quadrilateral fore-and-aft sail, the sails were attached to gaffs from the mast in a mid-ship line (gives increased maneuverability).

Lateen: yardarm, loosely affixed to a mast, allows sail to be shifted about to catch wind. Square rigged ships have lateen rigged foresail or jib mounted on bowsprit.

Bowsprit: a spar projecting from upper end of bow of sailing ship,

Lateen Sail: a triangular sail set on a long sloping yard, shaped right angle, good for maneuverability, allows ship to sail in directions other than the wind, however, catch less wind than a square sail.

Jib: any of various sails set forward of a forestaysail.

Flying jib: the outer or outermost of two or more jibs, set well above the jib boom.

Trysail: a triangular or quadrilateral sail bent to the mast, used for lying to, or keeping a vessel headed into the wind.

Periagus: sailing canoe, used in the rivers of the Caribbean.

Sloop: single mast rigged fore and aft and a jib all sizes from two-man boat to huge royal navy — most gas rigged, could hoist a square, or two squares when running before the wind, ideal for piracy shallow or low draft, used to navigate shallow water, out of reach of navy ships 30-65 feet.

Schooner: two masts fore and aft five-foot draft favored among pirates, narrow hull, do eleven knots in stiff breeze, capable of hiding in shallow waters, could carry eight cannon, four swivel guns, seventy-five men.

Barquentine (bars): small three masted square rigged fore, fore and aft main, and mizzen, not popular in Caribbean slow ocean crossing (important to plunder, not to have)

Brigantine (brig): two masted, workhorse combat choice of pirates all kinds of rigs, larger than barq, square sails eighty feet long, square fore and mast, also fitted for fore and aft carried ten cannon, one hundred men.

Galley: square rigged also had oars down on lower deck, each oar pulled by three men (usually slave ships).

Canoe: could be one hundred feet long, good in Caribbean rivers — slender, open boats, tapering to a point at both ends, propelled by paddles or sometimes sails.

Galleon: carried seventy-four cannon, two hundred men, four masted sharp blades at end of yards for ripping other sails that came close; also had

fighting platform, halfway up, both fore and main mast archers (fire was feared by all sailors), no open flame below deck, no firearms near sails, bow and arrow used on platforms rather than firearms, which could throw sparks to ignite sails.
Man of War: several kinds.
Corvette: two masts, brig rigged.
Frigate: three masts and ship rigged (full rigged), fast, having a lofty ship rig and heavily armed on one or two deck, smaller, twenty-four to forty guns.
Ship of the line: largest Man of War, three masts, ship rigged, three sometimes four decks, this ship was the fear of the ocean. No ship could withstand the broadside of 75 cannon. They were massive.

The boys were fascinated with the look and the description of the ships. It made them envision just what kind of ship each pirate had as he sailed into different situations. They could see the advantage of capturing various kinds of ships. Some they left at their special port, maybe at New Providence (Nassau), which was a pirate community, but always with a crew to watch over the vessel. They were pirates, after all, and stealing was their livelihood. Usually, there was honor among thieves and one pirate did not steal the property of another, at least not the large property. Stealing a ship would not be hard to discover. Maybe steal a pistol or gem, but not a ship.

The next entry they read was the one detailing weapons—knives and guns.

Most weapons belonging to the pirates were of the finest sold, they were in possession of them, because they stole them. When giving a prize for siting a ship, the mate was given a set of fine pistols. They were

more valuable than gold. They could mean the difference between life and death.

Cutlass: rough heavy broad bladed single edged sword,
two feet long blade, slightly curved, sharpened
on outer side resembled saber, only blade slightly
heavier and shorter. good for close combat in
small quarters.

Sword: elegantly curved, silver basketted, shark
skinned gripped dress sword, usually an officer
in the Navy.

Cutlasses: used by pirates because a single blow with
heavy cutlass would snap an officer's fancy sword
in two, they were used to slash or hack at an opponent. Easy to chop off a hand rather than running
through, swords not good on ships, need too much
room to use for stabbing an opponent, fighting in
close quarters, needed the chop of a cutlass.

Cutlass functioned as a tool.

hack down hatches

chop livestock

fell a tree

open a coconut

strike a spark to start a fire

skin a cow

split an anchor

Knives: cut rope and sails, pirates carried several
knives.

Dirk: dagger.

Stiletto: a short dagger with blade that is thick in
proportion to its width, pointed instrument.

Poniard: small slender dagger, both sides had an edge.

Dagger: a short swordlike weapon with a pointed blade and a handle used for stabbing, some had hilts and crossbars like a sword, to prevent hand from slipping forward many daggers designed to break the blade of an opponent's sword

Gully: big knife and eating utensil like butcher's knife.

Ax: used to climb the sides of ship, cut through lines, cut lines of grappling hooks, used in boarding, two to three feet long, sharp on one side, flat on other, other side used for sledge hammer.

Tomahawk: smaller than an ax.

Firearms: several types for different jobs and distances.

Musket: good sniping weapon, could clear deck before boarding fired together, as effective as cannon shot. muskets load through muzzle rather than breech (behind barrel). pirates made up charges beforehand. kept charges in pouch at belt five feet long, not used in boarding. took two hands.

Charges: gunpowder and wad of rag.

Blunder Buss: Like a hand held cannon, not like rifle, the muzzle was flared to increase damage and spread shot.

Pistols: most prized possession of our times. good ones like mine decorated stock with gold, silver or ornate carvings, mine are pearl handled hammer maybe shaped like lion or unicorn, or some animal from crest of owner, good ones stolen from passengers.

French Cavalry Officers Pistols Prized.

Muzzle loaders: easy, short.

Powder: carried in powder horn.

Ramrod or Rammer: usually attached to gun four-ten inches long.

Metal cap at bottom of pistol grip used for clubbing opponent.

Flintlock: single shot. Blackbeard carried six, already loaded to use in fight, avoided loading until sixth pistol fired, most carried prepared shot on belt.

Bow and Arrow or Crossbow: used in fighting platforms halfway up the mast for fear of sparks from flintlock setting fire to sails.

Grenades: containers filled with powder, lead, glass, and wick when lit, exploded everywhere.

Stink Pots: noxious chemicals, sulphur and other foul smelling smoke producing gasses to confuse and obscure vision, best with more smoke.

Cannon: usually six pound round shot, could have fifty on one side.

Now armed with the description and sketch of weapons and ships, the kids had a better grip on how things went during times of plunder. Luke recalled seeing several of the types of weaponry as he and Uncle Jabez fought the pirates to rescue Nathan and Mills. He wished he had read this part before, so that he could have taken advantage of opportunities to help in the rescue. He was a grown man in his mind, but the mirror told him he was still a little boy. He had to learn to be good with a whip, his bow and arrow, and his new skills with a rope. He was not ready for knives and pistols.

Blake got all caught up with the knives and decided to go around to the places in the house where he had seen them on display and learn to distinguish one from the other. It was useless knowledge they both cherished. It was the stuff of dreams. Never would they think to harm anything—not man, nor animal, nor bird.

Lunchtime. The kids put away their books and went to the cottage to find Ellie and tell her what they had discovered. Ellie was swooning over the details of Rhetta's wedding and knew the boys would not be interested, so she kept mostly to herself. Coincidentally, the boys knew that Ellie would not be interested in their find, so they also only told sketchy details.

As they ate lunch, they decided to go down into the caves again. They had the big shove pole from the boathouse, and they were going to look for the chest that Ellie had seen in her vision.

At the waterfall, they began to poke around in the pool. The pole was very long, allowing them to reach the middle of the water. It was deeper than it looked, and at the bottom, the constant falling strength of the water had caused the bottom to be a little rocky. As they stuck the pole down, only maybe two inches of the end came up covered in mud when they brought it back up. But they did hit bottom—and knew when they did—so any object of any height would hit solid, more solid than the bottom. They felt like they could find whatever was there, if there was anything to find.

The pool was larger than they anticipated, and there was a lot of poking going on. Luke, the strongest of the three, got so tired that he could hardly lift the sixteen-foot pole to bring it up and back down again. They sat down to rest. They had to talk Blake into not diving in. They reminded him that the last time he went underwater, he was on a dolphin with Poseidon's mask covering his face. As they discussed keeping Blake out of the pool, Luke began to think that maybe going in was not a bad idea.

As they sat down on the ledge beside the water, they became aware of six golden eyes fixed on them. The wolves had come out of their caves to see what all the commotion was about. Ellie gasped. What if there were water moccasins in the pool? Or even in the caves? They began to rethink all their innocence and the danger they could be facing. They decided that the wolves would know if there were snakes around. They would smell them. At that, they relaxed a little and decided that, from now on, they would not visit the caves unless the wolves were there.

So they began to search the caves to find exactly which crevices were occupied by the wolves. From now on, they would get the wolves before they explored, and if they couldn't find the wolves, they would wait until they did. Now that the wolves were around, and after a rest Luke began to poke around in the pool again. They could only do one side at a time, because the water was too wide across to get both sides, but with that pole they could almost reach the middle. Their original plan was not working out.

Luke had a brilliant idea. They would suspend the search until they could build a small canoe. In the water, they could search in safety. And the plan was hatched. They would concentrate on finding the right log, hollow it out, like they had seen the Indians do, and drag it into the grotto from the mouth near the sound. They were excited to build a canoe to search for the object in Ellie's vision. They also discussed what else they might find. After all, this was a popular area for the tribe.

"But what if I am wrong? What if I didn't see anything, and just thought I did? We might be just down here wasting our time." Ellie was doubting herself. After all, it had been such a long time ago, and she couldn't be sure.

Luke laughed. "We've got all summer to do this. If that chest has been there for two hundred years, weeks and months are not going to destroy it. We have plenty of time, and what else are we going to do for the summer?"

They all agreed. They would build a canoe.

"What about the boat from the pond that we brought over here the other day? Maybe we could use that. Then we could search right away." Once again, Blake surprised the other two with his suggestion.

It was actually a good suggestion, but there were a few glitches in the plan. What if the boat was too big for the stream? They needed to walk the entire area and measure to see if the boat would go all the way to the pool from the sound. Next, they needed a wagon to get the boat to the sound. How in the world were they going to do that without telling Grandpop?

From the looks of things, that chest would be hidden for a long time. They better satisfy themselves with reading until they could figure it out. The canoe was beginning to sound pretty good. They left the pole near the pool and started wearily back to the house. This time, they took the long way, toward the mouth of the stream, to the sound, encouraging the wolves to follow. That was not really necessary, since they were going to follow anyway. They made mental notes of everything they saw. They were looking for snakes and poking around with a stick they found for anything they needed to uncover now while the wolves were near them. Knowing that the wolves could handle anything that could harm them, they grew more comfortable.

By the time they made it to the mouth, it was time to get back so that their grandparents would not worry. They began their trip back upstream to the stairs. This time they walked on the opposite side of the stream, studying the things on the other wall. At one point, they had to wade across at a shallow part so that they wouldn't get caught on the other side.

Another thought: they had to build a bridge. This had been an eventful day. There was much planning to be an adventurer. Maybe that was why not too many people planned to be one. It was not as carefree as they had once thought. It took a lot of planning and thinking ahead. As they discussed their problems, they encouraged each other to be up to the task. They needed a bridge and a canoe. That's what they would do.

Arriving at the lighthouse, they saw Grandpop at the railing. He had been watching them come down the beach. Boy, was he a welcome sight. Home, no place like it. Safety!

That night Ellie had a dream:

She was looking into the pool where they had spent most of the day. She was accompanied by both boys, and all the wolves. Everyone was peering into the water at the bottom of the waterfall. As the water moved in the pool, it created small circles that eventually became calm and formed the stream that ran downhill. Luke was encouraging her to close her eyes and think.

"You saw it before Ellie, try to see it again," he was saying.

"But I'm afraid to get near the pool," she answered. "I'm afraid there are snakes."

Even in her dreams, Ellie was afraid of snakes. As she moved closer to the edge, she could see Weroansqua floating in a transparent gown that reminded her of the one she wore at the wedding. She was motioning for Ellie to come closer. Ellie heard her say, "Do not be afraid, there are no snakes in these caves. The wolves are the only living creatures in the caves. Powwaw cursed the snakes at Sooleawa's wedding and banished them from his area. Remember, Powwaw lived in these caves. Do not be afraid. You are in no danger here."

At that, Weroansqua disappeared, and a mist of silver and blue took her place. With a sputter of silver dust, the apparition vanished.

Ellie awakened in a start, and as her feet hit the floor, she moved toward the window. It was almost light. She could see the light coming from Dawnland, as the Indians called it, and its glow made everything blue. It was the beginning of the day. The sun was not yet showing its golden head. The morning was just blue. It had rained slightly during the night, and as the ground gradually sloped in front of the lighthouse, the reflecting pool it created caused there to be two lighthouses, one standing, and one mirrored on the ground. She heard a whisper.

"Ellie, Ellie," Luke and Blake were standing in the doorway of her room.

"You awake?" Blake whispered.

Ellie faced them and said, "I had a dream that we were in the pool."

"Us, too," said Luke. "We heard somebody say that the caves were safe. It was like a whisper from somewhere. Did you hear it, too?"

Both boys were anxiously waiting for her reaction. They had both awakened at the same time and quietly recounted their dream. Since Ellie had been in the dream also, they wondered if she also had the same one.

"I saw Weroansqua floating over the pool, and she told me not to be afraid of snakes, that Powwaw had banished them from the caves after the horrible incident at the wedding, with Sucki and the snake, the one the white wolf killed." Ellie was sitting on the bed now, the light from the break of day streaming through the window.

The boys moved to the bed and sat down, Blake scrunching up at the head of the bed with his back resting on the headboard, knees tucked up with his arms encircling them. He looked a little sleepy still.

"Ellie, do you think you can find the chest from here?" Luke's mind was working. "You think you saw it before when you were not with us. What about now, when we are all here, and can put our minds together with you? Powwaw said we would all be stronger together. Me and Blake can't do it alone. Only you can, but they said that together we could do things. We can do things together that we can't do alone. Whacha think?"

"Gosh, I never thought about that." Ellie looked interested. "Most of the time, I forget that there are things I can do that are a little strange. I probably should have tried it when we were there, but we were too busy, and watching you with the pole and thinking about making a canoe, I just forgot."

"Try it," Blake spoke and yawned at the same time.

"No, let's all of us try it," said Luke. "How should we start? Maybe hold hands, close our eyes, and picture the chest? Tell us what it looked like, so we can all think of the same thing."

"It was square and was smaller than the size of the one in the attic that had The Book, and it was brown, with leather straps around it, not like the ones of The Book's trunk, but that chest where you found the French pistols. It had two big leather straps across the top, and they fastened at the opening of the lid. That's all I can remember," she said.

"I know what it looks like. I can do it," Blake said as he moved in closer to the two and put himself on the other side of Ellie, placing her in the middle of the group.

They nestled up close to each other, holding hands, and Luke looked around at Blake.

"Don't say anything Blake. No matter what, don't say anything. Just think, no talking," he said in a stern do-as-I-say voice.

"I'm not!" Blake shot back, "and don't you say anything either!"

With eyes closed, the three concentrated on the picture in their mind and the grotto pool.

After maybe five minutes of silence, the calm was broken by three voices saying in unison:

"IT'S BEHIND THE WATERFALL!"

⋆ 17 ⋆

Pirate Style

There was much anticipation for the end of school. The kids began to take tools to the old house that would allow them to build a canoe. They had found the perfect log, and with Luke's rope, they looped it around one edge while Blue, the larger of the two horses, drug it out of the woods and into the boat barn. Grandpop never went into that barn. He usually only checked out the larger of the two structures. They collected a saw for evening up the ends, a hatchet, a large chisel, various hammers, and any sharp tool they could find in Grandpop's work shed that might serve to hollow out something made of wood. They set about making a canoe. It was hard work.

For two weekends the kids chopped and sawed on that log. The first problem they had was that every time Luke swung the ax, the log rolled over. They tried putting things on the sides to block the log from rolling, but it only lasted for a couple of swings, then it rolled. This sent them home tired every day that they worked on it, to the point that Luke could hardly lift his arms, he was so sore. Blake was full of scratches. Ellie was in the best shape, as she was not allowed to get a cut for fear her blood would run freely and not clot. It was beginning to be the worst idea they ever had.

There was no other solution than to ask Grandpop.

"A canoe? What in the world do you young-uns want with a canoe when you have a perfectly good skiff? And, don't tell *me* you are thinking about going near the water without a grown-up." Grandpop was puzzled, and the kids were sorry they asked.

"But, Pop," said Luke, "the Indians did it. It can't be that hard. Can't you just tell us? We aren't going in the water, we just want to build our own canoe."

"Well, let me see," Grandpop began. "First you have to find a log that is as tall as you are, and a little wider than your butt. Then you need to make it a little flat on top and bottom, so it won't roll on you."

Wow, the three thought, *Grandpop really does have all the answers. How come he knew it would roll away?* They couldn't believe how smart Grandpop was.

"But Pop, why do you have to cut the top? It isn't going to roll." Luke could understand cutting a flat part for the bottom, but not the top.

"You gonna get in it, or ride it?" Grandpop laughed. "You cut the top flat because you are going to be making the log sort of three fourths as high as the sides are naturally, and it gets easy to dig out."

"Oooohh," Luke's mind was trailing off to the picture he was forming. Of course, they were going to cut the top anyway.

"Then you saw off both ends, top tapering down at an angle to the bottom, to make your bow. It is hard to push a blunt log through the water, but if the front is shaped in a V shape, the water glides around it easy." Grandpop now was really getting into it, but what he didn't see on the faces of the children was that already it sounded impossible, and they knew they would have to figure out some other way to get to that chest.

Grandpop continued, "Once you have the log so's it won't roll, you start at the top, and begin to chip away in the middle to make a hole, and you keep widening that hole with an ax. You don't go but so deep. You just need a hole about eight inches deep and eight inches wide. Now you take some hot coals, like we burn in the fireplace, and put them in, and keep fanning to keep them hot—not a fire, mind you, just hot. The coals need to smolder and smolder until they start burning the inside just a little."

Now he had their interest again. The knowledge that they didn't have to chop out the whole inside made Luke smile. He, at that point, was so tired because the first instructions literally wore him out. Even though he was just thinking about it, he had already decided it was too hard.

Grandpop kept on talking, pausing every once in a while, looking up and thinking, then coming up with the next step. *Boy, was he smart,* they thought, *that's why everybody goes to him for construction advice. He must be able to build anything.* The steps were interesting, but all three of them had decided in their minds that it was just too hard!

"Then, each day, you dig out the burnt wood, easy to remove, and put in more hot coals, until you burn out a little more hole. Now, you have to stay watch over the thing. You can't have it catch fire. You also can't have the coals roll around and get to the sides. You need to arrange them in the exact spot for the inside—not too near the sides, not too far front. You just have to keep a stick on them all the time to make the inside perfect. This thing takes a long time, 'cause you need to let the wood soften in the burned parts in order to chip away the ashes for your inside. Use some wet mud or clay around the edges to keep the coals from burning away the sides and getting out of control."

Grandpop finally looked up from his pondering, and stared directly into three of the most astonished faces he had ever seen. "What?" he was confused. Wasn't he telling them what they asked?

"Well, Grandpop," Luke said, "maybe we didn't think you really knew how, but you do, and it just seems like you are saying exactly how to build one, and I guess we are surprised."

"Think I don't know how, do ya? Well, how 'bout we build one over at the old house this summer? I'll help, or I'll supervise. We'll build it in the old boathouse." Now Captain Charlie saw an even more surprised look on those faces. This time their mouths dropped open.

"You will?" Blake was standing now, and he jumped into Grandpop's lap. "That would be the best summer present ever! Would you really do that?" He was shocked that his grandfather would come up with that suggestion. So was everybody else. Ellie was fighting for a position next to her grandfather, and because of Blake smothering him, she could only snuggle up to an arm.

"Grandpop! That would be the greatest!" Luke was the most shocked and could hardly describe the reaction he was having to the answer his grandfather had given.

"What's all this commotion? I could hear you all from the kitchen. What's going on?" Grandmom came out of the kitchen, wiping her hands on her apron and looking like she didn't like being left out.

"Grandpop's gonna build us a canoe!" Blake fired out the answer so fast, Captain Charlie was shocked he had volunteered also.

"I said *we* were going to build a canoe, not me alone. I thought you wanted to build it yourself. I only said I'd help." He had to laugh at the mess he had just gotten himself into. But he knew his time at the lighthouse was short, and it depressed him a little. To tell the truth, it sounded like something he would like to do—right down his alley, and a chance to join the children in an adventure. He had been thinking about his age and his usefulness, and the thought of being young again around this silly group made him smile.

"Charlie! Are you?" Odessa looked at her husband like he had lost his mind.

"Of course," he answered. "If they are going to do this, they need an adult around, 'cause there are sharp objects and a little fire involved, and I don't want to deal with lost fingers and the Trent Woods going up in smoke." They both laughed.

Odessa hadn't seen Charlie laugh like that in months. She knew he was always in need of a project, and this really sounded like a good one—one that would be happy and giggly and productive and keep him around the kids. She only wished she could help.

It was settled. The kids would find a log—no problem, they had one—and when school was out, the construction of an Indian canoe would begin. Everybody was excited.

On the way down to the beach, as Grandpop gave his usual wave from the railing of the lighthouse, they laughed and laughed about the fun they would have over the summer. But realization set in that it still left the chest under the waterfall, and they didn't know if they could wait that long to find out what was in it.

Since they had to suspend the thought of the canoe for a while, they went back to their reading of the many journals left behind by Uncle Jabez and Aunt Rhetta. Ellie was almost relieved that they had to postpone the construction of the canoe. She was just getting to the girly part of Aunt Rhetta's journal, with the wedding and her time living in Richmond.

Apparently Aunt Rhetta had married a young politician, whose father was a friend of Charles Jr. and his wife, Eden. They had introduced the pair at a dinner party in their home, while Rhetta was still in school. The young man, Royster Sargent, was the son of an important man in the Richmond General Assembly, who had eyes on a political career in Washington, DC. Charles Jr.'s father had long retired from political life, but was still sought after for counsel when someone was thinking about a political career.

Roy, as he was called, was an extremely handsome young man, dressed impeccably, and was smitten the first time he laid eyes on the beautiful auburn-haired young lady from Miss Sophie's Academy. He had no idea of her background. He just knew he was in love. According to the journal, Aunt Rhetta had a lot to do with Roy's feelings, as she had fallen in love first. She was placed opposite Royster at the table, and her shy glances picked up on his innermost thoughts and revealed his interest, as every time she looked his way, he was looking at her. He was becoming interested in getting to know her better. She spent the entire evening trying to get into his mind, and obviously she did a good job, as, at the end of the evening, Roy asked Charles Jr. if he could call on his lovely ward. It was hard to contain Eden's happiness. She nudged her husband to relent and say yes. Rhetta was only seventeen, and finishing at the school. Eden was afraid she would be going back to the island before Royster had a chance to make his case.

By the end of the summer, they were betrothed. Uncle Jabez was not as excited as everyone else, for obvious reasons. Eden planned several occasions for Jabez to visit and meet the man who would rob him of his most prized possession. Finally, the date was set, and the mansion where Charles Jr. grew up was to be the place. All of Richmond society had been alerted. Rhetta and Eden took several trips to New York, looking for the perfect gown. They became a team of "sisters, older, younger." as both cherished having a female in this family of secrecy and adventurous men, until, finally, Uncle Jabez settled in his mind that this was a fact, and he acquiesced.

A year of courtship passed, which saw Royster and his parents visiting Hatteras Island on one of Uncle Jabez's ships, and staying in the magnificent mansion. Jabez and Charles Jr. suspended all business around the appointed time, as they did not want to either attend in bandages or have some public mishap destroy Rhetta's day.

In Luke's reading, he noticed more and more that Charles Jr. and Jabez were trying to move from piracy to society in their dealings. They had made a lot of money and made the acquaintance of many well-to-do contacts in their business—so much so that the transition from illegal to legal was rather easy. The days of the pirates were coming to a close, with the governments of the seaboard states employing the might of their naval powers to bear, and regularly displaying public hangings on shipping docks up and down the coast. Charles Jr. had the political connections to legitimize their merchant trading, and most of the officials were in their pockets, as they, too, had exploited the illegal trade.

Most of what Luke was reading now came not from The Book, but from smaller entries in less grandiose books of notes detailing observations that Jabez made. Maybe in his older years, as Luke had thought before, Uncle Jabez was just trying to chronicle what he had seen. It appeared he had really suffered during those first years of Rhetta's marriage. He was feeling lonely. The knowledge that he was alone began to bear on him, and he started writing his memoirs. It was not until Rhetta's child, Sabra, was born that Uncle Jabez's writings began to take on more of a contented existence.

His observations on the pirates were as interesting as his clandestine meetings.

Pirates, Jabez wrote, were by nature lazy and rebellious. They used foul language, and their bouts of drinking rendered them uncontrollable. They quarreled openly on land, and probably were more violent on land than at sea. They seemed to fight among themselves as viscously as they fought their enemies. They were morose, and capable of murder at the slightest affront. Most had come to pirating by way of signing on to an official navy of a country or being on a ship with a Letter of Marque for privateering. The life in the navies were unrewarding and cruel. The sailors were worked hard, with little food, no time off, and never allowed an idle moment. Some officer was constantly finding menial tasks for them to accomplish, such as scrubbing the ship, or polishing the brass, anything to avoid one single idle hour. Luke even read that in his *Horatio Hornblower* book.

When offered the opportunity to join in with the pirates or go back to the navy, the young man usually chose what he thought to be a more exciting life. It was an easier life, but far from glamorous. The entire ship was full of strong-backed, strong-willed lads in their twenties who were rich when they went to shore, and in several days of drinking and gambling and trafficking with equally unscrupulous thieving women, later they came back to the ship broke and in need of another pillage to continue their sorry lives.

They were constantly sick. They suffered from scurvy, the result of lack of vitamin C, found in fresh fruits and vegetables, and marked by swollen gums, livid spots on the skin, and prostration, which was extreme mental and emotional depression or dejection, not to mention loss of teeth. Many lost fingers, hands, and limbs to the chopping cutlass or the swift sword. They lost eyes to pistol shots, as well as flying debris from homemade grenades and flying wood in battle. There was never enough medicine or doctors to patch them up and make them whole. If something got severely injured, it was most expedient to chop it off, and usually the doctor on board was also the carpenter. They were never dry. The honeycombed hatches of the decks allowed water from rain, storms, or just the unruly sea to constantly seep down on them from above and eventually settle in the ballast area. This was where heavy bags of sand or rock or anything of weight to secure the stability of the desired draft of the ship were kept. This part of the ship needed to be constantly bailed out.

Surely the adventure was there, but the cost was heavy: They never had enough to eat. They drank excessively, as rum was easier to obtain than fresh water, and they found the need to go into battle drunk, in order to work up the courage or tolerate the pain, or both. Many who were forced up the masts, in either battle or rough seas, to secure the sails slipped and fell to their deaths, on the deck to a watery grave.

One of their punishments was the cat-o'-nine-tails, knotted strips of rawhide knitted together at the bottom to form a handle, and with the man tied to the mast, each sailor got a chance to swing the leather on the victim's back. If the ship had 100 men, it did not take long for the blood to flow, and as the last of the pirates got their turn, they were whipping a dead man. Curiously enough, walking the plank was not a part of anyone's punishment. The plank in question was a bridge used to go from one ship to another, balanced on both railings, in order to walk across the board. Planks were available, but if someone was going overboard, there was no reason for a plank. Pirates just hoisted the offending party overboard for shark bait.

Keel hauling was a dreaded form of retaliation. The victim was tied with a line to each arm and pushed off the bow. As the ship sailed, the almost drowned sailor was dragged along the bottom of the barnacled encrusted "keel" of the vessel and pulled back up at the stern. Either he was drowned or cut so badly that he eventually died a slow death.

The worst punishment was marooning. This happened to either one or more sailors. Charles Vane's crew set him off to die on a deserted island. The disgraced seaman was put on an island, known to have no inhabitants and hopefully not enough food, given a pistol with one wad of powder enough for one shot, and left there to starve, fry in the sun, be overcome and eaten by whatever animal lived there, thirst to death, or give up and shoot himself with the one shot left to him. This was the favorite pirate punishment. Some survived, as did Charles Vane, only to be picked up by a passing ship that he had earlier robbed. After a few days, someone recognized the disheveled sailor as being *the* Charles Vane. He was taken to Charlestown and hanged.

As well as a hard life, it was also a lonely life. There was little brotherhood in the "brotherhood of thieves," and when ashore, many picked up a companion to make their lives more meaningful. Hence, the parrots some associate with pirates come into the picture. They could be taught to talk, picked up language easily, hung in an iron cage, and listened to conversations in whatever room they were resigned to. They were so beautiful that a sailor would spend his whole share of booty given to him to own one. They could live to be ninety-five years of age. Usually a stopover in Jamaica or some other tropical port would provide an array of colorful species. They were good at imitation of sound, mistakenly thought to be speaking. They were satisfied to perch, either on a shoulder or on a stick in a cage. The blue parrot, the largest, was from Africa, and the green, smaller, were predominantly from South America. Their food was easily obtained and carried as it consisted of seeds and nuts.

The parrot required the same need for care as a three-year-old child, and also required grooming, feeding, and social interaction. This much attention was not known to the purchaser at the time of sale, and after a night of drinking a sailor might just get disgusted and let the thing go. Thus they were only "temporary" friends.

Monkeys were also a desired pet. They were so mischievous that their lives were short. They usually wore out their welcome faster than a parrot. Rats proved to be the preferred pet for the pirate if one were to feel the need for a pet.

The style of dress for a pirate consisted of what he stole. Most of the time, the striped shirt worn by the navies of the world were taken off the dead officer or sailor and donned by the pirate. Their elaborate waistcoats and silk vests were usually taken from a wealthy passenger aboard an unlucky ship. They also wore the breeches of the military or some nobleman, complete with silk stockings. Most of the time they were without stockings, and wore fancy buckle-topped shoes formerly belonging to an unfortunate victim. They all wore the three-cornered hat popular during the day with both gentlemen and the navy. The more important the person, the more braid around the edges. Sometimes it was edged in fur.

There was an account of the pirate Benjamin Hornigold chasing down a ship. After boarding her, he required everyone onboard—crew and passengers—to relinquish their hats. Seems after a night of drinking and celebrating the pirate crew had thrown their hats to the wind, only to realize they needed them. Well supplied with hats, he bid the company good-bye, and without any other affront, he sailed away.

Captains of pirate ships were happy to wear the military coat of a captured or murdered officer of the king, and the more braid, shoulder brushes, and gold buttons, the higher the rank. It was also not unusual for the most favored pirates—the captain, quartermaster, first mate, bosun, or someone who was in line to be rewarded—to wear the fine ruffled shirts of the gentlemen they robbed. The best coats were those with wide five- or six-inch cuffs, of heavy wool or velvet, the cuff being so thick it created an armor of sorts to protect from the slashing of a cutlass or sword. Tall, black shiny boots were worn by the captains but were cumbersome in a fight, so the average pirate preferred something less restricting. All stolen.

Most pirates wore vests, as they were popular during the day, and readily lifted from a dead body. The materials were of the finest silk, brocade, and velvet, embellished with elaborate buttons with golden braid and fancy collars. The jewels that were divided up among the men were usually worn, as there was no way to trade for money in exchange for drink, or in a card game as it was useless as loot, even a small amount. Jewels were truly the least desired payment for all their trouble. Sometimes they were given as money, depending on the port or the proprietor. The pirates kept necklaces, earrings, rings, broaches—all stolen from women on ships that were attacked. Some wore earrings but found that to be an inconvenience, as were the rings. Rings inhibited fighting and hampered gripping the cutlass. Therefore, they were not desirable as a prize to most.

The common headgear for fighting was a scarf, usually silk, to keep hair from obstructing the view of battle. Many fastened their earrings to their scarves, as it was less cumbersome. Some wore fancy belts, but likely as not, their breeches were held up by rope. Rope was dependable and comfortable, did not slip, and was accessible. The view of the pirate in town was one of a man with multiple visible scars and crusty, burned skin, making one think that they did not dress above the waist while on ship. The typical pirate wore a short blue jacket from a navy sailor and baggy culottes that had seen so much wear they were ragged at the bottom, having lost their elasticity. Some of their attire was exotic. Depending on the rogue, it was common to see red taffeta pants, or hats with feathers, or a crimson waistcoat.

They depended on striking fear in their victims, to just scare them into relinquishing their valuables. It was so much easier, and nobody got physically hurt. It was an age-old profession of not working to get what one wanted, but waiting for others to work, and then taking the results of their labors for oneself.

The life of a pirate was short. Blackbeard was only active as a captain near the Carolina shores for a little more than two years, but in that time captured forty-five vessels. He traveled with three or four vessels with as many as 400 men in total. Blackbeard offered every captured ship's crew the opportunity to join him, even those who were captured aboard slave ships. One of his most trusted mates was a former slave called Black Caesar. When Blackbeard died, he was considered old at thirty-eight. Most pirates, as they were young when they joined, died before the age of thirty, either at sea or on the gallows.

The captain's cabin on a pirate ship was opulent. If a ship had a forty-foot width, it was likely that the captain's cabin went the entire length across the stern just below the navigation deck, and even with the main deck. The desks, tables, chairs, and chests were of the most exotic wood and hardware. The furniture was taken from the finest ships of the French, Spanish, and English vessels that the pirate encountered. They had sets of beautiful china, recovered from chests en route to the fancy mansions of the governors and wealthy Caribbean inhabitants on the Spanish islands. The silver services, goblets, wine casks, and serving dishes were also stolen. They usually had windows with stained glass, and some had velvet curtains. The pirate captured a ship, and if it was better than the one he was on, he traded up, leaving the crew of the larger more detailed ship to sail away in the former, smaller, less affluent pirate vessel.

The charts and nautical tools were also of the best quality, as they were stolen from naval vessels, which had the best equipment of the time. They had spyglasses, sextants (an instrument used to determine latitude or longitude), compasses, and quadrants (used to measure the angular height of a star or sun, to help in navigation). They used trumpets for speaking back and forth between vessels, and pirates often did so as they passed each other at sea. Much information was gained, even at sea.

A pirate's most prized possession was his pistols. They were modern (still only single shot) and had the most elaborate handles, distinctive of the wealthy who were pillaged. Often they were the reward for the person who spied the next prize vessel. A set of excellent pistols was fastened to the yardarm as incentive to keep a sharp eye out for merchant vessels.

Skirmishes with a naval vessel were avoided, as the pirates were seriously outgunned. The naval man of war carried sometimes 100 cannon (using six-inch shells) on a side, and unleashed them on a ship to immediately sink it where it sat. The odds of besting a six-story monster like that were small, so the pirates wisely fled.

All pirate ships carried flags of all nations. It was a ruse to fool an oncoming vessel displaying the flag of a country into thinking that the approaching ship was friendly. They displayed either a flag of their same country, or a country with whom they were not at war. Along with the various flags of the countries, they also carried their own flag. Blackbeard's flag was a white skeleton carrying a spear in one hand and an hourglass in the other (indicating that time of death was near), and the spear was poised to strike a red heart. The background was black. Other flags of notorious pirates were sometimes a black background with a skull, and under the skull were either crossed cutlasses or crossed bones, all indicating death.

Charles Vane's flag was a white skull with crossed bones behind it, and an hourglass under, all on a black background.

Stede Bonnet's flag was a white full frontal skull, with a long horizontal bone under it, a dagger on one side, and a heart on the other side of the skull, all on a black background.

The pirate flag flown by Calico Jack also displayed a skull, with crossed cutlasses below, in a manner curling up on either side of the skull, all on a black background. Calico Jack, being somewhat of a dandy, had another flag, which was white, and the figures mentioned above were black.

The flag displayed by Benjamin Hornigold was simply a solid black rectangle, void of symbols.

Luke was fascinated by the trappings of the pirates. He thought of the young men who were enchanted with the life they thought they would lead. However, Luke, in his daydreams, had sailed from Hatteras to Charlestown to return Nathan and his brothers to their family. He envisioned the life they actually led, the true life, not the one they hoped to have.

As the three boys looked to the heavens, the scary part of the adventure was over. The interesting part had just begun. The boys were tired and had just had big hunks of bread, as they stretched out on the deck with their backs up against the wall separating the captain's area from the deck. At the top of the wall was the navigation deck, where Captain Johns was standing overseeing the wheelman as they headed toward Charlestown.

Luke looked at the clear night above them, dark blue with streaks of silver and some lighter blue clouds, with thousands of stars above them. Luke scrunched down to look straight up, the other boys followed suit, folded their raised arms behind their head on clasped hands, and marveled at the heavens.

"Know anything about star constellations?" asked Luke to nobody in particular.

"I do," said a voice from above," and Captain Johns grinned in the night as he stared ahead. "Tell me what you boys see," he said, "and I'll see if it is the same as me. I know these stars because I need to depend on them sometimes. Whatcha got, boys?" and he chuckled.

Luke smiled and settled in even more to stare straight up. "Well," he began, "I know the Milky Way is made up of 200 billion stars, and that is our galaxy." He grinned.

"Wow," said Mills, "show me."

Luke pointed out the faint streak of lighter sky that ran across like a porous sheet made of tiny stars. As he was talking, a shooting star, then another slipped across the sky, and Captain Johns chimed in.

"Uhhhh … shooting star," whispered Luke.

"They are not stars at all. They are meteors," the captain said, "which are small pieces of dust and other debris falling to earth from space. They travel

so fast, they burn up, leaving a trail of light." He could hear the interest in the boy's voices. "Luke, show them the Big and Little Dipper."

Luke began, "I read a book on stars and old gods, and they are all mapped out in the patterns of the stars. Look right there, see?" as he held up his hand toward the sky. "There's the handle, and down there is the square of the dipper. It is the oldest constellation in the sky. It is also the Bear, and when the gods pulled it up, they pulled it by the tail, and that is the handle." Luke held up his hands again pointing to another part of the sky. "That's the Little Dipper. It has, as a part of it, the most important star in the sky, Polaris."

"You are right, son. That one is used for navigation because it never moves, and is visible every night." Captain Graham Johns was staring at the stars talking, "It is always the brightest and is also called the North Star."

"Have you ever had to use it?" asked Mills.

"Sure have. Stars are most times all you have out here, and they are fun to know. There are animals, fish, symbols, horses, musical instruments, and they all mean something, and they are all fairly in the same place, so you know where you are when you see them."

"I know the ones associated with Poseidon, because I studied a book on him. He has a dolphin, let's see … uhh … okay, see that little group of bright stars there? That's a dolphin. It is the favorite of Poseidon. It saves men, that's why he is in the sky. Okay, now see that four making a square?" Luke was spreading his fingers in a frame, "That's my horse, Pegasus, Gus, I call him. He had wings, his father was Poseidon, god of horses. He came from Medusa's blood and carries Zeus's thunderbolts. See that blue one? That is my cousin Ellie's star. It is the hand of Virgo. It is called the 'Virgin's Diamond,' and represents healing. Ellie is a healer, but she doesn't know it yet." Luke was just rambling on, telling the things he read in a book and the things he looked at when he was on the railing of the lighthouse. He had memorized everything his grandfather had told him and looked it all up in the encyclopedia to make sure he knew shapes.

Here on the ocean—with the wind pushing the sails out, and all those stars floating by, and Captain Johns being interested also—it was like him and his grandfather, and instead of Ellie and Blake listening, he had Nathan and Mills, and Nathan's brothers, Gavin and Liam. He had learned a lot when he read the mythology book. He felt close to the sea, even wondering if his dolphin had followed. Rafe was on the top deck, and he hadn't moved since he got there. Sometimes the raven showed up and rode the yardarm, then disappeared. He didn't stay gone long, as they are also curious birds, and this was a once-in-a-lifetime adventure for the midnight black bird.

The daydream ended as abruptly as it had started, with Luke's thoughts returning to the plight of a sailor. They were mostly young in the eyes and face. He thought of how they got in that predicament. Thinking of the sailors, he knew the happy times were few, and fueled by strong drink and how they lived life in filth. The sea was usually the only bath they took, and when in port, and paying for a bath, the cleanliness was short-lived. Their fancy clothes were tattered and also filthy, but they wore them proudly. He understood their need for music. It must have reminded them of home and happier times. He did not feel sorry for them, and neither did he envy them. Jabez had kept a keen eye on the times in which he lived, and had passed down his information to Luke.

Most of the time in the attic was spent with his little brother at his feet, and he read aloud the things that were chronicled in the book. Blake rolled around on his pillows, striking different positions, as he lazily listened to the information Luke was garnering from Uncle Jabez's journals. Blake was as fascinated and impressed by his uncle as was Luke. Both had gained another hero. They might have been expecting to have as their hero one of the notorious pirates who dealt with Jabez, but the books gave them a hero of their own blood. Still, to both boys, Uncle Jabez, as adventurous as he turned out to be, was still not as worshiped by them as Manteo and Wematin. The two Croatoans had made quite an impression on the young men, and as they thought about it, they were torn as to which men exhibited the finer qualities.

The comparison was equal in fine qualities on both sides. They felt like they knew the Indians better, but here was a man who built this fine house and was as brave as any comic book hero they knew. They worried that he lived a lonely but exciting life. So far they had seen his friend Charles Jr. marry, but no mention of Jabez having lived with a female companion. They began to rummage through the many journals for some indication that he had been a happy man. They would keep up the search until they were satisfied.

It was not to be a long search.

★ 18 ★

The Brotherhood

The last day of school was an exciting day of gathering up belongings, helping Nett clean out her room, and one last time, Ellie and Blake swinging in the playground. They challenged each other to see who could buckle the ropes as they hung on tight. After several trips to the car, everything was loaded, and they were on their way home to the lighthouse. The old tower loomed in the distance, and they cheered, knowing how much fun was in store for them. Luke and Blake had their shoes off before they got to the compound. Grandmom was in the swing with a plate of hot cookies sitting beside her. Blake was so excited to get a hug, he almost sat in them. With mouths full of cookie, they all talked at the same time, speculating on what they would be doing for the summer.

The compound was a busy place, with the new arrival of navy sailors, who were also getting their first look at the mighty tower they were there to protect. The stream of young boys was endless going up the steps to survey the tallest brick lighthouse in the world. They met the children, and at Capt'n Charlie's suggestion, allowed the kids to show them around. The new sailors were impressed with the tour and the guides. The kids could answer every question they were asked, and elaborated on most of the information, even getting into the history of the wonderful tower.

- First built in 1803, but it was decided it was too short to be seen far out to sea.
- Adding to the short problem was the color, beige: it was almost invisible.
- It was originally 90 feet above the sea, now it rises to 210 feet.
- Originally it used whale oil lamps to light the tower.
- The additional height was added and the lighthouse was completed in 1868.
- The cost was $150,000 at the time.
- Twenty-three hundred ships have been lost along the graveyard of the Atlantic since the year 1500.
- Since there were no roads, boats brought materials through the Pamlico Sound they were called "lighthouse tenders."
- Several ships were wrecked in gales within view of the site, thus losing 150,000 bricks intended for construction of the lighthouse.
- The tower took 1.25 million bricks brought in by shallow-draft boats, which dropped them off at a special pier. From there, they were taken by horse and wagon, and a special tram railway track built from the pier to the site.
- The light equipment was taken away during the Civil War for safety of the lens.
- It was originally 1,500 feet from the sea.
- Coast Survey chart 35°15'32" N latitude, 75°31'44" W longitude.
- Light is visible for twenty miles.
- It was first painted with the upper half in red and the lower half in white.
- In 1868 a new, taller tower was constructed farther inland.

- The new lighthouse was built on a slab of pine timbers topped by a series of granite slabs.
- The new light was equipped with a new first-order Fresnel lens.
- The original was demolished in 1871 after completion of a new one.
- The new tower was painted in its candy-striped barber pole paint in 1873, making it equally distinctive during the day.
- The lens has 1,000 prisms.
- The new tower cost $167,000.
- In 1912 the candlepower of the light was increased from 27,000 to 80,000.
- The new light consists of a 36-inch aviation-type rotating beacon of 250,000 candlepower.
- It flashes every 7.5 seconds or 8 flashes per minute.
- All North Carolina lighthouses are painted in their own distinctive black and white pattern, allowing instant recognition of position.
- The only other lighthouse with similar paint and pattern is the lighthouse in St. Augustine, Florida, although it is visibly shorter.
- It stands 208 feet from the bottom of the foundation to the peak of the roof.
- There are 268 steps to the top.
- Its brightness now is 900,000 candle power from two 1,000-watt lamps.
- It warns of the sandbars that extend some fourteen miles out into the ocean off the cape.
- It is the first lighthouse to be built as a warning light to sailors.
- It weighs 4,400 tons.
- The light was suspended during WWII and relit after the war (a recent fact the kids were not yet privileged to, but the sailors knew it would be darkened).
- It was used as a "look-out" tower during WWII.

As the eager young tour guides finished their spiel on the information they thought the sailors should know, Blake chimed in, "And my daddy painted it by hand, and my Grandmom's family donated the land it was built on!"

The men sort of looked at him, and then rolled their eyes at each other in a manner that made Blake feel that maybe they were not taking him seriously.

"Well, they did!" he shot out, and turned on his heel with his back to the astonished lads.

Even as the children impressed the sailors with their knowledge, they had a knot in their hearts knowing that this special monument in their lives was about to spend some time without them. As they walked around with the new recruits to the service, they cautioned them about taking care of the special tower that the kids considered belonged to them. The kids had never lived anywhere else.

That evening, after the sailors had gone back to the base, the children went with Grandpop up to the top for an evening under the stars. They spent the warm evening with the breeze from the mighty Atlantic Ocean blowing slightly, looking at the heavens and talking about the constellations they could see on this particular night. *Oops!* There they go again, they even saw a shooting star. It seemed to be saying farewell, as they followed it across the sky.

Grandpop began to point out to the kids their own astrological figure in the sky. Sometimes it was hard to see it, but they had the telescopes out and usually they came close, but they did not forget what Grandpop said.

"Okay, Ellie, see that group of stars with the big blue star at the bottom? It stretches long out in the sky. Use the Big Dipper as a guide, follow the curve of the handle down to the southwest, until you come to the bright star. That's you.

"Now, let's see, Blake. Can't see yours tonight, but it is the Water Bearer—Aquarius, like *aqua*, the word, 'water' in Spanish and Latin. You were the cup bearer for the main god Zeus. He brings life to the group.

"Okay, my young man Luke, you and Ellie are great together. You are medicine and she is a healer. You are Scorpio, but your tail brings death. You are the protector always." He wrapped his arm around his grandson, to show that he, too, was a protector.

That night it rained—not hard, just enough to grow Grandmom's roses. When they awakened the next morning, Ellie rushed into the boys' room and made them follow her to her room, which faced the lighthouse. There was a beautiful double rainbow, stretching across the sky, each bridge on either side of the shining tower. At the bottom, as usual, there was a pool of water, showing the mirror of the lighthouse inside the two rainbows.

After breakfast, the kids saddled up the two horses and started down the beach. Grandpop was at the top of the tower, giving them a wave, his signal to be careful. As they rounded The Point, there were several men whom they knew, casting for fish. It looked like this morning's run on fish was plentiful, as they saw several pulled in, sometimes two at a time.

Luke and Blake went directly to the tower and the books. The Book had one more story. The colors were as bright as ever. They floated several images across the ceiling, only interrupted by an angel or two or three, as they turned to the final chapter.

I have much to say about my friendship with the pirates who trade with me. They have strangely become my friends, even as I know they are considered untrustworthy. I have had dealings with them from New Providence, to Jamaica to Charlestown, north to New York and Delaware and of course here on Hatteras Island. They have been generous, and helpful in many ways. I am now doing a business which is totally legitimate, there are no more clandestine meetings in marshes and sedges of the island, no more signals from the sea as to their arrival, no more wagonloads of stolen merchandise. I will miss the thrill and excitement of the unknown. I became fast friends with Blackbeard, Roberts, Johns, Daniels, and have known Bonnet, Vane, Rackham and Hands. I always knew they would die a robber's death, and I thank God that Charles Jr. and I did not meet the same end. We easily could have, but I do believe the pirates protected me. They provided this island with goods the people could not have afforded under the heavy taxes imposed by the government, and for that I am thankful. I remember the time Captain Johns and I did a deal which set Charles Jr. and I up for life. Trying to keep his job with the King as a Privateer, he gave Charles Jr. and I a chest of gold doubloons, I still have the chest he asked me to save for him. I have hidden it in a place that will never be discovered by thieves, but I fear he also has come to an untimely end. It has been two years since I have seen him, and I know he would come to retrieve his treasure if he could. Charles Jr. and I will keep his half of the treasure until I know for sure.

I recall times of drinking rum on the shore at the end of Hatteras Island, known as Ocracoke, with Teach and his crew. He says he will never be able to repay me for bringing him here the first time, and allowing him to find such a secret place. I knew Israel Hands, and am astonished he feels no ill will at Blackbeard shooting him in the knee and crippling him, as a joke. He says that he owes everything to his Captain, and would likely have been dead on the streets of London, had he not signed up with the Pirate. Hands spent his last years as Captain of his own ship.

I have traded swords with many men, but never one as talented as Blackbeard. I met one old pirate, a Captain LaPlume (Phew) who was a dealer in gold jewelry and precious gems, he traded money for gems from the sailors who came to him, allowing them to afford a night of drinking at his place. I also have kept him in a pretty penny buying from him, and thanks to him, have spread pirate gems throughout Richmond society.

Charles Jr., and I once went with Captain Phew to New Providence, an island off the coast of Florida. This was a pirate colony, and had it not been for the jovial Captain LaPlume, we might have met our end there, but he was so well liked, that the ruffians allowed us to pass without incident. Aside from his nickname of "Phew," due to his fear of water and lack of hygiene, Captain Phew was one who kept a clear path, as everyone moved away, his reputation and odor preceded him. He was also known to them as a man less talented to be a Captain than Stede Bonnet, as he knew nothing about the sea. His ship and crew were won in a card game, and it was well known that he ran his vessel aground several times. As a result of his ineptness, he never captured a ship, nor a prize. Finally the crew all left him in the port of New Providence, and he was forced to sell his vessel, and procure a ride back to the mainland on the sloop that belonged to George Daniels. Daniels being a local pirate from the banks north of here, dropped him off near here. He built a lean-to of a shop on the shores of Beacon Island, here he sold strong drink to those who had gems to trade.

Eventually he made enough money to buy a shop in a section located near the New York harbor, and as he was known by most of the thieves as a connoisseur of fine jewelry. He became as I had been, a buyer of pirate booty. We both succeeded in a treacherous trade only to work our way into legitimate society.

Charles Jr. and I met "Phew" again in Jamaica. We noticed a street fight near the shacks that line the shore selling rum, and as we tried to walk around it, for we did not involve ourselves in matters of no consequence to us, we saw a man cowering in the bottom of a pile of thugs, clawing at the ground trying to rid himself of the weight of several men. We sat down at one of the makeshift tables near the water and watched, entertained as he continued to inch his way to freedom. We couldn't help but stay to the end to see if he got loose. Each time he would get near the edge of the pile, another thug was thrown on the top, and with a grunt, the poor fellow was covered again. Finally, we took pity on the man, whose face was now planted firmly in the mud of the beach, and thinking him to drown in the mud, we reached down to give him a hand. By this time, the pile on top of him had grown to ten or more bodies, all groaning and without desire to re-enter the fray. As the fight ended, the pile was left, with this poor soul at the bottom, doomed for the night, until the unconscious bodies moved off him. We stepped up, and one by one, we picked up each drunken malcontent, and threw him off the pile, until we got to the bottom, and to the poor wretched soul lying flat, crushed, and now, under the mud of the path. We gathered his filthy body up, got him to his feet, and the warm Caribbean being within reach, we walked him over to the edge of the water and threw him in. He sputtered and splashed around, as we found a thatched lean-to on the shore, selling drams of rum. We sat down around an overturned barrel, and ordered a drink. "Phew" finally found his feet and started to stumble out of the water, still covered in mud. Charles Jr. stood up, and with his boot shoved "Phew" back into the calm water. We both took turns pushing him back in, until he was both clean and sober. At that point, we had him pull up a stool, purchased him a tankard of rum, and we talked long into the night. This was our first introduction to the misguided "Phew."

His introduction to the pirate colony on New Providence Island proved to be a valuable connection, during our business with the wrong side of the law. Benjamin Hornigold, the man who trained Blackbeard, Charles Vane and "Black Sam" Bellamy, had taken over an island that had been completely destroyed during the War of Spanish Succession (Queen Anne's War), located several miles off the Florida coast in the chain of islands called New Providence, the waterway through which most trading ships must go to get to Europe. This was an island occupied solely by pirates and the derelicts with whom they dealt. There came to be a Code of Conduct on this island, and a camaraderie of souls who frequented there. Hornigold intends for this to be a stopping place for the unlawful sailors of the sea. A place they can come to and plot with each other, discuss the routes of potential targets, and careen their ships without the thought of discovery. Here they can drink, fall into the streets, fight, barter, or sleep. There are merchants there who also deal in pirate booty, and anyone needing to trade with pirates would do themselves fine to visit there. We met the pirate captains that sailed the seas nearby. Hornigold continued to attack Spanish merchant ships and the plantations on the shores of Cuba, and in the Straits of Florida. They did so out of sailing canoes called periagus, and small sloops from their camps on Nassau. Here they had no fear of capture, and those in pursuit, dare not follow a vessel to this spot, for fear they would never return.

Charles Jr. and I met our Captain Phew one other time, one which proved to be beneficial to me. "Phew" now more the distinguished LaPlume, as he had cleaned up his person, and set himself up as a former pirate and to hear him tell it, quite a successful one.

The wealthy who visited his shop were impressed with his tales of piracy and the booty gained by commandeering wealthy vessels. Charles Jr. and I were amused at the tales "Phew" related to the interested prosperous New Yorkers. We listened to his spiel when a customer entered his shop, and as enthralled as they were, we cowered in the corner doubled over in laughter.

He since had gotten over his fear of water, and as a result had gone overboard with French cologne. We were want to sneeze, the fumes were so overwhelming.

We longed for the days of the ripe stench of uncleanliness. He had taken to wearing an eye patch for authenticity, and also carried around a wooden cane.

We knew of his ineptness, and the fact that he never once captured a ship. If the truth were known, he maybe never even saw one to capture, as he spent most of his life at sea, lost, without the knowledge of sea or sky. What an interesting fellow he was, we were delighted to be in his company, and couldn't wait to hear the tales he fabricated to tell the gentry of New York. We watched as he sold them gems for double the price, and knowing he paid little, we began to think we were in the wrong business.

It was there that I met Evelyn Strickland, a wealthy young woman from one of the prominent families on Long Island off the main of New York. I was certainly smitten, and garnered an introduction from La Plume. He more than gladly set up a meeting between us, and we shared many hours in the bustling city. I sort of left Charles Jr. wishing he had brought Eden, but he tolerated my absence very well. It seemed he knew this was a once-in-a-lifetime encounter. I had never seen such a beauty, and especially one with such high-born breeding.

She has raven black hair, and speaks in a soft voice that seems to be only for me. She is stylish and has become a friend of Eden, Charles Jr.'s wife.

They now spend hours shopping in the finest cities of the East, as Charles Jr. and I complete our business.

I am happy to see her love the people who are close to me. She and Eden have much in common, Evelyn's upbringing being the same as the aristocracy in Richmond. She was presented into society of New York, as her father is the owner of a large bank in the city. We met many more times as I frequented the city, each time now, Eden accompanied us, and it was a glorious time. When Rhetta left me to marry and live in Richmond, I thought my heart would never heal. Now, knowing how happy Rhetta is, I am considering happiness on my own.

Evelyn and I are now married, and settled in this wonderful house on the hill for several years now. She has taken over the job of finishing the inside, in the manner suitable for ladies of society, of which she is one. She and I have spent many wonderful days with Charles Jr. and Eden, and are quite content with the company of one another. She was educated in England, and here, we also have much in common. I have told her of my business in the past, and she was intrigued, rather than appalled. She is a welcome addition to the family, and loves Rhetta dearly. I do not make as many trips away from home as before.

Luke continued to read of the wonderful times Uncle Jabez had with his new wife. They traveled to places Jabez had never visited. Evelyn took him to Paris, London, and Spain. They even met Charles Jr. and Eden in London. Both Charles Jr. and Jabez were curious about the place from which most of their pirate partners originated, and they visited the haunts the pirates frequented. They went to the theater, often in New

York, and toured the museums of Paris, London, and New York. Evelyn was anxious to show Eden the exclusive shops of Paris, while Jabez and Charles Jr. wandered around the beautiful city. Luke read of the items they chose to go into the new huge house, and both boys pictured in which rooms they had found such treasures. They read of Jabez's nostalgia of the times both he and Rhetta shared in the house, and how excited he was at the birth of Rhetta and Royster's child, Sabra.

Uncle Jabez seemed to be at such peace. He was wealthy enough that he did not have to continue to pursue the trade business, but both he and Charles Jr. sometimes, took a challenge or two to find just the right item for a customer. The more dangerous the mission, the better. They both missed the escapades they had together when they were unattached.

One trip the two men took with their wives was to Boston, to show them both the sites of the town where they met, and the school where they both learned how to be gentlemen and businessmen. They had many contacts there and tried to reconnect with their former classmates. It did appear that there really was a most happy period of Uncle Jabez's life. But as Luke continued, he came upon the following passage:

> There has been a tragedy, the ship carrying my wife to her family in New York has met with a storm off the coast of Virginia and all is lost. I do not know if I will wish to continue without her. Rhetta has a child, Sabra, and it is the visits that the child makes here that is the only comfort in my life.

This part of The Book was sad, Luke stopped reading for a while. He talked with Blake about wishing that Uncle Jabez had not had to go through that tough part of his life. They both hoped that he stayed strong, and felt extremely sorry for the lonely man, who had been such an adventurous soul.

They continued to read and were glad when Uncle Jabez again contacted Rhetta and sort of started to put his life back together. It seemed that the child, Sabra, had filled the hole in his heart that Evelyn had left, and he took great joy in spoiling her. He became good friends with Rhetta's husband, and through Royster, he and Charles Jr. reentered the intrigue of politics. Jabez spent much of his time in Richmond, even taking an apartment there to be close to his family and his best friend. He spoke of the elaborate parties given in the Jarvis home, and there were ladies, thanks to Eden, whose heart was broken also; she had loved Evelyn and was crushed to see Jabez unhappy. She continuously introduced him to various beautiful and talented women of society, with whom he shared a dinner, maybe a dance, but nobody that could replace his wife.

Hatteras was growing, as was the business on the docks. After a while, Jabez sold his ownership of the area to the Austin family, but he remained a frequent visitor, usually around the hour when the ships came in. He still knew most of the captains and wrote as if he were happy.

> I no longer wish to chronicle my life, I am now remembering what it was. Rhetta also has met with tragedy, her husband has been killed in a duel. I fear that we both are cursed, except, there is Sabra. I have begged Rhetta to bring the child home, I know I would make a good substitute father, and Rhetta is of the same mood as am I. Neither one of us sees the need to smile again, it is the child that is our savior.

Uncle Jabez was successful in bringing Rhetta and Sabra home. It was like they both experienced a new life through the child. They took her to school, bought her a pony, and it appeared that the tragedies had become less crippling.

The rooms of this house are alive again, this time with the laughter of a child.

This child is much like Rhetta, she seems to see and know things beyond her years. Rhetta had finally confided in me as to our background from the indians. She has known for all of her life, and did not ever tell me. We are both cursed and blessed. The abilities of the child are remarkable. She too, like Rhetta, has an affinity with animals, and there are now two wolves who watch the house, one is old, probably the one who watched over Rhetta, and a wolf pup who spends his time howling at the moon. I am getting used to this strange family I have, and long to have been able to share all of it with Evelyn. I see her in my dreams, and know that she is still with me. I am busy making sure that I do not forget the life I have been lucky enough to live. Tragedy is a part of life, but with Sabra, I see that life is ever evolving, that death brings forth new life, and the wheel is ever turning.

That was the last page of The Book. Luke wiped away a tear and looked at Blake, who had his face buried in a pillow. They did not know how to tell Ellie. Then she crept through the attic door, and they could tell she also had been crying. Maybe she read the same account in the journal left by Rhetta. She had. The three sat silently, looking around them, thinking about this wonder of life and the heaviness of death. Ellie was reminded of her own mother, but she could not seem to be upset for herself. Grandmom was so special that she never felt abandoned. She was tearful for Uncle Jabez, and for Rhetta, but they too had something that breathed life back into them: a child. It was then that Ellie knew how much her grandfather and grandmother loved her. She read the hurt on the pages of Rhetta's book and listened to Luke tell of Uncle Jabez's broken heart, and she knew that there was always something to heal what was broken, and in that crack of the heart, love made a stronger bond— like the one between she and her grandparents. She wondered how long they grieved over their loss, and she was glad she was there to put the pieces back together.

The children closed The Book, with all its secrets, and decided that they would leave the house for a while, until they, too, could heal from their hurt for people they had never met. They learned to live someone else's life, and now they were experiencing their sorrow. Knowing how happy things eventually turned out, they had faith that life really did give, take away, and give again. They just needed to let time pass, and as it did, new happiness peered through the curtains of sorrow, just a little sliver at a time. Then the whole of the sun shone through, giving more and more happiness to wash away the pain.

On the ride back home, they were all a little sad, until they turned at the squeaking, clicking sounds they heard, and saw their dolphins, all three of them, frolicking in the ocean, trying hard to get their attention and doing silly tricks. The three kids dismounted and walked to the edge. Since it was warm, Ellie took off her shoes and leggings and waded into the ocean, just far enough for the dolphins to get near. The boys had taken off their shoes the minute the horses hit the sand, and they also were in the water, almost to their waist. Wet clothes were not a problem to them. They would be dry by the time they got home.

They could have sworn that the beautiful creatures were smiling, and then, as they got close, the dolphins turned toward the sea and splashed them with their tails. Now even Ellie was wet. How fun!

★ 19 ★

The Sunken Chest

The kids spent the first week of summer with Grandpop, helping to clean the lens and polish the brass of the lighthouse. They had been told they had maybe only a couple of months left to stay there. The war in Europe was raging, and according to letters from their dad, it was going to be a longer and more violent conflict than the one before. The navy boys were all over the place, and the kids did not feel as free as they had when it was only them.

The times they were not with Grandpop, they were on their horses, going back and forth to the old house, taking things from the keeper's quarters to the house on the hill. They often spent time on the granite steps and ledges around the huge tower, getting in as much playtime as they could. If they could have put their arms around it and hugged it, they would have. Luke regained his power with a bow and arrow and was busy teaching Blake. Grandpop was most impressed that he had made the arrows and the bow. It was not as fine as the one Manteo had made for Luke, but it was good enough for Blake to learn, Grandpop, who had more free time on his hands, made a target for the boys to practice with and stayed around most of the time while they spent hour after hour perfecting their aim. Ellie never did get strong enough, so she spent her time down at the shoreline, practicing her powers of communication with the dolphins.

She had gotten so good with her thought process that she could, in her mind, call Twylah to come, and the beautiful wolf would show herself at the edge of the bushes near the lighthouse.

She kept all of this to herself because, at times, she did not know if she should be doing this. But she felt that if she ever was in need of that power, for good, as Weroansqua had said, then she better know what she was doing. She remembered how that power had saved Sooleawa's wedding, when Sucki had conjured up the snake, and she wanted to be able to call on that if it ever happened to either of her cousins. She also remembered when she called for the dolphins to help Blake, and they did. This was a skill she needed.

Ellie had also spent a lot of time in the barn with the horses, and was able to direct both of them, Gus and her Blue, with her thoughts. They obeyed what she told them to do. Simple things, like, "Come here," "Stop," and "Kneel down," and Blue would get down on his front two legs, and kneel for her to climb on. This was something she had not shown Blake. She wanted to make sure she could do it before she let him in on the secret. She felt this was her strongest skill of all, so if the boys could shoot the bow and arrow with precision, then she could control the horses.

One hot summer day, Ellie and the boys were having a romp in the surf, and as the boys kept getting rougher with each other, and a little with her, she acted like she was disgusted with them, and stomped up on the shore and plopped down on the sand. She called the dolphins, and before the boys knew what was happening, they were faced with three playful dolphins, clicking away with their sounds and splashing the boys with their tails. Ellie sat on the shore, laughing and laughing, as the boys kept getting a tail splat in their faces. The game was too rough for her, but she enjoyed them getting pummeled with water from the dolphins.

"Ellie," Blake yelled, "I know you're doing this. Now stop it! Look at them, they are going to drown me!"

At that, one of the dolphins actually surfed in on a wave, and immediately, *Eeeehaaa!* The game was on, and the five of them, three dolphins and two little boys, surfed the breakers until they were so tired they could hardly gain the shore. They finally stumbled up to Ellie and plopped down beside her exhausted, as the dolphins merrily swam away.

"I wish we could go for another ride," Luke said. "I don't want Poseidon to forget about us."

"I don't think he will," said Ellie. "Looks like he heard you."

Ellie was looking at the blue and silver clouds, as they began to mingle with the puffy white ones that were over the ocean. Out from the sea, water sprayed up and in the mighty waves that were forming was Poseidon rising to half his body, spewing foam, covered in falling cascades of water, and throwing something their way. The glistening rocks landed near the place where the children sat, and as Blake clawed the sand to retrieve one, he discovered it was the crystal necklace he had worn before.

Travis, Brendan, and Micah covered their saintly mouths in a giggle, as they had not had fun with the kids since they discovered the old house, and they had been looking for an adventure on which to send them. They had been conjuring up one for the caves, but had not yet had time to do that since school let out. This sea adventure would have to do, because if the kids were to move away, they might not get another chance to watch them interact with their ocean friends. At least not here, at the base of the lighthouse. The saints also knew what was about to happen in these waters, and they would not be sending the kids into harm's way, so if they were ever again going to play offshore, now was the time to do it.

The three children slipped on the silver threads, with the crystal attached, as immediately the string began to form a suit of silver. Looking toward the ocean, three sargassum wreaths floated in on the oncoming wash. Each picked up one and headed down to the deeper water. As they neared the breakers, each had a chance to throw the sargasso mats over the back of their particular dolphin and watch as the mats formed a saddle. As the children climbed onto the mats, the thread whipped itself around them and formed a saddle underneath them and around the dolphin until it was a bridle, saddle, reins, and mask. Off they went.

The dolphin sped away with the three kids hanging on tight. Moira and Ellie began immediately to outshine the boys. They jumped and dived and jumped and twirled, until Ellie was getting dizzy. She gave Moira a little squeeze with her knees, and in her mind told her to slow down. Still, she could not erase the smile on her face from behind the silver helmet formed by the web of netting that the crystal provided. Finally Moira glided through the water close to the surface, with only a small dip under the waves, almost not submerging Ellie at all.

James and Blake were not to be outdone, and their tricks were also high and brave. They were quite satisfied with themselves until they dove under and went toward the bottom. They were surprised to see something going their way fast! Willi and Luke were about to swim a circle around them, and before James and Blake knew it, they were in a whirlwind of water, as the stronger Willi circled them so many times, James actually turned around. They were making Blake's head spin. Luke gave Blake a wave good-bye and off he went on his swift ride heading to parts unseen, leaving Blake leaning over and hugging James, and hoping he didn't slip off. They then continued their view of life below the sea, and Blake gave a hearty "hello" to the swarms of fish that schooled past him.

Meanwhile, Moira and Ellie were seeing how high Moira could jump, and Ellie's little heart was pounding out of her chest. It was unusual for Ellie to be allowed to have thrills. Everyone was always trying to keep her from any physical harm, but here in the water, with a white dolphin who was her friend, and given to her especially by Poseidon, she was experiencing the kind of stimulation that could only be enjoyed while in the water. There was nothing here that could hurt her or cut her.

As Moira and Ellie were frolicking, they were aware of many dolphins coming into their play area. As Ellie looked around at the dolphins surrounding her, she saw the fin of a shark, outside the circle of dolphins swimming slowly by. The shark did not advance toward the group, and Ellie felt a very safe feeling inside. As she and Moira had not yet noticed the awful creature previously, the other dolphins had as they swam near, encircling the pair and putting up a barrier on the chance that their fun would be interrupted by a predator. Finally the shark swam away, and the school of about ten dolphins stayed in the area with Moira until the shark completely left the area. The dolphins then went on their way, and the play continued without incident.

At last all were tired. The children and their rides were happy to renew their friendships. The day was still young. The dolphins surfed into the shore on a particularly large breaker, and the three dismounted. As they walked through the surf to the beach, their suits melted away, and when they reached the sand they were so tired, they plopped down on the beach and napped.

Ellie sat on the side of the quiet, dark pool, dangling her feet on the black, dark, blue water and watching the slight circles. Luke and Blake were on either side of her. Today was the day they would look for the sunken chest. They felt that Ellie could pinpoint the exact location. Her mind would work faster and more accurately when near water, so here they all were, feet in the water they were about to invade, and beside each other, with the knowledge that together, they were more powerful than apart. They had everything they needed in the cave with them: a couple of long poles and some rope, lanterns, flashlights, and dry clothes. They were anxious for whatever they could think of that they might encounter.

They were ready. The three moved close, and Ellie closed her eyes and tried to picture a chest. They had picked out one in the attic, which they thought had carried the gold bullion that Captain Johns had given Uncle

Jabez. They thought they had the correct one, because at the bottom of a particular chest of books, there was a gold coin. They thought that if the chests were the same, then the twin of the one in the attic would look like that. Ellie concentrated—she was getting good at it now—and almost dreamed herself into the pool, but Luke felt her move and blocked her from falling forward into the water.

"I have it!" she exclaimed after a while, and they all opened their eyes. "It's over there," and she pointed to a spot under the falls that was on the side of the area that was nearest them. "I think the chest is on this side of the falls, and it looks like it is sitting on some rocks, sort of out of the water, behind it, not under it. Luke, if you wade over there, near the rocks, and kind of get into the water, you can get behind the falls and feel around for a chest."

The plan had always been for Luke to get into the water. After Ellie had been assured that there was no danger of snakes, they all felt safe. Water was not a problem, as they were all good swimmers, even Blake. Blake could swim stronger than Ellie and had beat her every time Uncle Jack had put them to a race in the shallow waters of the Pamlico. Luke got up and stood next to the wall on the dry side of the falls. He inched over on the ledge, with arms spread and pressed against the rocks forming the wall, until he was almost under the falls. There was just enough rock for him to keep his footing, and he disappeared behind the water. In a minute he reappeared.

"I need to take a breath. It is dark, and I can't see anything. Give me a stick, not a pole—that's too long. Do we have a shorter stick?" He looked a little anxious but was still not ready to give up.

Blake searched around the cave with the lantern and found a stick about four feet long, and sturdy enough to hold its shape. "Do you think the flashlight will help?" he asked, as he handed the stick to Luke.

"Maybe, and if it doesn't, I'll throw it back." Luke took the stick and the flashlight and carefully slipped back behind the water.

Ellie was sending him thoughts, and courage, in her mind, and picturing for him to find the chest.

"I feel something!" Luke yelled back, and they could hear the stick as it poked whatever solid thing Luke had found.

Luke appeared back from behind the water and kneeled down to fetch the rope. "I think I can tie the rope around a handle, if I can get close enough." Back behind the falls he went. After just a short while, Luke came tumbling out into the pool from the middle of the waterfall, and came up out of the dark water sputtering. Blake pushed the pole in Luke's direction to haul him back to the bank. He still had the end of the rope in his hand.

"I just lost my footing, but I think I can do it. Just let me try."

Once again Luke disappeared behind the wall of water. This time it was longer, and he didn't fall out. In a few minutes, he came back from behind the falls, with the end of the rope in his hand, and as he walked on the ledge beside the falls to get back to the two, he obviously had something on the end of the rope. The rope stretched behind, getting straighter at each step he took moving toward them. At the end of the ledge, and now on solid ground around the pool, he motioned for his partners to come forward.

"Come on, let's pull. Grab hold of the end with me, and hang on. We are going to pull on something, and it doesn't have enough room to come out, so it is going to fall into the pool." He thought he had the plan.

Then Ellie said, "Let's tie the rope to that tree root, so if it falls, it won't pull us in with it."

"Good idea!" Blake chimed in, and got a curious look from Luke.

"Okay, gimme that end, and I'll tie it tight to this big root. I hope it doesn't break!" Luke tied the end of the rope several times around first one root then another, until they were sure that the weight of the chest would not pull the tree right through the ground down into the cave.

They pulled, and felt something move.

Ellie concentrated in her mind on the look of the chest she suspected to be the same size and look of the one behind the curtain of water. Her thoughts moved the object slowly on solid floor. She made the sheet bottom slide smoothly on the slippery slime of the ledge and along the wall of the rock. She kept picturing it moving with three fourths of its bottom on something solid. As they pulled, Ellie pressed the chest up against the wall and did not allow it to tip on the side next to the pool. She was hardly putting any strength in the pull, but on the position of the box as it moved steadily forward. They did not know it, but both boys were dealing with all the weight, because the ledge was slippery and wet for everyone. They were having a hard time holding to their own position. The chest continued to move along on the algae of the rock in the waterfall.

Once they had dislodged the chest and felt it move, the slide got easier.

"Pull straight, right near the wall. Maybe there is enough ledge that the chest can slide along the floor until we get it out." Luke settled himself first, leaning against the wall, to keep the rope straight, and signaled for the other two to pull. "Not hard!" he warned. "Gentle, little bit at a time."

The three tugged slightly on the rope. It moved again. They pulled again, it moved again. Maybe ten times they gently strained to make the object move, ever so slightly, until the end of a chest was visible.

At this point, the front of the chest was resting more on the ground than the vacant air of the fall's ledge, and now it was going to stay on solid footing until it was safely, wholly, out from behind the rushing water.

When the chest was settled on firm ground, the three kids collapsed on the bank of the pool and heaved a sigh of relief.

They all sat back to rest. Their relaxation was broken by Blake saying, "Ellie, did you do that?"

Actually, Ellie didn't know if she did or she didn't, so she just gave him one of her looks.

Ellie's relief came because she could also relax her mind and not think so hard. What she didn't know, but would learn, was that she did not have to strain so hard in her mind to get it to do what she wished it would. Her powers were growing as she practiced and came more readily than when she doubted that it would come to her at all. The boys were tired from strength exerted, but Ellie was tired from concentrating.

After a few minutes, they moved the lantern close so that they could see the whole piece. There was a shaft of light above them where the water originated as the result of a small stream which had narrowed near the hole down which the water traveled. This was a known stream that traveled through the woods near their house, starting from a gush of water that came from one of the many aquifers running underground on the island. The gush of water breaking the soil plane was on the Jennette property, in the woods, and therefore not one that was known by anyone outside the property. Uncle Jabez had also built a well that reached down to that aquifer to collect water for the house. He had protected the place where the stream began, knowing of its flow and downhill path to the sound. It was near the mouth at the sound, where the steam again showed itself and joined the Pamlico.

The kids had anticipated retrieving the chest. They had with them tools that were used to open the other chests in the house. They kept thinking, correctly, that the chests were the same, so they brought with them the very same key that opened the one that Uncle Jabez had been given. Logic came natural to them as they moved freely through the powers they had been given. Their thinking was close to their goal, and for them, with the help of their saints—who, by the way, were with them in that dark cave, having a good time sliding down and brightening the little water steam, giving the shaft of light they needed and helping them accidentally make the right decisions.

The lock of the trunk was rusty. Luke gathered up some wet mud from around the water and rubbed it in the lock, trying to scrape away the decay of 200 years of dampness. He assumed the lock was not gold but brass, and Grandpop had taught him that one cleans brass by constant rubbing. Inserting the key into the hole, he worked it for at least half an hour, until the inside of his hand was sore. Ellie wrapped a rag around his hand to ease the pain. Then, as she finished, she caught Luke's eye, and both simultaneously had the fleeting thought that she could do it. About the same time, Blake chimed in.

"Open it, Ellie. I bet you can. We will help you, or at least we can try 'til Luke's hand feels better."

They had all come to the same realization at the same time, and above them, snuggly floating above the ceiling of the cave, Travis, Micah, and Brendan smiled, as they finally had gotten through.

The kids concentrated on the lock, and Luke tried it again. This time, it turned, and the lock clicked. They wedged a sliver of rock under the brass coupling on top and pried open the lid. What they saw inside was entirely unexpected.

Inside the chest there were no coins. There were no gems, no silver, no golden goblets, no pearls, and no necklaces with huge rubies or sapphires. Inside the chest were huge wrapped objects protected in heavy sailcloth. They chose the one on top, and not knowing what it was, Luke handed it to Ellie, thinking she would be the one that would not drop it or destroy it as she opened it.

Ellie carefully unwrapped the cloth that surrounded the object. What she uncovered was a beautiful green statue of a fearful-looking Chinese man. The fearsome man had been carved out of one solid piece of whatever the stone was. It was heavy, and it was green, and part of the cloak the figure wore was the same rock but with strains of purple running through. How clever to have carved the piece and used the color in such a way. It was smooth and shiny, with an angry face: it looked mad. She placed it on the ground. Opening the next piece, next to the first was a cloth that covered something twice as large as the angry man, and both she and Luke lifted it from its wrapping. This was a beautiful elephant, on all fours with a very detailed trunk. It was white, and all the muscles of the elephant were obvious in the carving.

The next piece was longer and not as tall. It was a dragon, with perfectly carved scales, stretching long and low. It had wings on the side of its head where the ears would have been, and its mouth open like it was ready to shoot fire. This one was a light green, and on some parts it was a little white. On the hump, as the dragon stretched out, was a small platform, like a saddle. The next was a golden camel, with a saddle that was molded up like a real saddle. The gold of the saddle had been painted with designs of green and white and gold. The camel was standing, with head raised and mouth open. It was so beautiful, and more detailed than the others.

"All of the things in this chest are carvings, I'll bet." Luke smiled. He thought that the statuettes he was looking at were more beautiful than any chest of gold or bunch of rocks people called gems. However, on all figures, where the eyes were supposed to be were tiny gemstones. What kind they did not know. They just thought the treasure was the most beautiful find they could have uncovered.

"I'll bet ol' Captain PooPoo could have sold these things!" Blake blurted out.

"His name was Phew, not PooPoo … and it was actually La Plume!" Ellie gave Blake a side glance of disgust as Luke snort laughed behind his hand.

Blake looked at Luke laughing, and he was proud of himself for making a joke that shocked Ellie. Sometimes the little fella knew just how to snap everybody out of a mood. He was definitely 80 percent silly.

They decided to stop and take the things they had uncovered. Each one would grab one and take it back to the house. It would be easier to empty the chest if they took it piece by piece back up the stairs. So they rewrapped the figures they had uncovered and began the long task of taking each single prize up the pathway to the stairs and then to the house. They decided to leave the treasures between the walls for the time being, until everything was there. Then they would take them all into the attic, and maybe the chest would be light enough for the three of them to get it up to the room. They began. It took them most of the day. Their plan was to wait until they got to the attic before they unwrapped one more piece.

Finally the task was complete. They found the chest heavy, but taking their time and being careful not to scratch it, they completed that feat also. Next they removed the tools they had taken into the falls, until there was nothing left to indicate that anyone had been there.

At the room behind the fireplace, they rested. It was time to get back home. Their treasures was safe and their curiosity was satisfied, and they would get down the encyclopedia to see what they found.

Luke was looking at Ellie when he said, "Remember, Captain Johns said he was a privateer on the Red Sea, and had attacked a ship that he was not supposed to have stopped. If he was in the Red Sea, the ship he attacked was probably coming from China. So he thought the figures were worth more than the gold and decided to keep those things. Probably nobody on his crew wanted to share in any of these. They probably thought they were junk, and things like that were difficult to split up. What do you think?"

"I think you're probably right. They probably didn't want them," Blake said confidently in his grown-up voice, thinking that he was also included in the speculation.

Both Luke and Ellie snickered. Blake was so funny. Boy, was he going to be hard to get along with once he really got some sense. But the things they wanted to do definitely needed three, and he was an important part of this trio.

It was all they could do to keep this secret. This was bigger than the sword, and this one they were going to have to tell Grandpop, because they wanted both their grandmother and their mother to have these gorgeous statuettes. So they eventually had to tell. As they ambled along the beach on the way home, they discussed their secret, deciding that they would wait until they moved into the house. There was no way they could bring them to the keeper's quarters, and they actually did not want to move them.

At home, they took down the *Britannica* and, starting with China, they looked up carvings during the 1700s. For the figurines already uncovered, they could be jade or ivory or both. But eventually Grandpop would tell them.

Blake declared that if they were splitting up the loot, like the pirates did, he would take the dragon.

That night at dinner, they were unusually quiet. Grandmom thought maybe they had gotten wet and were getting a summer cold, so her suggestion was for them to go to bed early. Grandpop had the idea for a story, but they were not about to hear another one about a deer.

"Got any stories we haven't heard?" Luke asked.

Grandpop paused, then replied, "Let me see. Want to hear the one about how I got my name?"

EPILOGUE

It might be interesting to see if you have a genuine pirate in your background. Look through these names to determine your kin.

Blackbeard's Crew
John Archer
James Blake
Joseph Brooks
Black Caesar
Joseph Curtice
Stephen Daniel
Garrat Gibbens
John Gills
Richard Greensail
Israel Hands
William Howard
John Husk
Nathan Jackson
John Martin
Thomas Miller
Samuel Odell
Joseph Phillips
Lieutenant Richards

Stede Bonnet's Crew
Samuel Booth
Robert Boyd
John Brierly
Thomas Carman
Jonathan Clark
George Dunkin
William Eddy
Thomas Gerrard
David Herriot
William Hewett
James Killing
Matthew King
John Levit
William Morrison
Thomas Nicholls
Neal Patterson
Ignathius Pell
Daniel Perry

Blackbeard's Crew cont.

James Robbins

Owen Roberts

Edward Salter

Richard Stiles

James White

Stede Bonnet's Crew cont.

Thomas Price

John Ridge

Edward Robinson

George Ross

William Scott

Robert Tuccor

James Wilson

Other Pirate Captains in the Area

Captain Charles Bellamy: Not to be confused with "Black" Sam Bellamy. "They vilify us, the scoundrels do, when there is only this difference; they rob the poor under the cover of law, forsooth, we plunder the rig under the protection of our own course."

Captain Edward Low: North Carolina pirate, reported insane, horrible face as a result of sewing up his face himself. Black-flag ship, *Fancy*. Active for only three years, Sir Arthur Conan Doyle (author of the Sherlock Holmes stories) described Low as "savage and desperate" and a man of "amazing and grotesque brutality."

Captain William Fly: Captain only one month, former prizefighter. Led mutiny on ship *Elizabeth*. He was then elected captain, and personally killed the old captain and all opposition. He renamed the ship *Flame's Revenge*.

Anne Bonney: Sailed with Jack Rackham, "Calico Jack."

Captain Christopher Moody: 23 years old. Only a pirate from 1717–1722, hanged in London before he was 30. Called "Gentleman Pirate." Cheated his crew.

Peter Painter: Carolina pirate.

Captain John Rackham: Nicknamed "Calico Jack". He sailed with Charles Vane as a crew member. When Vane was thrown off the ship by the crew to be marooned, Jack was named captain.

Matthew Tryer: Carolina pirate.

Captain Charles Vane: Usually captured merchant vessels, pillaged another pirate off shores of Florida Keys, taking his find of a Spanish galleon reportedly filled with gold bullion. Angered Woods Rodgers, governor of the Bahamas. Hated by all who crewed with him.

Captain Want: Carolina pirate operating in the Red Sea

Captain Pain, Christopher Moody, John Cole, Robert Deal, Richard Worley, and Francis Farrington all pirated off the coast of North Carolina.

Many pirates spoke of Davy Jones's locker, or the bottom of the sea. Davy Jones scuttled his ship rather than be captured, and thus to visit Davy Jones's locker means to go to the bottom.

No cup was ever made of Blackbeard's head, and his body never swam circles around the ship, which was grounded on a shoal—not allowing for swimming anywhere, much less circling the ship.

One of Blackbeard's mates, William Howard, who served as quartermaster on *Queen Anne's Revenge*, purchased the island (peninsula) of Ocracoke in 1759. He lived past 100 years old.

Pirating did not quit after the Golden Age, in 1725. Rather, it continued in less active and different forms. The next book relates another time, when men rescued floundering ships by hand, when land pirates created a problem, when the sea became something to watch, to make safe, to tame, to use.

By the end of Book Four, the children would have made the transition to policing the sea, which was fast becoming a 'highway', as ships moved up the coast using what Benjamin Franklin referred to as a river running through the ocean (The Gulf Stream). From protecting their domain from a tower on the shore, to observations from a tower in the woods, they continue the vigil over the lighthouse, as it kept the same for them over all their years.

In Book Four, the brave deeds and heroic feats of the selfless surfmen of Hatteras Island are recounted, giving power to names like Barnett, Midgett, Dailey, Brady, Miller, Etheridge, Jennette, and Fulcher.

Also in Book Four appear the most interesting tales of the over 1,000 shipwrecks that happened off the coast of Cape Hatteras, in and around Diamond Shoals: the stories of the wrecks, the rescues, the people who were lost, and the families who waited for them to come home.

ABOUT THE AUTHOR

Jeanette Gray Finnegan Jr., Torok is a tenth-generation islander whose childhood was spent on Cape Hatteras when it was totally independent of mainland amenities. Jeanette—Jaye to friends—graduated from East Carolina University with a double major in English and history, and she did extensive graduate work at Old Dominion University in photography. After thirty years teaching both English and Advanced Placement U.S. Government, the author came home, back to the island, to live.

Jaye and her husband own the Dolphin Den Restaurant in Avon, one of the villages, and both spend the off-season writing. The five books in this series have been in the works for at least ten years. Previously Jaye photographed and produced a calendar of the island, from one ferry to the other.

The island is changing, and multigenerational families are dwindling. These books recall those moments that made life solid and depict a proud and innovative people, living on the edge of the world.

The stories are events that actually took place while growing up here. We know our history, and we found enough evidence of it as children. We would like to share it with you.

Enjoy the sights, sounds, and smells of this strip of land you obviously feel connected to also. This is what it felt like to live a natural life, surrounded by family and friends, few strangers, and lots of excitement. Growing up island was a special privilege with some unusual memories.